ALSO BY NALINI JONES

What You Call Winter

THE UNBROKEN COAST

THE
UNBROKEN
COAST

NALINI JONES

ALFRED A. KNOPF
New York
2025

A BORZOI BOOK
FIRST HARDCOVER EDITION PUBLISHED BY ALFRED A. KNOPF 2025

Copyright © 2025 by Nalini Jones

Penguin Random House values and supports copyright. Copyright fuels creativity, encourages diverse voices, promotes free speech, and creates a vibrant culture. Thank you for buying an authorized edition of this book and for complying with copyright laws by not reproducing, scanning, or distributing any part of it in any form without permission. You are supporting writers and allowing Penguin Random House to continue to publish books for every reader. Please note that no part of this book may be used or reproduced in any manner for the purpose of training artificial intelligence technologies or systems.

Published by Alfred A. Knopf,
a division of Penguin Random House LLC,
1745 Broadway, New York, NY 10019.

Knopf, Borzoi Books, and the colophon are registered trademarks of Penguin Random House LLC.

LIBRARY OF CONGRESS CATALOGING-IN-PUBLICATION DATA
Names: Jones, Nalini, [date] author.
Title: The unbroken coast / Nalini Jones.
Description: First edition. | New York : Alfred A. Knopf, 2025.
Identifiers: LCCN 2024030299 | ISBN 9781400042777 (hardcover) | ISBN 9780593803448 (ebook)
Subjects: LCGFT: Novels.
Classification: LCC PS3610.O6275 U53 2025 | DDC 813/.6—dc23/eng/20240830
LC record available at https://lccn.loc.gov/2024030299

penguinrandomhouse.com | aaknopf.com

Printed in the United States of America

2 4 6 8 10 9 7 5 3 1

The authorized representative in the EU for product safety and compliance is Penguin Random House Ireland,
32 Nassau Street, Dublin D02 YH68, Ireland,
https://eu-contact.penguin.ie.

For Drew, Phoebe, and Thalia

PROLOGUE

1640

The rainy season had come and gone, the boy's grandfather said, and then a last storm kindled over the western sea. The boy watched from the beach as lightning flashed from the bellies of distant clouds, blazing jagged paths to the surface. The grandfather could not see much but listened. It won't reach us, he promised, though waves raced in like couriers with urgent news. He did not fear for their boat even when drops began to pock the sand.

By dawn, the storm had passed. The sea and sky were milky-calm when the boy spotted the ship. He leapt onto a rock for a better view and counted three masts. Before him was the great bowl of the bay, pearly in the morning light, its coastal waters studded with fishing boats from Koli villages like his own. The tide was low, the shallows drained to ribbons of water. A litter of wild pigs rooted in drifts of seaweed, and women slapped their washing against rocks that would be exposed only a few hours. Children who had fanned out to find clams began to hop and point and wave.

The boy was in his thirteenth year and had seen such ships before, which the Portuguese called *naos*. They sailed the coast regularly, bringing men and priests with crates of European necessities; and bearing away silk, cotton, peppercorns, saffron, gold, porcelain, animals, furniture, or tea. But the voyage took many months and an arrival was always an occasion. Most of these vessels moored in the deep natural harbor of Bombai to the south, but some rounded the point to anchor close at hand, in the waters off Mahim, where the boy could watch them come in.

The village beach ended in spume and cliffs, a promontory the boy could not see past unless he ducked inland. He set off running to the high spit of land where the Portuguese were building their watchtower.

A last cool breath of dawn was caught in the marsh grasses, and the boy cut through the shaded courtyard of the Church of the Loaves and Fishes at the base of the hill. But once he began to climb, the sun broke loose of the treetops and fell hard on his shoulders. The boy was a fisherman, like all his line before him, but he imagined being a fish instead, swimming through air as though it were water. About halfway up he passed a work yard; a new chapel was under way for Stella Maris, a statue of Mary as queen.

Not even the oldest villager could remember the day she arrived. Long ago, priests brought her from Lisbon to preside over the growing parish of Santa Clara: not just Portuguese settlers but local converts—fisherfolk, paddy farmers, orchard tenders, merchants. The boy's grandfather told stories he'd heard from his grandfather: Stella Maris draped with fine red cloth, her crown studded with jewels, her robes touched with gold. She first sheltered in a mud hut, and every day the Kolis brought flowers to keep the air fragrant until her shrine was ready. All those who labored for her, from the stonecutters to the sweepers, were baptized before laying a single stone, and for a full year they were preserved from harm. No men fell ill; no women succumbed to childbirth; no one was taken when storms swept other boats away. They built the Lady Mary a house, said the grandfather, and the Lady protected them.

The boy did not know if he believed this. He knew with God all things were possible, but he also knew his grandfather liked to tell stories, making small changes the way a hand dipped in water made ripples.

His grandfather said that on the same slope lived a woman who befriended birds. These birds came to her for food, birds of great variety and beauty, birds who joined her in song. But the priests claimed the high ground for Stella Maris, and the birds disturbed their worship. The woman was relocated to the marshlands below, and one by one, her birds flew away. Soon only the injured remained, those with a crushed leg or broken wing, until slowly even the most grievous wounds healed. On the Feast of the Nativity of Mary, the remaining birds rose up in a cloud of song, circled over the hillside, and disappeared to the east. The woman vanished, abandoning her hut and all her belongings except her favorite blue shawl. This she had drawn around her shoulders, the grandfather said, at just the moment when she transformed into a kingfisher. She flew away and was never seen again.

This was only a story, but as the boy neared the point, he checked the skies anyway. It was possible to imagine some rare bright bird taking flight over the palms below, but he saw only gulls and crows.

The hilltop leveled to a broad headland that tumbled down on three sides to cliffs. Guards and laborers camped beside the base of the half-finished watchtower of Castelo do Riacho, and the boy skirted piles of stone that had not yet been fashioned into walls. From the eastern ridge, he watched the ship round the point into the bay. Gulls rode the updrafts while the ship followed the line of the promontory into the harbor. The morning air churned when they dropped anchor—men shouting, sails snapping, a great slow groaning as she turned on her line. When she was moored, the sailors began to sing, a rough, joyful sound, and the boy heard the names of Maria and Cristo in their song.

Soon small boats scudded back and forth in a brisk exchange of men and fresh water. The boy lingered, wishing he could see whatever goods and people were below deck. Eventually, they would emerge into the light, lift their eyes to the cliffs and the coconut palms, and become part of the scene of this harbor, his home. But he imagined that the hold of the ship contained pockets of air from far-off ports, so that for a little while longer,

PROLOGUE

the people breathing the musk of those cities belonged to places he would never see.

That night, his father woke him to catch the tide. Together they rowed to the mouth of the bay to cast their nets. The moon looked like a pebble worn smooth on one side, the kind the boy's grandfather rubbed when he told stories. But his vision had grown too cloudy for the boat; he feared he would soon be blind. The boy missed him.

Just before sunrise, they began to haul in the nets. One dragged. A shark! thought the boy, before seeing they'd snagged a block of wood—not waterlogged, though wet enough to sink below the surface—likely from the timber barges along the northern coast. "Quick," his father warned and the boy struggled to lift it by hand before the net tore. The boat rocked, his father plunged his oar to steady them, and the boy heaved up a dark shape, swathed in the net and streaming water. A few small fish flopped against it. The father put down his oar and stared.

His son had dragged a statue from the sea. Her robes looked nearly black, and her face was obscured by the veil of the net. Yet they knew at once who she must be.

THE UNBROKEN COAST

1

OCTOBER 1978

Francis Almeida, emeritus professor of history, rode slowly toward the shrine of Our Lady of Navigators. It was eleven at night, a ridiculous hour for cycling, according to his wife. Francis had not bothered to argue; he slipped away while Essie was occupied.

He had not expected a full house that evening. Only the last of his children lived at home, and Jude ducked out before dinner—a study group with university friends, he told his mother, though Francis suspected they would study chord progressions. His son, who played no instrument, had somehow joined a band.

Essie was too absorbed in her own arrangements to object. The following night, she would fly to America to visit their daughter, Marian. For days she'd been laying out various necessities: cardigan sweaters, jars of mango pickle, gifts for their granddaughter and the new baby, due in two weeks. Francis could not sit in peace for ten minutes without being drawn into consultations over what to pack in her cases.

Instead, the telephone. Essie rushed from the kitchen with half a potato in hand. She had learned not to hope for calls from their son Simon in Greece; "That is a wilder place," Francis once heard her explaining to friends. But she behaved like a lovesick girl whenever the phone rang in case it was Marian from the

States, a call they themselves could not place without waiting hours, often overnight, for a long-distance operator.

It was Daniel, Marian's husband.

"What do you mean?" Essie's voice soared. "When? Frank, Frank!"

The baby had come three hours before. Another girl, a healthy girl. Francis came to listen over Essie's shoulder. He felt a certain pride when he heard Daniel's voice. He had been the one to like Daniel, to insist on opening their home to the couple when Essie was set against him.

"But why didn't you call when labor began? Where is Marian—"

"Let him talk," said Francis, and she tried to shoo him away with her potato. Marian was resting. Daniel had run home from the hospital to check on Nicole, who would turn two in another month. In the next hour or so, they would move Marian to a room with a telephone, and he would try to place a call then.

Francis did not like to ask but felt he must be certain. "The baby is breathing well?"

"Of course the baby is breathing well, Frank! Otherwise he would have said."

Francis lifted his voice. "So no difficulties?"

None, Daniel assured him. A quick delivery. The nurse told them that the doctor had just been closing his eyes when she went to find him. He'd thought they had hours to go.

Essie laughed loudly. This was the kind of story she liked, one in which everything ended well. "What kind of doctor goes for a nap! And I believe it was eighteen hours for Nicole."

Daniel could not talk long; he must get back to the hospital.

"But who will stay with Nicole?" Essie asked.

"My sister is here."

Francis saw Essie's mouth tighten: Daniel's family, not Marian's, in attendance. But she carried on. "How is my little girl? Excited to have a sister? Tell her Grandma is coming on the big, big airplane."

Talk of airplanes sent Francis drifting back to his chair. He had heard all he needed. The child had come safely. Marian was well.

Dinner was a slapdash affair. Francis took his meal properly, but Essie stationed herself at the telephone, making call after call to let people know. She did not even fill a plate until Francis had risen from the table. When they heard the compound gate swing open, Essie lifted her head. "That will be Jude!"

But it was their neighbors, bringing a cake to wish Essie goodbye. The kitchen girl cut it into slices to serve just as Father Evelyn turned up, a leather jacket over his clerical collar. He used his pulpit voice, clear and booming, to congratulate them.

Soon the room had filled. With each fresh arrival, Essie recounted the story of the birth. Eventually the girl removed the empty cake plate and brought bowls of sweets and nuts.

The telephone rang just as Marian's godparents arrived. "Here, my girl, say a quick hello." The phone was passed among Essie and the other women. "I believe the doctor was fast asleep, isn't it?" Essie prompted Marian. Then a small note of insistence. "No, but the nurse said he had to be shaken awake." Questions about resemblances, temperament, the name—which displeased Essie, though she would neither yield nor argue in front of friends. "That may be the American way to view it, but we can think more carefully when I come." Finally, she passed the phone to Francis.

"Hallo? Hallo?"

Speaking on international calls felt like throwing words down a deep well, one splash echoing after another. And Marian's voice seemed faint; was that the connection?

"How are you, my girl? Feeling better?"

"She's not ill, Frank!" said Essie, and a few women laughed.

"And the little one? Curls, is it?" He laughed, trying to remember if Marian ever had curls as a baby. "Yes, why not? You call her what you like, my girl, we are happy. Here, your mother wants to speak. Lots of love."

The front room was hot and close, the air thick with talk. Once Francis made sure no one had an empty glass, he joined a group of men at the railing in the front of the house, where a bank of windows opened to become a balcony. A few smoked, tipping their ashes into the garden below. They did not require him to say much. They remembered the days when Marian was small.

"*Two* children." One of the men shook his head in a disbelief Francis recognized.

"And Essie is gone for how long?"

Three months, the full term of a visa. There had been no question of his accompanying her; one must stay to look after the house and Jude. But Francis had already met his elder granddaughter, Nicole; she was a year old when Marian brought her to Bombay. She liked to run the full length of the front room, from the balcony railing all the way to the kitchen, where Essie waited with open arms. If Francis leaned forward in his chair and put out a hand to catch her, she shrieked with laughter. She tried to mimic him when he stood on his head, resting her head on the cushion beside his with her feet firmly planted on the floor. Had his own children been so fearless and happy? Surely, they could not have been *unhappy* at that age, he told himself, but hadn't they always been quieter, wary? This child was delighted to jabber to the kitchen girl, who spoke no English. She leaned back against Francis when they paged through a book, as though she had known him from the start. She called out greetings to street dogs.

He thought of this later: the road quiet, a sandy noise beneath his bicycle wheels, dogs curled on stoops or banked against walls. Most of the Almeidas' friends had gone, but a few women lingered to apply themselves to the puzzle of Essie's suitcase: How many packets of tea, how many jars of vindaloo? Would there be time the next morning to replace the yellow baby garments with pink? On Linking Road, Essie could find full lehenga choli outfits for small girls, lovely colors, good mirror work; she must get matching; she must get sizes to last a few years.

The women crossed from one bedroom to another, great swaths of chatter sweeping behind them. The girl had finished collecting glasses from the front room and was dragging chairs back into place with the pointed irritation of one who wished to be sleeping. Jude had received the news that he was an uncle once more with absentminded incredulity, as though this had not been the expected outcome, and retreated to his rooms downstairs. Within minutes, the noise of his records came floating up through the open windows. Francis could not find a corner of his house in which to sit quietly. He was going out, he told Essie.

"At eleven?"

He wouldn't be long. Just a breath of air.

"Go and sit on the balcony!"

The church, then. He would light a candle for the baby.

"Don't be ridiculous, Frank. The gates will close any moment."

But her attention was already skittering. She turned back to the women, whom she had decided to consult on a family matter: surely they agreed that the child must have a saint's name?

Francis rode toward the sea, coasting past the Church of the Loaves and Fishes and straight into Varuna, the Koli fishing village.

A single road formed its boundary, which began at the foot of Seaview Hill and carried on past the church and a tight row of storefronts. At the heart of the village was a statue of Our Lady of Navigators. The area near the shrine passed for a public square but was really only a brief relaxing of the narrow track, as though the road exhaled before twisting past a few last shops and a spatter of huts.

The Almeidas lived half a dozen blocks away, in a well-planned neighborhood overseen by a Catholic housing association. But in the village the grid of streets dissolved to a more elemental arrangement. The curves of Varuna Road echoed the coastline. On one side were shops; on the other, crooked lanes—impassable by car—which flowed to the shore like rivulets of water. The houses had been built generations before, two stories high and one room deep, standing shoulder to shoulder, from a time when only fisherfolk would live so close to the sea.

Francis liked the sensation of moving effortlessly into an older footprint of Santa Clara. The history of indigenous peoples had never been his field; his period was the Age of Exploration. But centuries before the Portuguese or British came calling, people had walked this same patch of ground. He was on an ancient way. And in the middle of the night, the past and present did not feel so very distant. He could listen to the ticking of his cycle wheels and remember riding through Santa Clara with Marian strapped into the child's seat behind him. Only a pinch of years, nothing that signified in the great mound of centuries. It seemed he should be able to turn and ride back into a day when his children were not on the other side of the world. He paused briefly, a foot planted on the pavement; then a flash of movement drew his gaze.

A woman was running, nearly stumbling, up the lane. She clutched something to her chest—a baby, he realized when she passed beneath a string of lights and her foot overturned a pail of wash water before she reached the shrine. Francis watched as she approached the statue, the baby tight to her body, then bowed her head low.

He knew the origins of Our Lady of Navigators better than anyone; he had written its history for the church. In a report to Lisbon dated 1669, a Jesuit priest wrote that a Koli fisherman had cast his net into the waters and recovered a statue of Mary. Its provenance was uncertain, but Francis guessed it was intended for one of the niches in the vast Church of the Loaves and Fishes and went overboard in the harbor. Statues of St. Andrew and St. Peter, fishers of men, eventually filled the niches, and the Kolis built the Lady a shrine of her own in Varuna.

She was removed only once, when pirates invaded the bay and looted the chapel on Seaview Hill. They seized any valuables they could find, including a sixteenth-century statue of Our Lady, Star of the Sea. Accounts of the pillage described a scourge of starlings diving low to pursue the thieves as they tried to drag Stella Maris away. This legend, Francis noted, may have inspired the carvings of birds on the great wooden doors of the later basilica. At any rate, Stella Maris was too unwieldy to carry for long. The pirates wrenched the jewels from her crown, chopped off her forearm for the gilt object she held—likely a scepter, though no reliable descriptions survived—and abandoned her on the hillside. The recovered statue was tucked into a storeroom, where her desecration would not distress the faithful, and Our Lady of Navigators was conscripted into service, ascending from the village to preside over the chapel.

This state of affairs lasted until an outbreak of illness in the mid-eighteenth century prompted the fisherfolk to demand the return of their Lady. She had come into a Koli net as their protector, they argued, and cited legends of healing from the era of her discovery: pains eased, maladies cured, an old man's dimming sight restored. Their pleas intensified after several children succumbed to fever, and eventually the priests agreed. The crown of Stella Maris was restored with rubies, a new arm was fashioned with a detachable Infant Jesus, and she was raised once more above the altar.

Our Lady of Navigators returned to Varuna in a grand parade, borne high on the shoulders of the fisherfolk in a boat filled with marigolds. A century later, when the plague ravaged the city, Varuna fared better than nearby villages and the survivors gave thanks to their protector by building her a fountain. This water was not consecrated, but residents considered it to have healing powers. People dipped their fingers into the tiled basin when they asked for Mary's blessing and hung blossoms around her neck on feast days.

Standing astride his bicycle, Francis watched the Koli woman as she made the Sign of the Cross and turned to go. The baby was small, he could see. Not yet a year.

"The child is ill?"

The woman stared at him. Then she gathered the baby close. "She is better," she said fiercely. "She will be better."

Francis nodded. What more was there to say? He had lost a child, a daughter who lived only a few hours. It happened sometimes with twins, the doctor said. A problem with her lungs. There had been a long hollow silence when his wife was told the baby could not live. She looked at them as though from a great distance. Then she found her voice—"A priest, Frank"— and whatever else they might have said to each other was lost in the rush of what must be done. The older children, summoned to wish the child goodbye. Godparents, baptism, the prayer for the dying. The newborn boy wailing, unable to feed; the doctor urging Essie to try again. She could not lose them both, so she laid her hand on the girl's tiny chest before she gave her to Francis and fixed her attention on their son.

Francis carried his daughter out of the room, away from the tumult. He stood at the balcony so she could see a bit of sky. It was not yet dark, too early for stars. He had not known what to say to her, so he told her the names of her family. "You are Theresa, named for my mother. Your sister is Marian. Your brother is Simon. We just named your twin also; he is Jude." He held her long after she stopped breathing.

He watched the Koli woman disappear down the lane and wondered if her child would live. But when he stopped in front of the statue, it was not to offer a prayer. He was not a man to petition a statue or expect Mary to come to his aid. What he imagined instead was the crowd of villagers bringing the statue down the hill, the ship in which she came to these waters, the tools the sculptor used to carve the long stiff folds of her robe. Since his retirement a few months before, his days felt like a series of empty rooms he must wander through, one after another: classes he would never teach, children who had gone, grandchildren he would seldom see. The future would be lonelier than the past. But he could stand where others had stood, swept up in currents of history.

When his thoughts turned to Agnes, Francis did not push them away. It was what happened when slippages or collisions in his life left cracks; Agnes flowed into them like water. But he was a man of dignity. He did not indulge in regrets. Their history, like any other, was fixed. So he wondered small things. Was she awake also? What did she think about late at night? Did she remember they once walked here together?

He dipped three fingers into the water and made the Sign of the Cross. That was all. No statue could restore Theresa to him, or Agnes. But he was a man of ability and purpose, only in his sixtieth year, with ample time to look ahead. Tomorrow morning he would go to the jeweler's and choose gold chains for each of his granddaughters. He would accept the seat he'd been offered on the Santa Clara Historical Commission. He would see friends at the gymkhana, cycle to keep fit, fix up a regular game of cards. He could join his brother and their friends on a holiday to Goa, or go hear Jude's band, or mount a trip to visit Simon in Greece. Within a year or two, Marian would bring the little ones to visit; until then, it was enough to know they were alive in the world. He looked at the lines of the statue's face, her stern, mournful stare, and felt a wave of affinity for the Koli woman whose child might be dying. Let her live a little longer, he thought. Then he climbed on his cycle and rode out of the village.

When Francis stopped at the shrine on his way through Varuna a few days later, Our Lady of Navigators was simply another feature of the bright, busy street. A chicken roosted in the deep wedge of shade the statue cast, glaring at the people who stopped to dip their fingers. All along the road, fisherwomen sat on plastic crates to sell the day's catch. Francis glanced down the row, wondering if he might find the woman he'd seen, but almost at once he realized he would not recognize her. What he remembered was her lopsided run, the way she clutched her child, and the strangeness of their being alone, or nearly alone, on a street in Bombay. No one was ever entirely alone in Bombay. Someone was always walking or watching, selling or buying, jogging or scolding, drinking or begging, tending a fire, awaiting a train, wiping a windshield, hailing an autorick, sifting through rubbish, slapping a bullock, sleeping in a doorway. A dog ate from the street gutter. A man ducked his head for a roadside barber. Girls laughed on a balcony, their calls raining down. At all times, a child was watching.

But for a short while, until the Koli woman appeared, Varuna Road had been deserted. Francis had slipped free of his wife and neighbors, the city had rolled back like a wave, and at first even the young mother had not been aware of him. The whole episode felt like an obscure piece of history, something so far from his own life that he might never feel the force of it.

2

OCTOBER 1978

It was dengue.

The baby wailed as though she understood, and Flora tried to hush her. "But that is a monsoon sickness!"

"The virus comes from mosquitoes," the doctor said. "They breed in standing water—puddles, basins, a little water in the base of a flowerpot, that is enough. And they carry the virus from person to person, so keep covered at night. You should sleep beneath a net."

Flora felt the doctor was losing focus. "But for the baby, what?"

"Keep her hydrated. Give water if she won't take milk. And watch closely once the fever goes. That is the dangerous time. Any vomiting, any bleeding, if she suddenly goes cold—these are signs of severe disease."

"Is there medicine?"

A mild fever-reducer, nothing more. He took a lofty tone when he warned about dosages for infants and advised lukewarm baths to bring down her temperature.

This was why Flora did not like doctors. When she showed her neighbors the baby's rash, they all said better take her. Inez volunteered to watch Flora's son, Jerome. It was easy to feel she had made the right choice. But for the full hour Flora waited to see the doctor, she worried about the money she should not be spending, and how to feed her four-month-old in a crowded room, and what her husband, Dominic, would say about running to a clinic for a fever. And in the end, what cure did this fellow offer? A bath and a bed net. Flora left school after the eighth standard, but she herself could open a clinic if she wore a white coat and spoke of puddles.

She had not wanted a doctor for the birth, either, despite a series of troubling omens during her pregnancy. When she was six months along, she and Inez took Jerome to the seawall for the faint mercy of a breeze and watched while, bit by bit, the moon was snuffed out. Flora understood an eclipse was something to do with shadows, the same as she might cast with her hand, but the hugeness of this shadow—its inexorable progress across the poor moon—made her uneasy. A week later, a dark cat, very nearly black, crossed in front of her in the fish bazaar. The fountain downtown that bore her name was nicked by a taxi, jarring her with reports of *Flora Damaged*. A perfectly good lemon developed rot.

Then, in the week when the fisherfolk sniffed the air for rain and thought *Soon*, in the hour when the muscles surrounding the baby made a first loose fist and Flora in her market stall felt a twinge so slight that she only shifted on her stool and kept cleaning fish, Dominic's grandmother sifted a last bright pinch of crimson through her fingers, rolled down in the lane, and died.

Thunder grumbled, though there was no final cry from Pearl D'Mello. It had been years since she had passed from quiet to mute. But she was a fixture in the lane, sitting among the mounds of colored rice powder with which she created intricate rangoli patterns outside the family's doorway. The villagers saw grace in the last act of her body, which was to curve away from her latest design: Christ pinioned not on the Cross but on the soft bed of an enormous pink lotus.

Clouds piled offshore while Inez and Flora walked home from the market. Inez carried both their knives and consulted the sky whenever Flora paused to rest or to register strange inner workings.

"It *could* be today," Inez said, meaning the monsoon. But even as she said it, she thought maybe not. The sky was full of tricks in June.

"No," said Flora, meaning the child. She was not due for two weeks; this was only a twisting sensation that she attributed to waiting too long for a toilet. It was a common complaint that there were no decent facilities for fishmongers. Even when Flora walked the distance to the nearest, she must ask Inez to accompany her; at her stage of pregnancy, it was too difficult to squat on her own.

Another low growl of thunder. "They'll come in," Inez predicted with confidence. This time she was speaking of their husbands, who were not as slippery to forecast.

The air was dense with waiting. Merchants ducked out of shops to check the light. The undertaker at Seven Sorrows pulled a chair into the street as though preparing for a parade. Flora could not shake the sensation of fish scales stuck to her skin, even though she'd taken the flat of a knife to her hands and forearms.

When she and Inez turned onto their lane, they found a crowd of neighbors at Flora's doorstep. Flora was ushered to the body just as a blast of wind swirled plumes of colored powder into the air. Children began to whoop, thinking the monsoon had come at last. Flora looked past the sad curled fingers and bare cracked heels to the rangoli itself, a swoon of color with jewel-bright drops of blood falling from Christ's side onto the petals of a lotus. What could it mean, to imagine such things? Then came a pain so sharp that Flora had to brace herself against the door frame. Let the villagers believe what they would: it was not the death but the shock of that image that threw her into labor. Inez helped Flora inside while the neighbors debated whether to bring the body also: at any moment, rain could fall.

Instead, the clouds split like a bad lump of dough. The wind collapsed. Heat settled, as heavy as debt, on the lane and the bay and Pearl's small body, curled like a cashew and salted with pink and gold. Two-year-old Jerome, asleep in his cloth cradle with a neighbor to watch him, seemed to register a new weight in the breathless air. He woke and fussed until he was borne away, bawling, to a house up the lane, while Flora called after him, promising he could come home soon.

By the time Dominic was summoned from the docks, the neighbors who remained had arranged themselves into a vigil. They gave him a minute to absorb the loss of his grandmother before urging him inside, where his eyes widened at the sight of Flora in the household's one bed.

"Not now?"

"Why not?" Inez demanded. Old women died, babies were born; she had no patience for astonishment. Flora gripped Inez's hand as the pain cut through her like a heated blade, and Inez jerked a head toward the door. "You see to that side. I'll see to this."

Dominic obeyed, trudging up the lane to Seven Sorrows, where the undertaker rose from his chair in the road as if this, all along, had been what he awaited.

The house was bedlam—the undertakers on the doorstep, the pains worse than Flora remembered. After only two hours, Inez told Dominic they must take Flora to a maternity clinic. To Flora, everything seemed upside down, running to a doctor after Pearl died at home. She gave birth in a room of sharp lights and strange sounds. When Dominic came to meet his daughter, shouldering Jerome past the objections of the nurse, Flora felt the old woman's absence as a dim counterweight to a bright, soaring joy.

"Pearl!" Dominic decided with delight. It seemed only natural to name the child surging into the world for the ancestress who had just tumbled out of it. He held his son perched high on his shoulder, from which masterful height the boy stared down at the bundle that would be his sister. "See, Jerome. This is Pearl."

Flora felt less certain. She'd been fond of her husband's grandmother, who kept up a constant stream of small ministrations—the rice sifted, the beans shelled, the baby soothed. Occasionally, she'd offered pats on the shoulder or rubble-toothed smiles, affectionate moments that Flora would miss.

But—how to say it to Dominic?—Pearl had been so old. Old and then older, squinting, squatting, sifting, shrinking into herself so effectively that she hardly seemed to eat. If she hadn't tipped over and died, she'd have disappeared, ground down to piles of dust in a sad monotone of her bright powders. And what to think of her designs? Of course Flora admired them—so beautiful and precise—but a four-armed Christ unsettled her, she was startled by Ganesh as one of the Magi, and she did not know what to make of Mumbadevi in a Koli boat, casting a net with the apostles as Fishers of Men. Flora was Catholic, in a village full of East Indian Catholics, whose families had converted when the Portuguese baptized their ancestors nearly five centuries before. She regarded her faith as a collection of vows undertaken as seriously as marriage, and there was something porous, very near adulterous, in these visions of gods overlapping. Why not the regular rangoli fare: a peacock, a flower, a tile?

Still, Dominic felt tender about his grandmother, and Flora preferred not to object to the name while Pearl's soul might be lingering, susceptible to earthly slights. Then she looked at her daughter: smaller than her son at birth, wild damp hair, eyes shut to creases, so soft, so new, that Flora wanted to weep. She had not expected this of a second child; she had expected, without realizing it, a reprise of the first. Yet this baby's cry was all her own. Her face folded and unfolded to expressions Flora had never seen before. She could not bear to yoke her to a dried-up life. She suggested calling her for Dominic's mother, who had died young but was once a beauty.

"Celia Pearl," Dominic said, beaming.

Let it be, thought Flora, the old woman's name tucked inside to give her daughter long life. And since the child was sleeping, Flora slept also.

The next afternoon, gusts of wind swept through the city. Palms thrashed, dogs tracked spirals of dust, feral pigs burrowed into the brush. Laborers put down their loads and tipped their heads to the skies. A traffic cop broke character and grinned. Schoolgirls caught hands and stood rapt beneath the pageantry of rushing clouds; small boys flung themselves into the air. The light soured; then, for an instant, the city blazed white, like a film set, and the sky opened its throat in a long, hoarse rumble.

This was the hour in which Celia D'Mello came home, just as raindrops began to spot the road. She was tucked against her mother's chest, a shawl draped over her head when the downpour began. In moments, the village was wet and glowing. Men outside the Cooperative toasted the monsoon with wide, off-season smiles. Women threw back their heads to feel the rain on their faces. Children ran wild beneath good-natured scoldings. Inez and her husband, Clive, who lived above the D'Mello family, stood in the lane to greet them. "Hurry," Inez called, laughing, and Flora tried to lope a little faster.

Celia could see nothing but the skin near her mother's collarbone and the links of her gold chain. Almost at once, the bouncing exhausted her. She closed her eyes. She could smell her mother, milk and cotton and chai, and she could smell the first steamy smack of rain against the hard-baked earth. She could smell a long green breath as the trees and gardens of the city drank the rain and exhaled. All night and into the morning, the air of Bombay smelled fresh and clean. Flowers burst into bloom, impatient young shoots unfurled from the wet earth, rivulets of water flowed down the streets.

The shawl covering Celia was soaked when her mother stopped near their door, and her father suddenly picked her up and held her high. Celia opened her eyes, startled, and caught a glimpse of the sea and the sky stretching long gray fingers to each other.

"See our Celia," her father called to everyone in the lane. "She brought the rain."

"Madman!" her mother scolded and took the baby. But she was laughing as she flung back the wet rope of her braid.

By the time they reached the threshold, Pearl's masterpiece had swirled to streaks of color underfoot. Over her mother's arm, Celia saw light swimming with dark, the whole slick mass changing shape, kaleidoscopic, protean, frothing in the rain. She opened her hand to touch and was swung through the doorway instead. All summer they would tell the story of the rain falling on the baby's face while she blinked and blinked and never cried. It seemed possible that Celia had overcome every inauspicious sign her mother feared and landed among them, blessed.

For a full day, Celia's fever rose and fell with the tide. The boat didn't come in, meaning Dominic and Clive had gone to deeper waters and would not be back before morning. Inez stirred turmeric into warm milk, and Flora did what she could to get Celia to take a little. She bathed her, draped mosquito netting around the bed, persuaded Jerome to crawl inside. But the baby would not settle. All evening, Celia fretted, rubbing her eyes, tossing her fists, so that Flora had to walk with her. It was nearly midnight when the baby finally drifted to a thin sleep on Flora's shoulder, and even then, she kicked or cried out, jerking herself awake if Flora lay down. Flora had never known such a child for fighting sleep. Most nights, Celia would quiet only on her mother's chest, pinning Flora in place, as if to be sure she would not sleep through anything interesting. Surely such a child was not in danger of slipping away.

Then the fever broke. Almost at once, Celia collapsed into a sleep so thick that it was a kind of stupor. Flora put her in bed and watched her lie still and picked her up again. The baby felt limp and heavy. The morning was miles away, Dominic farther. Flora had not been happy when he took Clive with him, brushing aside her objection that Clive spent the better part of the week in a bottle. "You know him on land. On the boats, he's a different man."

Flora let that pass—Dominic had a blind spot when it came to Clive—but, alone with her children, afraid to sleep, and worried the baby's breathing seemed shallow, she thought of the two men out on the water as if nothing were wrong and felt a blaze of fear so sharp it might have been fury. Again and again, she touched Celia's cheek to make sure she wasn't going cold. The baby's lips were dry; had she taken enough water? She forgot to ask the doctor how long the dangerous period would last, whether she should let the baby sleep or wake to check her periodically, whether a person could be bitten again and reinfected.

Flora could think of endless ways she might fail to protect her child, and not a single one that would absolutely save her.

When she left the house, it was to see if anyone was about. The night was warm, but Flora raised Celia to her shoulder and draped a shawl over her to ward off mosquitoes. She left Jerome sleeping soundly, safe beneath the netting.

There was no one in the lane. But her neighbor's washbasin had a murky inch of water in the bottom—mosquitoes breeding right on her doorstep—so Flora flipped it over. Opposite was a row of flowerpots, and she tipped the water from every one. Where the lane ended, in a splay of huts along the beach, she kicked at any rubbish where water might collect: a bucket, a cast-off tire, a plastic tub where goats came to drink. "The middle of the night," her neighbor hissed from her doorway. "What is the matter with you?" But Flora carried on in a fever of her own. She finished their lane and the two beside it, and all the while she could sense the mosquitoes. A brush against her bare wrist, a thin shrill past her ear. She held the baby tight and ran, spilling water wherever she could, until she reached Varuna Road and looked in despair at the cistern where fish sellers dumped their ice to melt and flower sellers cleaned their tall black buckets. Everywhere she looked, standing water. She could not pour it all away. The wildness drained from her, and she swayed where she stood, exhausted.

When she reached the shrine for Our Lady of Navigators, she felt as if she had washed up before it. She put her cheek to her baby's head and waited to be filled with grace. Instead came questions. What about the sponge she'd used to bring down Celia's fever? What about the bucket? What about the water in Mary's cupped hands? She heard another mosquito, slapped and missed. The night whined with disease.

She stood so long without praying that she worried she would give offense. But she could not find words strong enough to beg for Celia's life. It was the work of Flora's whole body to keep her child alive—the basins she kicked aside, the nail she drove into the wall for the net, her footsteps back and forth across the room, her hand on the baby's back, every thought and touch and glance—and what kind of prayer was that? In the end, she said Hail Mary, wishing it did not end with "the hour of our death."

When she turned to go, an older man she had not noticed stood resting on his bicycle, waiting to visit the shrine. Good clothes, good cycle. One of the cottage Catholics from the neighborhood just inland, where families lived in bungalows with gardens. Was the child ill? he asked. He did not sound unkind or even abrupt. He spoke as though he understood. Was this a sign that she had been heard? Was his question a test of faith? Flora could not fail. "She is better," she told him.

She walked home in what passed for silence in Varuna, no longer tipping out water. She only wanted to get back to Jerome and hold both her children beneath the net. Had Mary been frightened when her son was newborn? Had there been mosquitoes in that place also? Priests spoke of her acceptance, but what did priests know of mothers? When Jesus was small and burned with fever, Mary must have held a damp cloth to his neck. At the foot of the Cross, she must have prayed for the nails to melt, for his wounds to heal, for different miracles.

Flora had never thought about such things before. They were not understandings she welcomed, nothing that told her Celia would live. Esperanza had lost a child in an accident with boiling water. The undertaker's son had a problem with his blood. A perfect infant fell asleep and never woke. Boys at sea, daughters in childbirth. Cholera, yellow fever, malaria, flu. When Flora prayed again, she did not picture the statue, or Stella Maris in the basilica, or any of the Marys she'd seen before. She imagined a woman moving silently through the village, gently overturning the pots and buckets Flora had left behind, then touching the statue's wooden fingers until they spread, and even that water trickled away, down the lane and into the great gray sea.

3

MARCH 1980

Francis had just been named chair of the Historical Commission when a petition to build on Seaview Hill was submitted.

"Here's another headache," said Essie.

This was her general view on matters regarding the Commission, which she understood as a way for Francis to earn no money while being of no help to his wife and no use to his family. She listed several ways in which an emeritus professor might better occupy his retirement: he could offer tuitions, for which he would be well paid; he could join the Investment Club and make more of his pension; he could arrange the repair of their damaged roof tiles; he could write a book, about some topic far from neighborhood politics; or he could devote his energies to the church and do some good in this world.

"I *am* doing good," said Francis.

"You think God cares for commissions?"

Their own parish was tangled in this business. A consortium of cousins—a Parsi family—had developed a scheme for the area's first business-luxury hotel. They had chosen a site on Seaview Hill, just outside the historic zone, where the Portuguese raised the Castelo do Riacho three centuries before. The ruins of the watchtower provided a mild attraction for tourists and a location for film directors, who framed shots of the bay with crumbling colonial stone.

The new hotel would be a few hundred yards away, on a wide spur overlooking the western cliffs and the Arabian Sea. The view, sweeping south to Malabar and north to Juhu, was unparalleled. Santa Clara was an up-and-coming suburb, out of the throng of downtown Bombay and attractive to film stars and executives alike. No chawls would need to be relocated, no squatters removed. The consortium was adamant: if they could not build on Seaview, they would pack up their plans and go north.

The dispute was over a small parish building on the proposed site. It was used only as a storehouse and had fallen into disrepair, but the church was reluctant to give up its foothold on a prime piece of land and submitted a claim to assert historical value.

A week later, Francis set off for a site visit. His bicycle chain had snapped, so Jude gave him a lift on his new motorcycle. As a child Jude was timid, apt to clutch Marian's hand or hide in corners, but he took the slope in a series of quick, fierce dashes that left Francis clinging from behind.

"Son, should you wear a helmet?"

"This is nothing," Jude called. He was twenty, Francis reminded himself. At that age, Francis had been engaged for the first time.

Still, he was relieved to be deposited on the hillside. Jude looped around and paused to consider the storehouse. "Doesn't look like much."

Francis looked also. "It's still standing." He felt respect for whatever lasted in Bombay.

While Jude roared down the hill, Francis greeted the layperson who would show him around. He knew her slightly, a woman who administered the system of temporary graves. She unfastened the padlock and opened the door into a dusty chamber. Francis stepped over cobwebs and dead beetles as they moved past boxes of papers gone cottony with age. The cartons stacked against a water-stained wall were spotted with mildew.

"These are?"

"I've no idea. Church records are kept in the parish office. These must be"—she peered at the boxes, as though to discern a word beneath the dust—"*unsorted.*"

"I can look?"

"If you like." She registered neither surprise nor interest. It occurred to Francis that a woman in her position—shifting the departed from graves to niches—would not be well served by curiosity. "But you'd better take them with you. You wouldn't want to work here."

This did not have the feel of a formal authorization. But Francis reasoned that anyone empowered to transfer mortal remains must be empowered to transfer boxes.

"What's this?" Essie called from the balcony when she saw Francis and the watchman unloading a taxi at their front gate. "Are you planning a bonfire?"

"These are archives," said Francis.

"*Ar*chives," she repeated to Marian over the phone. Marian placed a call from America every few weeks, "just to hear your voices," although Essie tried to pack in as much as she could. Francis occasionally tapped his pocket to remind his wife what such chats must be costing.

"You see what I put up with? And who do you think paid the taxi?"

It took Francis weeks to sort through the boxes: letters, construction plans, appeals, rosters, inventories. He moved a desk onto the veranda, where it was pleasant to spend his mornings. Friends and former students waved from the gate. He was on hand to collect the helmet he'd ordered for Jude. And he enjoyed the tug of curiosity he felt when he examined each new document. The days curved differently with work ahead of him.

"A wall of boxes. We are the eyesore of the neighborhood," Essie told Marian. "The housing association will be after us. But your father is happy doing the bidding of these Parsis."

"It is the church who filed," Francis reminded her.

"Only because these people are pushing in with their hotel!"

Essie had grown increasingly agitated, appalled by the prospect that her husband might rule against the parish. "And where will that leave us? On the margins of the church. We'll be outcasts in our own home."

In fact, the outcome was still unclear to Francis, the question more complicated than he'd anticipated. The storehouse had replaced earlier structures. The first dated to the Castelo era, a granary with thick walls to keep out rain and rats.

He sought out other sources: municipal archives, parish records, libraries. In one of the book stalls near Flora Fountain, he purchased prints of two antique maps. One was of Bombay as an archipelago of islands in the Portuguese period, their shape and number changing with rising waters. His map showed four. The other was of the single peninsula that emerged in the nineteenth century, with its long unbroken shoreline, after the British pushed civil engineering projects to make paddies of salt ponds and inlets. Francis framed both and hung them in the boys' old bedroom, which he'd taken over as his own. He liked to look at them when he first woke up and think about ways the city had transformed, the drowned land that had been reclaimed, the eventual coast.

"He's gone half the day, earning nothing and buying costly maps," Essie told Marian. "And what is the point? We all know we're sitting on reclaimed land here. Now my walls are covered in tatters and my veranda is covered in boxes. The dust is terrible—very bad for Jude."

It was pointless to argue on international calls, but Francis could not let everything pass.

"Jude rides a *motorcycle*. What is he breathing then?"

"You remember, my girl—how badly he wheezed when he was young!"

Jude barely glanced up from his newspaper. "I outgrew all that, Mum."

"Because I kept the dust out. And now your father drags it right to your doorstep."

"I sit on the veranda with no difficulty," said Francis, and Essie wondered whether neighbors thought it odd, a professor working outdoors as though he had no proper room in the house.

After the Portuguese decamped, the outbuilding passed to the church, co-opted around the time when Stella Maris began to attract pilgrims. It was used primarily for storage, though occasionally it served as a makeshift guesthouse for nuns, since women could not be accommodated in the more congenial quarters where priests stayed. When Francis found a letter that mentioned the arrival of six Franciscan sisters in 1830, he cross-referenced the archives of the Holy Name School, founded a few years later to educate girls in the Catholic faith. It was the school Marian had attended, first as a sturdy child in green pinafores and red hair ribbons, then as a willowy girl in green skirts and white blouses. The connection to his daughter brought a pleasing dimension to his work.

One afternoon, he paged through photo albums from those years: Marian in a confection of birthday frills; Marian at the piano; Marian flanked by her brothers, socks at her ankles. She resembled Francis more than he'd noticed in those hectic days. He wished they'd taken more pictures, something to lay beside his memories of the way she tucked her feet beneath her when she read; or her softness before a first cup of tea, her expressions slightly blurred as though sleep lingered like a haze; or her startled eyes the day he killed a snake with her field-hockey stick. Or even one photo of his other daughter, but she had died so quickly.

A week later, he surprised Essie by asking to speak to Marian. Usually he felt self-conscious on the phone; after the marvel of hearing his daughter's voice came awkward halts and echoes. But he hoped she'd be interested in his latest discovery: the Franciscan nuns who had sheltered in the granary were the founders of her school.

"Their first weeks in India," he told her, unexpectedly jubilant. "Imagine the heat—they had no windows."

"Like Sister Rita's office." That was the infirmary, an interior room. Marian laughed. "I haven't thought of that in years. It was so hot that girls were dropping in faints."

"There, you see, that is very good history!" Essie raised her voice to be heard. "You can't knock down the building now!"

But that structure had already been demolished. In June 1837, a cyclone battered the coast, tossing ships, trees, and houses from Colaba to Madh. Five days later, when Queen Victoria succeeded to the throne, two of her East India Company steamers had been lost, and the Konkan coast was littered with wreckage. The granary was leveled, the chapel roof damaged, and one piece of plaster fell so close to the statue that the near miss might have been a miracle.

By the mid-nineteenth century, Stella Maris had survived an ocean crossing, a pirate attack, an amputation, and a typhoon. She drew pilgrims in greater and greater numbers, both Catholics and non-Christians, and her fame gave rise to a thriving economy of roadside vendors hawking flowers, wax figures, and candles. But the chapel was too small, particularly after the extension of the railway line encouraged more travelers to make the journey to Santa Clara. In 1895, the parish launched an ambitious project to raise a new church. Their first step was to replace the granary with a storehouse, to house objects from the chapel during construction.

A year later, the plague erupted. Construction was halted, Masses suspended. Priests and nuns tended to the sick or succumbed themselves, and in 1897, the new outbuilding became an inoculation center and hospital annex. Its distance from the cramped chawls below was an advantage, and to the faithful, its proximity to Stella Maris offered other modes of protection. When the epidemic subsided, the roof was removed to let in sun and air and the interior scrubbed with lime. A new roof was laid, with the same red clay tiles that marked every building of that period, including Francis's house. The villagers raised a Plague Cross in thanksgiving for whatever mercy they'd strained from those terrible months, and construction resumed. In 1904, Mary, Star of the Sea, was completed: an imposing Indo-Gothic structure with twin bell towers. Fifty years later, the church was designated a Minor Basilica. Francis and his family attended the celebratory Mass, Simon little more than a baby, Marian small enough to sit on his shoulders when she tired of the climb. By then, the outbuilding had fallen into disuse.

Francis produced a detailed report—which exactly *nobody* would read, said Essie—to support his findings. These were straightforward. The current building dated to the nineteenth century, not before. It contained no features of architectural interest. A few foundation stones salvaged from the earlier structure were not significant. The Plague Cross a few paces downhill was a more suitable tribute to the patients and caregivers of the outbreak.

It did not follow that whatever was old must necessarily be of historical value, Francis wrote. The current basilica succeeded at least two earlier shrines, all on the same spot. The church had not been obliged to save the earlier chapel, or the mud-brick dwelling into which Stella Maris was originally conveyed. Santa Clara had been populated for thousands of years. Their neighborhood occupied ground where their ancestors once raised dwelling places. Every civilization built on what came before. Not everything old could be saved.

The Commission denied a historical designation, but this ruling did not fully clear the way for the hoteliers. The parish still had a narrow claim to the land beneath the building, by virtue of having occupied it for centuries. That question might have remained entangled indefinitely in court if Francis had not proposed a solution: a financial settlement (arranged as a donation) and a hotel room set aside in perpetuity for complimentary use by clergy visiting the basilica or by the Sisters of the Holy Name, whose brief stay on Seaview Hill might be considered historically significant. Both the parish and the consortium agreed to this proposal. The Sisters, who had refused to be drawn into the controversy, were delighted to accept. The Stella Maris Suite occupied a corner near the start of the hotel's shopping arcade.

It was a good outcome, most agreed, although Essie took a dim view of anything less than total deference to the church. She raised her eyebrows at the bottle of whiskey that the hoteliers sent Francis—more a courtesy than a gift, he reasoned when he decided to accept it.

"Better they should send us roofers," said Essie. The house would fall down around them if it were up to her husband to keep it standing. But when Father Evelyn mentioned that the church would salvage building materials from the site, Francis made a quiet inquiry. The next day, he took a taxi to fetch three boxes of period red clay tiles, more than enough to restore their roof.

Inspired, Essie laid claim to the marble threshold. She intended to build a shrine to Mary in their compound one day and fancied marble for the base.

Despite these successes, Francis felt restless the day before demolition. He sipped his imported whiskey and reviewed his report, persuaded once more that the Commission's ruling was correct. But his personal feelings were less absolute. He pictured the rows of pallets during the plague. He imagined the misgivings of the Franciscan nuns, perched on a hilltop far from home.

It was early evening, a pale-gold sky. After his glass of whiskey, Francis felt pleasantly light, his thoughts free to wheel in the skies with the crows as he cycled up Seaview Hill with his camera. He loaded a roll of film, stood back to frame the building, and pressed the shutter. He took close-ups of the door and cornerstone. A shot of the sea from the cliff-facing window felt a bit fanciful, beyond the realm of historical documentation, but why not also preserve the view? Then he rode downhill for one last photo with the Plague Cross in the foreground. Children were playing at its base, so he crossed to the basilica to wait. The sun had not set; there was still time, still light.

Outside the gates vendors sold flowers, candles, and votives for worshippers. A woman stood with her small son at the stall closest to Francis. The boy strained at her hand, whining to join the children near the Plague Cross, but she ignored him while she considered the selection of wax figures for offerings. She spoke sharply in Marathi when he carried on tugging.

"They're older, they won't want you."

The boy dropped her hand and gazed at the children with a longing Francis recognized. He remembered it all: the struggle into a clean shirt, the endless restraints, the sandal scuffing the road just to make a mark in the dirt. He might have been that boy once, enjoined to pray for some distant cause—ancient relatives, adult sorrows, his own future.

And here Francis stood, having landed in that future. He had survived when others had not. He had passed his exams, pursued a career, found a wife, fathered children: all that a man might ask. Still, the evening seemed dusty and threadbare, the light tipping onto the sea, his own purpose in coming up the hill nothing he could quite explain. What would Agnes make of it?

He looked at the boy. A little fellow, three or four. *Come see*, Francis mimed, tilting the handlebars toward him. The boy approached warily, eyes fixed on the cycle.

"You like it? Should we ring the bell?"

"Anthony!"

The boy looked at Francis, closed his fist around the front wheel, and stood fast.

Francis laughed. "Let him have a ride if he likes."

But the mother did not answer, speaking only to her son in great plumes of scolding about dirty hands and strange men while she uncurled his fingers from the tire with such force that she nearly knocked down the cycle, even while Francis held it.

There was a round hushed moment as the boy registered this loss; then he began to wail.

"One short ride—" Francis tried again, but the mother slapped the boy hard and bore the howling child away. Francis felt a flare of shared outrage, the boy's and his own. Why not a small treat? What did she mean by this *strange men* nonsense—a person of his standing! What was more natural than a boy riding a bicycle?

He felt better when he wheeled the cycle to the Plague Cross and the children came flocking to inspect it. They put their fingers through the spokes, spun the pedals with their hands, grinned at him. Francis took his photo before he lost the light, then let each child ring the bell before he rode home.

4

JANUARY 1982

Francis sat in a cane chair beside the pool of the Hotel Castelo, sipping a glass of juice and considering whether to follow it with a beer at half past ten in the morning. He had chosen a place beneath an umbrella, but light bounced from every surface: the paving stones, the glass tables, the pool itself. Even the voices of the children seemed to bounce up from the water, sharp and bright.

The pool deck overlooked the Arabian Sea and was a much-vaunted feature of the Castelo, open only to overnight guests and half a dozen neighborhood bigwigs: a hometown cricket hero, three film stars, a High Court judge, and Francis, who had cleared the way for the owners to build.

On a Tuesday morning in late January, his family had the pool to themselves. Marian stood waist-deep in the shallow end to keep hold of the baby. Tara was three, too small for swimming, Francis thought, but Marian dipped the baby's feet in the water until she laughed, then popped her into the center of a float to tow her through the pool. The child looked serenely pleased, giving Francis the impression of a queen on her litter, unruffled by acts of devotion. Nicole was more explosive, bursting into motion and chatter. She bobbed up and down on her own power, wearing inflatables on her arms.

"These are enough for her?" he'd asked when Marian blew

them up. This was the last of several operations to put the girls into the pool: a rushed breakfast, swimsuits, hair ties, sun creams, hats, sandals, trips to the toilet, and at last the five of them wedged into an autorick, jouncing up Seaview Hill, while Nicole counted the dogs they passed. A bag of towels in case the hotel did not provide, though of course the hotel provided. Snacks, though they could order food. Extras of everything. A last dab of sun cream. Dry clothes. Francis felt overwhelmed and a little cowed by the level of preparation.

But with all this, arm floats did not seem sufficient. Nicole was a solid child, tall for a five-year-old—this, Francis felt vaguely, was an American quality. It was the food, perhaps, or just the scale of things: cars with seats like sofa benches, highways with full lanes to overtake, massive shopping complexes. When he visited the year before, he could not get over the size of the grocery stores, aisles wide enough for carts in two directions, shelves and shelves of breakfast cereal or canned fruit (but nowhere a good sharp pickle).

"She'll be fine, Dad. At home she takes lessons with a kick board."

Was that advisable? he wondered but did not ask. He seemed more apprehensive than anyone else about the dangers to which the children were susceptible. Essie scoffed when he questioned the fish on their plates.

"We take the bones *out*."

"But at this age—"

"At this age! Your children ate fish before they turned a year!"

He always had to withdraw when she alluded to their own children: he could not recall the details of their upbringing. But he had held one daughter when she died. He had crushed the snake that might have bitten the other. He thought of the Koli woman who ran with her baby to Our Lady of Navigators, how easily a child could slip past help.

There was a flurry of splashing as Tara struck the water with both hands, paused to consider the effect, and began striking again. Essie sat in her skirt at the edge of the pool, her feet in the water, clapping for the baby. Occasionally, she looked at

Francis, her face radiant—"See those cheeks!" She was happy in a way Francis could not remember seeing before, happy to peel their favorite fruit, happy to clean them in the bath, happy to offer the treat of this swim. She had suggested it after a trip to Juhu—"See how they love the water!"—and pestered Francis to arrange it. The hotel required bathing caps for children; Essie was happy to buy a pair.

"I don't wear these at home," Nicole pointed out. She stood stiff with impatience at the edge of the pool, arms akimbo in their floats, while Marian restrained her long enough to twist her hair into the cap.

"Silly girl!" Essie said brightly, and pulled her close when Marian finished. "This is your home also."

Nicole submitted briefly. Then she said, "I'm swimming now, Grandma," with a formality that reminded Francis of the way Marian took care to be courteous in the house where she was born.

Essie only laughed. She'd been in her element since Daniel left for his semester in the States. Marian and the girls would spend another six weeks in Santa Clara, and Francis could see Essie pretending that this was her real life, the way it ought to have turned out, without the rupture of Marian's departure. She would rewrite it if she could, her grandchildren close at hand and Daniel scrubbed out, replaced with a neighborhood boy of her choosing.

He watched Marian catch Tara's hands and spin her around, the baby, mother, and grandmother all laughing together. He did not notice Nicole climb out of the pool until she was at his side, a squat column streaming water.

"Grandpa. Come in the pool."

"Me?" He laughed. He was wearing slacks and a button-down shirt, proper shoes to walk through the lobby. "You want me to go with you?" He could see the sliding wet tracks of her footsteps from the pool. It pleased him that she would try to draw him into their circle.

"How can Grandpa swim, darling?" Essie smiled widely. "In his pants!"

Nicole gazed at Francis. He could not tell whether she was persuaded by this logic or regarded talk of pants weak. For a moment, he thought of catching her hand and jumping in with her, shoes and all.

Instead, he beckoned. She came closer, looking like a fighter pilot in her bathing cap. He spoke in a low voice, only to her. "You have another swim, and I will order a beer. Then you can have a sip."

It was something she liked, something he knew about this child, who was both near to him and foreign. A secret she shared with her father and would now share with him.

"*Three* sips," she told him. "One, two, three."

Francis smiled. He hailed the waiter and ordered a King-fisher. At the edge of the pool, Nicole turned back. "Look at me!" she commanded, and plunged into the deep end while Francis watched, holding his breath until the floats dragged her back to the surface.

5

JUNE 1985

The fish market days at Santa Clara Bazaar were Tuesdays and Fridays, and on Thursday evening Dominic was still at sea.

The cottage ladies would do their shopping next morning. Flora would have to buy from the dock if he didn't turn up. "A day or two only, he promises," she grumbled. "Now see what!"

Three days was nothing out of the ordinary, Celia knew. All through May and into the swelter of June, her father must earn what he could, before the off-season. Her mother was only fussing because at the last minute he'd decided to take Jerome. Two regular crew members had begged off to attend a family wedding, and Jerome was nine, past the age when Dominic had begun taking overnight voyages. It was time to teach his son.

"Your poor brother! Missing his first week of school."

Her mother was driving Celia wild with this *poor brother* nonsense. Nobody said *Poor girls* when the term at Holy Name began before Jerome's school, St. Ignatius. For a full week, Celia and her younger sister, Evangeline, set off in uniform shirts that their mother buttoned right to the top, pinching their necks, in a flood of cautions about manners and studying and speaking up nicely, while Jerome spent airy days on the dock with their father. Besides, Jerome didn't care in the slightest about missing school. He worked doggedly, but he was always sinking a bit and trying to kick himself up again, as if he lacked an essential buoyancy which Celia, bobbing like a cork, could not imagine life without. She was six, nearly seven, certain about most things.

Among them: that she could work the boats as well as any boy. She knew fishermen did not take their daughters out to sea; she knew there was no point in complaining. But every time her mother sighed over Jerome, Celia compiled a fierce internal reckoning of all the ways he was an inferior choice. His thick fingers were no good for lines and nets. He needed to be shaken awake in the mornings. There was a slight, glazed pause when he had to tell his right from his left.

She imagined herself at the bow, enjoying the wind and spray, while Jerome was asleep or maybe seasick. Her father would hand her snarled lines, and Celia would untangle them with nimble fingers. Thank God you're here, he would say.

Instead, she was stuck at home: a cooking area in one corner, a bed tucked against the back wall with drawers beneath it, a small curtained cubicle for bathing, and a heavier curtain separating them from the lane. A cable snaked between the bars on the window for the television, and the electric lights were strong and bright. A half-dozen hangers with a few changes of clothes were strung up on another piece of cable. Sleeping pallets were rolled against the wall until they were needed. Her father had mounted a small case of shelves on the back wall for toys and keepsakes. On the long wall hung laminated photos: Celia's paternal grandparents, who died before her birth; her parents, who seemed strange and young in their wedding clothes; and a picture of her great-grandmother, as thin as a whisk broom. Celia's mother worried that Evangeline had inherited her silences. Near the door hung a print of the infant Christ, with pink cheeks and yellow curls, kicking his heels from the manger.

It was a good house for a family of five, built in the days when fishermen's homes were sound, with proper floors, stone thresholds, thick walls, and solid wood doors nearly always latched open. Some villagers lived in shanties near the shoreline with tarp-and-burlap roofs, but even those families had shining stacks of cooking vessels, pirated hookups for television, and occasionally a bicycle—awkward as a gangly teenager—right in the middle of everything.

No one place felt shut off from any other in Varuna, where children ran in and out of each other's houses and music from neighbors' radio programs wafted down the lanes. The whole village was Celia's home, and she seldom felt confined. If she needed more room—to let her thoughts unfurl all the way to the horizon without crashing into anyone's *We know best* or *This way only*—then a few steps away was the sea.

"Can I run down to the water, Mumma?"

"What, now?" Flora sat on the bed with Evangeline tucked against her, the day's labors finally winnowing down to what she could accomplish off her feet.

"I'll see if they're coming—"

"We'll know soon enough." But, yes, Celia could go. "Only practice a little with Lina first. You be a girl in her class. Who's a nice, friendly girl, Lina? You choose."

Evangeline looked pained. She had started kindergarten two weeks before but barely spoke to her teacher or classmates. Twice Celia had been called down from first grade to interpret her sister's silences. Finally, the teacher sent home a note: Was Evangeline fully sensible of what people were saying, was she delayed or limited, was she hearing-deficient? Flora went rushing into school the next morning. Yes, of course her daughter could understand, of course she could hear, nothing in the slightest wrong, doctor also can tell you. She can read already, books and newspaper both. Only she is quiet.

"Peaceful, actually," Flora corrected herself, thinking it a better word. "Perfectly behaved. You'll have no trouble with her."

But already Flora could sense a kind of cloud forming around her daughter, a stigma she was anxious to dispel. At night, she helped Evangeline practice useful phrases ("Good morning, teacher!"), and drafted Celia into role-playing sessions to encourage friendly chats with schoolmates. Celia knew these did no good.

"Go on, Lina. We'll make it fun!"

Celia thought of her brother, having adventures she would never have, possibly seeing dolphins. She sat against the wall and pressed her skin to the thick plaster, which felt clammy if not actually cool. "Maria," Lina finally said.

"Maria is a cottage girl?" her mother wanted to know, meaning did she live in the neighborhood just inland, a quiet grid of streets, all named for saints, with old-style cottages and bungalows. A cottage girl would know a different sort of life: a private compound in which to play, someone to help in the kitchen. She might have piano lessons. She would not clean fish.

Evangeline hesitated long enough for Celia to realize Maria didn't exist. "She's from Mahim."

"Mahim! Why is she coming such a long way?"

"Lina doesn't know, Mum. Let's just *start*."

"You're always rushing," Flora told Celia. "Go ahead, Lina. There's Maria in the courtyard, so go and say a nice hallo."

"Hallo," repeated Evangeline. She could not quite bring her eyes to meet Celia's. Celia did not know what was less endurable: her own boredom or her sister's embarrassment.

"Hi," said Celia firmly. "Let's be friends."

Her mother frowned. "Let Maria be shy, Celu. Go on, Lina."

"Would you like to play?" Evangeline said faintly. Celia could not imagine her sister actually choosing those words. Evangeline was watchful, intuitive—never blank. She had no gift for the banal.

Flora could sense the disconnect without understanding it. Perfectly natural thing to say, *Would you like to play*. Why should her daughter sound so unnatural, then? There was something mystifying about trying to prepare this child for encounters so straightforward that she could not fathom how to explain them. You just *make friends*, she wanted to tell her. All children do it. Evangeline was sweet, obedient, in no way contrary, yet she managed to thwart all Flora's efforts. Flora thought of the angel taking Zechariah's voice and wondered if extreme timidity could be a trial sent from God. It was certainly true that Flora felt tested, and the story promised a hopeful outcome: in a few months, perhaps, Evangeline's tongue would be loosened. But it was hard to resign herself to a miracle in which her daughter only fell mute in school.

"Maybe start with a joke," she suggested.

Celia brightened. Her friend had been given a book of jokes for her birthday, and they had been poring over them together. "What is the elephant's favorite sport?" she asked Evangeline at once. "Squash! What goes up and down but never moves? Stairs!"

Chickens, teachers, knock-knock who's there. Flora wanted to steer her daughters back to practice, but Evangeline had gone from looking as if she were being poked with a sharp stick to giggling like any child.

"What does a house like to wear? A-dress! How can you tell the ocean is friendly? It waves!"

Flora had been waiting for just the right tone, nothing too silly. "There, Lina! Such a good one for you!"

But Celia and Evangeline only looked at each other and laughed, as though jokes had leaked into everything around them, the whole world hilarious. Flora tried to join in, though she was not certain if they were all enjoying a happy night together or if the serious project of learning to make friends had been circumvented.

"Nice jokes. I think that's enough now. Time to settle down."

"But listen to this one. What do you call a pony with a cough? A little hoarse!"

More wild laughter.

"Lina, you say one," Flora tried again. "Pick your favorite. You like the ponies best?"

What was so funny about that? Flora wanted to know. But they could not stop laughing. Celia let herself topple back onto the floor.

"Stop playing the fool, Celu. Your turn, Lina."

Evangeline took a deep breath, then burst out giggling again.

"Lina, Lina! What did one pencil say to a—"

"Celu!" Their mother sounded so sharp that even Evangeline felt a touch of danger. She put her hand over her mouth, still giggling behind it. "We've heard more than enough from you. And such a good quiet name your great-grandmother gave you—what would she say?"

Nothing, Celia knew. She tried to control herself, but laughter rolled through her like sneezes, impossible to stifle entirely. Anyway, she was tired of hearing about the ancestress whose most striking quality was that she had been quiet, a hundred times quiet, a miracle of quiet, whose legacy of silence survived as a reprimand. Celia wished for a name with a lot of noise.

"I'm *helping*, Mumma. She likes it. Lina, do you want to see the book tomorrow? *Three Hundred Best Jokes for Children.* You can say them with us."

Evangeline nodded yes, so radiant with pleasure that Flora did not suggest more drills. She would prefer Lina to make friends in her own class, but starting with Celia's friends was better than nothing. At least the teacher would see that she could talk.

"Speak up nicely when you tell your jokes," she told Lina, and settled on the bed to hear the weather bulletin. No changes, no storms expected.

Celia waited until her mother switched the channel before asking again to walk down to the water.

"Now?"

"You said later."

"Why, Celu?" But she was in no mood for arguments. There would be no squalls near her son and husband for another night at least, Lina was leaning against her, and Flora felt drowsy. She had not slept well since Jerome had gone. "Quickly, then."

The heat had not abated, only softened. Still, the lane was full of people for whom sundown was release. Lights burned bright, turning the night the color of weak tea. Women talked over pots or nets. Wakeful children played on stoops. One father held a fussing baby; a couple of other men smoked while they chatted. A pair of women walked back from day work in other people's houses. A flower seller set down her basket and gave her last limp blossoms to the small girls who came running. Celia took a marigold.

She was greeted a half-dozen times in the lane, but the beach was nearly empty. A couple sitting on the seawall looked up, noticed Celia, and decided to leave. An old man sat outside a tin-and-tarp shelter, in a plastic chair with a cracked arm. Celia and Jerome played with the brothers who lived there, boys mad for cricket. She could hear voices past a cluster of huts on the northern tip of the beach—people collecting shellfish, maybe. The tide was out, the beach a soft composite of warm sand, withered rubbish, paper gone to pulp, and dried seaweed, with sudden slicing bits of shell and the occasional twist of rusted metal. Celia walked to the waterline. Past the oily yellow lights of Worli, the glittering fingertip of Malabar Hill pointed out into the darkness toward her father. She had seen the map of coastal waters that her father kept in an oilskin roll, but although she could trace the notches of the shoreline, she could not make sense of the thin lines flung out over the water like a net. When she looked from the shore, she only saw a few dots of lights past the mouth of the bay, each glimmer a whole boat. Daddy is farther than that, she thought.

She was not afraid, exactly. All her life, her father had gone to sea; all her life, her mother had listened to forecasts. But on nights like this one—smoky, moonless, the stars old and faded—Celia could not discern between sky and water to find the horizon. There was only a great rolling darkness, with no map lines to score it. What if her father and Jerome were lost? She had taken to testing herself with awful ideas, throwing herself over the clifftop of one fear or another and plummeting past the life she knew into a future in which she alone could save her family. She would become the type of hero her parents had never imagined—a girl who made her fortune in some unforeseen way—telling jokes to large crowds, perhaps. A whole year later, when all was well, her father and brother would wash up home again, to be astonished.

But for the moment, Celia stood in the muck, a small girl with sandpiper legs. The seas were calm; her father was safe, her brother lucky. The waves sighed as they gave up the shore. Celia kicked, spraying water. It was not so late, she thought. She glanced at the shack where the two brothers lived, but saw only their grandfather, still in his lawn chair, his broad leather sandals planted in a scree of broken shells and sand.

"Is Jay inside?"

"You should sleep," he told her.

Celia turned away. The lane was lively, the ocean unceasing, the reach of her own thoughts limitless, and the world full of people sending her to bed.

"I was ready to come after you," her mother scolded when she heard Celia outside the door, rinsing sand from her feet with the last of the wash water. But her mother sounded more distracted than annoyed. She was setting out baskets for market the next morning; she would buy wholesale from other village boats if Dominic and Jerome did not dock in time.

What was her brother doing at that exact moment? Celia wondered as she went inside, making cloudy marks on the floor with her damp feet. She wondered the same an hour later, when the room was dark and she could hear her mother's breath snagging softly on itself. What had he learned that she still didn't know? If he were home, they could play checkers; they had done it before, hissing "King me" and silently cheering while their mother was safely asleep.

"Lina," she whispered, nudging her sister on the sleeping pallet they shared. "Lina! Knock-knock."

But her sister was asleep.

6

JUNE 1985

Her father's boat came in just before dawn. Her mother left to help sort the catch before Celia or Evangeline woke. An hour later, Inez stopped in on her way to the market to be sure the girls were ready for school. Evangeline's hair was cut above the shoulders; she only needed a band to hold it back. But Inez plaited Celia's hair and tied green ribbons on the ends.

"There!" she said with satisfaction. "Such tall, tall girls, and still you keep growing. Isn't there a birthday coming?"

"Mine, mine!" Soon Celia would be seven.

"Monsoon baby. You make more noise than three storms." Inez tugged one of her braids. "Up the lane, then straight to school."

"Up the lane" meant the community center, where all the children of Varuna could go while their parents worked.

Celia waited until Inez had turned the corner, then caught Evangeline by the hand and towed her toward the beach.

"Will we be late?"

"Don't you want to see Jerome?" Their brother was the big news, back from his first overnight expedition. But Celia also hoped for a glimpse of their father while he and the crew were still on board. He was a different man on the boat, she sensed. At home, he rose yawning from naps, his attention drifting from the television to a mild interest in whatever lay close at hand.

"What's that, then?" he might ask Celia about a book in her lap or a handful of marbles she had won from friends. "Another book," he might marvel, without asking what it was about, or "Mind you leave some marbles for them," with no discussion of her superior skills. He frowned over money but did not complain as much as other fathers about subsidies or overfished waters. On the worst days he went silent, a gloom that could only be dispelled by visiting the Cooperative, or a drink with Clive, or his next trip to sea. In the monsoon season, the long blank hours could sour him.

But when Celia overheard him with his crew, he was quick and deft, even at the end of a tiring voyage. There were songs he did not sing to Celia, stories he did not tell her, jokes she never heard. She only caught snatches when he talked to other fishermen. She wanted to know those stories; she wanted her share of that man—her father but not quite. It did not seem fair that only Jerome should know him fully.

The docks were teeming when Celia and Evangeline arrived. Five boats were in, the smallest already unloaded and on its way back to its mooring. Children who had helped in the early hours before school went to scrub themselves clean and change into uniforms, and the first wave of women were off to sell at the market, Flora among them. But a dozen or so women remained, their saris tucked between their legs as they worked. Other women haggled over mounds of fresh prawns, squid, and bangda. Girls cleaned baskets full of Bombay duck, a native fish, before hanging them on bamboo racks to dry.

In a wedge of land near the seawall, children too young for school were playing with a ball, and two babies just old enough to sit up had been set down near their mothers' baskets, bobbing up and down as they grabbed at each other's knees. Older boys who had left school and crew boys from villages up the coast were busy on land and sea, scooping fresh ice from the communal cooler, hosing the boat decks, or filling bins with bulk fish for the export buyers.

Normally, if she had not been watching Evangeline, Celia would have been cleaning the catch before school. She did not mind those mornings, out in the sun and air with other girls her age, racing each other to scale the most fish. The smell got under her nails, but if she washed her hands well, only a faint tidal undertone remained. Once, when she was in kindergarten, she rinsed off too quickly, and when she reached the school courtyard, a cottage girl pinched her nose shut and pretended to choke. Celia froze only a moment—the stakes laid as bare as bone—before she curled her hands into great fishy claws and stalked the girl across the courtyard. She imagined the scent could shoot from her fingertips like a ray, so sharp that it would part the cottage girl's thick oiled hair. She drew closer and closer until the girl broke into a run. Celia did not bother to chase her. She learned to dig her fingers into a cake of soap before going to school, leaving crescent marks. The cottage girls learned something, too.

Their father was still on board, bent low to help the boys pitch the last of the catch from the hold, but when he spotted his daughters, he called in greeting without breaking the rhythm of his work. It must have been a good haul—her mother was already at market, and two other women were waiting to buy up what was left. One of the crew held up a large crab before tossing it into the tub.

While the girls watched, their father rubbed his hands on his pants and stepped to the boat rail to wave goodbye to a well-dressed man. The hotel buyers did not always come to the village docks, but their father was smiling; that meant a big sale.

"Look, Celu!" Evangeline pulled Celia's hand as Jerome emerged from the supply shack with an empty plastic tub in one hand. The girls ran to him.

"How was it?" Celia said. "Did you stay up all night? Were there dolphins?"

He shook his head no. His face had a numb look, as though he had toothache. When he spoke, his voice creaked a little. "Mum said you were taking Lina."

Celia shifted, impatient. "Where were you? Why aren't you with Daddy?"

Jerome flicked his head toward the hotel buyer. "He's Hotel Castelo. The driver's up the lane. They took twelve kilos of rawas."

"So much!" Evangeline looked awed.

Jerome tipped his head. Their father leapt down to the dock while the boys hosed the deck, and Evangeline ran to him. Jerome began to walk again, banging the tub against his leg. Celia kept beside him. "The trip was good?"

"We got bhekti also."

"What did you get to do?"

"Let me finish this—"

"But, Jerome!" She flung herself in front of him. "What was it like?"

He shrugged in a way that told Celia the whole story: he did not like being at sea; he could not talk about it; if he tried to put words to his distress, it would swell like a sponge in his throat. He would begin to cry, and couldn't she see he was doing all he could not to cry?

She could. She made a life's study of seeing him. Other boys are happy on the boats, why not me? said the shrug, and since she could not give shape to some different hope for him, any more than he could give shape to the reason he was unhappy, she said, "Maybe you won't have to."

But of course he would. Fishing was the center of everything.

"Did Daddy . . . What did Daddy say?"

"Stop pestering, I have to *do* this."

Celia was so mortified for him, about to cry on the beach in front of half the village, that she charged. Jerome rocked back as she rammed into his chest.

"What's the matter with you?" he shouted. "Get off!"

"Make me!" She could hear he was on firm ground again, his voice clear, the danger of crying past. She dashed off, and he chased her with a stream of old-aunty warnings: late-to-school, teacher-this, mummy-that.

"Then take Lina yourself!" She threw herself at her father's legs.

"I'm *working*," Jerome said, and Celia wanted to pummel him again.

"*Arre*, Celu!" her father said sharply. "Get your sister to school!" But his arm closed around her, a quick, damp hello, before she took Evangeline's hand and set off. She waited until they were out of sight to say maybe they'd better run.

7

JUNE 1985

On her seventh birthday, Celia informed her family that she had reached the age of reason. Her school principal had said so.

"Sister Regina? Why?" Flora tried not to sound worried about how her daughter had attracted notice.

To her relief, there had been no incident. Sister saw Celia and Evangeline at dismissal, and Celia was wearing the class birthday crown. "She said, Such a big girl now, and seven is the age of reason."

She tried to imbue the words with Sister's gravity, but her father laughed. "It may take a few more years in your case."

Celia said nothing more. She would have preferred her father to regard her birthday as significant, but it was a relief to hear him laugh. For two full months, fishermen were prohibited from going to sea, a government measure to safeguard small craft during the monsoon season. But if the rains held off longer than usual, the ban went into effect beneath perfectly clear skies. In villages up and down the coast, Kolis grumbled over the nets they couldn't cast. Her father's boat needed repairs, his columns of figures kept falling short, and he was trapped at home, chafing.

"What about you, Lina?" their mother asked. "Did you say hallo nicely? So Sister could hear you?"

Evangeline looked at Celia, who hurried to divert the conversation.

"Sister said seven is exciting."

"Did she?" Flora said. It would be enough if one daughter settled down and the other piped up, if Evangeline's troublesome cough would clear, if Jerome would stop looking miserable each time his father checked the weather. Flora wanted to take the sky in two hands and wring the slowpoke rain from it. But the clouds were as small as beetles, clustered beneath the belly of the sun. The air was parched. The heat shriveled whatever it touched.

"One more day at least," said Dominic, and Celia knew he was finished with talk of birthdays; he was predicting the onset of the monsoon. Banned from calm seas—where was the reason in that? Since boyhood, the fishermen of Varuna had worked at sea. They knew the waters the way they knew their wives. They could look after their boats.

Dominic switched on the television forecast. Rain did not worry him; he was checking for the jagged icon that meant an electrical storm.

When the report ended, he poked his head out the door. It was late afternoon, the sky yellowed, crows hoarse.

"Will you go?" Celia asked.

Dominic grunted, a sound that meant, I'm still thinking, or small girls needn't concern themselves, or I'm not yet ready to tell your mother. When he turned, he spoke directly to Jerome.

"Your schoolwork is finished?"

"Almost."

"Go on, then. Finish quickly."

Jerome put his head low over the book in his lap, looking as if he wished to crawl inside its pages. Celia imagined a turtle with a book-cover shell. She herself felt like more of a cat, slinking along the outsides of things, ready to leap.

"*I'm* finished, Daddy." If only he would take her.

"I'll go up the lane," her father said. "See what's what."

Her mother tipped her head. He was off to the Cooperative, where the men of Varuna could buy diesel from their own collective, purchase ice from their own factory, take a drink of their own toddy, arrange loans, exchange news, consider forecasts, issue complaints, settle disputes, and commiserate about acts of government.

Celia jumped up to go with him, but her mother had other ideas. "Go and check the racks, Celia, that's my good girl. No, Lina, you stay. That cough."

Her father walked up the lane while Celia took her basket to the beach. Rows of Bombay duck were strung from bamboo poles to dry, and she collected whatever was ready. She did not mind helping. But it felt to her as though the household needed fine-tuning to put things right. If Jerome had a cough instead of Evangeline, or if Celia had been a boy. Or if they could all come into clearer focus and her parents could see her, on the cusp of a new life.

"Your choices are your own now," Sister Regina had explained, though Celia did not see how. There were fresh starts, of course—a new school year, preparations for her First Communion—but her life was arranged in ways beyond her power to change. When she felt along the seams of her days, she could not find any hidden springs. She was on the hunt for some unexpected chamber, a door she could open to real excitement.

Or a birthday celebration. This morning, she woke to hugs. Her father pretended she was too big to lift before he tossed her up and caught her seven times, once for each year. Her mother helped her fasten a new necklace with a flower charm to wear to school. "Your special day, my girl," she said, and kissed her. Usually there were sweets, but no one mentioned any. If the weather held, Celia hoped they might walk up Seaview Hill together. Near the top, just past the Hotel Castelo, were balloon vendors and candy floss and hand-crank rides.

Instead, she brought home a basket of dried fish and found her father back from the Cooperative, his face set. He'd decided, Celia knew. Jerome was out, seeing to ice or fuel or nets for the voyage. Her mother was making a nervous clatter with cooking vessels. Her father did not glance up when Celia returned; he was packing.

"Come!" Her mother interrupted him, her voice loud and bright. "Celu is back. Let's sing to her before you go."

Jerome was gone already, Celia wanted to say but could not, because she was on a precipice, about to spill over into tears. Her father paused to sing, at least, while her mother hugged her from behind. Her sister did what she could with her thin little voice. But Celia could see that her birthday was finished before it began. This was it. She had not known how much she wanted until she saw there would be nothing more.

The song ended. Her mother squeezed her while her father described a special gift he had in mind: colored powders. "We can find some when I get back, and you can make your own rangoli."

"Or playing jacks is nice," said Flora. "Maybe a set of jacks."

"You should have seen my grandmother's rangoli. Magic, what she could do."

Celia didn't answer. There was nothing for her in such memories. She was not a girl for sitting and sifting.

But her father held up a net she had mended. "Already you're good with your fingers." He smiled, a real smile, and Celia saw an opening.

"Daddy, take the wooden boat!"

It was a last desperate move. The two-month hiatus kept most fishing boats anchored: all the diesel-powered crafts that fishermen used for voyages outside the bay. But the Koliwadas had fought for the right to use their old-style wooden boats in the shallows, and Celia thought her father might not need Jerome so close to shore. She would ask to go instead: a night with her father in her great-grandfather's boat.

"Don't be silly." He laughed when he saw her face go stony. "What's this pouting! What did Sister say? You're age of reason now."

Reason, Celia thought, was understanding what you couldn't even ask.

"We're back soon, baby," her father said, which Celia knew already, because after June 15, when the Coast Guard Act took effect, her father must use the diesel boat only in darkness. He must launch late enough to slip past any patrols; he must cut his engine and switch off his running lights as soon as he passed out of the bay. He must resign himself to stationary fishing, because it was madness to chase a catch and risk the fines. He must choose his spot well, where a man at anchor might bring up a decent net before dawn. He must forgo music and listen all night to the drone of the weather radio, scanning the skies for any sign of a storm. He must haul up in time to reach the bay before sunrise. If by some luck he brought in marlin, he would have nearly enough for his repairs.

He tugged Celia's ear. "Have a good sleep, birthday girl," he said, his thoughts already fixed on the voyage ahead. He had no time for small girls sulking.

Usually, Celia would have run down to the dock with him. Instead, she watched him go, her face so serious that she knew, if he turned back to look, he would not dare to laugh again. When he didn't turn, she felt cheated.

Inside, her mother was a fountain of talk about "one good catch; Daddy will be happy; then we can celebrate." Celia let the words pour over her and still felt dry to the bone. Nothing her mother said could touch her; she was busy with her own thoughts. She knew that when Sister Regina talked about choices, she meant the choices that belonged in religion class, choices to be close to God, choices to be good. But Celia wished for choices that were nearer at hand. She wanted to make her father turn in the lane and reckon with her. She wanted to astound him.

Her mother put on the television and switched from one channel to another, searching for something without the slightest hint of tragedy, no weather, no government officials. Within an hour, she fell hard to sleep. Evangeline slept also, her breathing sandy, her body tucked into the curve of her mother's.

Celia waited a few minutes more. The television still jabbered, but through the curtained doorway, she could hear bright shards of other people's lives: voices, motors, a stream of music. A small boy across the lane wailed. Celia was not disturbed. She was accustomed to a loose weave of noises around her at all times, reassurance that no one was ever alone. She was not in the least afraid when she picked up a small net her father left behind and slipped through the curtained doorway.

There was no chance she could go unseen in the lane, but she was lucky to encounter people who wouldn't fuss: a couple caught up in each other, a woman so eager to see her sons that she didn't send Celia home. Just before Celia reached the beach, she saw Aunty Janu's son, a man with wild hair and thick tufted eyebrows, sitting outside his mother's house with a bowl of rice. He wore his old boiler suit, though it had been years since he'd worked the oil rigs in Bombay High.

Stories were always buzzing about Aunty Janu's son. Some said he hadn't worked a day since his cousin, standing next to him on the platform, was blown away by a gust of wind. Others said something had broken loose and knocked the cousin straight into the water. Others said the cousin was not drowned at all but living in Andheri, where he fled after Aunty Janu's son threatened him with a knife. Some said it wasn't a knife: that Aunty Janu's son had stabbed a fork through his cousin's hand to the wooden table beneath, and his mother no longer kept cutlery.

Celia scuttled past. Aunty Janu's son was sitting with his legs stretched over the street gutter, where water ran down to the sea. Celia wondered if he could feel the damp through the thick canvas of his boiler suit. Was he mad enough to sit in puddles? Then his dark eyes swung up and caught her, like a boat held in a beam of light from the Coast Guard. She hurried past to where the lane splayed into the beach.

There was no moon, but clouds were rolling in, and the lights of the city were caught in a soft orange haze. The heat was caught, too, a long stale breath rising from the baked earth to snag on aerials, catch in tree branches, settle on roads and rooftops. Celia walked barefoot, making her way to the waterline. She could see only three dim lights offshore; her father and Jerome's would not be among them.

A few wooden boats had been pulled out of the water, flipped bottom side up like turtle shells. Half a dozen more were anchored, knee deep in low tide, for men to putter through the shallows looking for small catch: crabs, prawns, and lobsters. There were not enough, Celia's father said flatly. Even in the open water, Koli fishermen struggled to live on what the trawlers left behind. He made a story of it, a story of monster boats owned by fat-cat men who paid no attention to monsoon bans. Their pockets were so deep that they could pay off whomever they pleased. Their nets were so massive that all of Varuna could fit inside. Celia imagined the immense cloud of such a net falling over the village, snagging on the steeple of the Church of the Loaves and Fishes, drifting down over the courtyard of her school and catching on Sister Regina's shoulders.

Then the story collapsed into her father's tired voice: "They drag their nets across the sea floor so that even the baby fish are swallowed up. Not enough can grow. And what can we do? We are scraping by, and the catch for these guys is one lakh a day."

A lakh a day was unfathomable.

She walked through gummy sand, then waded out with the net held high. The *Pearl* was long and narrow in the water, a painted wooden boat with a small outboard engine. By the time she reached the anchor line, the swells came to her waist. But the water was calm, the surge slapping lightly against the side of the boat the way a boy's hand slaps the flank of a bullock to urge it on.

Her father kept a tarp over the boat, and Celia loosened the cord enough to tug it back. She hesitated, imagining small crabs. Then she threw her net inside and tried to hoist herself in. This was harder than she'd expected. The sides of the boat were creamy smooth, her own body low in the water. She made a few flailing attempts before her feet found a rock to stand on; then she heaved herself into a nest of rope and buoys.

It was a clumsy, clattering start. She felt like a small girl in a dark place, not her father's daughter after all. When the boat stopped rocking, she rolled the tarp back farther, until the stern was open to the sky. The bottom boards were painted blue and the thwarts orange, happy colors in daylight but eerie at night, like a clown in the wrong place. She tried to imagine her father's delight when he realized she could set a dhol net, even without wooden poles to stake it. She did what she could with rope and pitched the net over the side.

Bunches of mesh drifted up, looking slack and useless. She'd used the smallest net she could find, but it was still too large for shallow water. Never mind, she thought. The tide would come in, sweeping fish in with it. The net would work better once the water was deeper.

Until then, she could use the handheld net her father kept for prawns. Usually, her father steered the boat slowly while Jerome skimmed the water; usually, they preferred a tide running out. But the water was still low, and Celia could wade through the shallows; she had seen prawns caught that way before. She slid back into the bay.

For an hour, she trailed the net through the water and caught nothing. Every child in the village knew the bay was a sad old story. But Celia had envisioned a new ending, a loaves-and-fishes net. It was the girl-spy business of sneaking past her mother that would be difficult, she'd believed, or the pirate craft of climbing aboard. Once she achieved those, the fish were sure to follow.

She skimmed the net in a wide circle and brought it up empty. Again. Empty. Again. Empty. It was a lonely thing, an empty net. She wanted, of all people, her brother beside her.

The surge grew more raucous. When it began to play around her chest, she threw the net back into the boat. She had to hold fast to the anchor rope to haul herself in, and her arms were so tired that when she finally made it she sat panting, her dress plastered to her legs, her fingers pale and puckered, one thumb rubbed raw. She tried to cast her thoughts out, far from this moment, to when this aching part would be over. The stern swept up to a sharp point behind her and she leaned back into its narrow cradle. She could rest until the tide was high enough to bring up the dhol net. Fish would make everything right.

But already she worried she had reached the end. The fish in the bay were gone; she heard it in her father's voice. She gazed out at the water. The tide was coming in faster, the waves pricking up, looking almost alert, and she wondered how a sea could make such a secret of its dying.

What could be salvaged? She could not simply go home; some accomplishment must be wrung from all this effort. She thought of hauling up the anchor and casting the net farther from shore, but quailed; she was not fool enough to risk the boat. She curled her head into her arm and tried to shape a new plan, but her thoughts drifted up, useless and drowsy. The sky was soft and low, faintly orange. The sounds of the waves reminded her of her sister's breathing. Did her brother like sleeping on the boat?

When she blinked her eyes open, she saw bright clusters of lights moving far past the bay in open waters and knew the monster boats were out, their huge arms reaching behind them, their hands of hook and net raking the sea floor clean. She closed her eyes.

Then one banged into the *Pearl*. She woke, a startled animal jerk, and with wild eyes took in patches of where she was—the boat pitching, the dark tumble of sky—a different sky, the orange haze scribbled over with lead. Waves. Thunder. She saw a dark head a few meters away—the mustache, the fierce dark eyes—Aunty Janu's son.

"Celia!" he called her by name. "Celia! Come now!"

She tried to stand but was rocked hard. Before she could grab hold of anything, she pitched over the side.

Water in her eyes, nose, ears. Water overhead. She could not right herself, could find neither sky nor sand. She clawed water, broke the surface, breathed foam and cough and splutter, and was tossed under again. Her foot scraped a rock, but before she could stand she was swept away. Water flooded her thoughts, dragging her in and out; she saw Evangeline in the schoolyard, looking small in her checked pinafore. She saw her mother's back while she cooked, her father disappearing down the lane, her brother asleep beside her. She heard all the wet workings of her own body and the surge of waves around her and nothing else.

Then she slammed into something solid. Hands were at her

waist, and for a moment she thought she had conjured them: her father's hands, pulling her up. She was gulping air and choking, an arm banded across her chest, her cheek against the scratch of a bristly face—Aunty Janu's son, shoulder-deep in water. He said something she could not hear and shook her a little. Water ran from her mouth and nose. It was raining.

"Better?" She was still coughing but not as badly. He shifted her to his hip as if he were some regular uncle come to take her home from a party. "Hold on." She curled her legs tight around him and he turned to let the waves break against his side while he slowly carried her back to the boat.

It was a shocking distance. The sea had swept her halfway to the jetty. When they reached the *Pearl*, Celia thought for one panicky moment that Aunty Janu's son meant to put her back inside. She clutched at him.

Instead, he began pulling the tarp back over the boat, where rainwater was already beading every surface. It was a jerking, one-armed business, rain spattering the tarp with a sound like thrown pebbles. When he finished, he hefted her onto his shoulders so he could manage the cords with two hands. Celia ducked low and clapped her hands to his cheeks. They were rough, like her father's when he came back after a few nights at sea.

Aunty Janu's son yanked a knot tight and swung away from the boat with his hands closed hard around her ankles. He set off for shore, water churning around his chest. All around them, rain pocked the surface of the bay. "I left the net," she called, but he did not seem to hear. She wanted to turn and look for lights, her father's boat cruising into shore on the crest of the rain, but she was too scared to shift from her perch. "Is it a storm?" She lifted her voice. Sometimes there were cyclones. Sometimes waves battered the seawall until chunks of concrete fell away like wet sugar. Sometimes there were waves so high that a boat was tossed to pieces and the men were never found.

"Wait," he said. They were past the worst of the breakers. The wet boiler suit clung to his legs, a weight that dragged at his steps until, finally, she could see his bare feet in the sand. He walked to the seawall and lifted her onto it. They stood, wiping rain from their eyes and faces.

When Celia turned to the sea, it was fast and black, rearing up into waves. No boat lights. She wanted to cry. She wondered if Jerome was crying.

"You should go home," Aunty Janu's son told her.

"Daddy is there." She jutted her chin toward the sea. She knew what all village children knew: the Coast Guard would not assist a boat in defiance of the ban.

Aunty Janu's son looked at her through the rain—a rare open look, with none of what grown-ups had already decided in it. He had not scolded her, she realized. He had not asked her to be sorry.

"He'll come soon. The storm is passing. In another two hours, it will be light."

She stared at him, his wild hair and his soaked suit. His eyes were not so frightening, just keen. He pressed the back of his hand to his dripping mustache, as if he could dry any part of himself in the streaming rain. Celia decided she did not believe that business with the knife and fork. She moved closer and held on to his leg.

They sat together on the seawall. He blew his nose. After a while, the rain slackened to a mist. Aunty Janu's son drew a beedi from his pocket, found it too wet to light, and carefully replaced it.

"Maybe my mother doesn't know I'm gone."

"If she knew, we would hear her."

Celia hadn't thought of that.

"There," he said suddenly, and she saw a yellow spark bobbing in and out of view. The boat was close to shore, coming in steadily; they'd kept the lights off in case of the Coast Guard.

"Come." He slid down, and held out his hand to help her. "Before we hear your mother and father both."

"You are Aunty Janu's son," she told him in the lane, a way to admit she did not know his name.

"Jerome," he said.

"That is my brother's name!" The world was full of friends and brothers. The sky was still dark, but a thin blue seam appeared through the trees and buildings to the east, as if night were a bowl slipping off to one side, its terrors sliding away.

"I know yours. You kids are always shouting." He moved his hands like beaks and she giggled.

At her doorway, he took the damp beedi from his pocket once more. "Okay," he said, and, just in time, Celia remembered to thank him. He cupped her chin in his hand, then released her. Celia watched him go up the lane. She wished she could stay with him. Daybreak was near. Soon the vada-pav seller would light his stove, and they could eat from the first batch.

Instead, she slipped inside. Her wet clothes came off in a clump; silently, she put on dry. She reached over the bed where Evangeline slept with her mother and switched off the television. Then she curled up on her pallet, a cover pulled tight to her shoulders.

Her mother did not wake, but later came other difficulties. A net tied to boat lines would not go unnoticed. Celia must cut it loose when the tide receded, when the sea looked nothing like the place where Aunty Janu's son had found her. She must hope that, in the eight weeks of the off-season, her father would not register its loss.

Twice she was shaken awake at school; she must explain the note her teacher sent home. She must account for the state of her wet clothes, which her mother found in a heap.

"What kind of girl!" Flora moaned, when Celia confessed to waking in the night and walking down to the beach. Bad enough to say she was caught in the rain. "What kind of reason is this!"

Her father spoke sharply of locked doors. The catch had been light. The storm scared the boy. He was in no mood for silly girls, teacher's notes, small worries.

But what Celia remembered best was what she could never tell, the part of the story she tucked close to herself and carried through the lanes of the village; to school with her sister; to the market stalls and bungalows where her mother sold fish; even to her husband's house the day she married. It was the moment when Aunty Janu's son called her name. It was as if he had plucked it out of the wet air. There, in the midst of all that was huge, turbulent, inchoate, blind, she was seen. She felt that to be known was a kind of love, the kind she herself felt for Aunty Janu's son whenever she walked by his house with a cheeky pirate wave that left other children dazzled and terror-struck.

"If I like, I can march right to his door and take a ride on his shoulders," she told her brother a few weeks later, when a display of her superiority became necessary.

"You'd never."

"You think I'm afraid? I'm not afraid."

"You talk rubbish," Jerome told her, so she punched him hard and took off running.

OCTOBER 1986

The photograph was no bigger than the palm of Francis's hand, faded sepia on thick card stock. Albert passed it to Francis across the table at the gymkhana, where they were meeting for the first time in a year.

"Have a look."

Three figures beneath a mango tree. Francis touched the boy he had been, standing with Albert's sisters in their garden.

"You remember the day I took that?"

"Yes, of course."

He and Albert grew up a street apart. Albert was a year older, but they were given their first bicycles on the same Christmas morning and spent years riding from one end of Santa Clara to another. After Albert left to study in the south, Francis spent more time with his friend's younger sisters. Anna was the lively one, the girl who sneaked out of her house to turn up at a beach party in her pajamas. In the darkness, she seized the wrong bicycle to ride home, and Francis came to claim it the next day. He was nearly twenty years old—at university, reading history—a bit reserved, dazzled by her quickness. A few months later, at the end of the summer, he wrote to ask Albert's approval before going to their parents.

Their families liked the match. "Give her a ring if you like," her father said. "Only wait two years before you marry. Finish your studies."

Francis intended to ask her at the Castelo at sunset, his idea of a proper proposal, but they had walked too far down the Promenade to climb the hill before dark. Anna wanted ice cream, so they brought their cones to the seawall and looked over the long black rocks. Gulls alighted closer than Francis liked, and the slick green smell of low tide hung dank and heavy beneath the smoke of cook fires. A boy on a cart, his legs twisted and useless, knuckled his way to them to offer a secondhand newspaper full of the Nazi invasion of Poland. His voice rattled—"Please, ba, please"—until Francis found some coins. The sunset was bland, a wash of sooty peach over the horizon. Anna licked ice cream from the heel of her hand. The gulls menaced; the tide pools stank; war was coming; and Francis could not kneel on the seawall without looking a fool. Still, he asked; he could not wait. She said yes.

Three months later, Albert came home on holiday with a new camera and spent a sunny day taking portraits in the garden. A snap of his parents, known in the neighborhood as the long and the short of it. A snap of the two sisters, towering over their mother, a snap of his father and the family dog. He handed the camera to Francis to take pictures of the whole family; a blessing, his mother called them later.

When Albert took charge again, Francis and Anna posed together for their engagement announcement. Then Anna called her sister, Agnes, to join them: "Don't be shy!" Agnes stood a little apart from the couple in the photograph. She was a slender girl, two years younger than Anna, though a little taller. Anna was looking past Francis, laughing at Agnes; Agnes was just beginning to smile.

"You know, there are still mornings when I'm just waking up and I've forgotten. Then, suddenly, it comes back."

Francis nodded, though it was not quite like that for him. Certain ideas had shifted so deeply that even in sleep he no longer lost himself in the time of these photos. He made different mistakes: hearing his mother's voice, or glimpsing a woman in a yellow sari darting in and out of view in a crowd. Then he stirred on his pillow, and the ensuing years fell around him like so many stones.

The following April, a few weeks before Anna's twentieth birthday, she was walking along the crowded market road when a bus swung sharply toward the curb. She jumped to avoid it and was knocked into the path of a handcart piled so high with onions that the vendor hadn't seen her. There was a small fuss, passersby helping the fallen girl rise, the onion seller so distressed that he halted the bus, the bus driver indignant. It was only a minute before Anna was up again, a little dizzy but no broken bones, only a bruise where the cart had struck her hip. Could she walk, did she need hospital? The onion seller seemed ready to hoist her on his cart, but Anna laughed and told him no, no, she was fine. She waved to the bus driver, who put the bus into gear. She thanked the people who had helped her. She reassured the vendor, who insisted on taking her address.

She went home. She ate lunch without appetite. She lay down to rest for the afternoon and was still asleep at teatime, when Francis came back from university. "Come later and see her," her mother invited him warmly. An hour later, when the vendor came with a basket of onions, she had died.

It was early evening when Francis rang the bell again. He could see lights, he knew the family was home, but no one answered. Through the open windows, he heard wailing. For twenty minutes he waited in the garden, increasingly frightened but unable to step through the gate, as if doing so might upset some precarious balance. His first act as a betting man.

It was Agnes who came to tell him. He could see she'd been weeping.

"How?" he asked stupidly. "When?"

It did not seem possible that Anna could have slipped away so quietly. Surely he ought to have registered a sign, something to distinguish the moment she was still alive from the moment she was not. Agnes stayed with him in the garden, a hand on his arm, until he could compose himself.

"Come up," he remembered her saying. "Come sit with us."

Francis looked again at the photo. "A happy day," he said, before handing it back to Albert.

"Take it, if you like."

"But you should keep it."

"I have half a dozen more with the two of them. You remember how Anna was clowning?"

Francis did. She had jumped onto Agnes's back to peer over her sister's shoulder, their faces so similar that once Anna was sent home from school for impersonating Agnes in the confessional.

"I found copies of everything, even the two of you. You don't want *those*—"

"No, no." Francis laughed awkwardly. He had an archival mind; he could not bring himself to erase the record entirely. He'd kept the original announcement card with his parents' papers. But what could he do with the photo of his engagement to a woman he had not married?

Albert tipped his head. "Of course. But this snap is different. Not the two of you, nothing that looks too . . ." He searched for the right word and found none. "Family friends," he said instead. "Take it."

"Agnes won't want it?"

"No, that's fine. I've given her copies of the family shots. She said give this one to you."

"Did she?" Francis tucked the photo in his shirt pocket. "I didn't know she was down."

"Just for the weekend. Her train is tomorrow. She's staying up at the hotel; you know how she loves that. I told her, don't be silly, come be with us at the house, and she said, no, thank you, she wanted a swim." A bark of a laugh. "That is all your doing, of course."

Francis shook his head lightly, not quite a denial. "Should we meet up there tonight? I can book a table."

"Tonight we've got to go see my uncle in Grant Road. Dinner, the whole rigamarole. Even the boys are coming. We ought to have had you in before now"—Francis tossed his hand, *Not to worry*—"but these damn contractors, five in three days. I'll stop by tomorrow evening before I go, yes? Say a quick hello to Essie?"

Francis tipped his head—of course. "And the house? What does Agnes say to that?"

Albert shrugged. "She won't be living on the property. So for her it is more the idea of the thing." Albert was the only son, with three grown sons of his own. He was posted in Delhi, but in another few years he would come back to Santa Clara, and the family home was too crowded. No chance of buying in the neighborhood: nobody ever left. The Santa Clara Catholic Cooperative Housing Society, established a few years before Francis's birth, held a parcel of land eight roads wide—roughly from the Church of the Loaves and Fishes to the Church of St. Anne—to be retained for use by Catholic residents. The plots were generous, the bungalows made with materials that would have cost a fortune seventy years later. Their values had skyrocketed as the city spread north. Gardens that had seemed commonplace a generation before became small miracles. Families who wished to provide for their children were knocking down their houses to raise flat buildings in the same compounds, five or six stories high, so all could continue to live in the neighborhood. Generally, contractors took the ground floor as payment, which they turned over for profit or lived in themselves. It was not an arrangement Francis would have welcomed, a builder underfoot, but Albert viewed it as the best guarantee of well-made flats.

"I go to the bank tomorrow morning. The contractor takes the risk, not us, but there's paperwork to do with the inheritance. Meanwhile, Agnes wants to save our old mango tree." Albert grimaced. "I've told her: difficult to keep fruit trees in the middle of a building site. Still. You know Agnes."

Francis did not answer but tapped the pocket where he'd put the photo. "I've started taking photos myself these days. A little late."

"Not at all! Late for what? I should be doing more of it myself."

"I'm not photographing people." Francis felt unexpectedly

self-conscious. He had not spoken to anyone of his project, which had begun with the outbuilding. "Buildings. Houses, mostly, for a record of the neighborhood. You know I serve on that committee—"

"Yes, yes! We all answer to you. I can't touch a thing if you decide it's historical."

Francis smiled. This was Albert's way of puffing him up. The Commission had no jurisdiction over buildings erected after 1900. And Albert's cottage would not be the first pulled down; half a dozen had gone already. Although Francis had no official way to designate such houses as historical, he increasingly saw them as markers of a time that was passing, or had already passed. His time? How much of his own life was now history? So he took photos. A shot of each full home; a street view with the adjacent houses; and, if possible, architectural details: tile patterns, iron scrollwork, carved wooden doors that swung open like cupboards. He kept an album of these lost cottages and bungalows, a neighborhood archive to which only he contributed and which only he consulted.

He would need photos of Albert's house before it was knocked down. Perhaps tomorrow. He was formulating a plan for the morning, but by afternoon he would be free.

OCTOBER 1986

The morning's freshness had passed, the day taking shape beneath a thick rind of heat, birdcalls, road fumes, car horns, and street chatter, from which occasionally a single voice rose. The banana man made his way down St. Hilary Road, stopping at one gate, then the next, his back so bent beneath the bunches of fruit that he gave the impression of a tiny crooked tree. The great carnival din of children making their way to the school next door had modulated to a thrum of voices from classrooms and shrill yips from the games court. Cleaners and kitchen girls had long been at work. Housewives had gone to market, students were in their lecture halls, the city-bound had caught their trains, and Essie had finally set off for Linking Road when Francis decided it was time. He could not turn up too early, but if he waited too long he risked missing her altogether.

Essie had paused in the doorway to the bathroom on her way out, her handbag already on her shoulder. "Where are you off to? Not another shed?"

A storehouse, he thought, and scraped the razor over his jawline. "Albert is in town."

"There are cutlets for lunch," she said, slightly aggrieved, meaning Albert could come—there would be enough—but a pity about the cutlets, which were her favorite and would otherwise stretch to dinner.

"He's tied up with contractors. I thought I'd go by the house." Another long sweep of the razor. Francis tapped it against the edge of the sink, held the blade briefly under running water, and lifted it to his other cheek.

"Let him come for a drink this evening, then." She spoke more warmly, the cutlets secure.

"I'll tell him." Francis kept his eyes on his reflection. He was sixty-seven years old. His hair was thin on top, but that had been true for many years. He turned his face to one side, then the other, thin lines of shaving cream showing the tracks of the razor, and decided that, apart from the bald spot, he looked much the same as he had two years before. He was not so very changed since the last time they'd met.

The moment this thought formed, he cupped his hands beneath the faucet and splashed water on his face until he came up spluttering.

He rode his bicycle—he was still fit, he reassured himself—but he'd misjudged the heat. Sheets of hot air wavered over the pavement, and sunlight struck the basilica with such force that the stones seemed to vibrate. Francis had to stand on the pedals, each revolution its own hill, and he arrived at the Hotel Castelo damp and disheveled, flustered by the impulse that had brought him there. He stood a moment to compose himself, breathing in the rice-water air. The heat wore away the edges of things, softening the road and his crisp laundered shirt and even the years as Francis remembered them, so that one memory swam into the next, porous, disordered, unable to be contained. He left his bicycle at the foot of the low marble steps, nodded to the porter to place it in his care, and pushed through the revolving door into the chill gleam of the lobby.

The air-conditioning was a shock, his body reconstituting. Francis straightened his sleeves. The first woman at the desk issued a blank smile, but the second placed him at once.

"Good morning, Professor. How can I help you?"

A guest, he explained. An old friend. Perhaps he could ring the room? He gave the name.

"Of course. Let me look that up for you."

He waited while she consulted the register. It was a perfectly reasonable request, a perfectly reasonable visit. Still, he felt exposed, as if he expected at any moment to be asked the nature of his business. An old friend, he told himself again.

"I'm sorry, Professor. That guest checked out this morning. Did she expect you? Could she be waiting for you in the lounge?"

"No, no. There was no appointment. I only just heard she'd come, so I thought, why not . . ." He tossed his hand, a demonstration that he was not affected in the slightest. A pinprick of disappointment, nothing more. But the day seemed to lose its air, and seeping through him was a desolation he thought had passed with his youth. When had she left? he wanted to ask. By how many minutes had he missed her?

"The lounge is open, then?"

"Yes, of course," she said smoothly. "I'll call ahead to let them know you're on your way."

Francis sat for the length of a whiskey. The glass felt heavy in his hands, a good weight. When it was empty, he considered another, but a party of businessmen settled at a table near the bar—at such an hour, Francis noted, eyebrows raised—and their arrival served as a reminder of the progress of his own morning. He raised his fingers to signal for the check, but the waiter shook his head. "With our compliments."

The front-desk manager had given instructions, Francis understood. It happened when he was recognized. With this small erasure, Francis felt less like a man who had taken his first drink right after breakfast and more like a person of standing in his community. It was possible to get up and cross through the lobby again; possible to glance out to the pool deck (not there, of course; he had known better) and think of the days when he'd brought his granddaughters here to swim; possible to ride back down Seaview Hill, gathering speed to outrun any lingering foolishness—because what had he thought would happen?

What would have been said? A brief meeting, a chance to test the weight of his memories. He did not name what more he had hoped, only that it had been a painful awakening to hope so sharply for anything at all.

He whipped downhill in a froth of wind, the cycle juddering beneath his hands. He only kept from falling by leaning into a wide arc at the bottom, where Seaview splayed onto Creek Road. A moment later, he flashed past Holy Name School and tried not to think of Agnes within those walls, or anywhere in reach. She was gone, a story that had ended years before, one he would not tell himself again. There was no record of anything between them: a few careful letters and the picture Albert had given him of three young people in a garden. That was all. Francis had slipped the photo into the back of a small album of his grandchildren he meant to show Agnes. The album was tucked next to his camera in the bin on the back of his cycle.

He turned down one street, then another, winding slowly through the neighborhood as if to let the years between those days and this one accrue again. Still, he could not resist riding past the house where she and Albert had lived, which he'd visited daily as a boy. After she'd gone, he used to trick himself with the idea that she'd returned, was hidden behind those walls, just out of sight. He imagined bumping into her at a movie theater, or party, or choir practice. He looked for her on train platforms.

The house still had an air of concealment, the low roof hooding the veranda, the windows shaded against the sun. She could be inside. It was possible, a quick stop before her train. He felt a swell of hope as he imagined ringing the bell. Then he thought of Albert looking puzzled to find Francis on his doorstep, or a kitchen girl asking for a message, and he took out his camera instead. He framed the whole cottage and snapped. Side angles, then the number on the wall, the ceramic ornaments on the corners of the roof, the mango tree. Still the house yielded nothing. She was not there, he told himself, and wherever she was, she was not thinking of him. Once this made him angry, it was possible to replace the camera in the bin and ride away.

On St. Hilary Road, he coasted past his own house as though

it belonged to someone else. The years were too soft, a haze of what he ought to have forgotten. They offered no protection. He would ride until his thoughts were less disordered. He glanced back toward his gate to be sure he hadn't been seen, but naturally the watchman was nowhere in sight.

When he was struck, he had just turned his face ahead, wondering where to go next.

10

OCTOBER 1986

Celia was eight years old when she lost a shoe during a game of tag. The boy being chased caught the ball and became the rat, and instead of hurling the ball up again when the other children closed in, he took off running. Celia was determined to catch him even when he went beyond the Church of the Loaves and Fishes, the boundary she was not supposed to cross. When he tore through the churchyard and onto Creek Road, most of the children dropped away, but a last few pelted after him.

The pavement was full of obstacles—shoppers, vendors, boys sitting cross-legged and threading tiny beads outside jewelry shops. The road was nearly as bad. Celia cut a ragged path around pedestrians and street stalls. She felt the jolt of her shoe bursting off—then the smack of one bare foot hitting the road—but she didn't stop until the chase flung itself out half a block later.

Whatever had possessed the boy to run—a moment of manufactured fear, the wild grip of some superhero ambition—was spent by the time they reached the wall. He neither cowered nor tried to escape. It was over. The children streaming behind him coalesced into a small circle, panting, some bent at the waist. Celia turned back to find her shoe.

She did not see it at first. But she had dipped into the road to get around a man who sold underwear, batteries, and children's woolly toys, with a magisterial indifference as to both the range of his products and their protrusion into traffic—and that was where she found the shoe, flattened by a tire. As Celia peeled it up from the grit of the road, a horn blared, sending a quick liquid fear coursing through her. She jumped to the side, safe for the moment, but her troubles just beginning, because what, *what*, could she tell her parents? She took off the other shoe to walk home without hobbling.

When they crossed back onto Varuna Road, Celia stopped to examine the shoe once more. The sole was in shreds, the strap torn and hanging, the leather crushed.

A friend peered at it with her. "You can ask the mochi," she suggested. "Maybe with some new pieces?"

This was the sort of kindness that made Celia angry. Don't be stupid, she wanted to shout, but she managed to simply shake her head and pick at the buckle. The shoe was beyond repair. Before the chase, she had worn a small hole through the heel of its mate, and even that was the sort of thing to make her mother sigh. "What kind of girl? If you'd stop running and leaping . . ."

Celia could finish her mother's thought on her own. At eight, she knew the cost of things. She knew what the mochi charged for a new sole, because she had worn out too many. She knew how much more for a full new pair. She knew the way her mother would broach the matter with her father, waiting until after his meal, and she knew the way her father would count the money, one coin at a time. She knew he would take the coins from what they had set aside for Mr. Pujari, the moneylender. She did not know the full sum they owed, but she knew they had fallen behind. She knew how her parents' voices would drop when they wondered if another family might have a pair that would fit. She knew she must keep whatever she wore in good condition to pass down to her sister. She knew Evangeline would not complain when shoes were scuffed, or buttons lost, or elbows worn thin. Sometimes it seemed to Celia that it was the knowing that made her wild—the kind of girl who raced down a road without thinking what could go wrong—until something happened, and then she wished above all not to have done it, not to be the one who made everyone tired. "Can't you just be softer?" Jerome had asked her once.

Her parents were not home. It was not a market day, so Celia's mother must have been walking up and down the streets near St. Anne's, calling up from the cottage gates to sell to housewives and kitchen servants. On such days, Celia and Evangeline joined other village children at the community center after school. "But look after your sister, Celu. None of your nonsense."

She knew her mother meant they must play quietly, not tear through the village after idiot boys, because, four months after typhoid, Evangeline was still not right. The danger has passed, her mother told the children brightly. But Celia had overheard her crying to Inez. The doctor recommended light exercise, which sounded very well, her mother said, until you looked at the child. She was all ribs and pallor and knobby knees; her body seemed to lack the strength to assemble itself correctly. Even Celia could see that her sleep looked more like collapse than repose.

Celia was taken aside and issued firm instructions: she should include Evangeline in games. "But go gently, slowly." What games were like *that*, Celia knew better than to ask, and at any rate, her mother was already furnishing suggestions. They could toss a ball. Evangeline could turn the rope for girls who wanted to skip. They could play hide-and-seek without the running. That is hide-and-surrender, thought Celia. Some flicker of that idea must have reached her face because her mother's voice tightened. Did Celia *want* her sister to get well? Very well. Then she was not to run where Evangeline could not follow. She was not to let Evangeline overtax her strength. She was not to leave her alone and vulnerable to the slights of other children; she was not to say anything that might upset her; she was not to bully or argue or complain. She must put on a happy face, set a good example, encourage bright thoughts.

Staring at the flattened shoe, Celia had nothing bright to offer.

"You could wait to tell them," Evangeline said of their parents after school. "But what will you wear tomorrow?"

"Chappals." Celia spoke boldly, and Evangeline took her hand without a word. What could she say? School was a place for socks and shoes. The girls of Holy Name Primary wore green pinafores with white buttoned shirts beneath. Shoes, black or brown, and socks, white, brown, or green, which sagged at the ankles despite constant reminders to tug them up. In proper shoes, girls greeted each other; in proper shoes, they shared the scarred wooden benches of the classroom; in proper shoes, they ran laps around the courtyard with Miss Pinto at their center, consulting her stopwatch: "Well done, keep up." Would Miss Pinto pull Celia out of the circle while the other girls kept running, their glances bobbing to Celia's bare legs?

But there was nothing for it. Either Celia must tell her parents and endure the shame of needing new shoes, or she must avoid telling her parents and endure the shame of school in chappals.

"It's market day tomorrow," Evangeline said. "Mum will go before us." Their mother was always tugging collars and straightening hair ribbons, but their father was a more porous prospect. It might be possible to slip past him.

"Daddy won't see," Evangeline said. "I'll stand in front of you."

Celia twisted the torn strap until it ripped it off entirely. She wished she could throw one shoe after the other—bang, bang!—at the rabbity boy with his stupid ball. She did not want to be wild. She did not want to sneak.

"This one's not so bad," said Evangeline, inspecting the second shoe. "Should we give it to the ragpicker?"

She was right, Celia knew. They might get something for the leather. But if they haggled in the street, everyone would know. Their mother would hear of it the moment she came down the lane.

"Not enough." Her voice was sullen. "I'm throwing them out."

Evangeline paused long enough to be sure Celia would not change her mind. "We should go now, then. Before they come."

Their mother would be near St. Anne's, so the girls set off in the opposite direction, along the coast. Celia waited until they'd gone a fair distance before she found a rubbish pile near a construction site. Even then, she circled to the far side before casting the shoes away, to be sure they were absolutely out of sight. Let them be gone for good. With her next pair she would be someone new.

They walked back along the Promenade. It was a pleasant time of day, the sky touched with color, the tide rolling back from the rocks. They could smell the char of cook fires from a straggle of huts. The streets were full of people making their way home, or families already reunited, strolling in the gentle air. The world seemed soft and friendly, the sort of world that ought not deny anyone a pair of shoes.

It was a trick, Celia knew, a brief sensation of benevolence. All over the city, children went without. Still, the light changed and changed again, as delicate as rose water. The sky was different every time she glanced up to see it. She felt a shift, as though the ruined shoes belonged to the heat and blare that had passed. It was possible to feel hopeful without a precise idea of what shape her hopes might take.

Evangeline paused as a small girl emerged from a gated park on the shore, which the sisters had never visited: it cost a rupee to enter. The child was holding hands with her mother and another woman—an aunt, perhaps; they swung her between them every few steps. Her feet kicked up in party shoes.

"Pink," said Evangeline.

Celia watched. The shoes were smooth, like the curve of a shell. They barely grazed the ground before the child cried, "Up, up!" and again she was aloft, borne past them, giggling.

"Red would be even better," Celia said.

Evangeline turned to see the back of the small flying girl. "I like the pink."

Celia took her hand. If typhoid had killed Evangeline, she would have gone her whole life without wearing new shoes.

The sun sank lower. The sisters walked slowly, delaying the moment when they would reach home and all the wheels and cogs of the night would begin to grind: machinery to produce a new day that they already knew would go wrong.

OCTOBER 1986

Celia woke with the feeling that she must shake off a nightmare, and then the memory of the day before fell upon her like a length of chain. She heard the splash in the lane that meant her mother was washing; in another few minutes, she would set off for the docks.

When Flora came inside, she lit a tiny lamp. She did not want to disturb Evangeline's sleep, but when she saw Celia was awake, she crouched beside her.

"Rest a little more, Celu."

"You're going?"

"It's market day." Only hours before, her mother had been so frightened by the family's debts that Celia, pretending to sleep, had heard her weeping. It did not seem possible that the day could go forward in its usual way.

"Will that man come back?"

"That—" She stopped. "I'm selling today, Celu. This evening, we can give him something."

Not enough, Celia knew. Mr. Pujari would be back and back and back again. He had a soft stomach, and he took up too much of the room when he sat and waited for her father to come, speaking all the while about how important it was to keep on top of payments and what the bed frame might be worth, or Flora's gold chain.

"Better you should keep the boat, isn't it?" He smiled. "Otherwise, what?"

The night before, Mr. Pujari had stayed until eleven, drinking cups of tea with sugar. Evangeline finally fell to sleep on the bed, but Jerome and Celia waited up with their mother. When the sugar bowl was empty, Flora told Mr. Pujari that the children must sleep.

"Yes, of course," he agreed. "Children need their rest. Let them sleep."

"They sleep there." She pointed to where he was sitting. He shifted to make room.

Would he stay all night? Celia could not imagine sleeping beside his terrible soft stomach. "We have no more sugar," Celia told him. Let him go to some other house for his tea!

Her mother tightened her grip on Celia's shoulders. Her voice shook. "I've told you my husband is at sea, another day at least. He won't come tonight." This was a lie, Celia knew. He had not gone out in several days. He could not afford diesel.

"Strange," said Mr. Pujari. "The boat is here. I happened to notice when I walked to the dock. And your husband nowhere near it."

"He is with a friend! On a friend's boat!"

Mr. Pujari went on as though she hadn't spoken. "Such a pleasant walk. You're living like kings here, on the shore." At last he rolled himself up from the floor and tousled Jerome's hair. Jerome flinched. "Ah, big boy. Old enough to earn, yes?" He turned to Celia and laughed. "And this one! Her father's face exactly." He pulled a scowl in imitation and laughed again. Then he lifted her chin with his soft, wide thumb. "Tell Daddy I'll come soon for a visit. I wonder if he'll like to meet my friends?"

When her father crept in later, Celia pretended to sleep so she could listen. "He checked the boat," her mother whispered frantically. But her father had been hiding with Clive and Inez, who lived above them. They'd watched until they saw Mr. Pujari go. Even then, she heard her father say, he waited to be sure it was not a trap. Celia fell asleep thinking of lobster traps and her father caught inside one.

In the morning, her mother sounded like her mother again. "Don't worry, Celu," she whispered. "Daddy will go with Clive tonight. He'll have a share of the catch, and that will be enough to put this fellow off."

"But what if he comes this morning?"

"He won't come so early, not after last night." She patted Celia's cheek and smiled. "And we have no more sugar, right?"

Celia wished for nothing more than to sit up and hug her mother's hand, to hang on to her arm as if to a rope and be pulled to safety. *Everything is worse than you know*, she would say. *I lost my shoes.*

Evangeline coughed, and her mother sucked in her breath.

"Remember, boiled water only for her. I filled the bottle. Now, back to sleep." Her mother put out the lamp and took up her basket and was gone.

Her sister's breathing was deep and even; her father was snoring; her brother curled on one side, limbs pulled in like a turtle's. Celia thought of sneaking past her father in chappals only to be sent to the bench outside Sister Regina's office, where everyone could see who was in trouble. Would the principal speak to her parents? At any rate, her mother could not be avoided indefinitely, and her father was preoccupied, not blind.

She lay in the grip of one hopeless outcome after another until the darkness burned itself out and an ashy gray light meant she must get up. Later, she pretended to hunt for a mislaid tablet so that Jerome, who might notice her bare legs, would leave for school first. Her father was still buried in his teacup, unwashed and unshaven, a hand to the back of his neck. "Keep track of your things," he told her grimly.

The air was thick when Celia and Evangeline set off for school, as though the breath of every living thing had been woven into a steaming film. It was worse on Creek Road, where exhalations from cars and autoricks pulsed over the pavement. They walked single-file, Celia behind her sister as a scant measure of protection against the cars and buses that came rumbling within an arm's length. Evangeline's satchel was wide for her thin frame, and her water bottle seemed too big, bumping against her with each step. Neither girl paused when they passed vendors with racks of shoes, so many shoes that it seemed preposterous not one pair was Celia's. Everything was mismatched, the whole world badly done.

Students poured through the gates of Holy Name. Little girls came with parents or sisters or ayahs; groups of them arrived in packed rickshaws; bigger girls came in clusters of friends, banging into each other's shoulders. A father lifted his daughter to cross the road, and Celia imagined her own father appearing to bear her away to some place where shoes did not matter. The boat or the shore: anywhere but school.

But she must go. The stupidity of it made her want to rip the sky in half, the way she'd heard that, long ago, before becoming principal, Sister Regina tore a failed paper in two pieces and held them up for the class to see.

Inside the courtyard, students were moving in all directions or clotted in games or greetings. Teachers buzzed from one group to another. "Hurry, girls! The first bell has rung." Celia's legs were bare and hopeless, as long as stilts, as she stalked to the lower school with Evangeline. The feet with no shoes; the boat with no diesel; her sister so frail after months of doctors, medicines, bills. She moved along the edge of some new rage; anything could tip her in.

First one girl then another called her name in a friendly way. Celia smiled tightly but kept walking. When they reached Evangeline's classroom, she said, "Go on," in a rough voice. Evangeline obeyed, looking back over her shoulder with such pity that Celia nearly shook her; she wanted none of that, nothing but to stay so angry that it would burn away any embarrassment. She would leave school, she decided. School was intolerable.

She was pushing against a tide of girls at the gate when a voice sang out behind her. "Wrong way, Celia!" She turned and saw Sister Felicia. "Where are you off to?"

"I dropped my pencil case—"

"Quickly, then! Second bell will ring. And shoes tomorrow, please, Celia."

That was all. Celia's face felt hot and strange, like a mask. A new day rose up before her—a day she had failed to consider—in which no one really cared about her shoes. She could slide into her place in class, laugh with friends. This idea was so bewildering, and her own anger so entrenched, that she did not turn around. The watchman saw her leave and looked away, bored. Should she pretend to find the case and run back? She was fed up with schemes. If she went back, she would be marked late, scolded for all the wrong things.

When she rounded the corner, she did not feel free but banished. For a while, she drifted. The world with no particular place to go felt infinite in a way she had never known. Eventually she headed toward the shoe vendors on Creek Road, with a vague idea that she might work to earn a pair. Sometimes the men skimmed a dust cloth over their wares, or urged passersby to browse. Otherwise they stood chatting or squabbling, for which they would need no assistance.

Still, she tried. The first vendor had a checked shirt and plump face, not entirely unsympathetic. Did he need help?

"Get back to school," he said, grinning. The vendor beside him laughed loudly.

She had to walk past another half-dozen racks before they were out of earshot. Then she chose a stall at the far end. The vendor brushed past her offer, flicking his eyes over Celia.

"You want, you can buy."

"I don't have money. But—"

His hand came up, as fast as a snake strike. Celia felt his fingers against her collarbone as he tugged the baptismal chain there, pulling her small gold cross into view.

"You have enough."

Celia turned and fled. The man was not following, but she thought she could hear the first vendors laughing as she passed. She ran all the way past St. Anne's, first the church, then the adjoining college. A group of university girls in blue jeans were gathered near the junction with St. Hilary Road, singing a film song in silly bold voices, and Celia dashed past them, around the corner. A shout, a man's shocked face rearing up over the handlebars of a bicycle, and they were both down in a heap, Celia splayed over the front tire and the cyclist's leg caught beneath the frame.

She lay still, her chest flat against the wheel, her hand ground into the road. It was hard to breathe, as though her ribs had compressed and could not admit air. She blinked and saw a pedal spinning, the man's brown trousers. A line of blood darkened along his ankle. There were noises coming from outside her body, sliding all around her, but she could not chart them. She could not tell where anything was except her hand, electric with pain, and the patch of road beneath it.

"Little girl, can you move?"

She had no breath to answer. A woman led her to the side of the road, just past the gate of a school for boys. The pain in Celia's hand seemed to splinter her whole arm. "Wait here."

Celia leaned against the compound wall.

"Oh my God, are they okay?" A younger voice, one of the college girls. Jeweled sandals with heels. Celia closed her eyes. The shoes made her dizzy.

When she opened them, she saw a man crouched near the cyclist. The woman who had helped Celia was beside him, a shopping bag set down in the road. She had been to market, Celia thought. Maybe she'd bought fish from Celia's mother.

"Pow!" Above Celia, sitting on the wall, were half a dozen boys in uniform. One struck his hand with his fist.

"Direct hit! Dead on."

"This is nothing! I once saw a taxi go bang into a juice stand."

"If he had a motorcycle, they'd be goners."

"He might still be a goner. He might have broken his neck. Actually, you can break your neck falling two steps off a ladder."

Celia felt sick when she looked at the fallen man. She did not want to vomit in front of people. She could not see the man's neck.

"Is he killed?"

"Don't be stupid. He's moving."

It was true. Celia could see he was trying to rise. One of the college students lifted the bicycle and propped it against the wall near Celia. A man in his thirties and the woman with the shopping bag were on either side of the cyclist, easing him up. He was older, Celia realized. The top of his head was bald, a friar's ring of silvered hair below. He grunted, nodded to the woman that she could let go, and tried to brush the dust from his pants. "I'm fine," he said, but he could not shake off the younger man, who supported him as he stood.

"Go slowly, Professor. You've had a hell of a knock." He was trying to examine a small gash on the cyclist's forehead. "It's bleeding—"

"That's nothing," the cyclist said. "My camera—"

The man made a quick scan of the accident site and bent to retrieve it. "Right here." He fiddled with it, tried a switch, took a quick shot. "Working fine. I think *you* took the brunt of the fall, Professor. We must get you out of the sun."

"Hang on . . ." The cyclist peered down where the camera had been found, then checked his pockets, fumbling slightly. "I'm not sure—"

"There! You see? He's confused!" called a boy on the wall. "I bet he has amnesia. See if he remembers his name."

The cyclist looked up fiercely. "I'll remember *your* name."

Celia felt a wave of relief. She had not killed anyone; she had not erased anyone's memory.

The cyclist pulled a billfold from one pocket, replaced it, and continued to search the road, turning this way and that.

"You could be bleeding in your brain," the boy told him.

"What about the girl?" a different boy called. "She hasn't said anything."

Celia pressed herself against the wall as if she could disappear inside its cracks.

"Who are you? What day is it? You don't know, do you?"

"Hie! Down from there, all of you!" a teacher called and the remaining boys dropped to the ground—one, two, three, four—quick as bad ideas. As if awaiting that signal, the crowd began to disperse. The university girls turned toward St. Anne's.

The woman with the shopping bag offered to walk Celia home. When Celia said no, thank you, the woman crossed to take the hand of a small girl waiting beneath a clump of bougainvillea.

"You're certain? Then we're off."

Celia leaned back. She wanted to sink to the ground until the sensation that her body was faintly vibrating had passed. But the cyclist was coming toward her, frowning. The scratch on his ankle was not so bad, but the cut on his forehead was bleeding.

"I was carrying— There! It's gone into the gutter." He pointed into the narrow ditch that ran along the road, and Celia saw a small photo album in the sediment of leaves and garbage.

"Hang on, Professor. I'll get it." The younger man picked it up with one finger and thumb. It had a thin laminated cover, which he tried to wipe clean with a handkerchief. "Filthy down there. But the photos are fine."

The cyclist took it and flipped through carefully. Then he frowned, checking the road again. "There was a loose photo inside, smaller than the rest—"

"Let me walk you home, Professor. You should clean that cut. I'll get the cycle."

But the old man did not look up. He picked up a stick and poked aside debris in the gutter. "An old photo, black and white. Just check that side; I'll look here."

Celia saw the picture first. It had skittered near the school wall—not black and white exactly, but the colors of dust. The cyclist was busy with his stick, the other man lifting the cycle. She bent and picked it up, pain slicing through her arm so that she could not keep back a small cry when she put it in her pocket.

The cyclist turned, eyes narrowed.

"What's the matter with you?"

Was he scolding her for crashing into him or for crying out?

"I'm late for school." She could hardly speak with the pain in her hand and his eyes fixed on her. Would he follow her home, expecting money from her father for everything she had broken? She kept her hand on the photo in her pocket as though it were a last, desperate currency.

"Are you hurt?" asked the younger man.

Celia shook her head no. She needed them to wheel the cycle away, to leave her be, so she could think what to do next.

"Take your hand from your pocket," the cyclist ordered.

Celia kept the photo hidden but lifted her hand. She tried so hard not to cry that instead she whimpered.

The cyclist turned to the other man. "There. See the arm."

Celia flattened against the wall as the younger man approached. "Paining you, is it? Let's take a look." He put his fingers gently around the swelling above the wrist bone, and Celia made another small animal sound.

"Maybe *you* took the brunt of the fall," he said.

What was a brunt? Celia wanted to know. "I'm not taking things," she said in a hot, teary voice that she could not quite control.

The cyclist frowned. "Better bring her to my place. I'll come back for the picture."

Celia's voice pitched wildly. "I am going to school!"

"I'll get the cycle, Professor. You can't ride. The front rim is bent." Celia looked with alarm at the bicycle—damaged, just as she'd feared—and then the younger man put a hand on her shoulder. "Come."

She wanted to run in ten directions at once. "My school is that side," she said, her voice high and useless. "I am going to *school.*"

"In a little while," he agreed. "But first we must see to this arm. The Professor lives just there." He pointed to the compound beside the boys' school, and Celia hesitated. The stony heat of her hand was beginning to make her feel fevered all over. Maybe a little water.

They were a strange short parade, the old man moving slowly, eyes sweeping the ground, and the younger man wheeling the cycle alongside Celia. Each step jarred her hand, and the picture in her pocket bothered her. She did not like to see the old man searching. Perhaps she could leave it in his house, so he would find it when she'd gone.

"What is your name?" asked the younger man.

Celia did not tell him. If she kept quiet, nobody could press her family for money.

"We need to find your parents."

A bent spoke ticked as the cycle was pushed forward—not a loud sound, but implacable. When the ticking stopped at a wrought-iron gate, Celia felt a lurch of panic.

The watchman was not standing ready, but stretched out in a chair, possibly dozing.

"Hie! You! What are you paid for?" called the cyclist, and the watchman leapt up. He stared openly at the cut on the cyclist's forehead.

"You are bleeding there," he said, in a belated effort to be helpful. The older man growled at him to take the cycle and led them across the garden, past a veranda, to a flight of stairs that ran along the outside of the house. Celia stood at the bottom, feeling heavier and heavier as she watched him go up. It did not seem possible that she could ascend all those steps and walk into whatever would happen next.

"No," she told the younger man. She wanted to sink down on the first stone step; she wanted her mother.

The man misunderstood. "It's all right. I've got you . . ." And she was borne up against his chest. The pain in her hand was as sharp as a pencil tip, scoring a dark line right through the bone. She cried out.

"Yes, I know," the man said. "Nearly there."

He carried her the way Jesus carried the lost sheep, except that she wanted to spring out of his arms and be lost again. On the top landing, she could hear boys' voices from the schoolyard, and for the first time, she was visited by the idea that it was all happening at once—ordinary days, and days that changed everything. Somewhere a lorry might be flying off the road to the rocks below; somewhere else, a baby opened her mouth for a first taste of banana. At this very moment in Santa Clara were algebra classes; police arrests; medicines that worked; medicines that didn't. A wedding cake was being frosted; a child with pink shoes was laughing. At sea, someone with money for diesel was bringing in the biggest catch of his life, while a few streets away her father was dodging Mr. Pujari. Celia felt small and hollow, nothing of consequence. The world would shake its wide skirts and walk on.

"Come," the old man called, and they swung into a room with a ceiling so high it seemed to fall upward. Faint pink walls reeled as Celia was lifted to the sofa. The diamonds of the tile floor swam, one over the next. She closed her eyes and darkness lolled like a head tipping back. Somebody called for water. Evangeline must be ill again, Celia thought. Then the voices faded, and all she could hear was the ticking of the bent spoke in the lane, the bicycle slowly following her home.

Celia felt a hand on her head. When she opened her eyes, she saw a woman with spectacles and soft wrinkled cheeks peering at her. Celia's hand hurt with a deep cold ache, propped on a cushion with a bag of ice.

"Here." The woman offered her a glass of water. "Drink."

Celia obeyed, then held the glass tightly in her good hand. She was lying on an unfamiliar sofa in a small church of a room, airy, with a tile floor, high rafters, and a ceiling fan on a long stiff wire. On the walls were large pictures in frames, Jesus and the Crown of Thorns, the Virgin and the Infant, and art that did not belong to churches. In every corner, on every shelf, were framed snapshots.

"You've had a little sleep, but we need to wake you now. Another sip?"

Celia nodded.

"Why were you faint? Were you knocked on the head?"

Celia shook her head no and sat up, wincing.

"Can you speak?"

She nodded again.

The woman put a hand on Celia's forehead. "No fever. It's shock only, I think, or the arm is painful." She seemed to be speaking to someone who was not Celia, though Celia could not see anyone else in the room. After a moment the woman appeared to notice that also. "Frank! Where are you wandering off to? Sit down with that ice."

The old man emerged through a doorway. "She's hurt her arm," he said, and the woman swiveled, looking annoyed.

"I can see she's hurt her arm. It's a miracle that's all she's hurt—you charged into the girl with a bicycle."

"I keep telling you, she charged into me." Perhaps at some point he had applied an ice pack to his forehead, but now he was swinging it idly. "I've lost a photo, I'm going back down. But you'll have to call someone for the child, no?"

Celia stiffened, imagining police.

"What photo? Don't be ridiculous, Frank. You can't go out in this heat when you're bleeding from the head."

"It's only a cut—"

"If you've dropped something, it's been trampled by now. This madhouse next door—we've gone from a quiet road to a railway juncture. Now, sit with that ice." She turned abruptly to Celia. "You're Celia, is it?"

Again Celia nodded. Her hand throbbed, and she could not keep up with the speed of things: people in and out, strangers who knew her name.

"I've spoken to Sister Regina. She says you were missing from school today."

Was she a teacher also? She had the same stern, expectant look as Sister Regina, always waiting for a girl to do better.

"You're fortunate to go to such a nice school. Other girls aren't so lucky."

The man sat in a chair opposite, legs crossed. He cast his gaze here and there with the restless air of a person who hopes something interesting will happen, until he finally settled on Celia.

"Is she concussed?"

"*No*, Frank. You're the one with the lump on your head. She has run away from school. And I think she's left her voice in the road."

Truancy did not appear to hold his interest, but at the mention of the road he unfolded his legs and moved to the door.

"I'll be just back."

"Leave it, Frank! Such a fuss over a photo. You can make new copies."

"No, it was given to me." He spoke from the outdoor landing, but he didn't go downstairs, only crossed back inside, looking strangely lost at the door of his own house.

Celia thought of the picture in her pocket. This one mistake, at least, she could remedy as soon as nobody was watching.

"I knew your uniform at once, because my daughter went to Holy Name," the woman was telling her. "She had very high marks. Not once did she run off and worry everybody."

"Why did this one run off?" The man drifted around the corner and out of sight, but the woman stopped talking and waited for the answer as though the question was her own.

All at once, Celia realized she could not sit another minute in this impossible room. Chairs in rich colors, carved wooden tables, framed photos of people who never once, she felt certain, lacked a proper pair of shoes. She struggled to her feet, the bag of ice dripping onto the tile.

"I want to go home!"

The woman looked startled. "We're not keeping you, child. Sister Regina has called your family. Someone will be here soon."

It would not be the police. Her mother was coming, or her father. Celia blinked through tears. All the trouble behind and ahead fell away for a moment and she was left with that single promise, her mother or her father, coming.

"Sit down," the woman said. "Keep your arm still."

She brought a blue tin from the shelf near the kitchen. Inside were stacks of biscuits in crinkled white paper. Some were plain, some sprinkled with sugar crystals. They were the most perfect biscuits Celia had ever seen.

"Shortbread. My daughter brought them from England."

The man had disappeared again; Celia had not noticed him go. The woman could not have noticed, either; she was fully attentive to the biscuits. "These are my favorites." She pointed to a crimped round with unexpected reverence. "Go on, take."

Celia put an edge in her mouth and a golden sweetness almost overwhelmed her. She had not eaten since early morning.

The woman made a careful selection. Together they ate. "Try this one," she suggested.

It was a curious feeling, eating such biscuits in silence. They were biscuits for important visitors or a fancy-dress party. But Celia and the woman were quite alone. Between them, a sense of quiet ceremony arose. The room began to feel friendlier—the warm pink walls, the cushion beneath Celia's aching wrist.

"One more," the woman said thoughtfully, almost to herself. They finished those. Then she offered yet another, wordlessly but with a tiny conspiratorial smile.

Celia felt timid but no longer afraid when she pointed to the tin. "This daughter is the one who went to Holy Name? She stays in England?"

"She lives in America." The woman's mouth went thin and tight and she brushed away crumbs Celia could not see. "Her plane stopped in England when she came to visit."

Celia tried to think how far America was—from here to the train station so many times, from here to the city, so many times—and could not. "It is too far," she said, meaning the way her calculations collapsed. The woman agreed in such a tired way that Celia wanted to help her back to the way she'd sounded when she first talked about the daughter in school.

"What house was she in?"

But the woman did not answer. The cover was back on the biscuit tin, and certain thoughts that had been suspended began to quicken.

"You'd better come and wash," she said, and showed Celia to a bathroom near the kitchen. Then she lifted the melting ice pack from Celia's arm with a long, slow breath when she saw the swelling, as if she felt the pain herself. "Don't try to bend it. Just splash a little water on your face, you'll feel better."

"Frank!" she called as she left Celia. "Where has he disappeared?"

The girl in the kitchen said he'd gone down the back stairs to the garden. Celia thought of the man in the midday sun, glaring down at the dusty road, searching for the photo she held in her pocket. She tried to dash the thought away with running water.

Her hurt arm on the cool porcelain did not look like her arm; even her face in the mirror took her by surprise, the skin flushed, the eyes strange. As she stared at herself, she was gripped by the sudden fear that she would someday be unrecognizable, that she must change piece by piece, one irreversible thing after another. It was impossible to look at her arm, discolored, misshapen, and imagine it back to the way it had looked that morning. Nothing could be undone.

The woman was still in the kitchen when Celia finished, so she took the photograph from her pocket and tried to make out the faces. A boy and two girls, one of them laughing. She might be the daughter from Holy Name, Celia thought, or even the woman herself. The other girl had glasses and a waiting look, like she was thinking things over. The man looked straight at the camera. The same face as the man on the bicycle, she realized, only much younger. On the back, initials in faded ink: "A. F. A."

She meant to leave it on the table, but she heard voices at the gate and the ruckus of the dogs, and the woman came bursting in to say, there, her people had come. The photo was in Celia's hand as they went down together, and at the gate was Celia's mother, straight from the fish market, a plastic sheet still tied around her waist.

"Celu?" she said, her voice high, her eyes wild; that was all. Then she put an arm tight around Celia's shoulders and spoke only to the woman. There was a quick exchange about the accident—"You must get into an autorick . . . You must go straight to a doctor"—Celia did not attend to all of it. The woman was giving her mother money and her mother was taking it, thanking her, rushed and confused.

"Oh, the school bag," said the woman, "It's just up . . ." And she went to get it.

Her mother was bending over her. "Celu, your arm—"

A question and a lament, and Celia, who could not think how to answer for it, said, "She gave me biscuits."

She heard footsteps coming back down the stairs and leaned

hard against her mother's hip when the woman gave her mother the pack.

"Our name is Almeida," she said. "On St. Hilary Road—you'll remember? You must bring the child back in a few days so I can see how she does. I am Easter Almeida."

Celia thought of the back of the picture. "A.," she said.

The woman gave her a sharp look. "Go on, she's about to drop. This fellow will hail an auto." The watchman stepped into the road, and quickly, wishing she were already gone, Celia handed the woman the picture.

"I found this. In the road."

The woman's face, all words and motion, went still. She stared at the photo. Then she turned it over and stared again, until Celia must say something more.

"It was dusty, so I thought—"

The woman looked up at her, a strange, open look just for Celia, as though her mother had dropped away and the woman herself, with her gray hair and limp cheeks, was nothing but a puzzled girl.

"Is it you? The one laughing?"

"No," said the woman, Mrs. Almeida. "That girl died." Then: "Bring her back, don't forget," to Celia's mother, because the watchman had flagged an autorick, the gate was open, and at last it was time to go.

OCTOBER 1986

The elbow was dislocated, the arm fractured above the wrist. "Clean break at least," said Flora, as though thankful to be spared a messier crisis. Since the trouble with Mr. Pujari, she'd developed a habit of making bright remarks to cope with the insurmountable. "So quick with his hands," she commended the doctor, with no mention of the long wait. "Such a godsend," she said of the money Mrs. Almeida had given her, with no discussion of how to repay it. "Thank heavens, you're home," she greeted her husband, though clearly he should have been at sea, bringing up however many nets were needed to right the family's fortunes. Were there fish enough to restore them? Celia wondered. Even in sleep, she felt pinned beneath the numb weight of her arm.

The next morning, her father was still not at sea and still not thankful to be home. Her mother was still chirping. Celia still wore a cloth sling, with her left arm folded like a wing against her chest.

"At least she's right-handed. That is luck!"

"Such luck," said Dominic. He was not interested in silver linings; he turned instead to the dark cloud of his daughter. "So?"

Celia said as little as possible. She had left school to look for a pencil case; on the road there was an accident. Her eyes filled with tears. The story she wasn't telling seemed to catch in her throat; she could only nod. Yes, she collided with a man on a bicycle. Yes, he was hurt. Yes, the bicycle was damaged. Yes, she'd worried her teachers, her sister, her mother. Yes, she realized the arm might heal badly. Yes, she was wrong; yes, she knew better; yes, she was sorry. Yes, yes, yes.

Finally, in a voice so tired and gritty he might have peeled it up from the road: "Is it paining still?"

The medicine from the clinic had worn off in the night. Celia had awakened to a dull metal pain that throbbed in her arm and upset her stomach, but she shook her head no. She did not know what the tablets cost.

"Take, Celu." At last her mother's voice had lost its hectic cheer. She looked at Celia as if she could read each unspoken thought and would find a gentle remedy for them all. "The doctor gave them for you."

For two days, Celia drowned in heavy tides of sleep. She woke at odd hours to find her sister beside her in splintering daylight, or her father gone in the soft hours before dawn, then felt pulled under again. Nobody mentioned Mr. Pujari, but Celia could feel him creeping along the edges of what they didn't say. The pain in her arm rose and fell but never fully receded, and in her dreams she saw Mr. Almeida's photograph.

On the third day, she woke hungry. The pain had sunk to such a depth that Celia hardly felt it. It was mid-morning, Jerome and Lina at school. Mr. Pujari would not come, her mother said shortly; he was keeping her gold chain until they caught up with payments. They would buy it back soon. Her father had hired himself out on a friend's boat for a three-day voyage. He had nearly earned enough to buy fuel for his own.

"And by the time he's home, this visit will be finished," she added.

The Almeidas lived in the neighborhood where Flora sold fish, house to house. She stopped at each gate, calling up and spinning slowly with her basket on her head, like a fish waiting to be caught. When Celia accompanied her, they went together into the bungalow kitchens, but it was unsettling to approach the Almeida compound with a different kind of business. The watchman was not in sight, and neither Celia nor her mother called to hail him.

Instead, they waited. Celia thought of oxcarts stopped in the road, the way the beasts must stand and stand without knowing how long. She wanted to paw the ground and snort, or go clattering away, pulling her mother behind her. But Flora did not move, even when Celia tugged her hand.

"Will they want money?"

"They can want." Her voice was a flat road, going nowhere.

Celia knew she should leave it, but she thought of Mr. Pujari sitting in her house and imagined the Almeidas crowding beside him, a queue of people waiting to be paid.

"What will they do?"

"What *can* they do?" But the question jolted her mother into some manner of action; she smoothed Celia's skirt, straightened her collar, frowned at her bare legs. "You should have worn socks."

Celia did not answer. Of course she could not wear socks with chappals. She was right back to wishing for shoes. Then the watchman came to admit them, and Flora whispered, "Smile, Celu. Let them think you're a nice, friendly girl," and Celia knew her mother was scared, too.

The watchman sent them to the back, where a spiral staircase led to the kitchen balcony. A girl was husking coconuts beneath a clothesline. Trousers and towels and printed ladies' underwear hung in a limp parade over a small mound of coconut shells. The girl saw the sling and clicked her tongue. Memsahib was on the telephone, she explained in Marathi. Then she smiled at Celia. "You are looking better today."

A minute later, Mrs. Almeida's voice rang out: "You can come!" Flora and Celia did not move; they expected Mrs. Almeida to meet them in the kitchen. But the girl waved them on, and Mrs. Almeida called again, and Flora gave Celia a look so intent that a half-dozen instructions tipped out at once: Celia should not dawdle or stare or slouch or mumble or be too timid or be too bold. Then she grasped Celia's good hand.

The kitchen floor was plain cement, but they paused where the tile began, rippling across the front room in onyx, alabaster, and shady green. Celia remembered the way the patterns had whirled when she lay on the sofa, and then Mrs. Almeida turned from the telephone, looking distracted and not quite pleased to see them. "Here you are."

She did not ask them to sit; she seemed in no mood to sit herself. First she spoke in a resolute tone about what she wouldn't stand from bank managers; then she poked her head into the kitchen to instruct the girl about lunch. When, at last, she asked Flora about the arm—dislocated where; and fractured also; what prognosis; what was the cost—Celia and her mother stood braced together as if against a high wind.

"I brought a little for now, madam—" But Mrs. Almeida said, "No, no, later for all that," and turned to Celia.

"And you. Running off from school."

She said this as if it were not a question but Celia's true name. Celia did not nod or speak. Then, to her surprise, Mrs. Almeida asked about her teachers. Celia tried to answer nicely.

"And when you stay in class, you are studying well?"

Celia looked at her mother, who said, "She has good marks. Her daddy says she might stay to tenth standard. But *that* . . ." She tipped her head to say, Who knows what will happen to prevent.

"And you are learning English?" Mrs. Almeida turned back to Celia.

Celia did not know about the tenth standard, a level of schooling most village girls did not reach. She was smiling and trying not to smile, feeling shy from her mother's praise and the weight of this interview. She leaned against Flora's legs and nodded.

"Then speak up properly with your words."

"Yes, madam."

Flora switched to Marathi, speaking in a swift stream. "See, she is doing so nicely, and suddenly she runs away. I've spoken with her teacher. Nothing has happened, no troubles in school. Always before, Celu has been happy."

"I see." Mrs. Almeida gazed at Celia as though she were in a dusty old photo, a girl whose features must be puzzled out. "I know Sister Regina. She was just beginning at Holy Name when my daughter attended. She says you are an honest girl."

Celia shifted. She was nothing but long bare legs and her arm in a sling and dust and lies and hopeless mishaps, and still no shoes.

"You know Jesus sees all things?"

It was true. Even in this room, the print of Christ with the Crown of Thorns gazed down on her.

"I'll have the truth." Mrs. Almeida spoke as though ordering a driver to drive; she would not accommodate refusal. When Celia answered, she did not look at her mother.

"I lost my shoes. They are uniform. I didn't like to go out of uniform."

She heard her mother exhale and felt the room swell with a new mortification, not just her own but her mother's, too, and even her father's, out to sea on another man's boat without money to replace a pair of shoes.

"I see," said Mrs. Almeida again. "You are seven years old?"

"Eight."

"Small. She gets enough to eat?"

"Oh yes! Only, lately, there are bills. My youngest had typhoid, so we . . ." Her mother's hands fluttered in a gesture of nothing at all.

"I eat," said Celia fiercely. "Two, three helpings, whatever I like."

"Quiet, Celu." Her mother's hand pressed her shoulder. "We have a boat, madam. We eat."

"Come with me."

They followed her into a room that overhung the veranda like a balcony, with a painted iron railing below a bank of windows.

A narrow bed was pulled alongside the railing. Mrs. Almeida directed Flora and Celia to reach beneath it, and together they tugged a large suitcase into view. It was dusty on top, with stickers. PARIS, Celia spelled. DUBAI. She did not know NYC.

Flora took a step back while Mrs. Almeida unlatched the clasps. Celia gasped. Clothes and more clothes bulged beneath the canvas straps. Tucked along the edges: shoes.

"Some are hardly worn. In my day, we did not need so many nice things. But my daughter brings whatever her girls have outgrown. Usually, I give them to the church, but . . ." She turned to Celia. She had a smile like a teacher's, all her strict-stern giving way like a mudslide. "Let's see what suits you."

"Madam?" In the face of actual good luck, Flora's chirping faded to a whisper. "Already you've given us for the arm—"

Mrs. Almeida held up her hand. "Not all! I must keep some back." But she kept adding to their pile while Celia stared and Flora made a face between laughing and crying. "This is good-quality," Mrs. Almeida fingered a shirt, as if she were a shop girl convincing them to buy. "And this sweater. At Christmas, when the nights are cool—you'll use it, I think. It's not too heavy."

She unfolded garments one by one, slowly dismantling the stack. In the end, she only held back clothes for babies, a few pairs of thick pants—"These are better for boys, I think"—a batch of wool sweaters she would send north to Delhi, and dotted-Swiss dresses, blue and green. "These I may keep," she murmured, and put them aside from all the rest. The red dress with smocking she hesitated over, then held up to Celia's chest. Celia felt the fluttery shock of it, as if a bird had landed in her arms. A pink dress with white butterflies, a yellow smock with a ribbon belt. Two pairs of American sneakers with colored stripes. Four pairs of leather shoes, brown, blue, black with straps. "See!" Celia could not restrain herself. "For my sister and me both!" Matching navy-blue raincoats covered in cheerful green whales.

"What do you think of these fish?" asked Mrs. Almeida.

Celia brushed a finger over the pocket snaps. "Not like ours."

"Clever girl," Mrs. Almeida said, laughing, and Celia did not know how to contain her happiness. It seemed she must be a dozen happy girls at once, all wearing new clothes.

Mrs. Almeida called to the girl to bring bags. Celia wished she could put the shoes on top, where she could keep them in sight all the way home. But Mrs. Almeida had fixed ideas about packing; she put shoes straight to the bottom and told Celia to hand her one thing, then another: pants, dresses, skirts, shirts. A soft drift of cotton sweaters. "That's enough," she said when two bags were heaped over. "You will give me a good price for fish, I think," and began quizzing Flora about her market days.

Celia sat on the bed to look through the railing. It was painted creamy white, its grillwork a design of scrolls and circles, and she imagined portholes as she bent to peer down at the garden. If she ever came to have a big rich house, she would have just such a railing near just such a bed.

Mrs. Almeida sent Flora to the kitchen to confer with the girl about prawns and turned to Celia. "Let's empty that case. You can help me fill the bag for the church."

A few last garments lined the bottom. Celia lifted the edge of a shirt and felt something different underneath.

"See, madam!"

"Oh oh oh, that's where you landed! What a hunt we had for you!" Mrs. Almeida picked up the bright notebook. "There's no point in keeping it—she's filled out a different one. I can give this as a gift, just let me see . . . Ah, too bad, she's written her name.

"Can you read this?" She showed Celia the cover and helped her sound out the words: "Travel Diary." "This belonged to my granddaughter. This was her schoolwork when she visited. Every day, she wrote what she had seen and learned. She had a workbook for maths, and books to read, and this."

Celia did not entirely understand but nodded.

"She brought it all the way from America, and what do you think happened? She lost it! We couldn't find it anywhere. We had to find another in a shop here. Not as pretty as this."

"She finished, madam?"

"A month ago, she went back." Mrs. Almeida had soft cheeks, bags beneath the eyes, a face easily given to sadness. "You take this. It can be a present from her; see her name here? She is only a year or two older than you."

Celia ran a finger over the girl's name, the girl who had worn a blue raincoat with green whales, who had chosen this notebook and written "Nicole" in green ink.

Mrs. Almeida's demeanor became brisk. "Practice writing English words; then you can come and show me." This was clearly a command.

"Yes, madam." She could hear her mother, still in the kitchen. There would be no better chance for a private moment. Still she stumbled over the English words—what to call a man she had knocked down in the road?

"The uncle, his head is better?"

"Yes, yes. I had much worse when I fell two years ago. My whole hip was black and blue. Even now, when I walk any distance, that side pains me."

But Celia felt she needed to be sure about the photograph. "He is happy to have his picture?"

A pause, while Mrs. Almeida shut the suitcase, one snap after the other. "That picture was very old. I've given him a new one."

There was no time to ask if the bicycle was fixed. Her mother came, and they pushed the suitcase under the bed. Mrs. Almeida looked distracted once more. "No more running off. I will hear from Sister Regina if you do."

The bag handles cut into their hands as they walked to the village, such a shocking weight that Celia and her mother giggled when they had to stop and rest. At home, she and Evangeline spent the evening trying on everything. Her mother helped Celia pull a dress and raincoat over the arm in its sling. She wore real American jeans and sneakers so soft that they felt like cushions beneath her feet. They even found a large orange sweater that fit Jerome. When Celia pulled a skirt onto her head like a headdress, he put leather shoes on his hands and walked four-footed, and her mother did not sound cross at all when she spoke of wild animals in her house.

The next day, Dominic came home with money for diesel and a tired smile. What good were children's clothes to a moneylender? He was still behind in payments, still accruing crippling interest. At any moment, Mr. Pujari might turn up again. But it cheered Dominic to see his family happy.

"You see, Mr. Such Luck! Our luck is changing!" Flora was making plans. It was Sunday morning; they could go to early service and come home in time for her favorite television series. For over a year, she and Inez had been following the love story of Rama and Sita. When Flora missed an episode, she could easily catch up from other women in the village, but it was never the same as seeing for herself the heartfelt glances.

The dresses were hung with reverence. The raincoats, too wonderful to fold away until the monsoon, were kept on hooks in clear sight. That night, Celia went to sleep with one of the T-shirts in her good hand. It smelled pleasantly of cotton and the dusty suitcase and another scent, which Celia could not name but which she thought must be America. She wanted the whole day to stay as close to her, every scent and sound and texture saved: the shirt against her cheek, the snap of the suitcase latches, the smooth blank pages of the Travel Diary. For a week, she could not decide what sort of writing to venture first. What words would be good enough?

She began with "Nicole," the name of the girl who had lost the diary. She practiced on old newspaper until she could form the letters exactly as Nicole herself had. Nicole had used green ink and Celia had only pencil, but she cast a perfect grainy shadow of each letter. Next she chose "Tara," who must have been the sister; her name was on some of the clothing tags. "Mrs. Almeida" went directly below her granddaughters, so, on this piece of paper, they were not separated.

Mr. Almeida seemed always to be circling—ticking ahead on his bicycle or pacing through his house, unhappy to be still—and an inscription would fix him in place. But he must go somewhere, so she put him with his wife. Then she listed all that was marvelous in their house—"biscuits," "suitcase," "railing"—in spellings of her own. She did not like to write "photograph," but to do so seemed a kind of penance; tumbling after it came "bicycle" and "shoes." Beneath that she wrote her own name.

Once she began, every word suggested another. Lists grew like vines, trailing across the pages. From "Celia" came the names of everyone in her family. From "suitcase" came the clothes themselves: "dress," "blouse," "shoes," "coat." These seemed too plain, so she added words to describe each one. When she did not know the right words to use, she brought one piece at a time to school to consult Sister Vicky, who taught sewing. "That is piping," Sister Vicky told her. "These are pleats . . . smocking . . . lace . . . embroidery . . . plaid." "Rick-rack" made them laugh.

"Patch," "Stitch," "Seam," she wrote when Sister Vicky asked her to join the Holy Name Sewing Club, which mended clothing for children in need. Celia could think of a hundred more interesting ways to spend her time, but Sister Vicky's invitation left little room for argument, and Celia enjoyed this new story of herself: a fortunate girl with beautiful clothes, helping the poor. She imagined Mr. Pujari's sons in rags, begging for shirts with Celia's patches after their father's swift and total ruin.

So she was in the sewing room, teasing Sister Vicky to let her try the machine, on the afternoon that the PSV *Amar Raj* lost power in a navigation channel and collided with the MV *Vanda*, a container ship outbound from the port of Bombay.

The cargo of the platform supply vessel consisted largely of water-based drilling fluids. Think how much worse oil would have been, Flora might have said, if she'd been in a frame of mind to look for the bright side. But the magnitude of the disaster overwhelmed her, and anyway there was fuel enough. The *Vanda* was carrying about two thousand tons of diesel and lube oil. She was struck at midship, listed sharply upon impact, and began to spew. Seven hundred tons pumped into the Arabian Sea before the leak was plugged.

Dominic, with money for diesel at last, had gone three hours past the mouth of Mahim Bay with his small crew. They'd been trawling for hours, the radio reduced to a low hum on a day of clear weather, when they spotted the first container.

At first, none of the men were sure what they were seeing. A faraway ship, a trick of light—nothing to cause alarm. Then it came closer, one corner bobbing up, bright yellow, like a child's block, and far enough away to seem small and harmless. But it was moving swiftly, caught in a strong current, and soon the men could see telltale ridges. Dominic was puzzled; there was no storm, nothing to roll a ship or tear containers loose.

Eventually, it drifted so near that they could see a column of numbers on its corrugated side and painted red letters sliding in and out of the swells: "Shree." Dominic made a gentle adjustment to keep out of its path. He watched the container go past them and turned the radio volume higher.

For the next fifteen minutes, they listened to confused estimates, reports of crew evacuations, calls for more Coast Guard vessels to assess and contain the spill. Transmission by transmission, they began to understand. Shortly after someone used the term "oil slick" for the first time, they spotted a flash of red: another container. When a helicopter flew overhead, Dominic decided to bring in the nets before the tide.

They were not panicked, just a little more hurried than usual. Still: a moment's distraction, a taut line, and Dominic lacerated his finger so badly that it was nearly torn off. He wrapped it as tightly as he could to hold everything in place, packed the hand in ice once the fish were in the hold, but eventually he lost it at the middle joint.

That was the end of his life as a fisherman. It was not the finger; such injuries were common enough. It was not even the oil slick, which stretched for four kilometers from the site of the collision, fouling beaches and destroying mangroves; or not only that. It was all the days that had led to it, when Dominic did not have enough diesel to practice his trade, and the days after, days of salvage and clean-up, when fishermen were barred from the water and the people of Bombay warned not to eat from the sea. One hopeless day after the next, stacked up like containers on a ship. He could no longer bear the weight of them. He could feel himself begin to roll.

At first, he said nothing. A man was supposed to endure. He tried to think of better times, nights on the boat long ago, stars above and fish below and his father beside him, together in all that darkness. He had not minded feeling small when he believed God could see them. He used to imagine the faint green glow of their souls, sparking like the phosphorescent algae they occasionally saw, outlining the dolphins who sported on the bow waves.

But no more. What came to mind instead was the yellow container. Dominic was a fisherman, well schooled in chance. His idea of faith was to trust that what seemed arbitrary actually fit into a larger design, drawn by God. Until he could discern it, he hoped, he prayed, he looked for signs.

Had the container been a sign? It had appeared and disappeared in such a strange blank encounter that, for days afterward, Dominic felt tossed about, a box of lost goods. He had not indulged in doubts since the eighth standard, when there was a chance of a post with the Port Trust if he stayed in school. But he preferred to work for himself, in the way of his father and grandfather—and at that time, the boats still meant a good life. For years, he kept to his course, as though this life alone had been sanctioned by God and history, and all the while the fish were getting smaller, the sea more polluted, the fuel more costly, the trips more extensive. He could not even pray: What shape would his prayers take? It had been a simple thing to ask for his daughters' deliverance from dengue or typhoid—"Please, Lord, let this child live"—but how to pray for an ocean? "Dear God, restore the mangrove swamps"? Still the big industry trawlers would rake through the breeding grounds; still the government would turn a blind eye. Still people would come to the Mithi River with their cooking vessels and oil drums, their raw sewage and industrial waste, their goats and cattle; still the poisonous waters would dump into the bay. "Lord, prevent oil spills"? Later, Dominic would come to know that it had taken thirty-two separate instances of noncompliance with navigational rules, contraventions of the Merchant Shipping Act, and outright breaches of maritime law, plus a series of mechanical failures and a confluence of wind and tides, to send the yellow container floating past him—on its way nowhere, with God knew what inside. To pray for one thing in such waters was to pray for a thousand things to be untangled and set right, for history itself to be reworked. He did not believe it could be accomplished. Jesus himself was a small, scant hope, walking on water from an infinite distance, picking his way between the troughs of waves. Dominic D'Mello remained a fisherman to this extent at least: when he lost faith in the sea, he lost faith in God.

Celia knew only that her father spent a week pacing up and down the lane, taking too many drinks with other fishermen, who were also at liberty to take too many drinks, or sitting in a silent black gloom that her mother called praying. Celia had not known prayers could be so angry.

While he was gone, Mr. Pujari came to take their television. That was a Saturday night. Celia knew that her mother had been waiting all week long for her Sunday-morning episode of *The Ramayana*. She waited for Flora to send Mr. Pujari away, but Flora only gathered her children close. When Celia shouted at Mr. Pujari to get out and come back the *next* day to steal from them, Mr. Pujari laughed. Her mother snatched her arm, as though he might try to take her next.

A week after the spill, Dominic announced that he would no longer need diesel to make a living, but CTC tea. "That is, 'cut, tear, curl,'" he added, as if that were the point that needed explaining. Inexpensive to stock but a good, bold taste. Flora began to weep.

In the days that followed, Celia also felt tossed, but more deliberately: her father, Mr. Pujari, or possibly God had tipped the family out of the life she had always known, for obscure reasons of their own. She herself had been one of them.

"But you said *clean* break!" Flora insisted when the doctor told them the bone had slipped out of place.

"This happens sometimes," he said.

An X-ray, an IV to numb the arm, a closed reduction to reset the bone, a second X-ray, a cast instead of a splint, more bills to settle. Two days later, her father sold the diesel boat. "At least no surgery," her mother said. "At least we have the dinghy still."

She was fooling no one. Her eyes filled with tears at the idea of a tea stall.

Clean break, Celia did not write. Dislocation. Reduction. She had taken to composing ghost lists, words she did not want in the diary. Range of motion. Nerve damage. Laborer. Debt. In the real diary, she wrote all the kinds of fish her father had caught, the words for various methods and nets, the parts of the boat. She kept a mental tally of how many episodes of her favorite television show her mother had missed: three. It troubled Celia that her mother would not walk up the lane to the Cooperative, where small crowds gathered to watch the program together. Flora had kept to herself since the sale of the boat.

Finally, Inez bought a new set and persuaded Flora to watch with her.

Celia never heard about the container her father saw. But although most of the fallen containers sank to the bottom, a few, with buoyant cargo, stayed afloat, to be carried away toward Pakistan, Oman, Somalia, or to crack open on the rocks offshore. Salvage crews worked to drain hazardous chemicals, and up and down the coast, people cleared debris, timber, soggy bales of cotton and jute. Packets of tea steeped the waters off Marine Drive; empty gas canisters caused a brief panic in Back Bay; a flotilla of Western toilet seats swept in for the kids of Worli, who grinned through oval white frames for newspaper pictures. Birds gorged on buffalo meat from a burst reefer on Elephanta. Juhu beaches were closed until a banked container of guar gum was towed off a sandbar.

Celia and Jerome spent hours with baskets on their hips, scouring the shoreline for something worth saving. They did not find much at first: chair legs, rotted cashews, a few of the Worli bathroom fittings. But eventually a container of plastic novelties broke apart just off Khar, and Jerome and Celia were among the first children scuttling over the low rocks to collect key chains, bubble wands, and strings of colored plastic beads.

The beads they found turned out to be rosaries with dangling plastic crosses. Celia and Jerome came home with full baskets and masses of chains around their necks and shoulders. "See, see!" Their mother scooped up great armfuls of plastic treasures and let them rain down again. She was weeping; she could not get through the days without weeping. The sale of the boat had left her so rudderless that she could not even share her husband's relief at having paid off Mr. Pujari once and for all. She could not understand how they would eat unless by divine mercy, and as if in answer, the sea festooned her children in prayer beads. She attributed this grace to Our Lady of Navigators, who had been raised from these same waters.

This sign that Mary was watching over their family even after they had abandoned the sea brought Flora such comfort that Dominic promised to call his new business the Holy Rosary Tea Stall.

For a few weeks, the sea coughed tar balls, like an old man with black lungs. Dominic constructed a stall on Varuna Road. Flora constructed brave remarks. Evangeline waited for strength that might never come. Celia waited to see if her arm would heal. Only Jerome was cheerful, happy with the water guns from the container and the prospect of a life onshore.

The Holy Rosary opened a month after the spill, with a selection of tiny photo frames, key chains with Ganeshas or Buddhas, colored whistles, bubble wands, and a rainbow array of rosaries alongside its more orthodox offerings. By this time, the container had been identified as belonging to Shree Devi Enterprises of Bhopal, but there was little left to claim. The goods had been dispersed, first by tides and then by beachcombers, the shore picked clean. The container itself lay rusting on a shelf of rock, its corrugated yellow flank exposed in low tide, until it was towed away and scrapped four months later. Other containers became more permanent features of the coastline. At the collision site, a long jagged row of them settled on the sea floor, forming a makeshift reef. A container to the north, beached high on a sandy spit, was commandeered by squatters, who squabbled with the authorities proposing to clear it away until rising waters ended the argument.

When the cast came off, Celia's arm looked odd to her, the skin flaking, the muscles thinned to strands, like a piece of driftwood with a knot at the elbow. The doctor recommended exercises, and slowly the arm came to feel like her own again. She had not intended to go back to the sewing club, but once the boat was gone, she found comfort in unexpected things. The satisfaction of picking up a torn shirt and putting down a mended one. The weekly ritual of asking to use the sewing machine and hearing Sister Vicky say not yet.

She still slept with the raincoats hanging overhead, but they no longer meant what they once had, or perhaps they had picked up new, inadvertent meanings. Celia wanted to hold the day of the suitcase so tightly that nothing would be lost, but she no longer remembered all the stickers on the suitcase. Tenth standard, her mother had said, but how certain had she sounded? Mrs. Almeida had spoken of a new picture, but did she say what happened to the one Celia had found?

Even what Celia kept firmly in mind twisted to new shapes. She would never forget the moment when she first saw the smocked red dress, but after feeling the hem brush against her knees, she could not quite recapture the breathlessness of her surprise. At night, when sleep did not come, she imagined she was in the bed at the Almeida house, peering out through her porthole in the painted grille of the balcony railing. But those memories became tangled with the boat her father had sold, the way her mother cried over it.

That was the difficulty; any one day could be subsumed by another. Nothing was safe, not even words in her own hand. What she wrote on the first page of the diary seemed altered by what she wrote on those that followed, and by what she left unwritten. In the end, she abandoned her lists and began sketching garments she might make with Sister Vicky.

Celia wondered about Mr. Almeida every time she climbed the spiral staircase to the kitchen with her mother. Flora continued to sell other men's catch to Mrs. Almeida and a few longtime customers. It was not much money, just a way to keep to a life she knew. The prawns, at least, were their own: their wooden boat was good enough for the shoals.

Mr. Almeida was seldom home mid-morning, but the kitchen girl smiled whenever she saw them, or pretended to be shocked by Celia in her finery from the suitcase. Once, she touched the pleats of a skirt with a cloudy look and said, "Chota baby." Then in Marathi: "Nicole is the bigger girl. Always running. But Tara is happy to sit with me."

On that day, the gift of a fish pleased Mrs. Almeida so much that she invited them to stay. She offered packaged digestive biscuits—not shortbread, although Celia could see the blue tin on the shelf. She wished for a taste but felt that she and Mrs. Almeida understood each other in that regard. Such biscuits were not an everyday occurrence.

"You are writing in your diary?" Mrs. Almeida asked.

Words and pictures also, Celia told her.

"You can show me next time," Mrs. Almeida said. "Bring it with you."

Celia returned a week later, wearing a pair of shoes that once belonged to Mrs. Almeida's granddaughters. Nicole's, she liked to think, as though that sister belonged especially to her. There was a pleasing symmetry to it: the running sister for Celia and the quiet one for Evangeline. When she thought of them, it was not exactly as girls—as girls, they lived far away and were strangers—but as more intimate presences, connected to her. She walked in their shoes.

She came straight from school, in the uniform Mrs. Almeida had recognized on the day of the accident. Later, Celia wondered if it was the best time to visit. Mrs. Almeida had risen from her afternoon sleep, but her hair was sticking up in the back. She seemed rumpled and out of sorts, even after her tea.

When it came time for Celia to open the diary, she balked at showing Mrs. Almeida the names of her granddaughters. Mrs. Almeida was looking too soft, as though she had left some essential armor at her bedside. So Celia turned to the second page of her lists before handing her the book, but Mrs. Almeida looked carefully through all the pages, touching a finger to the names of her own family.

"Very nice." Her voice reminded Celia of the way her father spoke to her when he was actually thinking about money.

But the list of teachers roused Mrs. Almeida. She read the names aloud, telling Celia about those she remembered and asking questions about those she didn't know.

"Nicole and Tara. They learn Marathi, madam? Hindi?"

"English." Mrs. Almeida looked so startled that Celia did not ask when they would come again.

"Here, madam." She pulled two small packages from her backpack.

She intended the rosary for Mrs. Almeida; the white beads reminded Celia of pearls. The picture frame with a key ring was for Mr. Almeida, so his photograph would not be lost. But in the end, she gave both to Mrs. Almeida. Mrs. Almeida was there, and Mr. Almeida was not, and maybe Mrs. Almeida would share of her own accord.

The rosary pleased her especially; she kissed Celia to thank her. Celia hoped to find Nicole and Tara in the armada of framed photographs around the room, but the telephone rang and Mrs. Almeida answered it. After a minute, she put a hand over the mouthpiece. "Okay, child, tell Mummy you've done well." The kitchen girl gave Celia a sweet lime, and the visit was finished.

Halfway home, she spotted Mr. Almeida on his bicycle. He wore chappals and brown trousers, the kind she remembered from the day of the accident. Celia nearly ran to greet him; she wanted to tell him about his present. But it had gone to Mrs. Almeida, so she stayed where she was, watching until he rode out of sight.

13

FEBRUARY 1987

Francis sat in the gymkhana, at the corner table set aside as his own. The typewriter was left undisturbed between visits, and any stray papers he might leave—wandering off to have a quick word with friends, intending to come back but forgetting, sometimes, in the flow of conversation—were collected and placed on the teak shelf near Reception. He paid a little extra for this service, money his wife would consider thrown away. "You have the whole house, Frank," she told him when he first retired. He moved from one room to another, hoping for peace. But Essie was always barging in to interrupt him. Someone's daughter was getting married. What was the meaning of this bill? Dinner guests were arriving. Her fishmonger no longer sold fish. Once, she came marching in to point out a stain she would find difficult to remove. That was the day he packed up his typewriter in its old case and walked to the gymkhana with it, his fingers aching from its weight. He was a Golden Boy, a member of fifty-plus years. He had taught many of the younger members at university. If he wished to work at a quiet table where he could order a drink whenever he liked, the gymkhana would accommodate.

At the moment, he was finishing a project for the Hotel Castelo: not a scholarly work but a gentle history of the watchtower from which the hotel had taken its name. He knew the sort of thing: suitable for a brochure or lobby posting, a touch of heritage for curious guests. The brevity of the piece, the swiftness with which it swept through the centuries to its jaunty conclusion—the establishment of the hotel itself—was another reminder that much of his own life had passed into history.

Francis was accustomed to tunneling backward, to considering the forces that had shaped his life from a distance of centuries. He thought of history as a light, shining into the murk of what had been forgotten; he thought of the years he himself had lived through as clear and bright. But, increasingly, he saw that time would darken them also. He was eleven years old in 1930, when Gandhi began the Dandi March. In April, Francis's father took him to Juhu to see women gather salt from the beach, a day Francis ought to have held fast in memory. Instead, he could only summon a few brief impressions: women collecting brine at the water's edge; the small packet of rough salt his father bought; a child down the beach, holding tight to a kite-string. Francis had felt a pang of envy; he wished he had a kite. On the walk home, his father explained that the police had attacked women harvesting salt on Chowpatty, and Francis could still recall his pride in being chosen for an outing with a touch of danger, while his younger brother, Peter, was left behind. But that was all he remembered. He and his father must have gone home, Peter must have been disappointed, and the vast machinery of empire kept grinding, until the years revealed it had begun to fail on those very beaches—salt in the gears. It was mortifying to recall with perfect clarity the image of the crisp red kite, floating high above the history Francis could have captured with his own eyes.

Even his own history was difficult to pin down. He remembered arriving late to the family party his parents hosted for his twenty-first birthday; he remembered his mother's expression when he turned up at last. But he could not remember where he had gone. Anna had died a few months before; had he been with Albert? His parents worried about melancholy and counseled distance, but even when Albert returned to the south, Francis turned up at Anna's house a few times a week. It became a refuge, a place where memories of her could gather unimpeded. He liked to hear Anna's mother call him *son*. He liked to sit quietly with Agnes without any need to explain what he might do next.

Agnes was a quiet girl by nature, not one to charm or chatter. For a long time, it had been possible to overlook her, and then, slowly—Francis could not locate how or when—it became impossible to think of anyone else. He was adrift when she left home nine months after Anna's death. She had grown so thin and quiet that her father did not think she had the stamina for university studies, though she begged to begin a course. Her mother decided a change of scene might help Agnes rally and sent her south to stay with cousins.

She was gone four months. By the time she returned, she and Francis had exchanged several letters, in which neither spoke directly of love. But a life with Agnes felt like the only possible way forward, an outcome so natural it hardly needed discussion. She cared for him, Francis knew. He remembered her hand on his arm in the garden. He remembered that when he arrived at the vigil to join family and friends in the prayers of the rosary, she crossed the room to sit beside him. He remembered her at Albert's wedding, where he stood as best man. Agnes wore a yellow sari, a flower in her hair.

She took an overnight train home three days after his term ended, arriving in the city at daybreak. Francis stopped by after breakfast, but she was resting for a few hours. "Come for lunch," her mother urged, and he spent the interval trying to tick past the hours. It was strange, after the work of the semester, to find himself spinning aimlessly through a sunny morning. A badminton game, a bath, a struggle with a book whose pages he barely registered. He rode to a jewelry store and considered three or four trays of rings before deciding they should choose together.

Still, he arrived back at her house too soon. He turned at the head of the road and looped for several more blocks before letting himself return.

Agnes was in the garden with her cousins when he finally came to the gate. While she was away, Francis had wondered whether he would always be struck by her resemblance to Anna, but when she waved he did not see Anna at all. He imagined away the cousins, imagined the moment when he would take off her glasses and kiss her.

Lunch was a noisy, happy affair. The whole family came flocking to welcome Agnes home. "Sit," her mother encouraged Francis. "This is your home also, son." Her eyes filled with tears, but she blinked them away and smiled.

It came as a small shock to be reminded that Francis's place among them was still as the boy who would have married Anna. Impossible to describe what had changed, or how; impossible to speculate what her parents or even Albert would think. He wanted only to be alone with Agnes, the one person to whom he would not have to explain. She sat near the center of the table, and although Francis kept constant hold of the sound of her voice, he tried not to look too long in her direction. He preferred to wait until there would be no need to trade in hidden glances. But he felt a kind of charge whenever her eyes met his, and a secret glow in the moments just after she looked away, the way, after a circuit was broken, the wire could still flare orange for a second or two before fading to gray.

After lunch, the aunts retired to rest while the younger set played cards. Agnes's mother went to lie down but kept popping up again: a message she meant to give, a question she meant to ask, a letter she meant to show. She put a hand to Agnes's arm or head or cheek, as if she could never be done assuring herself that her daughter was home. There would not be a chance to see Agnes alone, Francis realized, but even after he said goodbye, he lingered beneath the mango tree in case she might slip down to the garden. It was May. Much of the fruit had been harvested green, but those left to tree-ripen were beginning to blush, weighing down the branches.

The next day, he kept away. By the third evening, he began to regard their prolonged separation as a test and his endurance as an answer—however arbitrary—to the one question that remained: Had he waited long enough? Had enough time passed since the loss of Anna?

It was nearly a week before he suggested a walk. She agreed so quickly that he knew he had his answer. When a friend appeared at the gate, Francis forced himself to talk a little before walking the short distance to the park near the fishing village where he and Agnes would meet. He was thinking that, by this same hour the following day, he would go to her father. Or perhaps they would hold off, say nothing for a few weeks, let the future swell between them.

Instead, her hand on his arm. Her voice quiet but steady. Yes, it was true she felt a connection to him. They were good friends. Close friends. But she'd heard a stronger call. She was certain. She was sorry. "Who knows? They may throw me out." She tried to laugh, but her voice was shaking. He kissed her on each cheek, and then he truly kissed her. Again. Again. She leaned against his chest, and he put his arms around her in full view of anyone watching. For a minute, he thought he had won: they would walk back together, the beginning of everything.

Then she pulled away, smiling as though already grieving for him. "I have to go."

He could not remember much of that season. Listless days. Games, bets, cards. Friends who joked they could not get his attention. "Francis. Francis!" His father sitting him down one rainy night to say Anna was gone, poor girl, but Francis had mourned long enough. He must look to the future.

Francis waited until his parents had gone to bed, when the trees lashing in the wind and the muddy streams coursing down St. Hilary Road made it possible to believe that nothing was really set in stone. Then he took his cycle into the wet. The gardens were waterlogged, the lawns flooded like paddies, the streets streaming with runoff. He rode in great wild rings around the neighborhood, skids and dashes, throwing plumes of water high from his tires before he turned down her road.

He had reached her house when his wheel caught a clump of sodden leaves. The cycle went down in the mud, and Francis struck his forehead against the handlebar. He stood, dazed, looking up at her dark window, and then he sat down hard against the compound wall and closed his eyes. He did not know how long he stayed there, letting the rain beat against his shoulders. He drifted to sleep, if it was sleep. When he opened his eyes, he brought his hand to his head to feel the lump and laughed to see the thin thread of blood on his fingers. It was nothing, nothing at all. He had changed nothing. There was no other end to this story. He must pick up his cycle and go.

Francis? His father pulled his chair so close that Francis blinked. *Son, you understand what I'm telling you? It's time to stop looking back. Your life is ahead of you.*

Yes, said Francis.

MARCH 1987

The Holy Rosary Tea Stall on Varuna Road was touch-and-go. At first, Flora kept her market stall to tide the family over, buying from other boats and calling out to shoppers from the slick tiled platform where fishwives squatted on low stools, their knees spread wide around dark-stained chopping blocks, the catch fanned out before them.

Directly beside her was Inez. Inez and Clive had no children of their own, a situation no one discussed but which Flora slowly understood to be permanent. Inez was ten years older, Clive older still, but their age alone did not convince Flora. It was the affection Inez cultivated for the D'Mello children that taught Flora no miracle was coming: Inez's grin when she measured Jerome's height against her own, her delight in Celia's clowning, the ways she contrived to put a little extra on Lina's plate. When Clive brought in full nets, Inez gave Flora a standard crew share, as though Jerome had been one of the boys aboard.

"That is too much . . ." Flora tried to argue but lost the words. The world seemed designed to bring her to tears, both its abrasions and its moments of softness.

"What's too much between friends?" Inez was in high spirits. All Varuna knew that Clive had spent the weeks of the monsoon in a wet season of his own, so it was a relief when boats could launch again and Clive was restored to a proper routine. He was a little man, bandy-legged, not too difficult for Inez to navigate when he drank. He muttered remarks that nobody admitted to hearing. Some nights, when the mutterings gathered force and burst from him in small puffs of ire, Inez came down to spend the evening with Flora, and Dominic went upstairs to take a drink of his own. He could steer Clive's thoughts away from various disappointments—*No sons, not even a girl!*—and toward memories both men enjoyed: sightings of sawfish, octopi, sharks. The day Clive released a beaked sea snake from his net. The storm they had survived when one was a man and the other a boy.

Occasionally, they spoke of Dominic's father, who had died on his boat with Clive during one of the rare voyages when Dominic stayed ashore. He was struck down with chest pains so far from land that there was nothing for the crew to do but lay their hands on his head and arms so he might feel he was not alone.

Even when Clive was drinking, he shielded Dominic from the confusion of those final minutes. Better the son did not have to remember a wet stain spreading on his father's pants, or fright rising in his eyes. Clive considered it an act of mercy that such memories had lodged with him, not Dominic. He would not undo such mercy with talk.

Dominic only spoke of his father's death when he also drank too much. "The one time I didn't go with him. I never said goodbye."

"No time for goodbyes." Clive shook his head to clear it. "What was that song he used to like? About the lady and the moon?"

Downstairs, Flora and Inez rolled their eyes at the choruses that rolled above them. If the men drank enough, they slept where they sat and Inez stayed the night below; in the morning, the women fried fish. Eventually the men came shuffling down—cheeks slack, eyes sour—and ate.

The families had been entwined so long that they could not possibly untangle their debts. They crewed on each other's boats, borrowed from each other for fuel. For months, Dominic forgave the rent without mention of the clinic for childless couples. Later, Clive hid Dominic from Mr. Pujari. When Clive's television no longer gave a good picture, Inez came downstairs every Sunday morning to watch *The Ramayana* with Flora. After Mr. Pujari took their television, Inez purchased the new one they shared. There was no beginning or end to what they owed each other.

But the tea stall upended Flora. Before her husband sold his boat, she held to the notion that she and Dominic were better off—landlords, not tenants, even if they never asserted themselves in such a way. Without the boat, without the prospect of a good net changing their fortunes, week after week of accepting favors began to wear on her. And it was crushing to see the ease with which Inez filled her baskets. The catch was good, a season that might have righted them if Dominic had just held on. Flora tried not to sound reproachful when she said he must be missing the boat.

"I don't miss the debt." What else to say about losing a boat that came from his grandfather to his father to him? "I don't miss Pujari."

Flora agreed with *that*. But Dominic had a way of refusing to look around corners. For how long would he plant himself in the flimsy shelter of his tea stall, buying milk they could ill afford to serve with his tea? Would they lose the house if the tea stall failed? "At least set up near the market," she begged, but he insisted on the village road. Too much competition near the market.

"That is because there are customers there!"

Instead, he took a spot beside the undertaker and promptly made a deal to provide tea for the bereaved at a reduced rate.

"Why not?" Flora said to Inez. "He is trying to kill us all."

"Right at the head of the road," said Dominic, aggravating Flora with his new man-of-business voice. "Easy for boys off the boats, easy for anyone coming from church, easy for families at Seven Sorrows. Very good foot traffic."

"The traffic is feet first," snapped Flora.

Increasingly, her spirits depended on her weekly viewings of *The Ramayana*. She and Inez watched together, the pair of them rousing the children for early Mass so they could be home in time for the show. Inez was drawn to Rama's heroics, but Flora preferred his wife, Sita, who picked her way over painful rocks to follow Rama into exile. Flora did not share Sita's habit of tender speeches, but it was her private feeling that she was enduring rocks of her own. Her husband had exiled himself from the sea, and what choice did Flora have but to follow? He might as well be lost in the forest for all the attention he gave to their prospects. "Things will pick up," he said blandly.

When? Flora wanted to know. What future could they wring from a tea stall? For what could they train their son? What match could they find for Celia or Lina? The girls must marry from the fishing villages dotting the coast; they must hope to attract a fisherman's notice, not only with their faces but with their proficiency. Inland, a bride's family might need a dowry. But in the Koliwadas a skilled fishwife was an asset, commanding respect and sometimes even a bride price. If Flora did not see to their training, her daughters would be disinherited along with their son.

Evangeline was still recovering her strength after typhoid, but Celia had far too much time on her hands. "Doing *what?*" Flora asked again and again, when Celia turned up long after the others came home from school. Friends, Celia said airily, or clubs. Such friends, thought Flora, unsettled to learn that Celia sometimes stopped to chat with Aunt Janu's son. No one was certain he was dangerous, but why choose such a big frowning type? And what good could come of clubs? Her child should mend clothes for beggars until she became one herself?

"You'll fall behind in class," Flora warned, though a bit uncertainly. Celia had a quick mind; she seemed to keep up without trying. Even the cottage lady, Mrs. Almeida, encouraged her, summoning her regularly to check on her reading. One afternoon she gave Celia a book, something Shakespeare, in which Celia's own name appeared. Celia showed Flora the printed version of her name before putting it away behind the glass-fronted shelf where the family kept their treasures. She said

Mrs. Almeida would help her read the full book later, when Celia was older, which was all very well, except that when Flora felt uneasy about her daughter, she found herself wondering what became of the other Celia. Was it a happy ending? "Why not try reading it now?" she suggested. "Your teacher can help you."

Celia made a face. "No," she said to her mother, in a way Flora would never have spoken to her own mother. "We read different books in school."

"Then mind you do your work properly," Flora said sharply, feeling she had lost hold of the conversation. So there were books and other books; what could she say to that? The point, she felt with distressing new urgency, was that Celia must continue to do well in school. She would need every advantage. They no longer had a boat to secure her future.

So a few weeks later, when Celia came home from school with two notes pinned to her collar, Flora felt a throb of recognition. Here was exactly the trouble she'd warned against, come to pass at just the moment that Flora's prayers for Evangeline appeared to have been answered. For months, Flora had begged Evangeline to make friends, and this very afternoon the child was off at a birthday party.

Flora removed the notes from Celia's collar and opened them both before handing them to Jerome. She had trouble with written English.

"Go on, read them to me."

"No!" Celia tried to snatch them away, but Jerome waved them overhead. "Give!"

"What'd you *do*?"

"Reading. *Extra* reading." This was a dig. Jerome tunneled through words so slowly that Celia sometimes reached over and flipped his page.

Jerome poked his hand higher. "Teachers don't write notes for that."

"Not about *you*." A quick fierce leap; she scrabbled at his wrist.

"I bet they say something worse about *you*."

"Celu—" came the warning but too late; she was up and scratching like a cat until Jerome howled and Celia tore one of the notes away.

"Rat," she shouted. "Blowfish!"

"Celia!" Her mother's voice cracked like thunder. Celia rolled back. She could have lunged at Jerome again: his round shoulders, his hand cupped to his cheek. When he let it drop she saw the welt, threaded with blood.

Her mother's gaze took in Celia's whole body. "What is *wrong* with you." This was not a question, Celia knew, but a reminder that she was past understanding.

Her mother held out a hand to Jerome. "Come, son, let me help you," which told Celia she might as well be gone.

She left the house, and then the village, and then kept going. At first she was only trying to outrun the girl she always ended up being, but on Creek Road, she felt a wild impulse to march to the train station. She searched her pockets and found no money for the fare, nothing but a torn note. And she had snatched the wrong one. "Could Celia please bring a 2-meter length of fabric to school?" What would her mother have made of that? Celia imagined leaping aboard a train to stand in the open doorway, where she had never been permitted to ride, while her mother huffed along the platform, streaming apologies as the train picked up speed.

It was the other note Celia had meant to recover, the one informing her parents that she had been caught reading an adventure story beneath her desk during math class. Celia knew the truth was far less damning: she had been reading her library book, and the pale workings of the classroom receded, and when math began she could not tear herself away from the mysteries to be solved. It was not only a matter of villains and kidnappers; she wondered about the whole world that rose from its pages. Why should brothers and sisters go to school far from each other in England? Where were the villagers when the mother fell ill and left the children with a bad-tempered servant? How did they pack food in sacks without everything spilling? The story galloped ahead, and Celia could only hold on tight.

She was shocked when her teacher seized the book, startled to find herself back in her classroom. She half-imagined her teacher would congratulate her on such exemplary focus.

Instead, she spoke of a girl who *sneaked*. A girl who *put herself above children trying to learn*. A girl who was *thoughtless, inattentive, disrespectful, sly*. Celia let the words break over her like waves. It was impossible to be understood. She must simply endure while what she knew to be true was scribbled over by what a grown-up decided. She must stand in the corridor for the rest of the period, then take home a note telling her parents all the wrong parts of what had happened.

It was so easy to disappoint people that she could have choked on it. And then came Jerome, with his blowfish cheeks and his curled rat-fingers.

She had not even remembered to bring the book when she fled. It was at home in her backpack: *Five Run Away Together*. Running away seemed easier for the Famous Five, four English children and a grinning dog, who set off for an island refuge with tins of food and a wooden boat of their own to pilot. In Santa Clara, the only places Celia could think to go were the toy shop and the old Castelo wall. But she had no money to spend, not even on ice cream, and the bay splayed before her like a million ideas she'd already had. She needed a mystery to solve, a larder to raid, a bicycle to pedal madly. She needed Julian to toss her a ginger beer when she arrived someplace new. *Five Holiday in Varuna*, she imagined. The Five would stay in the Hotel Castelo and notice Celia sitting on the wall, reading a book with uncommon focus. Who is that intelligent girl? the boys would wonder. Anne would offer an ice cream. Soon they would ask her help tracking down the head of a crime gang. I know the man, she would tell them, Mr. Pujari. Dick would clap her on the back. They would jump into a taxi and go racing downtown, straight past her mother's warnings about big-city this, anything-can-happen that. Flora was forever telling the story of the girl whose earrings were torn from her ears by a man who promised sweets and led her down a lonely lane. Which lane? wondered Celia. She was so restless her skin itched; so restless she could scarcely look forward to finishing the *Five* adventure. She would not be able to keep herself in check; she would swallow it whole, and that would be the end. The book would not be able to contain her.

She was wandering up Creek Road, failing to resign herself to the toy store, when she heard her name and saw Inez approach with her loose, clown wave.

"Where are you off to, all alone?" Inez sounded pleased that Celia was so grown-up, which pointed Celia in a new direction.

"I'm looking for fabric," she said, and showed Inez the note from Sister Vicky. The script wobbled a little, like Sister Vicky herself. She was not as steady as she used to be, Sister told Celia, when she found her outside the classroom, disgraced, and suggested that Celia walk her to the sewing room.

It is not a club day, Celia reminded her, but had to stop talking so she would not cry.

That was when Sister Vicky explained about her shaking hands and her weak eyes also. "Do you know, I can't even manage a pair of scissors? After this year, I will not be able to teach."

Celia looked up, shocked that Sister would share anything so sad and true without wrapping it up in a lesson. But Sister only said, "Let's see if you can cut a pattern yourself."

"It's a special project," Celia told Inez. "Sister will teach me to use the machine. That is usually sixth standard."

"Clever girl!" Inez beamed. "Only where's Mumma? You're not on your own?"

"Today I'm only looking," Celia said, then thought to add that her mother was helping Jerome. This was not untrue, she decided. Everyone knew Jerome needed help and then more help with schoolwork. Flora could not read the assignments, but she could tap her finger on a page when she sensed his thoughts were clouding over.

"You won't find anything good this side," said Inez. "Come with me!"

They walked to the street market on Linking Road and spent nearly two hours in the fabric stalls. In the end, they found a pattern that looked so nice in two colors that Inez said to take both. That way Celia could make a kurti for Evangeline also, and how could Inez give a present to one girl and not the other? Only let the second be a surprise. Celia was already feeling a twist of unease over what her mother would think of this expedition, but when she hesitated, Inez said not to worry. She would keep the extra fabric at her place until Celia was ready for it.

As a treat, they rode home in an autorick. Celia watched the streets streaming by, the blurring lights, the overtaken buses, all the many, many steps she didn't have to take. But her thoughts kept tipping to the thin blade of her mother's voice. She wanted her mother to see the cloth and feel proud. She wanted Jerome to know she was sorry.

Instead, Jerome was nowhere to be found. Her mother looked up at Celia with her mouth pinched tight when Inez came hallo-ing inside.

"She's been with *you*!"

"So late! I know. But we've picked up the cloth she needs."

When Flora said nothing, Inez filled the room with talk of colors and patterns and such fun choosing. "She has a good eye, this one."

"Thank you," Flora thought to say. A good eye? While teachers were angry and Flora was combing the village lanes, wondering where the child had gone. After two hours, she'd sent Jerome to check the beach. He did not refuse but asked, "Why can't we have some peace?" as he left.

"I must pay you back," she told Inez.

"Don't be silly!" Inez put her arm around Celia's shoulders. "Soon this one will open the Holy Rosary Tailor Shop and keep us all in fine clothes."

"She doesn't need to be a tailor in the third standard," Flora said. She meant to say it lightly. But Inez's face changed—a rare uncertain look—when she said good night.

―――

Her father read the note while her mother watched. After a minute, he turned the page over and saw nothing. "So you need me to sign?"

"That's all you have to say?" Her mother's voice rose dangerously, but her father didn't appear to notice.

"Celu, listen properly in school. Save your books for later."

"Okay, Daddy."

But her mother surged up like a great roused dragon, filling the room with *I cannot believe* and *How can you sit quietly when.* Celia stayed where she was, on the floor, coiled small.

"Okay, okay." Her father closed his eyes. When he opened them again, he said, "It's not so terrible for a schoolgirl to be reading."

"Not *school* books," said Jerome.

"From the *school shelf*," Celia flung back.

"How can she learn maths if she's looking at books?" Flora demanded. "Celu, where is this book? Give it to me. There—you see! This is not for learning anything. Who is running away?"

"These are the Five." Evangeline pointed to the cover. "Four children and the dog also. See? The dog is their friend. They live in England." Evangeline smiled so sweetly that for a moment it seemed their mother might be swayed.

Celia would have been grateful if she weren't so fed up with the entire family. Did her brother have to buzz around every small mistake? Did Evangeline have to be such a no-trouble child that ordinary girls like Celia seemed hopeless? And why was everything bigger than it should have been? One book, and her mother was shouting at her father. Did this happen in other families?

"What do English children have to do with you? There are no nice books about India? Nothing about girls who know how to behave? Nothing about fishing?" She turned to her husband. "She had no time for this nonsense when we had the boat. Now we begin to pay the price."

"Price! What price? Every father in the lane wishes he could have this problem!" He took a pencil from the clutter on a shelf and scrawled his name at the bottom of the note. "There. Finished. Celu"—he spoke so sharply that he did not seem on her side—"take this away."

Celia had to reach past her mother to take the note. The whole room seemed rigged to explode.

"No price," he said again, and Celia thought of the way he used to be after a good catch, joking, easy in his movements, a different man.

It was more difficult to make a kurti than Celia had imagined. The sleeves were the tricky part. If she could have made sleeveless, she might have been finished in two days, but Sister said sleeves were better for church, so she might as well learn. The sewing machine made a great clacking hum that startled Celia the first few times, and one of the senior girls had to thread the bobbin for her. When Celia had finished the basic construction of the blue kurti, she went up to Inez to begin work on the pink.

Flora could not refuse to buy from Clive's catch, but she made stiff work of it. Inez had not dropped by in the five days since the trip to Linking Road.

"Mummy will be proud of you," Inez said, and Celia understood she meant later, when her mother stopped being angry about something so large that it might as well have been Celia herself.

A week later, Celia presented the finished kurtis to her mother. She brought them home in a used plastic shopping bag that Sister Vicky had given her, with dusty creases across its rainbow colors. Sister smiled when they folded the garments inside. "See, just like store-bought."

"Here." Celia handed her mother the bag and watched as she withdrew the kurtis. The banded yokes had taken a full session each to cut and stitch.

"But where did you get these?"

"I made them." Celia meant to sound friendly, but her voice was a room of sealed doors and barred windows. She wanted her mother to do the work of opening them. She wanted her mother to explain how Celia could love her family but still land in their midst like a ball of burning rags. She wanted her mother to decide these tops could make up for the book and the note and the scratch and the shouting. She wanted to present a new version of herself, a girl who smiled nicely and shocked them all with her skill. The intensity of what she wanted could have bent iron.

But certain bars remained in place. So she stood, unsmiling, waiting for her mother to unlock what she could.

It took Flora a little time to understand. What *was* this bag, and the garments inside it, and this moment with her daughter? Even after Celia disclosed that she was taking sewing lessons, she stood tense and wary, watching Flora in a way that Flora did not recognize. Were these lessons a secret? A remedy for books? In Flora's confusion, she looked away from her daughter and at the pink top, turning it over in her hands, running her fingertip along the hem.

"That is for Lina. I used the *machine*."

"Did you?" Flora took care to sound impressed. "This is not the club?"

"No." Celia sounded scornful. "That is for mending, not making new. This is special."

"Sister Vicky is giving you these lessons? At no cost?"

Celia tipped her head yes.

"And the fabric? Inez bought both?" Pink, not what Flora would have chosen.

Yes again.

"Acha," Flora said. She imagined Inez and her daughter sifting through bolts of fabric, making faces at what they did not like. Maybe they shared a glass of sugarcane juice on the way home, the sort of treat Flora could not afford but Inez did not hesitate to offer. Flora looked at Celia, still small for her age, but growing, growing, and held the blue kurti to her shoulders. "This one is yours? It's looking so nice!"

Even she could hear the way her doubts about these lessons had crept into her voice, or possibly something lonelier, a sense that other women were exerting themselves to see to her child and she might no longer be at the center of things. She summoned herself and smiled. "You must wear it to Mass this week. Go and put it on. Let me see it properly."

Later, Flora would empty the emergency stash she kept in a leather pouch, deep in a cardigan pocket. She was not sure how to press Inez to accept repayment; she could not pretend two lengths of cloth were different from other favors that passed between them. But when she went upstairs, Inez took the money quietly.

"She wanted to surprise you," Inez said. "So I thought—"

"Yes," said Flora. "Thank you."

"A little trim would make it nice. I saw ribbon with gold thread—if we go back, I can pick it up for her."

"I'm taking her myself." Flora did not intend to sound severe, so she pushed herself to say more. "Can you believe she's come home with a new pattern? Another two meters."

Inez raised her hand slightly, offering back the money. "You have enough? You can always—later—"

"I have it," Flora said, a near lie. Then another: "You should come if you like."

Inez sat in the graying dark, her pots neatly stacked, no sign of food, no brewing tea. When she shook her head no, Flora felt ashamed.

Just this once, she thought, another lie, because this would not be the only time she would feel reluctant to share her daughter. There would be other days when she wanted to hoard this child, who had once felt so wholly hers that Flora hadn't minded who plaited her hair or gave her a bit of ribbon. She was not certain what had tipped the balance, but she sensed certain possibilities passing out of reach; or maybe it was Celia, passing out of Flora's hands and into the world's.

But she would have this evening with her daughter. She would buy the cloth she could not afford. She would buy it herself.

"Come down at least," she urged. Inez did not respond, and Flora struggled to find a way back to their easy exchange. "Such a help if you could sit with Lina. Jerome is at the docks, and the master of tea won't be back until God knows when. Lina might feel lonely. But if you're not up to it—"

Inez tossed a hand—*No, no, that's not it*—and gave a frown that became a kind of acquiescence. In a few minutes, she said.

Flora was nearly out the door before Inez called her back. It turned out she had already bought the gold ribbon for trimming.

"Don't give it to her yet, though. Wait until you've done your shopping."

"But let it come from you," Flora said helplessly.

Inez shook her head. "This is better." She held out the package to Flora. "I *like* to pick up little things for them. I *enjoy* myself."

Flora could not find a way to protest. She had come upstairs intending to find a single clear moment in the swish and ebb of their households. Instead, she remembered a game she had played as a child, trying to hop on the exact spot where the water met the sand, even though it changed with every wave.

Inez looked away. The sounds of the evening came drifting through the balcony like smoke. "I have no daughters."

Later, Celia bounced from one side of her mother to the other while they walked to Linking Road. It was all Flora could do to keep her out of ditches. They checked half a dozen stalls before they chose a print. Then Celia picked up another, in Flora's favorite shade of green. "For you, I'll make full salwar kameez."

"Not tonight," Flora said, laughing, as if they could buy as much as they liked but preferred to be patient.

The streets were lively and friendly; the walk was long but not unpleasant. Celia passed the time by ticking off plans: an outfit for Flora, a top for Inez, another for Mrs. Almeida. "That will be a good surprise," Flora agreed. Then Evangeline again. "But what about you?" Flora asked, and Celia tipped her head— maybe yes. "Are you tired? Should I carry that for you?" But Celia held the parcel tight to her chest, reminding Flora of the time they gave her a balloon when she was small. How they laughed to see her hug it with both arms. The string trailed behind her all the way home.

SEPTEMBER 1987

Anthony Correia was ten years old before his mother permitted his father to send him to the neighborhoods around Creek Road, a few kilometers south of their village. This was not an acknowledgment of Anthony's age or growth, but a lucky chance. The boy they had hired to make deliveries cut his foot on a length of pipe when he was unloading paint cans. He bound it well beneath his sandal, but within two days the wound began to fester, and on the third day he could no longer pedal the cycle.

"Let Anthony go," his father decreed, and since the orders must be fulfilled and there was no time to find a better replacement, his mother could not object. Instead, she shook her head grimly and said things like "Does he know how to cycle properly?" and "Look at the size of him," prompting Pinky to make cooing baby noises.

Of course he could cycle, he wanted to tell his mother. Nobody asked you, he wanted to tell his sister. But neither had a disposition that accommodated dissent. Better to keep his mouth shut and let his thoughts wheel beyond his family to the freedom ahead. For hours he could slip away, and who could say how long a delivery should take? Not his father, with his bad heart. Not his mother, with an unexpected new fight. The boy with the bad foot had come hobbling to the shop with his own mother in tow to present various medical receipts. While Anthony prepared the day's orders, he heard his mother argue that the job encompassed only the loading and unloading and ride between, not every place the fellow chose to put his foot.

The shop cycle was heavy, with a cargo platform between two rear tires. The delivery boy could manage up to sixteen cans on one run, but Anthony should start small, his father decided.

"He'll end small, too," Pinky said. She lingered to see him off, speaking sweetly of training wheels.

"You're late," Anthony reminded her, since she must go to school when he need not. Fishermen kept their sons on the boats when required, their father reasoned. Was a cycle so different?

But Pinky hoisted herself onto the cargo bed and lolled back, swinging her feet. Anthony should give her a ride, she proposed. "Maybe that will build up your muscles. Maybe then you can take *two whole cans*."

A bearded *goat* wouldn't marry you, Anthony could have said. He had composed this insult three days earlier while spying on Pinky and her friends, who were discussing what they hoped for in a husband. Pinky made loud pronouncements about her requirements for height and dancing. And a good beard, she added in her know-it-all way. Who would ever want her? thought Anthony. His sister was a thin bit of wire, twisted to every kind of sharpness.

Instead, his father said it was high time she took herself to school and learned to be of use to her family. Pinky made a show of hugging Anthony goodbye so she could whisper "Bad heart" without being overheard. Their father's condition might be passed down to either one of them, their mother had warned, and Pinky enjoyed predicting Anthony's demise.

"Watch out for hills," she said with mock sorrow, and when Anthony shoved her, she wagged a finger. "Try not to *exert* yourself."

"Try not to fuck yourself," Anthony said, but only later, testing the sound of the word in his mouth. He was panting a little as he tried to get the cycle moving. It was his second run, and already his leg muscles burned, a weakness he was glad Pinky could not see.

For the rest of the morning, he ferried small loads of paint back and forth to the boatyard, a short trip made longer by the embarrassment of delivering only six cans at a time. "Here comes half a coat," the boys at the yard hailed him, until it became a kind of name.

The boatyard was where his father got his start. As far as Anthony could tell this was an accident, though his father called it good business and his mother called it the power of prayer. They were fisherfolk, like most of the villagers. Then, one day, after a voyage, his father woke from a good sleep, washed his face and teeth, drank his tea, and collapsed. Anthony was three and Pinky six when a doctor told their father his condition was grave. He must live quietly, eat carefully, drink seldom if at all. The physical life of a fisherman would overtax him; he must find a different occupation.

The diagnosis came just before the off-season, when Anthony's father had laid in a supply of marine paint for his family's two diesel boats. His first move was to recoup his losses by selling paint to other fishermen. He could make a profit, he realized, because they were used to overpaying for freight charges. If they could buy within the village, nobody would order from outside again. He sold his boats and used the capital to buy a shop and inventory.

What Anthony remembered best from that period were the long rumbling rides across Santa Clara. Pinky was enrolled in school, but Anthony was too young, so his mother took him with her to make offerings to Stella Maris. The bus deposited them at the foot of Seaview Hill, and they walked up the winding slope to the basilica. At the roadside stalls, she chose wax offerings to give proper definition to their prayers: a terrible bulbous heart, looking nothing like the shape Anthony recognized, and a symbol of prosperity, which interested Anthony more: sometimes a wax storefront with the word SHOP stamped across the top, sometimes a five-hundred-rupee note, as thick as a slab of butter, with a colorless impression of Gandhi's face.

At the outset of the construction boom, the business expanded to house paint, and her selections expanded to wax buildings. Anthony wanted wax airplanes, but that was for travel, his mother said, and where would he ever have to go? When he touched the figure of a tiny wax doll, she pulled back his hand. No more mouths to feed.

It was to this neighborhood, finally, that Anthony cycled on his own, the cargo bed deliciously light with sample-sized cans of exterior paint for a building site near the Church of St. Anne. The area was full of new construction, old bungalows coming down so fast that they might have been scythed for harvest; multistory flat buildings rising like a bristling new cash crop. Anthony rode along the coast road, enjoying the pleasant arc of the shoreline and the smooth paved surface of the Promenade. It was a wide path meant for pedestrians, but what single rule could apply to such a river of people? Rules were never the same for beggars and the wealthy, children and grown-ups, squatters, police, bullies, film stars. There were dogs without leashes, a child launching a kite, roller skaters, a wandering cow. When people seemed annoyed with Anthony, he blasted his bell and veered as sharply as the three-wheeler allowed, rattling the samples strapped together in the back. He made a game of it: pretending he was an airplane pilot avoiding sticky lumps of clouds. He imagined they'd feel like candy floss, smearing the cockpit with a sugary film, clinging in shreds to the wings.

In his pocket he had money enough for candy floss, or possibly a glider plane if he passed a toy shop. The contractor at his last delivery had tipped him, a piece of luck Anthony did not report to his father when he picked up the final order of the day. He planned to look on Creek Road after making his delivery. He was passing packs of schoolgirls, a reminder that Pinky would soon be home, and the longer he stayed in Santa Clara, the better.

When the Promenade ended, he huffed inland for a few blocks, looking for the street his father had described. This was the part he dreaded: finding his way. He worried about road signs, and asking directions, and people laughing at him. Already he had passed two half-finished buildings behind knobby grids of bamboo scaffolding, neither ready for paint. But if he delivered the samples to the wrong site, would the workmen simply accept them? Would Anthony be blamed for the loss? It's near St. Anne's, his father said easily, but all the streets were near St. Anne's. For a moment he felt a kind of hatred for his father: his slack hands and soft chest, his mild foods and nest of cushions, his mother's "Don't upset Daddy," as though a bad heart could be roused to strike.

He was looking for St. Helena Road but turned at the junction of St. Hilary, thinking the names were so close that the scrawl on the receipt had misled him. But when he reached the right number, he saw only a bungalow. No workmen. No sign that anyone cared to try patches of color, from parchment to papaya, on the outer walls. The only activity was two houses down. A man with a bicycle—a real one, two wheels—pointed a camera toward the cottage in front of him. As far as Anthony could see, there was nothing to photograph. He rode a little closer.

"Is there a snake?"

The man was older than Anthony's parents, with iron-colored hair.

"No." His look was so close to a frown that Anthony nearly rode on. Then the man turned to indicate the far side of the road. "There *was* a snake once, just there."

"What kind—"

"You!" the man said suddenly and Anthony started, as though he'd been caught napping in school. A teacher would pull a boy up by the ear; the rules were different for teachers.

But the man wasn't speaking to Anthony; a schoolgirl behind him was waving. She was younger than Anthony, skinny legs, round face.

"Back again, is it? Who have you run down lately?"

"Nobody!"

"A wild elephant, that's what you are. Charging into people." He spoke with severity but the girl grinned. "And this fellow is hunting snakes."

The girl cast an appraising eye over Anthony and his cycle. But when she spoke again it was to the man alone.

"You are choosing paint? This is your house also?"

"No, no. This family is on holiday."

"Then who are you visiting?"

Anthony felt they were losing the point. "There was a snake that side," he told the girl.

"Ah," the old man said. "That snake came long ago. Before you were born."

"Was it a cobra?" The girl, butting in again.

"A tree viper. It coils around the branches and only drops when it's ready to—" He smacked a fist against the heel of his hand, the hammer blow of a strike.

"Deadly!" said Anthony.

"Maybe if you went straight to hospital—"

"Did it bite anyone?" the girl asked.

The man shook his head no.

"But you saw it yourself?" Anthony was determined not to be misled again. "What did it look like?"

"Bright green. Hidden in the leaves of a fruit tree. I only saw the head when it hung down."

"It could still be nearby," Anthony said. How long did snakes live? The street was full of trees.

"I killed it," the man said, and Anthony felt a surge of heat. This old man in his flapping slacks could finish off a viper, and his father could not even ride a cycle. The rules were different for bad hearts.

"Tell us!" said the girl.

"I don't stand about telling stories in the road," the man said sternly.

"Look!" Anthony pointed to a jet passing overhead. At night, planes were reduced to clusters of lights. Sometimes he spotted a row of three or four, queuing up at intervals over the sea as they came in to land. But in daylight he could make out the engines beneath the wings and the colors on the tails. He could not see the windows but he knew they were there. He rose up on the cycle and waved.

"They can't *see* you," the girl told him, and Anthony dropped his hand as if bitten.

"If they're low enough—" the man began, but Anthony bore down on the pedals and the cycle lurched forward. This was the wrong house. He was wasting his time with these people. "Hie, you! Watch out!" the man shouted, dragging the girl back, and Anthony jerked past them.

It was choppy, starting from a dead stop. Anthony was four houses down before he found a decent rhythm, and still he wasn't moving as fast as he'd like. The man was shouting, but it was easy to pretend not to hear, easy to imagine his ears were full of the roar of his own twin engines. He thought how wrong the girl was, how the pilot looking out the cockpit would see everything at once: the shop and the boatyard, the basilica and the airport, the delivery boy limping home with his mother, Pinky and her stupid friends. He would see Anthony cycling two streets away to the construction site before setting off to find a toy shop. From such a height, a pilot would only have to blink once before the man and the girl were gone.

"Every time you come around, I'm nearly killed," Mr. Almeida grumbled, but Celia was used to him.

"That was not me," she said. "That boy is to blame."

"What did you think would happen, starting fights in the road?"

"I was only telling him."

"And who are you to tell him? What do you know about airplanes?"

"I know about boats," she said seriously. "When a boat goes so far, you can't see anything on it."

Mr. Almeida grunted.

"You have been on an airplane?" she asked.

"All the way to America."

"Over the water?"

"Over this sea and then another. Even in a plane it takes many hours."

"What did *you* see?"

"Mostly clouds. But when you take off and land, you see what's beneath you, like small toys."

"So, next time, if I stand high and wave, you could see *me*."

Another grunt. "I am getting too old for such trips. And when you reach, everything is different. Even the food. My daughter cooks nicely, but you can't find the right things there. When Essie goes, she takes a suitcase full of spices and pickle."

"She likes to go?"

"She misses them, so she goes."

"Are you missing them?"

"I?" His laugh had a touch of modesty. "Yes, of course, I am missing them. But they can visit me here. That is better."

"You send them pictures?"

Mr. Almeida looked puzzled, so Celia pointed to his camera.

"No, no. This is something else. A different project." For a moment, it seemed that was all he would say, and then he explained that soon the house in front of which they stood would be knocked down. A new flat building would go up in its place.

Celia looked again. It was simply a house, the kind she passed on every side in this neighborhood, but knowing it would soon be gone made it both more vivid and somehow less real, as though it were already a story of itself. It was a bungalow, not as big as many of the others, with a triangular roof that gave it a cottage look. She wondered how it would feel to live away from the sound of the sea. "Do you know the people?"

"Oh yes." He waved his hand in a way that took in the whole neighborhood. "I know everyone here."

"But you're taking a picture when they're gone? You don't want them in the picture?"

He smiled. "The people I remember well enough. But when the house goes . . ." He pointed to a flat building down the road. "Do you remember what house was there once?"

She did not. He took a small plastic album from the bin on his cycle and flipped through the pages until he found the right one.

"I knew that house! I liked the color."

"I liked the door," he said.

Celia turned the album pages. "Will they come this year? From America?"

"What?" He sounded surprised. "No, not this year. Maybe next."

He lifted the camera again and snapped a photo of her. "There. Not just houses. Now I have a picture of an elephant."

This pleased her. "I am *Celia*," she reminded him.

"It is not my job to remember the name of every child who runs me down in the road," he said stiffly, and she giggled again.

She thought about this photo on the way home, looking up at the places where the rooflines leaned back and she could see the sky. Occasionally, there was a plane, and she imagined Mrs. Almeida crossing the ocean with jars of pickle and masala in her suitcase. Tucked safely in a book was the photo of Celia, crossing the ocean also.

Francis finished a roll of film taking photos of the cottage and cycled to Creek Road to drop it off. When he came out of the photo shop, he saw that the idiot boy who'd plowed right past them was perched on his cycle at a toy stall. Francis thought of warning him to take better care, but the boy was across the way, and Francis was not in the habit of collaring strange children to lecture them on safety. The boy would have to fend for himself, and if the thought briefly struck Francis as forlorn, he reminded himself that he'd already launched his own children into the world. He'd put his daughter on an airplane before he ever flew himself, a journey so far that he remembered feeling, for the first time in her life, that she would be beyond his help. The best he could do for her was a one-way ticket and a favor from a former student, who waved Francis and Essie through Security to sit with her in the departure lounge.

Marian was going abroad for graduate study, looking younger than her age. She wore a coat too warm for the Bombay night and too thin for the cold of New England. She would stop in London first for three days. "London!" Essie kept exclaiming. Over and over, she checked to make sure Marian had the right address for a cousin who would show her around the city, as though this was the point of concern: the stop in London, not the looming years in Massachusetts. The flight was delayed—Francis began to worry about malfunctions—and for nearly two hours, Essie held their daughter's hands in both her own. Eventually, Francis dropped his own hand, as heavy as the months ahead, onto Marian's shoulder. He still remembered the way she leaned against him.

She'd planned to spend two years in the States—two years only—but just when he was about to wire money for a return ticket, a letter arrived. Francis could not remember reading it, only feeling its blows. She'd met a boy, an American named Daniel. Daniel had finished his dissertation and accepted a teaching position. They would marry in June; they would live in Ohio. It sounded like a bit of nonsense in a song, Francis thought. Fa la la la la. Oh hi oh. The couple hoped Essie and Francis would fly over for the wedding. They'd put aside money to help with the tickets.

Essie ranted and sobbed. She spent three weeks filling notepads with letters, insisting that Marian come home. She applied for a visa to go at once to confront her daughter and used the full arsenal of Francis's connections to expedite its approval. Francis had never seen her in such a rage; he could not defy her openly. But on the day the visa was granted, he waited until she went out before he placed a call to Marian.

"Do it now, my girl," he urged her. "Don't wait. Or she'll arrive and put an end to it."

Marian wept. "I wanted you with me, Dad." He remembered the words exactly as she said them. But they both knew the strength of her mother's hold over her.

Before Essie could book a flight, Marian and Daniel were married. Francis put on a stunned expression and dodged his wife's hysterics with nightly visits to the gymkhana. He played cards with his friends, the stakes just high enough to make a difference.

Over the next several weeks, matters did not improve. Essie burst into tears at the slightest provocation and consulted priests about an annulment. She refused to take any interest in Marian's trip home, when she would bring Daniel to meet them all. Essie did not make up the extra bedroom. She made no special preparations for meals. On the night of the couple's arrival, she refused to leave her room.

Francis went to the airport in a borrowed car. He had a fleeting impression of Daniel, tall and thin, with winter skin and large round glasses, before Marian occupied his full attention. He had not seen her in almost two years: a thin, girlish figure in a sweater. Her eyes wide, her hair cut to her shoulders. Around them, the passageway was jammed with people coming out of Customs, shouting to cousins and brothers, raising sleepy toddlers high in their arms. Francis stared at his daughter, trying to understand that this girl was married, this girl was gone.

"Dad. Dad?"

He hugged her then; he kissed her hair. "You'll be warm in that sweater."

She laughed a little. "It's cold on the plane."

"Cold? Is it?" He felt that he'd lost his footing, that he must learn again to be her father. "Here, my girl, give me the cases." He would have carried everything, Marian herself.

She had always been a decorous child, meticulous about dress and manner, but she stopped to hug him again right in the center of the aisle. People flowed around them, pushing past with carts, plastic-wrapped suitcases, boxes tied with twine.

When she finally let go, she wiped tears from her eyes and looked over his shoulder.

"Is Mum outside?"

He drove them home, aware that Essie's absence had set Marian reeling. She gave Daniel the front seat and sat in the back, anxious and alone. Daniel asked mild questions about slums and roadwork. A sulfurous breeze blew through the open windows, warm and soft against their faces. Francis found himself wishing the drive was longer.

They reached home after midnight to find that Essie had extinguished every light, locked every door. Jude was on the veranda in his pajamas to greet his sister.

The next fortnight was a cycle of shouting, crying, fainting spells, and martyred silences. Essie did not address a word to Daniel; to Marian she recited her litany of disappointments. Francis escaped each morning to work and each evening to the gymkhana. Daniel spoke mostly to Simon and Jude. He paid no attention to Essie's insults beyond an occasional appraising glance. He was not lavish or fawning, but maintained a level civility—thanks, could he help, good night—and proposed daily excursions to get Marian out of the house. Listlessly, she took him to Elephanta, Juhu, the Hanging Gardens.

One afternoon, he asked Francis to join them. They were going to Dharavi, where Daniel might buy a briefcase. Would Francis come with them?

"I can't," said Francis. Instantly he felt the weight of their disappointment. But his friends expected him at the card table. He had been playing well, he had been winning. He could not resist the hold a streak exerted over him.

"There's no time to tell the boys. They'll be waiting for me—"

"That's fine," said Daniel, but Marian turned away.

"Come on, Simon," she called her brother. Francis noticed how slight she seemed, as if the American winters had drained her. "Let's go."

That night, he returned to find the house in uproar. Essie sat sobbing on the stair landing. Francis could hear her from the road. She would not move when he came up, only leaned over to let him pass. Simon and Jude had taken refuge in their bedroom.

"What happened?" he asked his sons. "Where's Marian?"

Jude cowered on the bed. Simon stared into a magazine. He raised his eyes for a brittle moment. "Gone," he said, and returned to his article.

"They left," Jude said. "They went to the airport hotel." He said it the way he might have said Buckingham Palace.

Francis tightened his fingers around the money in his pocket. He had won, though not so spectacularly as he had hoped. Not enough to keep from wondering if he ought to have gone to Dharavi. "For a drink, maybe," he suggested.

Simon looked up sharply but said nothing.

Francis did not squeeze by Essie a second time. He went down the spiral staircase from the back balcony and walked around to the veranda. The ground story was bolted. "Hallo?" Francis called while he fitted the key. He felt like a fool, talking to closed doors. "Daniel? Marian?"

The suitcases were gone. So were the shoes near the door, the toiletries in the bathroom. It was a warm evening, but Marian had taken her heavy sweater from the wardrobe where she'd kept it ready for the return flight.

Francis thought, This is the end. This is the way she will leave us. He thought, I will have no daughters left.

Later, he would not know how he managed it. He felt transformed into something swift and powerful, a current even Essie could not withstand. He ordered his wife to her feet, ordered her to write a note of apology. He did not remember what he shouted to effect this miracle, but he threw his winnings in her lap. She stared at him, stunned.

"I like this boy," he shouted. Was it true? He thought possibly yes. Finally, she rose, stepping on the bills still scattered on the landing, and went to her desk. Francis waited for her to disappear inside before he stooped to retrieve them. His head was buzzing, and he could not understand why he felt like a sneak, pushing the bills into his pocket.

In the front room, he watched her with her pen, thinking of all the pages she had covered with her rants and demands, her accusations of betrayal. He imagined the weight of those letters on Marian, great fat bundles arriving day after day, and wished he had thought to write a note of his own. *This is your father's home*, he could have written. *You are always welcome here.* He could have written to her husband. *This is your home also.*

Instead, he took a taxi to the hotel to deliver Essie's note. At Reception, he asked first for a room under Almeida before remembering they would register with Daniel's name.

"I can call up for you, sir."

But Francis smiled and shook his head. "No need, I'll go up."

It was Daniel who opened the door, nodding, not quite saying hello, before stepping aside so Francis could enter. Marian sat on the edge of a bed, looking drawn and ill. Her sweater was thrown across a chair, the suitcases still packed.

"I'm sorry, Dad . . ." She began to cry.

"What's all this?" He sat beside her as though she were small again, a child to be talked out of any grief. "Sorry for what, my girl? There's no need to be sorry. We are the ones who can be sorry."

"I've tried to talk to her, but I can't—we can't—"

He put his arm around her narrow shoulders and tried to calm her before explaining: all that business was finished. "See, I've brought a note from Mum." Francis glanced at Daniel, who stood by the door. "Everything is settled now. You can come back, both of you."

Marian leaned close to Francis while she read Essie's note. Then she looked at him, uncertain, before turning to Daniel.

"What should we do?"

"I think we should try."

"Come." Francis tried not to sound as urgent as he felt. "Come, we'll go together."

He insisted on carrying a suitcase, insisted on settling the bill for the hours they had stayed. The figure appalled him, but he paid it the way he would have paid a ransom, grateful for the chance. They might have changed their airline tickets; they might have slipped away for good. As it was, his daughter was married, she would live in America, but she was not quite gone.

At the gate, he let Daniel take the bags while he paid the driver. When the car pulled away, he stood in the road, breathing in the deep twilight, looking at the house his father had built. For the time being at least, all his children were in it. Marian was waiting for him on the veranda. Daniel was rummaging through a backpack to find the hotel chocolates he had brought the boys. Essie called down from the landing to ask a little sullenly if *anyone* wanted tea.

"Thank you, Dad." Marian looked at him the way she used to as a girl, as though he could make anything better.

He led the way upstairs, thinking of the tree viper. He had seen the danger, picked up a field-hockey stick, killed the snake.

The whole episode felt simple. He had not imagined any other outcome; he did what a father should do. He had not realized until later how rare that feeling would be.

———

The small foam gliders came in orange and blue. Anthony chose blue. He rode to the start of the Promenade and parked the cycle by the seawall so he could launch his plane away from the street and trees and other children. It was low tide, no fear of losing the plane. The first several times, the glider didn't catch the air well; it came twisting down on its nose only a few steps away. But eventually he began to get a feel for the right kind of throw and sent it soaring over the low, flat rocks. He gave himself ten good flights, one for every year of his life, before he leapt down to retrieve it for the last time. It was nose-down in a crevice, and he worked it free carefully, taking care not to damage the foam.

It took him a full minute, maybe more, to realize the cycle was gone. First he saw it was not in the spot where he'd been launching; then he told himself he must have taken a crooked path over the rocks and scanned the wall all the way to the end. Nothing. He felt a throbbing panic as he looked in the other direction, where he knew he hadn't gone. Nothing. Nothing. He wanted to run, but in what direction? Even standing on the wall, he couldn't see far enough: the crowds and the movement and a bus rumbling past; what was behind the bus? How far could anyone have gotten? He'd turned his back three minutes at most, and how to explain *that* to his parents? Then he couldn't run, because his pulse was thudding and his body could only curl into itself. He sank to the wall. Was this his father's heart? If it was, would they forgive him?

He did not know how long he sat waiting for something different to happen. Twice he vomited onto the rocks. The second time, a small boy with a runny nose grinned and pointed, and Anthony snatched up his glider and moved farther down the wall. He sat hunched against the setting sun, looking up occasionally in case it was all a mistake, until he realized there was nothing to do but go home.

"What do you mean?" was where it began. His father rose up from his pillows. His mother pushed past him to go stand in the lane and see for herself the evidence of no cycle. Then shouting and more shouting. I was sick, he told them. I got off when I was sick. The hollow feeling came back so badly that it seemed he might be sick again.

Later, his mother shook her head and said things like "I knew it would go wrong" and "Bad idea from the start." His father asked a thousand questions: "But where, exactly? And you heard nothing? Did this sickness go into your *ears*?" Pinky made retching noises whenever he came near. Anthony waited until the following day, when he was alone with his mother, to ask if his heart was weak, and she said, "Not your *heart*." He waited a minute longer to ask if there would be a doctor, and she sighed before saying that the one bright spot in this mess was telling the delivery boy to stay home for good.

For Anthony, the bright spot was the glider. He hadn't dared bring it home, so he'd stashed it near the village, concealed in a cracked plastic bucket that he found in a rubbish pile and dragged behind a tree. He felt a rush of triumph when he recovered it two days later, still in mint condition, and the power of this secret was not entirely extinguished the following week, when older boys wrenched it from his hands and sent it skittering onto the roof of the school. Crash landing, they jeered, because of course it could not be retrieved.

The rules were different for older boys. But within a few days they had forgotten, and the glider became Anthony's secret again. For months he pictured it, poised above him every time he sat near the window of his classroom, needing only a good wind to send it soaring. While he waited, he thought of all the ways his life would change when he grew tall enough to send bullies packing, strong enough to twist Pinky's arm until she squealed, rich enough to take a taxi to the airport to watch planes take off all day and night. It was all coming. The rules would be different for him.

DECEMBER 1990

Finally the tea stall began to prosper. But before Flora could enjoy her relief, her husband opened a second place, twice as big, half a dozen blocks inland. He struck a deal with a baker and chose a corner site across from the College of St. Anne: a roofed pavilion with a counter in the back, a display case for baked goods, and a wedge of floor, open to both roads, with room for tables. The biggest expense would be metal doors, which would roll down from the roof to secure the pavilion when the café was closed. But the baker helped him find a good supplier, a fair price.

Baker? Tables? Could they sit still for two minutes without flinging themselves into risky new ventures?

"There's no risk. University kids will come flocking. They drink tea all day long."

"Then it's a toilet you want, not tables! With tables, they can sit and sit with a single chai and never move. And who is this baker?"

"It's a family business, near the station. They do buns, sandwiches, bread"—he turned to wink at the girls—"brownies, pastries, cakes. Whatever we need."

"But what family?"

"The father started the place, now the son is running it. He is Farooq."

"Farooq?"

"Farooq Khan. Nice guy. He'll deliver."

"Why start up with Muslim people we know nothing about?" This was just his way, Flora thought, overlooking everything. "Why not a Catholic baker?"

He laughed. "What Catholic baker? I found the best. You wait and see."

Dominic called the new location the Rosy Café. A simple name was best, and there were no more rosaries to sell.

He expected another argument, but Flora agreed. "'Rosy' is not so many letters for the sign maker. Anyway, why ask for trouble?"

"What trouble will come to a tea stall?"

Flora clicked her tongue. "I don't like these Tiger people." She knew the name of the Shiv Sena, but it was the painted face of the tiger, leering from placards, that always seized her attention. "All this Hindutva talk. See what I've heard in the lane: in some parts of the city, they're going into shops and demanding money, saying, Only we are sons of this soil, what are you?"

"Son of shell, at least."

"Already they may be unhappy with Catholics. And now you're working with Muslims."

But her husband told her she made too much fuss. That was downtown, maybe. From the sea, Bombay coalesced to a bit of coastline he used to be able to blot out with his thumb. On land, it was another story: a multitude of cities, infinite cities, shimmering one on top of the next, the way fast cars could sail along flyovers without disturbing the shanty colonies that sprouted around their concrete pilings, or the way he himself, on the rare occasions when he went to town by road, could look out on one side to the Mahalakshmi Race Course, then look out the other and see the Haji Ali Mosque—its causeway submerged in high tide, and in low tide a living bridge, coursing with people. The city held them all in her huge cupped hands: gamblers and pilgrims, migrants and Maharashtrians, Hindus, Muslims, Buddhists, Catholics, Parsis, Jains, Sikhs, and Jews. Even Santa Clara had never been one thing or another—fisherfolk by the shore and a slaughterhouse near the station. There were Muslim butchers as well as bakers; Muslim shops lining the road to the market; Muslim neighbors in Muslim building complexes, Muslim merchants selling fishing line, notions, stationery, toys. Mosques, churches, fire temples, Ganeshas, the hodgepodge of Creek Road. How could you untangle what had twined together over centuries?

So, when he heard about Hindutva rallies where huge crowds shook their fists, spilling over with rage, he shook his head with genuine sorrow. There would always be angry young men and fat-cat politicians to goad them; always madmen spouting nonsense and desperate men listening; always money to be made by someone at the top, thugs at the margins, and skirmishes for an unlucky few. Bombay would absorb them as Bombay absorbed all else—invaders, migrants, kings, and infantas, all manner of gods, even visions of itself, a city of several islands contrived over centuries into thinking itself one.

"Stop worrying," he told Flora. "We are Kolis, the first sons of this place."

A year later, with the Rosy Café thriving, Flora experienced an entrepreneurial awakening of her own. One day, when the fish from Inez looked especially fine—firm and plump, a nice color and a fresh smell with just a touch of salt—she kept back enough for five or six families and cooked them. It was a little extra ginger paste for the marinade, more garlic paste also, an extra handful of spices—hardly a cost at all. The oil she was heating already. The rice flour was only to coat. She kept some for her family and offered the rest from the original tea stall, served piping hot on newspaper sheets, dripping oil and lemon. As fast as she could make, she sold.

Within a week, she had a scheme to sell fish-fry. She loved the bustle and shouting of the docks, and she enjoyed the sharp pleasure of a good price when she dealt in large enough quantities. The family had most of the setup they needed at the original tea stall—with a little more space and extra burners, they could manage.

As soon as Dominic agreed, Flora leapt at the chance to move down the road, away from Seven Sorrows, whose clientele, she admitted, had created a useful demand for tea, but whose proximity to a food establishment did not seem like a good omen. This was a happy outcome for everyone, since the undertaker had brought his wife's family into the business and needed room to expand.

Flora chose a spot closer to the Church of the Loaves and Fishes and decided to replace the faded Holy Rosary sign with something fresh and new.

"Pomfret," she said with satisfaction. "An English word—that is better for cottage people."

"Why not Prawn?" asked Dominic, so solemnly that Celia knew he was teasing.

"Better not." Flora wrinkled her nose. "I can serve prawns, but for the name, a bottom-feeder's not so good. Anyway, a fish is simple for the sign maker to paint, and 'Pomfret' has a nice fat sound."

Celia was thirteen, intent on fourteen, which would bring her one step closer to real life. Every day, after school, she changed out of her uniform and helped either her mother or her father, except Fridays, when she went to sew with Sister Vicky, who had retired from Holy Name but lived in the motherhouse at the base of Seaview Hill. Her eyes and fingers were not strong enough for sewing, but she could guide Celia through projects.

Within months, Flora's restaurant began to gain a reputation among the neighborhood cottages for fried pomfret and butter-garlic crab. The stall did not have set timings; they only sold until the food ran out, usually by mid-afternoon. Hired drivers pulled up for takeaway while their clients ate at the Hotel Castelo; so did the autoricks from Linking Road or Creek, and occasionally even a blue Cool Cab, whose driver rolled down the windows briefly before blasting the A/C for a downtown fare.

Some people wanted to eat straightaway, standing outside as at a roadside dhaba, so Flora bought stools to set up along a rough wooden counter. Evangeline sat with a pot of blue paint and copied the sign maker's fish on top of each one. She had no black paint for the eyes, but her father said the fish were better off blind. "Otherwise, what are they seeing when somebody sits?"

As Pomfret grew and Flora needed more help, she and Inez settled into a partnership, splitting the take when they worked side by side to cook for the afternoon rush. Celia preferred to spend her afternoons at the Rosy Café, where she encountered a wider range of people. The students were her favorites; hearing their talk was like opening a book to a page in the middle and trying to find her bearings. But the café drew priests from the church, too; professors from the university; ladies with shopping bags; staff from the Hindu boys' school on St. Hilary Road; customers waiting for the mochi to turn up and unlock the wooden box that opened into a cobbler's workshop; the mochi himself, whose arrival timings were uncertain but who was entirely regular in his consumption of ginger tea; bank tellers in straight skirts and nylon blouses, seeming softer, slightly blurred, outside their air-conditioned cubicles; drivers, who sometimes took a long lazy break over a single cup and sometimes beeped to have their orders brought to the wheel; travel agents, who looked as hardened as criminals after wrangling with airlines and Indian Railways; clerks and poets; the quietly fashionable middle-aged woman who owned a fancy clothing boutique; and half a dozen jewelers, who sent boys running back and forth with trays to serve their customers. A cottage boy with curly hair came with his friends from St. Ignatius most afternoons, and Celia wondered if he realized that twice she had given him extra biscuits. Muslim shopkeepers came in twos and threes, smiling beneath their beards as they greeted Celia and her father. "Dom!" they called him. "Come and sit with us."

They had become his friends through the baker Farooq, who arrived each morning on his motor scooter to drop off the café's supply of snacks and pastries with an egg patty or sometimes even a brownie for Celia and Evangeline. He wore all white and a white topi with gold thread, which made him look like one of his own sugar-dusted confections. Celia liked him.

Every week or two he brought them a present of biscuits,

brushing away Dominic's objection. "It's nothing, nothing!" His beard was grizzled, and he looked stout and kingly, easing back on his scooter. "A little sugar keeps the energy flowing. Right, girls?"

"Thank you, Uncle!"

Sometimes he opened the large case mounted on the back of the scooter to show them cakes for fancy parties.

"Time for a look?"

Celia's favorite was a golden anniversary cake, showered with perfect icing fireworks. "So big," breathed Evangeline.

Farooq replaced the cover. "Big enough for all your friends? Your birthday is coming when?"

Evangeline flushed, but Celia took their chance. "She is May and I am June, so we can share nicely."

Her mother would have shushed her, but men had different ideas of manners. The baker laughed, and her father said, "Enough, you beggars!" and waved them off.

It was Celia's job to take dishes from Pomfret to the Almeidas every few months. Flora no longer sold door to door, and it had taken several joint visits to ease Mrs. Almeida into accepting Inez. "We are partners," Flora explained. "Same same. It will be like I have come, giving good prices."

Mrs. Almeida smiled sadly. "I am an old woman," she said by way of apology. "And see, I have no daughter here to help me, and my son does not understand the burdens I bear. So every small change takes its toll. I am used to this one and her ways. We have—how to say it?—a *connection* over many years."

Flora promised their connection would carry forward, while Inez tipped her head in agreement. She did not offer her own view, which was that the fish, which had already come from Clive's boat, would be very much the same. She kept to Flora's prices, and eventually, over the course of many months, Mrs. Almeida permitted herself to feel reassured. She gave both Flora and Inez small gifts at Christmas.

Pomfret was closed for New Year's Eve, but Flora spent the morning preparing food for the village celebration. Just before midday, she sent Celia to the Almeidas with three large take-away dishes: "Then she may not have to cook so much this evening." Flora had been dismayed by a fuller understanding of Mrs. Almeida's troubles, an aging woman with two children gone and one son at home who remained unmarried. So sad, to keep a nearly empty house.

But when Celia arrived, it was evident the house was not empty, or at least that it would be full again by nightfall.

"Everyone has come," the kitchen girl told her. She was at the grinding stone, making a masala paste, but she let the pestle loll to one side while Celia took the cover off each dish to show them to her. Nicole and Tara were *so high*, the girl reported, lifting her hand above her head. "Men are looking short beside them. And they are eating very much." She tucked her head in a quick, proud nod. "They are happy with my food."

"Where are they?"

Out, the girl said. All downtown, in two big taxis. Only Badasahib stayed behind, and he went to the gymkhana.

On the way home, Celia walked by the last of the holiday vendors, who had been selling their wares all month on the roadside near St. Anne's. A few Santas still lurked among a thinning grove of electric-green tabletop trees. Gold-foil New Year's banners and paper bouquets of poinsettias were pushed to the front. Illuminated stars rested on their pointed tips in a range of colors and styles.

The vendors ignored Celia; a schoolgirl was a poor prospect. But at the last mat, a boy near her own age called out to her.

"You want a star? You want a Santa cap?" He perched it on his own head. The cap was floppy red with a cotton-wool border, ridiculous, but Celia hesitated.

"Last one. Very cheap."

Maybe for the village party. Maybe to make Sister Vicky smile when Celia visited her at the motherhouse, another of her Pomfret deliveries. Sister did not have much appetite, but the lovely smells filled her up, she told Celia, and she enjoyed a taste before she shared her meal with the other nuns. Or maybe the hat would suggest certain jaunty possibilities if she wore it to the Rosy and the cottage boy who came with his friends from St. Ignatius would have reason to notice her. Celia knew she was not beautiful—she had a forehead like the beach at low tide and a chin like a double knot, tying up her baby face as firmly as her mother once tied the strings of her hat. Still, she liked to imagine scenarios in which the boy realized that she was lively and fun-loving, a girl of spirit. Maybe that was too much for a hat to accomplish.

"No," she said. "Not today."

"Why not today? What day, then?" He would not take back the hat; she had to drop it on the blanket and walk on. "This is the day!" He watched her go with mounting annoyance, waiting to see if her departure was a ploy. When she didn't turn back, he startled her by shouting in English. "Bitter watch out," he called. "Bitter not cry."

That night, the whole village would turn out to the beach to celebrate. Oil lamps would dot the seawall, with dozens more set afloat just past the moored boats, the glints of their flames spreading farther and farther as the flotilla drifted from shore. There would be a feast with music and dancing, and offerings of flowers and coconuts to throw into the waves. This was the way Kolis honored the sea at the start of the fishing season, so why not on New Year's Eve also? For three hundred years, the villagers had worshipped Jesus, who spent his days among fishermen, a friend to them all. But they lived in a village named for the Lord of the Sea; why not offer Lord Varuna their prayers also? Why not let Jesus share his coconuts? It was a night to hope they all would prosper without a fixed idea of which great force should accomplish it.

At home, errands finished at last, Celia wanted nothing more than to run down to the beach and help her friends stuff the village straw man, who would represent the old year ablaze in the midnight bonfire. But her mother had become a kind of fountain, showering her children with frantic instructions. They must bathe, all of them; would there be time for the girls' hair to dry? They must wear their Christmas hair ribbons, which she had taken care to find in colors that matched their new clothes. They must be ready long before the festivities began, because their neighbor was bringing his camera to take a snap of the whole family, looking their best.

Evangeline dressed first, her hair only a little damp, her limbs not so stick-thin as they once were, a soft color in her cheeks. She looked just right, Flora thought with satisfaction, remembering the teacher who suggested keeping Evangeline back, when she was only quiet and thoughtful; and the doctor who shook his head over her chances when she had typhoid. Flora wished they could see this girl, brimming with health. "Here, take a little of my good cream for your face and hands," she said tenderly. "Jerome, into the bath," she ordered. "Celu"—she spun to locate her elder daughter, who was braiding her hair with soaked patches on her shoulders—"see this girl, hair still dripping! What did I say to you? Go stand in the sun and brush it."

Celia wanted only to finish before she missed her chance to stuff the old man. One of the boys had got hold of a bundle of firecrackers, which they meant to bury deep in the straw man's chest. "I'm going to the beach. It'll dry in a few minutes."

"How can it dry in plaits?" But what point talking sense to this child, who would argue a wave back from the shore? "Come, you've forgotten your ribbons."

"Mum, please, I'll do that later—"

But her mother insisted. "Later, you'll go one way and your brother will go another, and if I can find you long enough to tie a ribbon, it will be in the new year. Come."

She leaned close, so close that Celia could feel the heat of her breath. Wherever Celia looked, she was seeing a part of her mother's body that it didn't feel right to examine without some small preserving distance: the round cheeks so like her own, the soft pouch beneath her chin, the fine hairs on her upper lip. Celia tried to settle her gaze someplace safe—her mother's eyes—and saw the way the flesh beneath the lower lashes had begun to sag, the twin wedges of dry skin near the corners. Her mother had never been a beauty, but she had been to Celia the beginning and end of all bodies, a body that meant this is what women are, this is how they look, this is their smell and feel. She had known complete faith in her mother's body once, leaning her head beneath her mother's hip, curling one arm around her thigh. She'd felt not only safe but more solidly herself.

Now she fought a traitorous urge to duck. For mother and daughter to see each other so closely that something like shame or pity passed between them—she felt mortified for them both.

Flora clicked her tongue. "You're getting a pimple," she said. "You need to take care of your skin; otherwise, your whole face will be spots. Put a little lemon juice, then we'll rinse it before we go."

There was no end to her mother's fussing. "Mum. Don't make such a big thing of it."

"What big thing? A small lemon."

"Nobody cares. Nobody's looking at me."

"Why not? People should close their eyes when you're coming?" Flora decided not to mention the family photograph. "Try the lemon. And later this week, I'll pick up tea-tree oil." She felt a surge of magnanimity as she looked at her child, this big frowning girl who had once curled tight inside her. Her own mother would never have offered such remedies, but Flora knew from the start that she and her daughters would be different. There was a pain in her chest when she was carrying Celia, she remembered, an ache so deep that she couldn't decipher it. Nothing like that had happened with Jerome, so she thought it was unrelated to the pregnancy, a heart symptom or a liver complaint. When she could no longer hook a sari blouse, she braced herself for the worst and went in tears to the clinic. "Any other symptoms?" the doctor asked, pressing one place and then another on Flora's belly with such strength that Flora imagined the child born with thumbprint depressions. She hoped the tender scalp was tucked away, safe.

"The ache is here, I think, yes? Nothing to worry about." He brought her hand to the place where her skin creased in a tight line and her belly began its rich arc outward. "Right here. Feel? Baby is making place, forcing apart the rib cage."

Flora walked home, stunned. That the baby was making itself was one thing; that the baby was remaking its mother, prising apart bone and changing her interior landscape forever, was a revelation for which her first pregnancy had not prepared her. "The ache will go when the baby drops," the doctor told her. But the ribs would stay as the baby left them. Sometimes it seemed to Flora that this was what God intended, that Celia should open her up, carve new places inside her, so that whatever the mother knew could flow easily to the daughter, nothing tight or cramped or hidden between them. Her daughters had teachers for schoolwork, Celia had Sister Vicky for sewing, but let them come to *her* with what really mattered: their friends, their bodies, the small things, like new hair ribbons, that would help them feel proud. Her girls would have an ally in all the petty wars of adolescence, skin eruptions, menstrual cramps, sandpaper moods, the foolish beauty treatments Flora would have liked long ago. Finally, there was money enough. She would give her daughters what she herself had never had.

But here was Celia, not smiling and thanking her mother, not running to get the lemon, not looking anxious or hopeful in the conspiratorial spirit Flora expected.

"What's the matter? Legs stuck in the mud?" Her voice was warm and teasing. "Come, I know it's a big day, you're unhappy to have a mark on your face, but this will help. And lemon gives a nice smell."

Celia swallowed a dozen things she might have said about how this day was as cramped as any other; how she was losing her chance to meet her friends on the beach; how she didn't want to think about her face or the cottage boy who would never notice it; how foolish she'd feel, spritzing herself with lemon as though she were a bit of fish, or the sort of girl who cared, or *her mother*—but it was useless to say any of it. Her voice was skintight when she said she didn't want it, could she please just go?

"Yes, go. Why not?" Her mother's voice rose so suddenly that a latch in her throat might have broken. "New clothes, new shoes, new ribbons—but nothing is good enough for this one. She turns up her nose."

"It's not that, Mum," Evangeline tried. "She just—"

What? thought Celia. But her mother was past intercession.

"—and hear the way she speaks to her mother! When I was a girl, I'd get one tight slap." She opened her jar of good cream and dabbed it on Evangeline's forehead. "There. Rub it well. And take a little for your hands also. At least you can appreciate." She thrust the jar into Evangeline's hands and began whirling about the room, one end of her dupatta trailing lower than the other. Celia wanted to stop her and straighten it, to stop everything in motion. If her mother could just keep still for two minutes. Instead, everything was moving too fast, the whole afternoon going full-tilt in the wrong direction.

"Mum, I didn't mean—"

"One picture," she said, with a sadness so sharp that Celia felt the cut of it. She wished her mother would just be angry again, give Celia something stout and strong to knock against. But this was their way: her mother crumbled to sadness, and Celia was left undone. Sometimes Celia wondered what would happen if she lost her temper entirely. She imagined herself a punishing flame from which her mother must flee without turning back or else weep herself to salt.

"One picture of us looking our best. That is too much to ask?"

Celia looked at Evangeline, who handed her the jar of cream before going outside. Celia put a little on her hands and cheeks, careful not to take too much.

Her mother was picking up things and putting them in new places. She lifted her voice to carry through the whole room so she did not have to look directly at Celia. "You're ready to go, then go. I'm not asking you to wait."

"No," said Celia. "I want to stay." This was suddenly true, though she knew of no way to convince her mother or understand it herself. All her rush had drained away, and she was left wanting less than she had just minutes ago. If she went to the beach, a certain story of New Year's would end here. An argument would be what her mother remembered.

"The cream is nice," she said.

"Coconut milk." Her mother's voice was still hard. "Where is your father? What can be taking so long? He should have closed by now—"

"I can go see," Celia offered.

"Be quick, then. And careful." She meant Celia's good clothes. She turned away when she said, "That color is nice on you."

Outside, Evangeline stood with her face tipped to the sun. "Why not take the lemon?"

Her sister's voice was mild, with so little reproach that she sounded like nothing more than a girl who felt curious about strange, wild things. Celia didn't answer.

"It's not so hard to make her happy."

This was both so true and so hopeless that Celia could do nothing with it. She started up the lane, away from the beach, telling herself never mind, the straw man must be finished.

She looked first in the Cooperative, the likeliest place, but he had not come yet, said Clive. Clive himself had clearly been there for some time, well into his glass. "See this girl! Growing up." He looked her up and down and clicked his tongue, as though she had transgressed. "A few years and she'll be back, saying, Where is my husband?"

He laughed loudly and Celia turned to go, but he dropped a hand on her shoulder. "A daughter to me, this one. But another year or two and she'll be . . ." He rocked very slightly, until it became clear that whatever else he intended to say was lost. One of the men put an arm around him.

"Come this side," he said, and Clive released Celia with a small tremor.

"A daughter!" He reached out to touch her hair.

No, she thought, confused, her hair was still wet. She pulled back while the man told Clive, "Okay, okay, we'll sit awhile," before turning to Celia. Not to worry, he told her. If her father turned up, they'd send him home.

"Why home?" Clive thundered, but Celia left the man to answer.

The sun outside felt better, everything more itself. Her father was not at Pomfret. He was not at the dry-goods store, which was about to shut early for the night, or the undertakers', where he liked to drop in for a chat; during the years when he was establishing the tea stall, he had grown to like the family. They were a quiet, decent bunch, he told his wife. They didn't talk a widow into nonsense. They let a grown man cry without making him feel a fool. The father, a man near Dominic's age, was adept at knowing what not to talk about. Before the café took hold, when Dominic faced long stretches without customers, the undertaker read newspaper articles aloud to help pass the time. One of his sons had frequent nosebleeds, and he used to hold the child against his chest for ten, twenty minutes sometimes, calmly repeating newspaper stories, until the bleeding stopped and together they could go inside to change their shirts.

Celia was on Varuna Road when she finally spotted her father, coming from the direction of the café. He held up a folded foil star to greet her. "We'll surprise your mother."

"Where did you get it?" Celia asked. Maybe the boy with the Santa hat had gotten his sale after all. It would be nice to think that what looked like chance had its roots in something kinder, an unseen hand balancing what could be balanced. She knew that, even in the Bible, the poor stayed poor and the rich stayed rich. Still, she hoped God made slight adjustments. She liked to imagine Him at work on the edges of things, small deft mercies no one would notice.

"Was it the boy by St. Anne's, at the very end?"

"One of those guys."

At home her mother threw up her hands about the time, but her father smiled and unfolded the star. The arms were patterned with holes and a silhouetted Holy Family sprang into view at the center: Joseph with a staff, Mary with a veil, the manger with a tiny haloed curve.

"You wanted this type?" Flora asked. She was not sure about a Holy Family made of paper, their blank faces no bigger than thumbprints. "The plain ones give a better light."

"The Christmas ones were half-price. And I like this." He

turned to Celia—amused, conspiratorial, his look as good as a wink—and she wanted to laugh, not at her father's expression, exactly, but because she saw it would be a good night. There would be no quarrels or hurt feelings, no silent walks up the lane. Whatever her mother didn't understand about her father would be an occasion for fondness.

"Yes, okay. Why not?" Flora watched Evangeline twirl the star from its string. "Just see how this girl has shot up! That is why we need a photo, everyone getting so big. But it's too much at once—she'll outgrow her own strength."

"How can it be too much? Her legs must reach the ground," Dominic said. "Anyway, let her keep growing. Whichever girl is taller in the next ten minutes can help me hang the star."

He strung a lightbulb inside it and hoisted Evangeline onto his shoulders to hang it. Celia turned off the lights—the room went dark—and the brown thumbprint faces turned golden. Bits of red light scattered across the floor, and then Evangeline reached up and set the star spinning so that the room whirled like the inside of a kaleidoscope. Celia began to laugh. She had the brief sensation of floating up past her dreams of the cottage boy and the memory of Clive's hand, past all the hopeless welter of wishing to be changed but not so changed. This would be the new story, she realized; the star and the photo, her mother smiling, her father coming just in time.

17

MAY 1992

Francis could no longer manage a steep hill, but he rode his cycle as far as he could before wheeling it the last stretch to the Hotel Castelo. In the bin was a biscuit tin, where he he kept a small collection of personal photos and letters out of Essie's reach.

He knew he occasionally misplaced things, but his wife's housekeeping posed a constant threat. He caught her once, sifting through all the photos he had taken of the neighborhood, putting everything out of order. "Look at all these, gathering dust." She flapped a single picture at him. "And only one with a *person*."

That was the village child who had once pitched into his bicycle—he could never remember the girl's name. Essie kept that photo aside, but God only knew what would have happened to the rest if he had not come home in time. He transferred his entire photo archive into shoe boxes under his bed.

In the lounge, he was ushered to his favorite table and swiftly furnished with his favorite whiskey, pleasing reminders that, ten years after opening, the hotel still acknowledged their connection. He generally met friends at the gymkhana, but on certain evenings he felt the need to be alone with what no one else knew or remembered; nobody but one.

He ran into Agnes occasionally. They were both from Santa

Clara families, invited to the same weddings and funerals, but without the opportunity for private conversation. So he was startled, perhaps something more, when he had received a card from her five years before: Was he free to join her for a drink?

He told Essie he was meeting an old colleague, put on a suit, took it off again, settled on a fresh shirt and tie, and took care not to turn up too early. When he arrived, Agnes waved to him from a corner table, her robe and habit incongruous in the sumptuous lounge. She ordered champagne for them both, laughing at his surprise.

"Usually I like a shandy. Tonight I'm drinking for her." Only then he did he realize it was Anna's birthday. She would have been—what—

"Sixty-seven," Agnes supplied. "Do you remember her eighteenth?"

He did, he did. She wore a pink top—

"Always pink for her. That was her favorite."

"And her nineteenth, with the ukulele. Whatever became of that?"

Agnes wasn't sure; she wished she had it still. Maybe it was among Albert's things, packed away during the construction of the new flats. Her nephews and their families would soon live one on top of the other. The youngest was Francis's godson. It was easy to ask about him, easy to tumble into conversation. Agnes was working in an orphanage. She was full of stories, brimming over with questions about his own children.

"It's getting late," she said at last.

"You're staying with Albert? I'll take you home." He would leave his bicycle, walk her back.

"No, no, I'm staying here." She grinned at him. "Such lovely rooms they've set aside for Sisters of the Holy Name."

"I'd nearly forgotten . . ." He'd ordered a whiskey after their champagne, then another. The world had softened, certain edges pleasantly blurred.

"It still comes as a shock, how everything changed when she died. She would have been your wife. You would have been my brother."

But Francis put up his hand to stop her. For years he had told himself a different story, a truer story. "It would have been you. You would have been my wife."

For a moment, Agnes said nothing. Then she tipped her head. "We were all so young," she said, and it sounded like an apology. She motioned to the waiter and ordered another champagne, her second. "The first was for her; now this is for me," she told Francis.

"Good," he said, so heavily that for a moment he felt sheepish. What he meant was: *good*, let her put herself first for once; *good*, she would stay with him longer. But Agnes didn't seem to mind. She was the sort of person who never did mind, he told himself, and the thought seemed to have the quality of a revelation.

"Back then, I used to think that only one life could be the right one, the life God intended. But now—"

"What?" The fog of whiskey lifted: in its place came a sharp focus, a hyper-clarity. He was in his late sixties, but not everything had been decided yet. There might still be things that happened next.

"Now I think it's not so set," she said. "Maybe there are a few happy lives for any of us. If Anna had lived. Or if she'd run off with someone else." He smiled, acknowledging that Anna had been capable of it. "Or if we had married." Agnes spoke slowly, giving each word its weight. Francis stared at his hands on the table before moving one lightly against hers. They did not look at each other, only sat in a stillness so close to overflowing that with one drop more, Francis knew he would spill out of his own life.

"Maybe God intends only that we make the best of whatever life we choose." Her hand shifted away; she raised her glass. "To you, Francis. To your children and grandchildren."

She left the nearly full glass when she kissed him on the cheek, such a swift, soft goodbye that he did not have time to pull her close. For a long time—a third whiskey—he sat deciding whether to follow. His children were grown, Jude nearly thirty. His wife had no place in the blazing intensity of this moment. Ideas about right or wrong were rendered so feeble as to seem absurd. But he was afflicted by a different stillness from the one that had fallen upon them together. He tried to imagine Agnes's face if he turned up at the door. What he saw instead was the way she stood on the edge of the dance floor at Albert's wedding; or the steadiness of her gaze when they talked in her garden; or her smile, a little sad, a little mischievous, when she ordered the champagne.

She would open the door and—what? He finished his whiskey, picked up her glass, swallowed hard. The taste of old coins. He did not get up. He did not get up. It was nearly intolerable, knowing she was within reach. What stopped him was the prospect of her dismay if what she wanted was to think well of him.

Eventually, his eyes drifted shut. Someone—a waiter or clerk—shook him gently. Francis was helped to his feet and led to an empty room. Sleep dragged him through the next hours, until he awoke to a smear of light and a headache as thick as glass. He washed and tried to smooth his shirt, knowing it was too late. Still, he found the room and knocked on the door. She was gone. All that was left was the blinding ride home and the hail of scolding from Essie: where had he been, why hadn't he called. The room was free, a courtesy for his contributions. Of course he hadn't called; why should he wake her? He ducked beneath her voice to go into the bath and tip cool water over his head. He felt shame in nearly equal measure: both for what he'd wanted and for failing to act.

Since that night, he had returned to the hotel every year on Anna's birthday. He tried to tell himself he had no expectations, but he looked up whenever anyone entered the lounge, hoping to see Agnes. He had somehow misplaced the photo Albert had given him of the sisters in the garden, so he brought the biscuit tin with its strange cargo of old letters to search for it in peace. The photo might easily be folded inside a slip of paper, overlooked.

He sifted through them carefully, rereading the letters Agnes wrote after Anna's death. These contained nothing significant, nothing to savor beyond the fact of her writing them. *Love, Agnes.*

    No photo. He could not remember the last time he saw it, a lapse that pained him. He was left with what he *did* remember, those evenings beneath her mango tree, the yellow sari she wore at Albert's wedding. She'd tucked a flower into her hair—not the usual sort of garland, a single large blossom. Francis did not know its name. But this was not something he had forgotten. This was something he had never known.

18

DECEMBER 1992

All Varuna agreed that summer had been Clive's worst monsoon yet: two months onshore in a jug, drinking through the money he'd set aside to sustain them until Inez took what was left to Dominic for safekeeping. By the time he could return to sea, Clive had lost his one good suit and his grandmother's fine brass serving tray in drunken wagers. This was a seasonal affliction, the villagers knew. The fishing routine would soon assert itself—not a cure, exactly, but a steadying. At sea, he managed, his eyes small and tight, his face as grim as headache. For the three or four days of a voyage, Inez could sleep peacefully.

But something had shifted. After weeks of voyages, Clive was unable to right himself. His earnings leaked from his pockets: more toddy, more wagers. Inez took to seizing whatever money she could. Clive disappeared for hours at a time, listing sharply on his short walks home.

Flora was increasingly anxious for Inez, who worked at Pomfret on non-market days but could not earn enough to absorb Clive's excesses. They were two months behind in rent, a debt which Dominic would forgive but which worried Flora. Silently, she tallied what had been lost to them: Inez chiefly, but her own family as well. She and Dominic had Jerome's future to settle: a concern she did not know how to navigate. What would it cost to give him his start? All over Varuna, villagers were trying to educate their sons for a living onshore, something beyond the boats and oil rigs. Boys enrolled in typing courses. One bought a machine to cut keys and established himself as a village locksmith. A pair of cousins joined the postal union.

For old-timers, for whom fathers and sons formed a long chain of fishermen, it was as if the final links had been sheared away and the ends of the chains loosed, swinging wildly into the world beyond. A village boy began as a known quantity: steady hands, or a head for mechanics, or a boat to inherit. Then that same boy became something else entirely, apprenticed in a field no one had heard of. What was a sound engineer?

Nobody was surprised that Jerome preferred vocational training to upper secondary. He enrolled in a three-month certificate course in food-and-beverage services at the Bombay Institute of Hospitality Technology (BIHT). "BITE," Celia called it. Sometimes she bared her teeth and gnashed the air near his ear.

Flora clicked her tongue. Celia had a way of going too far, forcing Flora to defend this BIHT even though she felt suspicious about what lay beyond the Koliwada. "All the way to Dadar, son?" It was unsettling to turn her back on the sea and imagine a new set of dangers.

As soon as Jerome earned his certificate, he enrolled in a second program in hospitality arts. (HA, said Celia.) But what was the point, Flora wondered, when he could work in their own stalls without any training?

"This is for bigger places," Jerome told her. "Where I can get a paid post."

"Why not?" said Dominic. "He could land up at one of the hotels."

Flora felt uncertain. But fisherfolk regularly sold to hotel buyers at the docks. It was not so disorienting to think of her son on the other side of that exchange, the one with clean hands.

"Let him work at Hotel Castelo," Inez proposed with a great fat laugh. "He can let us into the parties." This comforted Flora, who wanted to keep her son close at hand.

Still, they strained over the tuition. "We're fine," said Dominic, and for the moment it was true. But Flora knew how quickly things could crumble. It was the swiftness she remembered best, the vertiginous drop to a place of no return. And then, suddenly, the baskets of plastic rosaries. How *had* they lost the boat in the end? Was it typhoid or upkeep or the long weeks of fouled waters? Was it their daughter knocked down in the road? She did not know how to guard against its happening again. She did not like to play games with fate, surrendering the rent money that might sustain them. And she did not like to think what would happen to Inez if Clive kept on.

"You could go with him," Flora suggested to Dominic. She meant to sea. "One overnight. Maybe if you are together—"

"There's no trouble on the boat. On the boat he's fine. The trouble is on land."

"The trouble is in *Clive*," said Flora.

But a fisherman fishing was not an emergency in a village where the catch might still pay off. Inez herself went to the docks and bought fuel for a longer run. "Let him stay at sea until he loses his taste for this madness," she told Flora. Clive had a solid boat, decades of experience, no trouble finding a crew, a fair chance of a windfall if he moved past the empty waters near the coast. When they came back after a six-day voyage, the nets were full, his hands steady, his eyes clear. He finished on the docks by midday, reached home when the sun was high, and threw himself onto the bed for a good long sleep before going up the lane to celebrate with the boys. For two days, he did not come home. He began at the Cooperative, then went off with a couple of men from a village in the north. When he came back, nearly all the money was gone.

"He had it?" Flora asked Inez, without quite asking why. A month of rent at least, she thought, gone God only knew where doing God only knew what.

"He had to pay the crew."

A three-day trip, a thinner catch. A week later, Inez came home from the market and found two men angling the bed frame down the flight of steps along the outside of the house.

"Where are you going with my bed?"

"Not yours anymore," one of the men told her. He was short of breath from the effort of negotiating the turn onto the lane.

"That is my bed," Inez said, but her voice sounded faded and old.

The men carried the frame to the road and balanced it across a motor scooter, the headboard sticking out one side and the foot the other. The driver perched in front, the passenger sat behind to hold it steady, and the motor scooter moved slowly away.

Inez was sitting with Flora when one of the men returned forty minutes later for the pallet, which he rolled and hefted onto his shoulder to walk up the lane. Women on either side looked up from their buckets or rose from their stoops to stand and stare as he approached. The lane was so narrow that he was forced to move through them as though pushing through branches in a forest.

Suddenly, one of the women cursed. Then another. One old woman with a face as tight as a fist screwed up her mouth and spat, spraying the man's heel and breaking his stride. Another dumped filthy water from her washbasin at his feet. He kept his eyes down so that he did not have to see their faces.

Inez made no move to stop him, only spoke in a monotone. "My father gave us that bed. Sons of bitches." Flora thought of her own strange paralysis on the day Mr. Pujari unhooked the wires of their television.

When Clive turned up that night, he said nothing about the bed, just lay down with a blanket in a corner and slept.

"He lost it in a bet," Inez told Flora. "He'll sell the floor next."

A delegation from the Varuna Cooperative visited the next day to encourage Clive to leave the bottle aside and build up his health. Dominic spoke, and two other men. Clive took it quietly, nodding and nodding. It was agreed that he might be served a glass or two, no more. But Dominic had a fisherman's sense of what it took to turn a boat around. He did not believe the problem would be so easily solved. When Inez came to him with her plan, he agreed to help her buy a large metal wardrobe with locks on both doors and a built-in safe.

"She can fit a whole bedroll inside," he told Flora. "If she locks things up, they won't lose everything."

Clive was at sea when the wardrobe arrived. It was too wide to fit through the door, so Dominic and a few other men rigged a pulley to hoist it onto the balcony. There was a party spirit to the enterprise: people watching, men laughing while they worked. When they heaved it off the ground, a boy darted forward to pretend he was lifting it, and the men shouted to get back, all of you. So the children formed a ring around the spot where the huge piece dangled overhead and imagined the ways it might crash. Everyone cheered when it landed safely.

Later, Inez came down to report that she had packed away her valuables. She looked like herself again, Flora saw, bright looks and quick smiles. It was the second Sunday in Advent, a festive season; Flora thought they should all play a game together. But Dominic would not move from the television. Something has happened, he said. A mosque torn down in Ayodhya. "They say it's the birthplace of Ram."

"Oh, Ram." Flora spoke of the warrior avatar in the same way she might speak of an uncle who could no longer surprise her. She and Inez had been devoted to the story on television, but neither cared for hotheaded demonstrations. They abandoned the television to chat on the stoop.

Celia stayed with her father and watched scenes flash across their television. A rally, roiling with men. Then the crowd surged and charged through barricades, flooding the short rise to the mosque. Another flash: men spread across the walls like vines, filling the niches, lining the roof. Some brandished axes, others hammers or metal rods. Another flash: gaping holes in the courtyard walls, crumbling brick innards, the mosque half devoured. Men tore at stone bare-handed. Another flash: rubble and dust. Then the images jumped back to the start, the mosque whole again. But it looked different to Celia. The domes rose up, blind and baleful, like three gray eyes closed against the sight of the men rushing in.

Her father said nothing, only watched as the footage looped

in a coil that seemed to keep tightening. Finally, he got up, looking grim. He was going out, he told the women.

As soon as he left, Flora called to Celia to switch off the television. "That's enough of that," she said, as though he'd carried off the newscast with him. All this madness in a place where the D'Mello family knew nobody and would never think to go. This was what the world did: press in on you with its bad-news this and so-sad that, snatch away what little time you had to see to your own affairs, fill your head with pictures you wished you'd never seen. Jerome was out with friends, but Flora and Inez coaxed the girls to join them for a walk around the neighborhood. All the cottages were strung up with holiday lights. Why not look at something happy instead?

———

Flora knew Clive's boat must be in when she heard footsteps on the stairs in the first gray light. "Sleep, Celu," she said, since the noise had roused them both, and without a word, Celia turned over and closed her eyes.

That was what woke Flora properly, the joke of her daughter listening to her for once.

The walls and floors were thick, well buttressed against heat and rains, but it was pleasant to hear the faint trace of voices and movements above and recall the days when Dominic used to return at dawn. Flora listened for the sound of the metal wardrobe door and thought she heard it; a sign that Inez must have taken charge of the money Clive brought home. An interlude, then more footsteps; that would be Inez going to load her baskets for market. They used to walk together when both their husbands were fishing, and for a moment Flora felt the pang of their separation. She had enjoyed the hush of such mornings, the surety of her hands as she sorted the catch, the sense of fellowship. She thought of following Inez to the beach, but it would be some time before the share for Pomfret was ready, and until then, Flora, with no catch of her own, would be reduced to standing outside the circle like a gull. She let her eyes drift shut instead.

That morning came the first uneasy reports of demonstrations from villagers who had been downtown the night before. Nothing seemed amiss in Santa Clara, but one of Flora's friends saw an injured body conveyed by handcart to JJ Hospital.

"But where is the trouble?" Flora wanted to know. She had run through her fresh fish by the time the girls returned from school and hung the sign that Pomfret was closed for the day. If none of the village boats came in by evening, she might take the early train the next morning to buy from Sassoon Dock. She and Inez occasionally went together, riding with other fishwives in darkness, and returning when the light was still shy over the city. Sometimes they found a place on the scarred wooden benches, but usually they sat cross-legged on the floor beside their baskets, rocking lightly against one another with the motion of the train.

"Better stay put," said Dominic, who closed the café early. People weren't stopping, he told his wife, but really it was that the Muslim shopkeepers, his friends from the line of stores behind the market, did not appear. He carried on serving students and neighborhood clerks, those with no need to venture even as far as the train station a couple of kilometers away. Then Farooq came with a bag of odds and ends and said he was shutting the bakery until the city calmed down. "Stay a minute," Dominic urged, but Farooq shook his head, hardly looking at him. No, no, he must get back.

Flora waited at the head of the lane, looking out for Jerome, thinking what a terrible idea Dadar had been all along, and why hadn't she kept her children safe in the village? Jerome finally turned up, looking shocked and pale; on the train, he had seen a man bleeding badly from a head wound. He and Dominic went to the Cooperative to see what other news might sift into the village, and Flora sat talking on the stoop until the rumors began to drive her mad and she ordered Celia and Evangeline to come with her to the beach. They would see if any boats had docked. "Now?" asked Celia, who could never simply do what she was told, and Flora snapped yes, pretending to be worried about Pomfret, when what she really wanted was to turn her back on the city and look to the sea, whose storms she understood.

They were on their way back when they ran into Inez, her arm in a splint.

Flora put a hand to her chest. "Not broken?"

Inez tipped her head yes. Celia saw the flash of dismay on her mother's face as she urged Inez inside.

"Paining badly?"

"No, no. Not bad." Inez sounded as if nothing was out of the ordinary. "It was aching this morning, so I wrapped it. Then it began to go numb, and I thought maybe a proper bandage. I went to buy it and the fellow said no, no, better go to clinic. And now see what!" She looked with disdain at the sling.

"You remember when Celu broke her arm? They put it in one cast. Then—after how many weeks!—they said the bone went wrong anyway."

Inez wagged her head. The village was full of such stories. It was like Jesus on the Mount, she told Flora, only, instead of loaves and fish, trouble and more trouble. Doctors were never satisfied.

"But how did you break it?" Celia asked.

"Celu, don't . . ."

Inez spoke to Flora. "It's only because he took me by surprise. Usually he'll sleep ten, twelve hours, like a dead man. But I went out on the landing—such a stink coming off him!—and when I went back inside he was standing dead still and said give him the key. Of course I'm not giving him the key!" She leaned back against the cushion. "He's forgotten all about it now."

On television, the state channel broadcast footage of the South Africa vs. India cricket match in Cape Town. There was no mention of a disturbance in Bombay as Muslim demonstrators took to the streets to protest the destruction of the Ayodhya mosque. A mob stormed the police station a few blocks from JJ Hospital. Near Null Bazaar, shops were looted and set afire. Petrol bombs shook Dharavi. Bullets were flying in Bhendi Bazaar. In Bharat Nagar, north of the Mithi River, a bus was burned to a smoking hulk. All over the city, rioters took up choppers, knives, soda bottles, sickles, and, spikes. Violence broke out in Nirmal Nagar, just up the tracks from the station where Flora might have waited for the train the following morning.

Instead, she and Dominic went upstairs with Inez. "To help her settle," Flora said. "She may need help changing clothes."

Jerome threw a blanket over his head to sleep. But Celia waited until her mother came back to ask if Clive had broken Inez's wrist.

"No! No . . . He went for the key and knocked against her, maybe, I don't know. He wasn't steady. She must have put out her hand when she fell. That is the way you break a hand, you know," she added, as if this had been the lesson she intended all along. "You come crashing down on it with all your weight."

"Then why is Daddy staying?" Evangeline asked.

"To sit with Clive awhile." Flora picked up her tunic to change for bed. "When he woke this morning, all that business with the key was finished. He didn't remember a thing. He said, 'What's this?' when he saw the cupboard. Inez told him she got it for a good price, not to worry, and she's kept the key safely so it isn't lost. He accepted, no problem."

Celia stared. "But what about her *arm*?"

"The arm will heal. Go on, get ready for bed." Then she stopped and stood as she was, in her bra and salwar pants, her belly sagging softly. "Say a prayer for her, Celu."

Celia was thinking of the time she broke her arm as a little girl, when her mother still had a place in the Santa Clara fish bazaar and Inez worked beside her. The women were busy, the hours long and loud. But Inez called Celia to her side and found small ways to let her help. She held whole fish in place and let Celia use her good arm to cut off the heads and tails. Fish after fish, even though it slowed her down. Celia felt proud to use the big knife.

She was not thinking of a prayer, exactly, just remembering the knife in her hand, the thwack of the blade against the wet chopping block, the way Inez grinned when flecks of blood landed on their cheeks.

19

DECEMBER 1992

For the next few days, the D'Mello family did not stray far from the tight fist of Varuna. The small Catholic neighborhood of Santa Clara had not imposed a curfew, but villagers kept to the village, and cottage people stayed shut up in their homes after dark or moved in small, swift huddles to other people's houses a street or two away. Nobody lingered at a café. There was no point keeping the Rosy open.

At first, Pomfret was possible. Flora bought fish from the village docks, wrapped in newspapers full of stories that seemed like they must be from some other place. Inez fried fish with one hand. She and Flora heard news from cab drivers and the trickle of customers from the hotel. Clive was out at sea.

The Catholic schools in Santa Clara carried on, so Dominic walked the girls to Holy Name. The sun was bright and common. People met in the lanes to exchange stories of what they had seen or heard, and Dominic brought home any newspaper he could find, borrowing copies from the undertaker when the newsagents sold out. Flora wore down the hours with questions and more questions. How many more days until someone put a stop to this, were Catholic places in danger, what did Dominic think, what did teachers say, what was Jerome studying, what were the girls doing?

Playing cards, said Celia shortly. She lost a game to Lina,

then listlessly won the next. "It's better with three." She poked Jerome's leg with her foot. "Come on, play."

"I'm working."

"HA!" She said, an indictment of the hospitality arts. He wasn't working at all, only poring over a slick catalogue from his program. "The Future Is Bright," it promised.

"Don't pester, Celu. Let him study. You also could look at your schoolwork—"

"I'm not pestering. And he's not studying."

"Enough." Dominic tossed down the newspaper. "I'm taking a walk."

"A walk?" Flora blinked. "Where to, in all this?"

"In all *what*?" said Dominic. "Nothing is happening here."

"Daddy, can I go with you?"

"Now see! You've set off Celu."

Dominic pulled on a vest. "Come if you like," he told Celia. "It's fine," he told Flora.

"You don't know what's fine," said Flora, but only as they were leaving.

They followed Varuna Road to the Church of the Loaves and Fishes. Celia wondered if her father meant to take her inside—to light candles for each intention, the way her mother did. They could light candles all night and never be finished, she thought. There weren't candles enough for a whole city.

But he strode past the courtyard gates without stopping. Even on Creek, the shops were padlocked, security grilles down. Restaurants were closed. Traffic thinned to a few cars and autoricks. People were hurrying off the streets, not pouring onto them seeking the lively yellow bustle of a Bombay night.

Her father led her to Seaview Hill. "We'll go up and take a look."

They climbed at a good pace, mostly in silence. Celia did not know how to break it. It was as though her father had become someone she did not know, someone to feel shy around.

"You had your school concert," he said abruptly, nearly a question.

"Yes." The basilica loomed ahead. "Sister Vicky came in a wheelchair."

He nodded. In all this madness, there were concerts; why shouldn't his daughter sing in them?

"And what about classes? You're doing well?"

He sounded like a distant uncle. Celia told him yes and scurried ahead to match his stride.

"In another six months, Jerome will finish his course."

She knew.

"He's thinking of training for a cruise line. Steward, that sort of thing. He's spoken to you?"

Celia shook off the small hurt in admitting he hadn't. It had been a long time since she'd felt allied with her brother—since they were children, when she saw herself as almost his age, almost a boy. Evangeline was far behind, the frail one, the baby. But the balance had shifted to "Jerry and the girls."

"It's good money," her father said. "A good life. He'd be gone maybe twelve, fifteen months at a time. Then home a little while. He could save his full salary."

"But, Daddy . . ." What was he talking about? Why was everything she knew twisting out of all recognition? "Jerry hates boats."

It was a truth nobody had admitted aloud. She half-expected the words to cause an explosion.

But her father only laughed. "What boat? This is a floating hotel. Bigger than a whole street of flat buildings."

Celia felt whatever else she might say scrambling away from her.

They walked past the Hotel Castelo, past the ruins of the tower, to where the hill ended in a low cliff at Land's End. Celia could see people scattered along the length of the seawall, guests who'd wandered up from the hotel, men who sought a safe vantage point from which to view the riots, even a few couples who lingered after the sunset as if this were an ordinary night.

Celia's father led her to a place where no one else was sitting. The bay had a bit of chop, he said mildly. He was looking toward Mahim, so absorbed that Celia could study the line of his jaw. His mustache needed trimming, and he had stubble on his chin. Above his ear was a small patch of gray hair, no bigger than a thumbprint.

Time seemed to have slowed since the riots began, the days and nights suffused with waiting. Now, listening to the waves strike the rocks below, Celia felt a vertiginous sense of its acceleration. Her father would grow old. Her brother would leave home.

"And what about you? You're not far behind."

"I don't know." Celia could not get her footing in this encounter. Did he think she would follow Jerome into hospitality arts? Would she train for something else? Would she marry at eighteen or nineteen or twenty? She thought nineteen might be best. She thought three or four children, and her mother near at hand to help look after them.

But that would only come when her parents were ready to solicit proposals, or when boys liked her enough to propose on their own. She sometimes took walks with the older brother of one of her classmates. He was not a real prospect—the family wasn't Catholic, nothing could come of it—but he liked her smile, he told her one day when he found her alone, and then he laughed, making her laugh. Before that, she'd never really thought about him, but when he suggested they could meet for a walk, she thought why not. He paid the entrance fee for the park near the Promenade and led her to a stone bench facing the sea. They bumped noses when he kissed her, and she began to laugh, but he tried again so quickly that there wasn't time.

What she felt above all was exultation that this had finally happened to her. It took the second and third kisses for her to begin to pay attention: the graze of his cheek, his fingers moving lightly from her shoulders to touch her arms. She was glad to be kissed, glad to know that much more about the world and herself. She wished sometimes he'd hold her more tightly. She would not have minded a performance of love. But even when she tried to stretch her own feelings into something more interesting, she knew their evenings were a bit of sweetness, nothing more. She thought of him not as a boyfriend but as the boy she kissed.

Her father was speaking about office jobs, computer courses, something out of reach of the weather. The sea pitched below, and Celia's thoughts tossed like waves: the sewing room, shears, scraps, patterns. "I like sewing," she said, then hesitated. Most village girls left school by the end of the tenth standard. "If I stayed in school, I could train to teach sewing."

"Junior college, then." He spoke as if it had always been a choice. She doubted he'd ever really imagined his daughter could be a teacher, but the present chaos seemed to have loosened something in him. Everything was shifting. With a single gust of wind, they, too, might be set afloat into a wild, untethered future. "Why not? Otherwise, you'll be running off to sea with your brother."

"You want him to go?"

"Later he can come back to the Rosy. For now, let him earn something. Why should he stay?"

Celia had never heard such things from her father before. He had always been the proud Koli who saw no reason to leave Bombay. "We're living where everyone's dying to come," he said when he heard of boys going off to Bangalore or Delhi or out of India altogether.

Now she followed his gaze to the curve of yellow streetlights that marked the southern coastline. She didn't know what she was looking for—flames, maybe—but she saw nothing beyond a row of lights pointing out over the water. "What are those lights? Is it police?"

"Headlights. People park cars along the beach and shine their lights into the bay. To defend us from attacks by sea."

"Daddy?"

"Even in the village they're talking this nonsense. Those fool Putra brothers aren't fishing, they've taken their boat 'on patrol.'" He snorted. "So that settles it. We'll sleep safe tonight." He tapped her shoulder, time to go. "It's just talk, girlie. These idiots are standing guard? All that happens is their batteries die. In the morning, they push their cars home."

Even a week ago, Celia would have trusted him entirely, but she had seen him stunned by the riots. He had not believed that Bombay, a world city, a city of trade and sophistication, was capable of such brutal partisan attacks. He had dismissed her mother's fears and Farooq's. There was no escaping it: her father had been wrong. Celia looked out at the black sea, where the headlights could not reach. Her uncertainty struck her as so disloyal that she held his hand as they started down.

They neared the Hotel Castelo, and he paused. "Should we go in?"

Was he serious? He was wearing loose trousers; she a cheap skirt and old chappals. No proper shoes.

"We'll get an ice cream. The biggest you've ever had."

The brass door revolved, as inviting as a carnival ride. Inside, the women behind the counter would narrow their eyes. Porters would stare. A security guard would come swiftly forward to ask questions. "I don't think we can."

"Why not? I have money. Let them check my pockets!"

Celia imagined the rubber chappals squeaking on the marble floor. "No, Daddy. No, thank you."

She didn't realize she had disappointed him until they were at the bottom of the hill and he laughed a little. "Never mind. Soon your brother will be king of the cruise lines. He can take you."

A week later, the riots appeared to have run their course. City officials and journalists fought over totals: this many dead, this many injured; this many Muslim, this many Hindu; this many stabbed; this many burned; this many struck by police-issued bullets. Christmas was less than two weeks away, and vendors hawked trees and stars. The café reopened, then the bakery. Jerome and Dominic spoke in low tones about cruise lines but put off mentioning anything to Flora. Inez locked her cupboard each night. The worst was over, she told Flora. Clive was drinking, but he was no longer betting their lives out from under them, and he said not a word about the bill from the clinic. The sun kept on, like a child with only one simple tune.

20

DECEMBER 1992

On Christmas Eve, Jerome broke the news about the cruise line to Flora. By then, Evangeline had been told, not so much behind her mother's back as in deference to her feelings: the family must be ready to comfort her.

"Maybe after lunch?" Evangeline suggested. "That leaves enough time."

Nobody had to ask for what. Flora loved Midnight Mass, the proud walk through the village, the greetings to other families, the carols and lights. No one liked to ruin her pleasure. They expected a storm of weeping and resistance, but best to finish with it before the day tapered to evening and they must all get dressed.

"A bath might help?" Jerome said in his mild, drifting way which passed for thoughtfulness but made Celia want to slap him. Her mother would rinse away what, exactly? Her only son would go to sea; by all means, fill the buckets.

This was how Celia felt lately: ready to snap at whatever was soft or stupid, and everything, nearly everything, was. The week before, her brother had shown her the brochure from the training center and tapped the section on stewards. "I thought of looking for a trainee post as crew cook, but even for that they want hotel experience. Plus, the kitchens will be hot."

"And you couldn't do security. That would be *dangerous*." She meant it as a cut, but he took her seriously

"In the end, you're dealing with troublemakers." He sounded so prim, so bloated with knowledge from the University of This Single Brochure, that she wanted to pinch him the way she had as a child, using her nails. "I can start as steward with only three months' training once I have the hospitality-arts certificate. And stewards get high tips."

He began listing opportunities for advancement. From deck steward he could rise in food-and-beverage service to become a waiter, or, with a further course in interpersonal skills, he could choose promotion to cabin steward.

Celia considered the photos. A pastry chef brandished a piping bag. A bartender raised a cocktail glass. "Make New Connections," read the caption beneath a steward, a guard, and a housekeeper, everyone grinning in uniform. It was like the start of a joke, the kind her brother didn't get.

"They look like idiots," she said.

His face closed.

"All this is happening on a *boat*, right? You could hardly last two nights with Daddy."

"This is different."

"How?" Celia refused to feel sorry when he looked stung. Jerome could dash off without a hint of regret, but *she* must be careful not to wound *him*? She suspected that the worst harm anyone in her family could inflict was to speak a shred of truth. At any rate, the brochure seemed uppermost in his concerns: he refolded it tenderly, as if afraid to damage the *Career Opportunities* inside, then sat in glum silence. He had a way of planting himself in the muck of any fight until his sheer brooding bulk seemed to make its own argument. *See how sad he is! Why can't you be nicer?* She couldn't.

"You do understand: you're *living* on the ocean?"

"Celu! Look at the size of this." He pointed to a photo of a ship. "You think it's the same as our boats? Out there, you have no idea. We were . . ." He stopped and waited for the right word to rise up in him, something commensurate with the dread he'd felt as a boy. "Small."

There was more; he could not say it all. The smell of diesel in his hair and fingernails. The putter of the engine, the hollow clicking of the winch. The blocks of time like hills to scale, the minutes to cast a net, the hours waiting to haul it in. The loneliness. He felt the pall of it at night especially, with only a few scattered lights of other boats in view. There was so much ocean that it seemed wanton, such an exorbitant sky. In rough seas, when his father leapt up to secure a line, his feet on the deck rail did not seem enough to keep him on board. The boat, the fuel, the nets, the boy, the man: with a single lazy heave, all could disappear.

He knew his father had a different feeling. Most Kolis grew up serene on the water, certain in their movements. They felt fine being small, content with their modest claim on the great bounty of the sea. Jerome knew all this yet found no peace in it.

But on a cruise ship, he would be among thousands. He pictured rooms blazing with lights, lights strung along every passage, great blossoms of lights hanging from the ceilings. Even if he stood facing the ocean, he would only have to turn his head to see a glittering stack of lights behind him, towering into the sky. Such a ship would leave a wake ten times as wide as Varuna Road. It would cleave through a stiff chop with Jerome feeling nothing but the thrum of the engines. In rough seas, he would be buffered on all sides by procedures and contingencies. His father would come to know Jerome could go to sea, same as any Koli with his foot on a rail.

He liked the ocean, he told Celia stiffly. On big enough boats.

Celia didn't bother to remind him how big the ocean was. It was only a matter of time before their mother heard his plans and put her foot down.

But on Christmas Eve, when Jerome said, "Mum, I found a training course," Flora listened without interrupting. He offered her the brochure, and Celia heard the headings in her mother's voice. "See the World." "Tax-Free Earnings." "Renewable Contracts." She saw her father's gaze, flicking between her brother and mother, and she began to feel complicit in a wrong they'd all perpetrated: conspiring to present her mother with a glossy scheme to take away her son.

"'A Festive'"—she showed the brochure to Evangeline, who supplied the word—"'Atmosphere.' That is what?"

"It's like a party or a holiday. It means there'll be a happy feeling."

"Like today."

She smiled so artlessly that Celia said, "It's only an idea, Mum. It won't really happen." Her father and Jerome both stared, but Celia would not be quelled. It was ridiculous, expecting her mother to take in such news on Christmas Eve. It was a kind of bullying.

"If I finish my course in May, I could start training this summer," Jerome said.

"Summer," Flora repeated. She passed her finger over one of the headings. "'Free Room, Free Meals, Free Travel.' You want to travel, son?"

It was a question Celia did not expect. She could see Jerome hadn't, either. He nodded.

"I never knew," she said.

There was a pause. Celia wanted to fill it but wasn't sure with what.

Then her mother looked up at Jerome—a mild look, nothing forbidding in it. "It's strange," she said. "When you were a baby, I knew every small thing you wanted. There was a cup you liked to bang against my pots. You put out your hand for it even before you could speak. And when you did start speaking, I knew where every word came from." She smiled. "Most came from me. You listened, and then you said them yourself. Like a parrot, but no beak, nothing sharp. Only cheeks." She blew out her own, round and full, to show him. Then she let out the air and turned to her husband. "This is good, you think? A good program?"

Celia blinked. Her mother was conceding. Her father began talking about tuition: he would never go back to a moneylender, so Jerome might need to wait.

"If Clive could only pay us . . ." Flora began.

"We'll have it soon," said Dominic swiftly. "A little here, a little there." This was the way you moved up in the world, he assured her. Jerome would make back their initial output after just one cruise, two at the outside.

"Then I'll be helping you," Jerome said. He looked soft and young, in no way ready for the future he was proposing. Yet Flora beamed. Dominic suggested opening a bank account in a serious man-of-business voice he never used with Celia. Evangeline loosened in the way she always did when a patch of tension cleared, opening like a flower to happy relief.

Only Celia was left feeling wronged. She was not certain of the exact terms of the wrongdoing, but the feeling was unmistakable; it flowed into a deep trench of other recent troubles, an underground stream of what she was expected to endure with good grace or what she could never mention in the first place. She even felt the sting of things that hadn't happened to *her*—Inez and her cupboard, the mosque torn down, the wave of riots—all ways that the world imposed what Celia did not want to learn. Things tore apart so easily, and she was wounded by knowing it, and wounded again by how quickly her family had agreed that they, too, would be torn apart.

"Why can't he work at the Hotel Castelo? He wouldn't need all this money for training."

But her mother had plunged back into the brochure. "Free uniforms they give you, son! Free laundry!" She laughed at the wonder of it. "I'll be sending you my saris."

"Sending *where*?" Celia said. "The middle of the ocean?"

"Can you visit the ports?" Evangeline asked.

"Oh yes, that's part of it—right, son?" Anyone would think that Dominic had dreamed up the "Offshore Excursions" policy. "And your visas are looked after. Everything is managed for you."

"Okay!" Flora clapped her hands. "Time to get ready. You first, son. I'll heat the water."

A bath did not help. Nor did the outfits her mother laid out: peach for Celia, Evangeline in rose. Nothing could make Celia feel fresh or pretty; she was all eyebrows and elbows. The family set off an hour early to satisfy her mother's hopes of five seats together, but at the head of the lane, Flora clutched Celia's arm—"Mind, Celu! your good shoes!"—as Celia stepped into the edge of a dung pile.

Her mother urged the others to "Go! Save places!" while Celia tried to scrape her sandal clean. A moment later, their neighbor Esperanza paused to greet them, her family fanned out behind her in a Koli phalanx. Flora smiled to hear that Esperanza's oldest sons would soon take over the family boat.

"Good boys! And we also have news. Jerome will train for cruise ships."

Celia dragged her soiled shoe against the road and Esperanza clicked her tongue. "You should pick up your feet properly. Your shoes will last longer."

"Such a dragon," her mother said when Esperanza was out of earshot. "But beneath it all, there is a heart."

"Why are you going on about cruise lines?" Celia grumbled. "She doesn't care about that."

"Of course she cares. But do you think it's a little sad for her? Her sons won't have such chances."

"Jerome might not even do it. He might get some other job, here."

"Which one?" Flora said absently. "There's something he likes?" She scanned the crowded street. "I thought we'd be early enough, but—"

Celia felt a small body slam against her. Her ankle buckled and a little boy in raw silk ricocheted into the road.

"Careful!" her mother warned her, as if Celia were the one banging into people.

A flare of pain caught and held, like a candle being lit. The road was crowded, her mother kept waving, boys were stupid, Celia's ankle *hurt*, and nothing felt like Christmas.

"Why did you tell them Jerome will go? It's like you're pushing him out the door."

"What pushing? Who is pushing?"

"Why can't he work in the café with Daddy?" Celia meant

to sound sensible. But her voice slid as if she might cry, the last indignity of a walk begun in cow dung.

Her mother spoke as if Celia were small again. "We are here, Celu. The Rosy is here. He can always come back and pick that up. But for now he wants to try something on his own." She shook her head. "So many boys are going off to the Gulf, the States, England. That is the main point. If Jerome went to one of those places, he might stay. This way, he is always coming home."

It had not occurred to her that her mother was thinking in such directions, beyond what Celia had imagined herself. She struggled against the threat of fresh tears. "Wait," she said tremulously. "Wait. I have to . . ." She leaned against her mother while she rubbed her ankle. "Okay. We can go."

Yet for a moment they stood, Celia's head on her mother's shoulder, her mother's arm supporting her. "Such a pretty color, this peach," her mother murmured. "See how it suits you."

When they were walking once more, she shook her head. "Such a girl for limps and lumps! You can hardly make it down the road without falling."

That's not true, Celia very nearly said. It was as if she were wired to object; she could feel it crackling through her like an electrical charge. But she was exhausted, the way she used to feel after weeping as a child, and it was pleasant to lap up whatever tenderness her mother offered. It was not so hard, she decided. You let people be a little wrong about you. You sidestepped those moments as though they were a mess in the road. You tried to move forward.

"Breaking bones—"

"Only once!"

"And always making light. Even when you were small, even with your arm in pieces. What a fright you gave me! One look at that wrist, gone the wrong way around, and I thought I would faint. But does this girl say anything about the pain? Nothing. You were chatting about the sweets they gave you."

"Biscuits." When Celia remembered that day, nothing was

strung together. There were only moments, a handful of beads instead of a necklace. The downed bicycle, the blazing light, the schoolboys, the floor tiles. The picture of the girls who were not Mrs. Almeida. The cut on Mr. Almeida's forehead. Her mother's face, tight and fearful. And, detached from any pain or terror, choosing biscuits with Mrs. Almeida.

"You can take them a few dishes this week for the New Year."

"Mum, you remember Mrs. Almeida's daughter? The one who left the suitcase? She went to America, and now her children are living there." Celia did not know exactly what she was trying to say: that her mother might be right about Jerome, but also how quickly everything reversed. The granddaughter brought a travel diary to the place the mother called home.

And somehow all that shock of movement was contained in the person of Mrs. Almeida. She had given birth to a daughter, raised her, watched her go, and was left waiting for grandchildren to visit or not. Such a life felt remote to Celia, unfolding only a few streets away, but so far from the experience of a village family that it startled her to find those spheres colliding, her mother jostled into a life that resembled Mrs. Almeida's even a little. Both had children who could go.

"They may visit for the holiday. We'll send enough for them also," her mother said easily.

They rounded the corner and saw the church grounds where Mass would be held: tiny white bulbs overhead, potted poinsettias, and a Christmas tree with cotton wool stretched along the branches for snow. Illuminated stars were strung across the entrance, where a boy in a vest and his tiny sister shouted with laughter, trying to catch crescents of light in their hands.

"Just like you, that little one," Flora said. "Never looking."

Hundreds of folding chairs covered the clay field, nearly every seat saved or taken. They walked slowly up the center aisle, people eddying in every direction. Flora worried there was nothing left; then suddenly Jerome sifted out of the crowd like an apparition, the ghost of Christmas seats. As they followed him, Flora indulged in triumphant speculations about what would have happened if she'd listened to Dominic. "We would have split up, three and two, but even those are nearly gone. Ten minutes, that's all the difference."

Suddenly, she seized Celia's arm. "Look!"

The altar was a great barge of white and gold with masses of poinsettias at its base. The choir was gathering, but Flora pointed to the crèche.

"There! You see?"

Celia saw only the usual fare. The Holy Family at the opening of their makeshift stable were almost life-sized. An angel was mounted to the roof, a star suspended above. The Wise Men were still a traveling party, far off to the east in a ring of poinsettias; little children dashed among the gold-foiled pots to touch the camels with their painted blankets. The Kings would only reach the stable on the Feast of Epiphany, but during the Processional, the Infant Christ would be borne up to the straw-filled manger, where Mary and Joseph had already set their gazes.

"Look at the sheep!"

There were ten or twelve, artfully placed, so it took a moment for Celia to realize that one was a dog, a living dog. People in the front rows saw it also: a stray, dun-colored, its back pressed against a hollow lamb the way street dogs stretched along walls to sleep.

Usually, Flora would have gone directly to the altar to genuflect, but she did not like to pass near it. "Anyway, the singing will start," she said, sounding doubtful.

"It's only a dog," said Celia. They had passed half a dozen street dogs on their walk without the slightest danger. "And it's sleeping."

"Still," said Jerome, "it really shouldn't be here."

"How would a *dog* know that?"

"Don't worry, Celu. We can see the crèche at the end."

But it was the dog that interested Celia. She tumbled into a vision of a living Nativity, the resin figures replaced by the beasts of Santa Clara. Dogs like this one, feral pigs rooting in the straw, battle-scarred cats. The donkey would become a goat. The sweet-eyed cow would be a bullock with painted horns, shifting its thin hindquarters. A rooster would climb to the roof to crow the good news. Celia felt she ought to replace the Holy Family with beautiful people, but what flashed to mind were the beggar families camped along the church gates, as if they had been swept there by a giant whisk broom clearing the road. Mary would have thin arms. There would not be a manger, only a baby tucked in the pallu of her sari. Maybe a little cart with wheels, if Joseph was missing a foot.

"Celu! This way!"

Her mother and brother moved down the side aisle and Celia knew she should follow. But she paused when she saw a priest in long robes hurrying toward the crèche. He carried a walking stick, though he was too young to need it, and conferred with some men sitting in front. They got up with an air of taking action. When he passed the stick to one of them, she realized they would use it to drive off the dog.

Suddenly Celia loved the dog, the dog she could hardly see and would not exactly want to touch, the dog whose sleep in all this hullaballoo seemed so improbable that it must be either sacred or profane.

A few steps forward, a tentative jab toward the Nativity lamb, and the dog twisted up, barking. For the first time, Celia saw its pup, who lifted its head but did not stand.

Confusion rippled through the first rows. "Poor thing." "Easy." "Careful!" The mother stepped forward so the pup lay beneath the tent of her chest, but she kept her eyes hard on the stick. A long, low growl.

The priest urged the man to try again, but the moment he raised the stick, the mother lunged, barking, and all the men recoiled. It might have been a bit of fun, a quick chase through the Nativity scene to run off a stray, but a dog protecting her pup would stand and fight.

"Better leave it," one called.

"It can't stay!" The priest raised his voice. "The Procession of the Infant comes right this side. If the dog is still here . . ." But his speculations were evidently too upsetting to speak aloud. A bitten ankle? A botched Nativity? A note of crudity in what ought to be glorious? Would people *laugh*?

Maybe the shepherds kept dogs to protect their flocks, thought Celia. It was such a big story—the hosts of angels, the courses of kings. Surely, there was room in it for a dog or two.

The dog lowered herself, her body pointed toward danger like a drawn arrow. The field, from her crouch, must have seemed hopeless: battalions of shoes, the chaos of lights, the terrible stick. Such a thin dog, all teeth and nerve. A single blow, a few good kicks, and she would be finished.

Perhaps the priest realized that also. With a quick, haunted glance toward the choir, he held out his hand for the stick. The other man gave it.

Go, Celia begged, a prayer to the dog. *Run, go!*

The other man circled toward the manger, drawing the dog's gaze. Slowly, the priest raised the stick.

"You there! Put that down!"

Celia saw a dark suit, a green tie, a ring of gray hair. Mr. Almeida.

The priest kept hold of the stick, but one end sank down. "Professor Almeida? Professor, it's Joe. Father Joe. Freda Mendes's son. You taught my brother—"

"What the hell is this?"

Mr. Almeida was not shouting, but he spoke the way other men spit in the road. Celia drew closer, until she was only a few paces behind them.

"This dog has come in. And we have to—"

"Thrash it with a stick?"

"Clear the area for safety. We've been trying to drive it off, but the dog won't go."

"Of course the dog won't go. There's a pup." Celia had never heard a priest addressed in such a way before, as though he were exceedingly stupid. "And you lift a stick to them!"

A younger man joined him. "Dad, go and sit. Mum is waiting."

Mr. Almeida paid no attention. "Hundreds of people in this field. All these *things*"—he tossed his hand at the crèche—"and you can't make place for a dog? You go after her with a stick?"

"Dad—"

"Son, with a *stick*!"

The priest appealed to the younger man. "We can't let dogs run wild at Midnight Mass."

"You can't beat them, either, with all these children watching." Mr. Almeida's son spoke mildly, as if they had already reached an understanding. "Come, Dad."

"Something's wrong with that pup," Mr. Almeida said. "It's too weak to stand."

"It's living on the streets; it's diseased," said the priest. "What if it bites someone?"

Mr. Almeida looked at the priest just long enough to turn away. "Son. Is there any meat left from dinner?"

His son looked startled.

"Just a little meat," Mr. Almeida said. "She's thin. She'll bring the pup."

"There's sorpotel," his son said slowly. "The carols won't start for ten minutes."

"Meat!" the priest said. "You want to feed it?"

But something had shifted. The Almeidas were talking only to each other.

"Why not? I'll come back in five minutes."

Celia looked doubtfully at Mr. Almeida, who did not appear to be capable of getting anywhere and back quickly.

"That's silly, Dad. I'll go."

But the priest shook his head. "You have the First Reading. All readers need to be in place before the carols begin. If you go, we may use the alternate."

Mr. Almeida's eyes flicked over the priest with no more regard than if he'd been a plastic shepherd. Then he addressed his son. "You can't go. We'll never hear the end of it. She's told everyone you're reading." He turned, casting about for some better prospect, and saw Celia. "You!"

She felt a jolt at being recognized. "Celia," she reminded him.

Mr. Almeida tipped his head. "This one will go for us. She's always dashing through the neighborhood."

"Dad, you can't send a strange girl!"

"What strange girl? This is a girl we know."

On an impulse Celia asked, "Is Nicole here?"

Mr. Almeida's son blinked. "No. No, not this year." He looked at his father. "Dad, never mind the reading. This girl doesn't—"

"I want to go!" She thought of the dog. She thought of Jerome, going wherever he pleased. She thought of Mrs. Almeida and the suitcase, the favors her mother could not repay in fish. "I'll be fast."

"Not so fast you knock people down," Mr. Almeida warned.

"Professor Almeida, as a parish—"

"Just remind her which house, son. Once she's back, you can manage the dog. I'll tell your mother you're helping with the procession."

The priest retreated in a sulk, his stick poking out like an awkward remark when people stopped to greet him. Mr. Almeida's son gave careful instructions: the gate, the servant, the platter in the refrigerator.

Mr. Almeida cut him off—"She could have come and gone by now!"—and nodded at her before he went to rejoin his wife. He walked stiffly, like something whittled from wood, to their place in the first row. When had they arrived to get such good seats? wondered Celia. She could hardly conceive of an hour early enough.

The Almeida house was only two blocks away. Celia rattled the gate to hail the watchman. The kitchen girl was surprised but gave no trouble. She scooped food into a plastic shopping bag, and Celia went clattering down the front steps, remembering the day someone had carried her up.

By the time she got back, the congregants had pleated into rows. Families arranged themselves: grandparents with grandchildren, arguing siblings set apart. Even the crowds in the back had coalesced, standing expectantly in the places where they would stand for the next two hours. There was the sense that they had gathered close, like the shepherds long ago, to witness a marvel.

Mr. Almeida's son smiled at Celia and took the bag.

"Now we'll see."

Celia watched while he made a wide circle behind the dog, then tipped a little food to the ground. The dog lifted its head.

The choir leader tapped the microphone. Celia could not delay any longer. She took one last look at the dog, low to the ground and creeping toward the food, before she hurried down the aisle to her family. "Celu, *where* have you—" But her mother broke off as the carols began. Celia felt proud when Mr. Almeida's son gave the First Reading.

In line to receive Communion, she looked for them: the dog and the pup, Mr. Almeida and his son, Mrs. Almeida with her quick, wide smile. But their family had lined up on the far side of the field, and she could not see through the sifting columns of people. *Body of Christ, amen; Body of Christ, amen.* She checked every lamb, her eyes sweeping over the manger where the Infant now lay. *Body of Christ, amen.* She stepped forward, lifted her tongue. *Body of Christ. Amen.* The dog and the pup were gone.

DECEMBER 1992

The dog devoured the pork Jude dropped in a trail to lure her, then picked up the pup and followed Jude at a careful distance to a spot outside the entrance, where he emptied the rest of the food from the bag. Two hours later, when Mass was finished, she was in the same place, the pup lying beside her. She stood and stared as they passed.

"Clever dog," Francis told Jude.

They didn't notice her following them until they turned to wish the neighbors good night and caught the movement beneath a clump of bougainvillea. She kept to the side of the road, carrying the pup by the scruff of its neck, stopping when they stopped. Essie clutched Jude's arm.

"There's a dog there, stalking us!"

"It's only going the same way we are."

When they reached their gate, the dog deposited the pup by the post and watched as they made their way across the compound. Essie pointed.

"It's still here."

"Is it?" Francis spoke airily. "It must be hungry. I'll find a bone, or some such—"

"Don't be ridiculous! Once you feed it, it'll never go. Off with you! Shoo!" She flapped her hands. The dog remained fully attentive, as though Essie's performance required an appreciative audience, then shifted her hind legs to sit. "Son, run it off. People are coming to see us; what if it attacks?"

"It's not even barking," said Francis. "Let the poor dog be."

The family stayed up deep into the night, with friends stopping by, a holiday toast, a phone call to the States, where the grandchildren were preparing for Christmas Eve. Jude checked the road from the balcony, but even with holiday lights, it was too dark to see.

In the morning, the pup was dead, and Jude did not have the heart to drive off the mother. He let her into the compound and fed her at the back of the garden.

The next three days were an endless wheel of "You must be joking" and "Absolutely not" and "I put my foot down."

"I also have a foot," Francis reminded his wife. He hardly knew what he meant by it, only that he was not a child to be forbidden things.

"But what kind of dog is this? A pi-dog, filthy."

When he proposed to give it a bath, Essie screwed up her face and spoke of disease. So Francis carried the dog into the bathroom, scrubbed her vigorously, and bundled her into a towel to take to the vet. He came back by auto a few hours later, the dog subdued in his lap, the bill settled in cash.

"But how much did you spend?" Essie demanded. "And what are you doing with my good towel?"

Francis warned her not to shout: the dog had been given several shots and must rest.

"Not in my house!"

"This is *my* house," said Francis, an impulse he regretted, since it prompted Essie to recall her arrival as a young bride. It was a story she always began by recounting the death of her father when she was six. Then came the slow unraveling of her mother and her reliance on an uncle, who stepped in as a guardian and persuaded Essie to agree to a match. She sighed when she speculated that her own father might have advised her differently.

"You see, Frank was engaged for a short time to a neighborhood girl, and this Almeida clan felt loyal to her—"

"Mum, we know all this. Who are you talking to?" Jude was deep inside his newspaper.

"Son, what can you know? You never heard how these people spoke to me."

Francis had no particular memory of his parents troubling Essie, only the usual friction: occasional slights, quarrels as thin as sandpaper. But he saw no point in saying so. He preferred to hold his memories sacred, not drag them into arguments. Instead, he wandered onto the balcony, coaxing the dog to follow, and spread a thick towel beside the narrow bed pulled alongside the railing. This was used for seating, but occasionally Francis napped there for the breeze, the way he and his brother used to when they were children. The dog circled heavily, then dropped onto the towel.

"Not my towel, Frank! Actually, I had just turned down a boy . . ." Francis knew this story so well he could recite it. The fellow intended to live on his father's plantation outside Coimbatore, which had seemed too remote to Essie. "No proper parish. Only a small family chapel," she lamented with the air of one who had missed her chance. "What could I do? Later, he built his own textile mill and became *very* wealthy . . ."

The drone of her voice was soothing. "Rest," Francis advised the dog, sliding a cushion beneath her chin. He lay down himself, remembering the days when he and his brother pretended the balcony bed was a machan, high in a tree, from where they kept watch for tigers. The dog groaned softly, and Francis put a hand on her head to settle her. Soon both were asleep.

The late-afternoon air was thin, not cool, but Francis woke wishing for a blanket. He sat up, rubbing his face, and it was only when he saw the crumpled towel that he realized the dog was missing. Jude was nowhere to be found. No noise from the kitchen; Essie and the girl must be resting. Francis did not want to call the dog and rouse the household; one small misstep and Essie might actually cast the poor dog out. Besides, she did not yet have a name.

"Here, girl," he tried softly. Then he heard a voice in the garden and looked over the railing. Essie was sitting directly beneath him on the veranda steps, only her feet in view. The dog was sniffing the edge of the lawn.

"Not in the flower beds," Essie warned. "Stay this side." The dog circled back, a show of obedience that Essie acknowledged with a grunt. "You are no breed at all," she informed the dog sternly. More circling, more sniffing. When the dog finally squatted, Francis expected another scolding, but instead Essie got up. He watched from the back as she walked through the garden and bent down with a bag to pick up the mess. "Come on, you," she told the dog. Before she turned to face the balcony, Francis withdrew into the house.

Seven years after Anna's death—far longer than his parents had hoped—Francis agreed to a meeting. The girl was traveling with a family his cousins knew. She was the right age, educated. Her uncle sent her on a holiday to Bombay, and they met at a wedding, then again at a cousin's house. They spoke first about Shakespeare, then London, a place Easter—Essie—hoped to visit someday. She did not have Anna's charm. There was nothing like the ease he felt with Agnes. But he sensed a taut intelligence beneath her conversation, which might mean they'd be suited. And he no longer thought of marriage as he once had. It had become a matter of manhood, the way a man should move forward from what he could not have to what he could. He wanted not to be alone. He wanted to learn to love a wife. He wanted children. He told his parents he was willing.

Once the proposal was settled, Essie and her uncle came to his father's house, the place where she would soon live. She sat on the edge of a chair and looked at the walls and floors and shelves. She asked about the books. At the end of the meeting, she held out her hand and her uncle laughed. "Come, my girl!"

She flushed. Francis stepped forward to kiss her on both cheeks and then she turned so quickly that her hair swirled behind her. She'd worn it loose, swept back with a clip. This style, he later understood, would not have been her choice. But he still remembered the sight of her as she walked away, the thick fall of her hair brushing against her kameez. A strand caught in the mirror work and Francis wanted to reach out and free it. He did not obey the impulse. But for the first time he told himself, "That is my wife."

22

JANUARY 1993

The mob violence abated, but Bombay flared with tension. Muslims turned out in large numbers for Friday-evening calls to prayer, which had always rung through the city but were suddenly branded a menace. Hindu separatists conducted massive demonstrations, blocking roads with angry crowds who demanded an end to roadside namaaz. In some cases, the speeches led to looting and arson.

Then on January 1, the newspaper *Saamana*, launched and edited by Bal Thackeray, published an open call for Hindu aggression. This was swiftly answered by individual attacks: a knifing, an assault with iron rods, a Muslim hutment set aflame. Shiv Sena activists marched on the police station in Jogeshwari, demanding security for Hindus, before some of the protestors broke away to attack a mosque.

The murder of four Mathadi workers on January 5 lit another fuse. Their union called for a bandh, and speakers who assumed the killers were Muslim urged Hindus to take up arms and defend themselves. Meanwhile, Hindu separatists posed as government officials to survey neighborhoods, or used voting registers to determine with chilling accuracy which residences belonged to Muslims.

On January 6, a month exactly after the riots began, the forecast was for smoke. This was a measure of haze, when smoke from open fires and the exhaust from motorways hung in the still air. But it seemed to Dominic that something was tightening over the city, keeping all the foul air in: a skin that needed puncturing. He thought of the forked lightning icon that he used to watch for on the weather forecast and imagined the sky cracked in half: the fissure, the relief.

That night, a city official and a police constable with a sword led a Hindu attack on Muslims in Mahim. A second wave of riots began. Choppers, iron bars, petrol bombs, kerosene cans, acid bulbs, bottles, swords, and broken tube lights all served as weapons. Neighbors were beaten or burned alive. Fires blazed throughout the city. Army columns were deployed. Fifteen days later, when the riots finally subsided, nine hundred were dead and more than two thousand injured.

A few more skirmishes, a few last police firings, then all thinned to rumors. The police and military remained on alert. Each day without violence was laid over the next, a paper-thin balm across the gaping wounds of the city.

The quiet was precarious. All over the city, the first thing anyone registered about anyone else was: *Hindu or Muslim.* Even in Santa Clara, nameplates came down from some of the flat buildings. Ladies from the cottages hesitated before getting into taxis. Shopkeepers kept a tense eye on anyone lingering. Flora made do with what Varuna fishermen caught for Pomfret. Farooq did not resume his morning deliveries until mid-February. The bakery windows had been smashed, he told Dominic. Broken glass and animal dung covered the floors, and one of his ovens had been damaged by a homemade explosive. The oven saved them, Farooq said. If the explosive had not been contained, if the fire had spread, the whole place would have burned.

For weeks, fears of a next attack clouded the streets.

Then, on March 12, at 1:30 p.m., a bomb exploded in the basement car park of the Bombay Stock Exchange, killing dozens outright while survivors fled beneath a rain of debris and shards of glass. Within minutes, another detonated a few kilometers to the north at Katha Bazaar. Then a petrol pump in Dadar, next to Shiv Sena Bhavan. For the next few hours, serial blasts rocked the city: the Air India building at Nariman Point, Fishermen's Colony in Mahim, Century Bazaar in Worli, Zaveri Bazaar in South Bombay, the Plaza Cinema in Dadar, the Hotel Centaur in Juhu, Sahar International Airport, and the airport Hotel Centaur—twelve sites in all.

Celia was in the sewing room at Holy Name when a suitcase detonated in a guest room on the eighteenth floor of the Hotel Castelo. Moments later, a homemade explosive shattered a lobby window. The glass splintered with a loud crack that set people screaming, but the window remained in its frame, and the only injury was to a woman who fell while running away. Investigators determined that the lobby grenade was thrown from outside and must have landed near the window by accident; a strike on the entrance would have caused far greater damage. But there were no good witnesses. The doorman was assisting guests, and the woman with a lemonade cart just down the hill saw nothing out of the ordinary. The day was hot. People were buying lemonade.

Twenty minutes later, when school was dismissed, the road was crowded with parents rushing to fetch their children, shoppers hurrying from markets, worshippers fleeing churches, and people streaming down Seaview Hill, away from the blast site.

Celia broke away from her friends to see the hotel for herself. Creek Road was a maelstrom of sirens and voices, but as she climbed, the chatter fell away. People making their way down moved swiftly, their faces set, their voices low if they spoke at all. A few vendors outside the basilica were moving their carts away from the gates. An autorick buzzed past, carrying only luggage.

When she reached the hotel, what she saw from the road did not seem so bad. The broken window looked menacing, the revolving doors had stilled, but the building itself was intact. It was only when Celia walked farther uphill and looked around to the sea-facing side that she realized the extent of the damage. A long jagged wound ripped through the back wing. She could see the insides of rooms, some destroyed, some oddly composed: a vase that still held flowers, a fully made bed on a torn bit of floor. Debris had fallen to the cliff below, and in one of the lower rooms, where the windows were blasted away, a curtain made a limp attempt at surrender. Before Celia could climb the rocks for a better view, a stone-faced police officer waved her off.

It was off-season, a quiet week. In mid-afternoon, none of the guests had been inside the wing that suffered the most damage. A half-dozen policemen in khaki clustered near the entrance, taking no discernible action. A crew of three bellmen had set up a ladder and were gingerly taping the cracked glass to hold it in place. Hotel guests had been evacuated, although a few lingered across the road. "I've paid for the full night," said one man loudly. The reception staff huddled together, their uniforms powdered with dust, and did not bother to answer. Another guest asked a police officer if she could retrieve her handbag. The lemonade woman was talking to a reporter.

It later came to light that the attacks had been coordinated by the Muslim leaders of an organized-crime syndicate. Some conspirators framed it as an act of retribution for aggression against Muslims during the riots. Most of the explosives were packed into cars and motor scooters, abandoned in strategic locations, and detonated by remote control. In the hotels, the terrorists booked rooms in which to leave suitcase bombs. In Mahim, they threw hand grenades straight into crowds from the windows of a Maruti van. At the airport, they lobbed grenades over the perimeter wall. In Worli, a former taxi driver staged a jeep stuffed with explosives near the passport office. The blast leveled shops and blew apart a double-decker bus, full of passengers.

The explosives entered the city through secret cavities in cars and scooters, the sort of spy plot Dominic enjoyed in television programs. Celia overheard him talking with his friends about how the terrorists smuggled arms and ammunition into India by water, and she remembered the cars they saw from Land's End, parked along the great curve of the bay, their headlights seeking out invaders.

In fact, the explosives and weapons shipments were found to have landed south of the city before being transported into Bombay. Customs officials, landing agents, and policemen who smoothed their passage were convicted on a range of charges, from bribery to conspiracy.

The Famous Five Scotch a Bomb Scheme, Celia imagined as she walked back down the hill, and pictured the children hailing an autorick to follow the bad guys. "Hurry!" urged Julian, and the driver jockeyed in and out of lanes until they came to a dead stop, trapped by the clogged roads. Then the bombers crossed Mahim Creek, into the part of the city where autoricks were not permitted, and the children jumped out—"Oh, I say!"—while Timmy barked and barked and the villains escaped.

Still, the thought of Timmy reminded Celia to stop at the Almeida compound on the way home. She had visited several times during the riots, to deliver meals when Mrs. Almeida could not risk the shops and to check on the dog from the crèche. The dog was three or four, according to the vet, undernourished but gaining nicely. The Almeidas called her Bella, and Celia gave her a bright-green collar.

"That's the color of my house at school," Celia explained to Mr. Almeida, and he said, "Why not? You saved her." Then he called to the girl for some boiled chicken and let Celia feed the dog, piece by piece.

On the day of the bombing, Celia found Mr. Almeida in the garden. He seemed confused, looking for his daughter, although Marian was not visiting.

"Did you hear about the hotel?" she asked.

"No, she's not at the hotel. I brought her back from that place!"

Just then, Bella came pelting through the yard and jumped up to lick Celia's hands, barking joyously. "See, she knows you," he told Celia, and whatever uncertainty he felt about Marian seemed to dissipate, as though swept away by the brush of the dog's tail. When Bella sat on Celia's feet to keep her from leaving, Mr. Almeida began to laugh.

"Crazy girl," he said, meaning the dog, or Celia, or even his daughter, gone so far and missing all the fun.

SEPTEMBER 1994

Francis Almeida was seventy-five years old, a man of property and a pillar of his community, on the day when he was reduced to stealing his own bicycle. This indignity was entirely the fault of his wife, who made such a fuss after one small tumble that it was pointless to reason with her.

Still, he tried. "It's nothing," he told her the morning after his fall. "In a day or two, I won't feel it."

"What day or two?" Essie said. "You think you'll spring up like a jack-in-the-box? You'll be hobbling for weeks."

He tossed his hand but did not take up the argument. It was true that he was subject to occasional aches, but he kept fit for a man of his age. A twisted ankle would heal.

"And you were totally disoriented. You had no idea what was happening."

"Of course I know what's happening!"

At times, perhaps, he skimmed over brief lapses in memory. He could not always remember the name of the dog or the place he had left his billfold. "Here, girl," he called, and the dog understood. But these were natural aberrations, which Francis attributed to the distractions of his household. There were tradesmen after sales, priests after donations, contractors after his father's house, fishwives with baskets. The ancient watchman threw open the gate to an endless stream of people. The telephone sounded a fresh alarm whenever the tax accountant had a question or the salon rescheduled. Even his daughter, Marian, once a girl of good sense, rang constantly from the States, as if overseas calls were coins to cast into a fountain. Sometimes he listened while his wife chatted with her about nothing at all—the accountant's query, the hair appointment. "We are fine," he assured Marian when he took the phone. "You can call once a week to see. Save your money."

Jude was always bringing friends around, or girls he didn't marry. Francis had begun to feel an irritated concern for them, getting older with each party, a hectic tinge to their spinster laughs. And Essie could talk and talk and never stop.

". . . a miracle if the ankle heals. And you may need scans if you've knocked your head."

"What scans?" It was a minor accident. He struck something—the roads were in a constant state of upheaval—and his wheel caught the edge of the curb. He only felt a little jarred; in another moment he could have stood by himself.

Instead, arms encircled him. "Come, Uncle. Slowly." He was led to a seat at an outdoor café. He'd twisted an ankle, making it difficult to walk, but otherwise he was fine. The cycle was fine. No schoolgirls needed medical attention. He would have hailed an auto, except he could not find his billfold. He was patting his pockets when one of the men asked for his phone number. Francis was so annoyed that he had no cash—in his other trousers, no doubt—that the number went right out of his head. He had to sip some water before he could remember.

Eventually, Jude appeared, asking what happened. Francis shook his head. He watched his son angle the bicycle into the car and thank the people at the café. "Come, Dad, let's go." Home, Francis thought, but they drove to a clinic. For forty minutes, they waited to see a doctor so young he did not even recognize Professor Almeida.

"Anyway," he reminded Essie, "Doctor says I'm fine."

"And will Doctor look after you when you break your neck? You have no idea what you put me through, Frank. I pick up the phone and a stranger tells me you're flat in the road. Thank

God, Jude was here; otherwise, what? I should carry your cycle on my back?"

It was Essie's way to ask useless questions; Francis saw no reason to answer them. He turned his attention to breakfast. Chapatis were kept warm beneath a plastic cover, but he did not have the appetite he once had. Now he preferred a lighter start: yogurt, a little sliced fruit. Their regular girl, who lived in, had gone back to her village on holiday, so Essie had brought in a local woman. She was constantly dropping things but cultivated a prison-guard demeanor to ward off admonishments. Once, Francis saw her use a piece of chipped ceramic to clean her fingernails while Essie scolded her.

Essie paused as the woman poured his tea, a nerve-racking operation.

"I've spoken to Jude," she said when the woman withdrew. "And he agrees with me—"

"Where *is* Jude?" Francis wondered.

"He's gone to a locksmith. Frank, you can't go cycling all over town, crashing in the road. This is the end."

Francis's hand began to shake. He put down his teacup.

"End of what? I've had one small fall."

"Not one. Remember? You hit that child Celia and gashed your head."

"What nonsense! *She* ran into *me*."

They heard a crash in the kitchen and Essie shook her head. "There, you see!" she said. "All this shouting. You've set her off."

Francis refused to look at her. A man sits down to breakfast. At his own table, in his own house. His servant has fingers of stone; somehow he is to blame. His wife lectures him about bicycles; what does she know about bicycles? His son doesn't even turn up to ambush him, only sneaks away on mysterious errands to locksmiths. All before a sip of tea.

He lifted his cup again and tried to anchor it against his lip, but he wasn't quick enough.

"Look at you. Your hands are shaking! You're banging cups all over the table. How can you manage a cycle?"

Francis pushed back his chair, upsetting his tea.

"Frank!"

He knew what came next: a big show of mopping up, a speech about cleaning up behind him. Let her say her piece to the teaspoons. Let the servant fling every last dish to the floor. Bad ankle or no, he was off to the gymkhana.

He stayed long past his custom, taking lunch in the club and forgoing his afternoon sleep to doze in a cane chair on the veranda. The light had changed when he felt a hand on his arm. "Sir. Sir." Francis struggled to sit upright. Had he missed a lecture? Whose office was this? "There is a function this evening, sir. We are setting up this side. Will you come to the restaurant?"

The feeling was like lifting a foot to the rung of a ladder and finding nothing there. Francis put his hands to his arms against a slight breeze. Fans were suspended from the ceiling in a soldierly row, thin cables trembling with the motion of the blades.

"You'd like tea, sir?"

He was at the gymkhana. How long had he slept? He permitted the boy to help him rise.

He felt more himself after a chat with Roddy D'Souza, who used to work in Finance at the university. They thought of playing a few hands, but Bertie never turned up. Eventually, Roddy drifted home while Francis lingered, the sky fevered with sunset, until a band struck up on the far side of the property. Wedding guests came pouring in as he limped home.

Jude was on the veranda with a glass of beer, scratching the dog's belly. He was clearly waiting to break the news, but Francis walked around the compound to see for himself: his bicycle, trussed to the railing of the back stairs, near the damp patch where the servant dumped wash water from the kitchen balcony.

"I thought it was safest here. Or we could clean out the shed and keep it inside."

Francis made his way to the front steps, which began in the garden.

"Dad—"

He shook off Jude's hand as though it were a stinging insect and held fast to the railing.

"It doesn't have to be forever."

It was heavy work to reach the landing. Each step meant a sharp twinge when weight fell on his ankle. He wished Jude would leave him decently to his private struggles, but Francis could feel him hovering a step or two behind, like an anxious thought.

"I'll talk to Mum once your ankle's better. You gave her a fright, you know."

Francis grunted. He had no interest in a report on the softer feelings of his wife.

"And me as well, Dad. And Marian. We all want you to be safe."

Oho, he thought, they've called Marian. But he swallowed this further betrayal without a sound. A single word would be a concession. They did not wish to consult him in matters central to his own interests; very well, let them stumble through the days without further contribution from him.

Upstairs, Essie waited to receive him with an unusually conciliatory air.

"Frank," she began.

His ankle throbbed, but dignity insisted that he walk straight past.

Her voice rose. "Don't be foolish, Frank. It's for your own good."

Francis recognized the phrase from the days when she'd meted out punishments to the children. He'd avoided such scenes, though occasionally, when the fault was grievous enough, he was conscripted into service with his belt.

Once, he had led his son—one of the boys, but which?—to the back of the compound over nothing more than a skipped tutorial. There had been a cricket match in the road, a fresh shirt ruined. Francis made a point of not interfering with every twist and turn of managing the children, but when the boy stared up at him—he remembered! it was Simon!—he felt a thrill of recognition. Here was his son, looking so much like Francis's own brother; here were just the sort of tricks he and Peter got up to as boys. Essie would not hesitate to bring down a government over a stained collar, but Francis knew better. Whatever maternal claims she made about schoolwork or washing, she had no idea what boys owed each other in a cricket match. He motioned to Simon to come close, told him to cry out in case his mother was listening, and struck the leather against a tree.

Francis expected relief or gratitude. Instead, the boy looked first at the tree and then at his father with an incredulous frown. It was an expression Francis could not place, fully outside any resemblance to him or his brother, and he felt the whole business sliding away from him. He smacked the tree again; again Simon didn't make a sound. This was the trouble with children: one brief foothold, then a cavernous drop into unknowing. In future, he resolved to leave them to Essie. But first he jabbed Simon in the arm, eliciting a single soft cry.

"Louder," hissed Francis.

Suddenly, the boy caught on. "Go," he whispered, with a wild, electric grin. For ten more strokes against the tree, his loud pained cries rang through the garden. Then he pinched himself to bring tears to his eyes, and in perfect accord they mounted the stairs.

Simon had left India in 1974. He'd gone to England on a student visa for graduate study, but he dropped out during his first year and took a job with a backpackers' travel agency. For the next few years, he led budget tours through Africa and the Middle East, traveling to places where Essie's pleading letters did not seem to find him. Eventually, he graduated to specialized tours of Greece and Italy, sending postcards from the Forum, the Acropolis, the Spanish Steps. This was not a career Francis could have imagined, but he was pleased by the echo of his own interest in history and searched the book stalls for a map of classical Athens to hang beside his historical maps of Bombay. Finally came a partnership in a tour company that Simon helped launch. Essie kept his postcards in an album to show visitors. "He's running his own business," she enjoyed telling people.

Simon rarely came home, but Francis trusted the strength of their alliance. Jude was led by his mother; Marian let distance make her overly cautious; but Simon would never have taken his bicycle.

This thought carried Francis through the next few days, housebound with his ankle. He refused to speak to Essie or Jude beyond small matters of necessity. He did not go to the phone when Marian called. He sat with his chair angled toward the television, from which position he could also see the kitchen doorway. "Hie, you there!" he called whenever the servant filled her washtub. "Other side! Not on my cycle!"

After a week of such treatment, Francis decided he'd endured enough. He waited for the house to empty, with only the dog to follow him from room to room, gazing up at him as though she could read his intent. "Clever girl," he said. She was happiest morning and night, when all the people of her house were safely gathered in one room. She was a dog of such intelligence and loyalty that he was thinking of breeding her for the pups. "*Breeding* her," Essie repeated to Marian. "A *street* dog. He's gone absolutely bonkers."

The padlock key was not on the hook with others of the household, or on the telephone table beneath old bills, or in Essie's wardrobe, which he was irritated to find open. Despite his warnings, she kept her gold in a flimsy case on a back shelf. She might as well tie her bangles to the compound gate, he thought, singing out to thieves like wind chimes.

Thieves were a perennial concern. Francis knew he could be forgetful, but the incidences of missing money were so frequent that he'd begun to look beyond his own inattention. Was he being robbed? He had assessed his property and concluded that a thief who got past the gate would not encounter much resistance. Jude kept the downstairs locked while he was at work, but Francis and Essie occupied the upper story, and the door was only locked late at night, when Essie retired, as though she considered herself a match for intruders. All day long, anyone might venture upstairs: delivery-wallahs, chance visitors, and workers contracted by his wife, usually the cheapest sort, who cast appraising eyes over the furnishings. The constant come-and-go had accustomed the dog to strangers. She was still protective, but she alone could not save them, and Francis dreaded an encounter in which she might be kicked. So he hid any cash that he drew from his pension. He poked bills into shoes and clothing, pushed a stack to the bottom of the bed, stashed a packet in the biscuit tin where he kept old letters.

But his own security measures could not help him find the key. He considered trying to break the lock, but he balked at the idea of standing in his garden, hammering at a padlock for all the neighbors to hear. Instead, he sought out the servant. She was meant to be preparing the midday meal, but he found her on her hands and knees, picking pieces of mutton from an overturned pot of food. The dog pushed eagerly past Francis's legs.

"No broken glass? Let her have it, then," he said.

She grunted as she sat back on her heels. "That was your meal."

"I am eating out today." He made a point of sounding authoritative. "Listen, where is the key to that lock down there? I'm taking my bicycle."

He expected resistance. But, clearly, the impoundment held no interest for her; she pointed to a nail just inside the back balcony, where the shed key hung from a string. The shed was where they kept garden tools, spare roof tiles, and other odds and ends, including a slab of marble Essie had salvaged but hadn't actually *used*. This would be the fate of his bicycle, Francis realized, if he didn't intercede. It would sit forgotten like the drift of shawls Essie kept for the moths, decades' worth of stockpiled gifts from the States, biscuits she saved until they went bad.

The padlock key was on the same string, in plain sight. The dog feasted on mutton while Francis retrieved it. Good, thought Francis. A treat would ease his departure. The day gathered itself into form.

He picked up his camera from the front table, and when he couldn't find the case, he tucked it inside a cloth shopping bag. While changing into outdoor shoes, he happened upon the biscuit tin at the bottom of his closet—a piece of luck, since he had not been entirely sure where he'd last put it. He counted out five thousand rupees with the sense that he had returned to himself: a man with money in his pocket and the independence to go where he liked. First a trip to the locksmith: high time he took charge of his belongings. Then a ride through the neighborhood with a fresh roll of film and the list of landmarks he meant to photograph: certain long-standing shops, the basilica, the Castelo ruins. He'd jotted down several on the back of a brochure he'd written long ago for the Hotel Castelo, a history piece they used to keep in their lobby. It bothered Francis that he had never taken a photo of the hotel in its heyday, the way he remembered it best. If he had time, he'd make a quick stop at the liquor store before meeting the boys at the gymkhana.

The padlock took only a minute. The watchman performed a small obligatory fuss, waving his hands as though Essie were there to see him, so Francis opened the gate himself. He felt a twinge in his ankle when he mounted the cycle, a brief instability, but soon his legs moved evenly. The watchman called after him—thin, useless cries—as Francis rode down St. Hilary Road. It was just before noon, the air bright with the babble of schoolchildren. He took no chances. He pedaled away from the market.

———

By evening, Francis had not returned. No one had seen him at the gymkhana. He had not visited any friends. Essie scolded the watchman until he seemed more bandy-legged than ever beneath the weight of her shouting. Finally, she dispatched him to his post and took up her own on the telephone with Marian. Jude kept bullying her to leave the line open, but once he'd gone, the strain of the empty house was too much to bear.

"Babe, you see what I live with? I'm sitting all alone here. No, I've sent the servant home. What help can she be? She fed our lunch to the dog."

Friends fanned out, but still no word an hour past sunset. Did the bicycle have lights? Marian wondered, which irritated Essie. How could she keep track of every little thing?

"No one considers my own health. You forget I will be seventy this Easter."

Essie was born on Easter Sunday in 1925, and celebrated her birthday on each subsequent Easter, no matter when it fell. She had informed her children well in advance that she expected them all home for the celebration of her seventieth. "You should buy your tickets now, otherwise the fares will go up," she added, but Marian did not even acknowledge this reminder.

"Would he go to church?"

Essie was compelled to remind her daughter of certain home truths about her father.

"Maybe to Uncle Peter's grave? Or what about the university?"

People are looking, Essie reminded her. Neighbors and friends, since all but one of her children had flown. "And what can you do from so far?"

Marian rang off, then called again ten minutes later to report that she had contacted the history department. He hadn't turned up at his old office. "I won't tie up the line, Mum, but I'm sitting by the phone—"

"He won't call, babe, I'm telling you!"

Jude might check in, Marian insisted, or any of the search party. "Please, Mum. Leave the line open."

Essie put down the receiver and sat, considering, before dialing her cousin in Bangalore.

Outside, darkness settled. The city redrew itself with different colors and outlines, different bits hidden. Roads coursed like rivers, orange in one direction, white in another, and the sky was paved with billboards. Lit windows rendered skyscrapers in mosaic. On the main roads of Santa Clara, shops looked fresh and vivid, roused from their afternoon torpor. People flowed through the huge arched doors of the churches, leaving shoes heaped on the steps outside.

A few blocks from St. Hilary Road, headlights fell on the broad back of a woman whose sari looped between her legs in the Koli style. She kept to the center of the pavement, neither yielding nor quickening her pace, so the car was forced to crawl behind her as she turned onto Varuna Road, which took them through the heart of the fishing village.

Suddenly, there were dozens of people. Children on balconies pushed their feet through railings and shouted down greetings. A cyclist slid so close to the open window that the driver pulled in his elbow to let him pass. The driver was not Jude—Jude was at the train station—but friends and neighbors were involved in the search. Linus had taken Professor Almeida's history class.

The car nosed past a tiny dry-goods store that opened like a cupboard, past an undertaker, a butcher, and the shrine to Our Lady of Navigators. Linus checked the men outside the barber shop, some freshly groomed, others waiting for a cut. He scanned the courtyard of the Church of the Loaves and Fishes, still crisscrossed with people lighting candles for the night. Then he started up Seaview Hill.

He drove past stalls as bright as lanterns as the car approached the basilica. Two beggars came the moment he stopped: a boy to pass a rag across the windshield and a girl to cup her hands at the window. *Please, ba, please.* Linus looked past them to the creamy marble courtyard. No sign of the professor. He would make a quick sweep of Land's End and turn around. When the car moved ahead, the children jumped aside to escape its motion.

A girl in a Holy Name uniform walked down as he drove up. She glanced back over her shoulder: hoping a boy would follow, guessed Linus. She looked the age for it, sixteen or seventeen. Farther on, he saw another half-dozen girls in the same uniform, laughing and weaving in a loose circle as they passed the abandoned hulk of the Hotel Castelo, where no one would think to go, except that no place was ever empty, no one ever quite alone in this city.

A year and a half after explosions and looting had closed its doors, the hotel still squatted, directly between the sea and the proposed site of its sleek new successor, awaiting the settlement of multiple lawsuits. Linus glanced at the cracked windows, remembering the dances, the swim parties, his first imported vodka, and saw a thin figure huddled against the boarded-up doors.

He wasn't sure until he pulled the car so close that the man shrank from the glare of the lights. Of course he knew Professor Almeida by sight—the whole neighborhood knew him—but it didn't seem right to see him alone at this dark and shattered place. What Linus remembered best was the man at the lectern. In those days, Professor Almeida had a rich voice, the voice of a storyteller, and once he shocked the entire assemblage by singing. Linus had never forgotten it.

Marian tried calling back for over an hour, but the line was engaged. Did that mean a hospital? When she finally thought to call Jude on his mobile, he had just heard from Linus. Five minutes later, she reached her mother at home.

"Still nothing, babe—"

But Marian cut her off. Found. Very well. Though it wasn't right that Marian knew before Essie herself had been told. Everything was out of whack: Frank hailed as a returning hero, and Marian delivering the news from half a world away, somehow vexed that Essie had dared to call her cousin.

"They are family. You think I should keep them in the dark? That is your father's game, not mine."

Then Marian expected her to carry messages. "Give Daddy my love. Tell Jude I'll call soon."

Later, Linus reported that Francis seemed confused but allowed himself to be led to the car.

"I'm looking for someone. I don't know, she may be here—"

"At the hotel, Professor? You want to find her at the hotel?"

The word seemed to agitate him.

"No, no! I brought her back from that place. I have her suitcase—where's it gone?" He turned to look behind him.

"Come, we'll find it. It may be home already."

"I took her home!"

"Then come. Come. We'll see her there."

They were both in the car when Francis looked back toward the Castelo and frowned. But this time he spoke mildly. "The lounge is closed, is it? I was meeting a friend, but I may have got the days crossed. We were meant to have a drink." On Creek Road, he asked if they could stop at the photo shop; he must drop off a roll of film. He began searching his pockets for the canister, until Lionel suggested they might go the following day; the shops were all closing.

When they reached St. Hilary Road, Jude and Linus conducted a hushed conference in the garden and decided not to mention the hotel to Essie. They steered him past her without stopping.

"But where did you disappear, Frank!"

Linus waved them on and sat with Essie in the front room. "Now you see one small peep of what I go through," she told him.

Jude helped his father to bed. Francis lay back quietly, one hand on the dog, who jumped up beside him. When he was settled, Jude brought the phone so he could speak to Marian.

"Where are you, my girl?" he asked, as though she were the one who'd gone missing.

With Nicole and Tara, she said. She hoped the mention of his granddaughters might anchor him, but he seemed to mistake them for school friends, as if she were a student at university again, sleeping over in town.

"And you're staying the night? Come early tomorrow."

The bicycle was gone, and whatever else he'd carried with him. There was nothing more they could uncover about what had happened. At any rate, Jude must go, he told Marian; people were stopping by, making sure all was well. He'd left Mum in the front room with a few neighbors and a schoolgirl from Holy Name.

"That kid from Varuna. I don't know how she heard."

"Mum's been making calls," Marian said wearily. But there was no point trying to manage her mother from across the globe. The crisis was over: let Mum play town crier if it made her feel better. She wondered if anyone had contacted Simon, but she didn't want to keep Jude any longer.

She hung up the phone. It was late morning her time, the same bright hour in her part of the world as when her father had disappeared, as though that whole clutch of time had been pinched away. She wondered if this was how life felt to him, time folding in on itself, days pleated away, distant years suddenly touching. When she called the next morning, he was still asleep. Her mother narrated the whole saga as though Marian remembered nothing at all. "I know that, Mum—" she tried to say, but Essie snapped that Marian could not possibly understand her ordeal from so far away. Then she picked up her story just where she had left it.

"Are you coming soon?" Francis asked his daughter when she called again that evening. "I'll ride to the station to meet you . . ." As though she were a girl still, ready to perch on the back of his bicycle for the short trip home.

24

SEPTEMBER 1994

A young man in his prime coasts past on a bicycle. It would make a good start to a film, thought Anthony, the hero cruising downhill while girls turn their heads to watch him flash past. He could see the scene: a sudden downpour, a stranded girl, a drenched scarf pulled over her head. And suddenly the hero on a bicycle, offering a ride. Her hesitation would last a few song beats, overcome by a clap of thunder. Then they'd wheel through the city: plumes of laughter through puddles, a splashy dance in the lanes. He began to hum "My Name Is Anthony Gonsalves," the song that gave him his name. He had just turned seventeen; he wished he could wave to beautiful girls as he rode past. Instead, he ticked past teenagers with mobiles, tourists with backpacks, and two men in cheap shirts who glanced up and away.

At first, he worried about a clamor behind him, maybe a hurled stone, but he kept his face low until he'd gone a sufficient distance from where the bicycle had waited to be his. He'd found it propped against a tree, no lock in a city of thieves, no one about but an old man looking through the cracked windows of the Hotel Castelo. One glimpse from behind—thin legs, thin hair—and Anthony reckoned the bicycle couldn't be his. Was such a man even fit to ride? The hotel had been closed for over a year, yet he was peering through the shattered glass like a madman.

While Anthony watched, the old man disappeared around the corner of the building. For a snatch of time, their patch of road was empty. He laid his fingertips on the handlebar, waiting to see if the old man returned. If he did not, if the bicycle—a good, working bicycle—had been abandoned, then Anthony could claim it the same way he might pick up a dropped coin or a piece of fruit that had fallen from a cart. The wheel of luck, turning toward him.

It took only seconds: a leg thrown over the side, his feet finding the pedals. A shopping bag was bundled in the bin over the rear wheel, but Anthony didn't bother to remove it. He took a last glance over his shoulder and pushed off hard. Nobody was in sight when he started down the hill.

He knew how to ride. As a boy, he'd ferried paint from his father's business on the shop's three-wheeler, until that was stolen and they bought a cargo trike with a motor. But the slope was steep. He kept tight hold of the hand brakes, arced wide on the curves. Just before the basilica, a family stretched across the road, holding hands like a row of paper dolls. In a film, Anthony would have scattered them in a show of lively spirits; the father would throw a comic fist, the little brother would grin with envy. In life, he veered to avoid them, and the mother shouted, "Slow down, you hooligan!"

He would have made it if not for the schoolgirls. But he came rocketing around the curve, saw the church rising high and the bright blur of flower stalls, and suddenly girls surrounded him, in every direction. Anthony braked; the cycle lurched; girls shrieked; and he spilled onto the road.

He heard laughter and sat up, a hand to his hip, where he'd come down hard. A dozen or so girls were closing in. Upperschool, near his own age. He could feel their gazes heaped upon him like so many accusations.

"What's the matter with you? You could have killed us!" a girl with glasses scolded.

Anthony wrenched himself up and righted the cycle. It was a clumsy escape, twisting through the mass of girls. "Get out, go," he muttered, propelling himself with his feet on the road.

They backed away, leaving a ragged channel. But before he could nose through, one called, "Wait!"

Anthony felt a jolt worse than the fall—had he been found out?—and then she held out a cloth bag. "You dropped this." She made it sound like a joke, another way to laugh at him. He barely registered plaited hair and a round face before looking at the bag.

He didn't want whatever it was. He had the sick feeling that came whenever his luck went bad, a vertiginous sense that the world was tipping him slowly off its surface. But the bag had fallen from the bicycle; he couldn't leave it as though it didn't belong to him. He imagined a family's shopping inside—onions or potatoes—and was suddenly assailed by the idea that he had stolen something. What would his parents say when he turned up with a bicycle? For a moment, it was hard to hear over the thrumming in his ears, as if he were underwater and voices above the surface could not reach him. It seemed possible he would drown.

The bag dangled from the girl's outstretched hand. Anthony wanted only to tuck it away and be done with it, but he took it so abruptly that she flinched.

"Jackass!" called the girl with the glasses, and Anthony bore down on the pedals to hurtle through new waves of jeering and laughter.

He got around the next bend, out of sight, and then his hands began to shake so badly that he had to pull aside. The slope behind him blocked the view to the south, so he looked toward the Promenade and forced himself to concentrate on how small everything below seemed: people and boats, buildings and roads. It was low tide, the rocks strewn with washing. Even saris spread to full length looked like scraps at the foot of the sea. He tried to shrink the schoolgirls to their proper size: a blur of fuss and chatter, faces he could not recall. An old man picking his way around the Hotel Castelo was nothing to him. An old cloth bag and a secondhand bicycle did not signify.

The trembling stopped, though Anthony still felt unsteady. This sick, hollow feeling would last an hour or more, he knew; that was always the way with these episodes. But he was exposed on this hillside, where the schoolgirls—or anyone who wanted to give him trouble—might appear at any moment. As soon as he could manage it, he rode down and headed inland.

He revived a little when he reached the main road. Nothing had happened, not really: nothing that could be traced back to Anthony. He was a boy like any other on a bicycle. And any fool who left his things unattended stood to lose them. But traffic was heavy, horns blared, cars panted exhaust, and his breathing still felt ragged. When he saw a policeman at the junction ahead, he turned off to circle a small park.

Slowly, the cycle revealed itself to him. Hand brakes. Rubber grips. Chrome bell, which Anthony glanced at warily, as though it might ring of its own accord. He left the circuit of the park but kept to quiet streets near the college until he happened upon a café with outdoor tables. He sank into a chair, the bicycle propped beside him.

He had money in his pocket for tea, money for a roll from the bakery case. When the guy serving him looked over, Anthony could raise his fingers to agree, yes, another cup, without worrying about the cost. Even the price of a good bicycle might have been absorbed without much difficulty.

It was true that, once, such an acquisition would have been significant. A cycle, or the loss of one, would have had a different weight. But the Correia Paint Shop was thriving. Anthony's future was settled; he had gone directly into the family business after passing his exams for lower secondary, and it would all pass to him when his father's heart gave out entirely. His sister, Pinky, worked in a salon—not out of necessity, but as a way to avoid the computer accounting class their father kept pushing. "Then she also can come to the business," he argued.

Anthony and Pinky had experienced a rare moment of perfect accord in thinking Pinky was better off in the salon.

"She needs all the help she can get," said Anthony.

"I can't work with buffoons," said Pinky.

So she carried on painting nails. This was viewed by their father as a temporary irritation, by Anthony as the logical outcome of a childhood devoted to fruitless beauty treatments, and by their mother as a way to bring Pinky into contact with wedding parties of a better class.

Regardless: There was money enough for her to marry well. Money enough for Anthony to drift into the business and decide it was no more boring than school. Money enough to dissuade him from considering other options, beyond the vague belief that he was meant for something better than paint and stains. Money enough so that Anthony could pursue meetings with contractors—most real, a few invented—all over Santa Clara, which gave him time away from the constraints of his family. Money enough for the computer accounting courses that Anthony, like Pinky, managed to sidestep, explaining that he preferred to learn on the job while he continued to keep the books with pencil and paper. Money enough to omit cash payments from the records occasionally, when his pockets were empty and he felt in need of a quiet reward for his loyalty. Money enough for a bicycle, if he wanted one. Did he? He looked across the café table at the cycle, as though at an unlikely companion.

He sipped tea until his stomach settled. After a time, he took the cloth bag from the cycle's bin and reached inside to find two keys, one on a string; a padlock; a tourist brochure; and a camera.

The brochure was nothing. The lock and keys went straight back into the bag. But the camera was a bewildering discovery. He had imagined groceries, dry goods, a shoe in need of repair. Instead, an object of real value. Anthony had never considered owning a camera before. If photos were required, his mother marched them to a photo stand in their village. When he began to feel queasy again, he reminded himself that he had never sought a camera; he had simply benefited from an accident of fate. And who wanders away from his belongings? A man ready to discard them. Anyone with money for a bicycle and camera could afford another bicycle and camera.

He paid the bill and set off with fresh energy. The bicycle

could take him all over the city. The possibilities of a camera seemed limitless. He had accepted his place in the family business without argument, but he chafed at the tedium of paint and more paint, meetings and more meetings. His father's slowpoke expansion into sealants and caulks wearied Anthony to the point of collapse. He envisioned something bigger—he was not sure precisely what—but something that would put him inside one of the luxury flats they painted. Perhaps this was the first step.

When he rang the bell to scatter a pack of schoolboys, it was if the cycle had found its voice. He rang it again in sharp, coarse blasts as he approached three women dressed in salwar kameez, the colors of ice cream. Mango and Berry looked away, but Pistachio giggled. Here was a woman, a real woman, different from his sister and the schoolgirls on the hill. Anthony slowed down—"Hallo, beauty, hallo, hallo"—before flashing past.

He coasted by the Church of the Loaves and Fishes just as the bells began to chime, deep and sonorous. Bright chains of flowers were strung along the gate, and when a marigold blossom drifted onto his arm, Anthony put it into his pocket. Already, he felt different, slipping beyond the small, tight plans his parents were forever weaving. He had found—he had been granted—a bicycle. In this spirit, it was easy to believe in signs, easy to believe his course was sanctified. God put the cycle and camera in his path. A bit of roadside fruit, an unexpected windfall.

Anthony pedaled more freely, each new belief begetting another. He believed that past injustices were payment for this sudden bounty. He believed his life was tipping toward fulfillment. He believed the world, which had given him so little, was making reparation at last.

The cycle made quick work of the distance home. At the end of the Promenade, Anthony headed toward the point of a snub-nosed promontory. On the inland side, the city flooded right up to the road: larger buildings crowding behind the low houses of the fisherfolk. In front, jostling for space like eager children, were small establishments from an earlier generation. To the west were rocks and water. An occasional eruption of huts composed the lower reaches of the Koliwada.

Anthony pulled aside at the edge of a ragged field, where as a boy he had hidden a glider. A sign promised new construction, its depiction of sleek beachfront luxury fading after months of municipal tangles. Anthony's father had quietly avoided the Koli efforts to block the developer, certain he would get the paint contract if the building went through. Meanwhile, the lot became an encampment for temporary workers who raised shacks and settled in. There were children, chickens, people churning in and out—a whirling come-and-go with abrupt, almost mysterious, instances of stillness. A goat tied to the signpost chewed on its own rope. A mound of rubbish smoldered.

Anthony lobbed the lock and keys into the smoking rubbish. He tore the brochure into pieces, then kicked them near the embers, where they were certain to burn. After a moment's thought, he put the camera into his pocket and threw the bag away as well. He wanted no discourse with the previous owner, no hint of who that might have been. But the camera was easily tucked away, an acquisition he need not mention to his family. He would put it aside until he found some use for it.

The sun broke like a yolk against a low bank of clouds, spilling tender color across the bay. The road narrowed to a track, and clotheslines formed a broken canopy overhead. Old women sat outside, sifting rice or tending babies, chatting in broad voices. Children kept a ball aloft with whatever they could use as a paddle: a hand, a notebook, a piece of driftwood. There was just enough room to ride.

Bicycles were common; many villagers had them. But not Anthony. Children ran after him. The old folks looked up as if a breeze had come. Anthony greeted them without stopping. Through a gap at the end of the lane, he saw the sea, glassy in the evening light.

This was the way he arrived at his parents' doorstep, still astride the cycle. He'd spent the ride planning what to say: he'd been saving for some time, he'd made a deal with a man too old to ride. The words he settled on sounded clear and unassailable, easy to believe.

SEPTEMBER 1994

Some girls jumped and squealed, making the most of a reckless boy in their midst, but Celia only watched as the bicycle lurched through the Holy Name Choir. She couldn't see the boy's face—he was hunched over the handlebars—but she had a brief impression of flopping hair and startled eyes before he took off. He pushed the bag he snatched from her into the rear bin. Idiot, thought Celia. He didn't even thank her.

But this was not a day to bother about boys. The choir had been invited to sing at the Feast of the Nativity of Mary, its members released from class to spend the afternoon rehearsing at the basilica. It was pleasant to mill about on the flank of the hill, composing nonsense lyrics to the hymns while they waited to file into the cool nave.

Two hours later, Sister Ignatius let them go, though she was still agitated over certain ragged passages. Celia and her friends bought ice creams and spent the afternoon at Land's End, talking and laughing, until the sun dropped to a low bank of clouds. Light spilled along the horizon like a seam of lava, then cooled to pale mineral blues. The girls began slapping mosquitoes.

It was dark when Celia left them, later than she should have stayed, but not so late that her mother would worry. Still, her pace quickened as she approached the Hotel Castelo. She did not mind the deserted building by daylight, when it looked only dingy and broken, but at night its bulk seemed sinister, blotting out so much sea and sky.

The Castelo was just ahead when she heard a voice coming out of the darkness, as thin as a bit of raw wire, singing.

Celia jerked back. Her mother's warnings about lonely corners and girls who were interfered with came back to her. But the voice itself, once she listened properly, did not seem menacing. Cheerful, quavering, thrown up against the great dark mass of the Castelo. Madman, her mother would warn, but Celia stepped closer. The wide steps had a pale luster, and she could make out a dark figure sitting on one side.

He kept singing—something in English, though Celia could not catch all the words. She moved closer. "Oh no, the rowboat," she heard, then a small laugh she thought she recognized. He began to sing again, and Celia rushed toward him, because what could have happened: Why should he be here, washed up against these steps?

"Mr. Almeida?"

He broke off in the middle of a lyric. "Yes. Hallo." He spoke naturally, as if they were meeting at his own front gate.

"It's Celia. Celia D'Mello, from Varuna."

He laughed again, rueful. "I've had so many students . . ."

This happened sometimes when she visited, a little fogginess. "I'm friends with Bella, you remember?" She knew he would place her at once if the dog were here to greet her. "My mother sends fish sometimes. And you took my photo with your camera."

Still he looked blank. It was difficult to explain who they were to each other, she realized. And she did not like to remind him of the accident, as though, years later, he might take up his scolding. "You called me wild elephant," she said instead.

"Acha, acha," he agreed. "Listen, my girl, have you got the time? I'm waiting for this place to open." He tossed a hand toward the ruined lobby. "Every evening, it used to be. I don't know what they're doing now. Remodel, what."

"It's shut down. People say they won't fix it up again."

"Rubbish. How can they leave it in this state?"

"Mr. Almeida, is someone coming to get you?"

"I must get inside, actually . . . I don't know where she is . . ." He looked up and down the road, twisting back to see the doors plastered with warnings. Celia was startled when his gaze came to her. "But what's this, my girl? You need a ride? I have my cycle." He smiled kindly. "You go to Holy Name. My daughter also; do you know her there?"

"No—I mean, yes, but . . ." Celia was not certain what to do. Stay? Find help? It was clear he was not right. "Mr. Almeida, why don't you walk down with me? We can go together."

"No, thank you. I'm waiting for someone. She'll come anytime."

She tried once more. "We can go find Bella. You know, your dog, Bella?"

Again he refused.

Celia hesitated. "Then I'll go by your house and tell them you're here."

"No need, my girl. I have my cycle. I keep my own agenda."

"You'll wait here?"

"Yes, yes. I'm waiting."

He seemed fine for the time being, humming as she left, but she saw no trace of his bicycle. She passed a car on its way up, and for a moment, blinded by the headlights, she wondered if Mr. Almeida could have been telling the truth about a meeting. But as the car passed, she saw it was a man driving, not a woman.

She hurried down the hill, making plans. She would stop at the café to let her father know she was going to alert Mrs. Almeida. Her mother would be more sympathetic—she had a soft spot for the family—but her father was closer and would grasp what was happening quickly. Her mother would delay her with a hundred questions or try to send food.

She spent an hour at the house on St. Hilary Road. When she got home, she answered what she could: Yes, Mr. Almeida was back; no, nobody knew why he'd gone; yes, he seemed to recognize her in his confused way; no, she didn't see his bicycle. That must have been lost already.

    The bicycle was never found. Nothing could be recovered in such a city, nothing lost without being claimed, nothing discarded without being consumed in Bombay's vast gullet. People found uses for mildewed books, torn plastic, empty rice sacks, broken radios, cut sections of pipes. Ragpickers swarmed through the streets collecting scraps, and waste buyers gave one rupee apiece for empty oil cans from hotel kitchens. A schoolgirl lost a ribbon and a beggar tied back her hair. Women gutted fish and cats hissed over viscera. Shipping containers of recyclables from the West were hauled to the vast slum of Dharavi, where workers sat cross-legged and sorted mountains of plastic, their fingers quick as flies. They washed the plastic in steaming vats, crushed it in machines of their own making, and spread the granules on the rooftops to dry: a glittering mosaic of what would soon be reconstituted. The bazaars were filled with what was cast off or stolen: compasses that didn't know north, keys without locks, bolts of all sizes. All parts of a chicken were eaten. After Eid, mounds of sheep and goat hides stiffened in the sun, awaiting transport to the tanneries to be stitched into wallets, belts, and satchels. Vultures fed on bodies in the Towers of Silence, though there were no longer enough birds to pick the bones clean. Wild pigs rooted in drifts of garbage, strewn across the beach like banks of seaweed. Goats filled their bellies with newspaper and fruit rinds; crows lined their nests with shreds of cotton. Ambassador cars were resurrected, time without end. Mochis reinforced the worn soles of shoes with rubber from old tires. The earth from leveled hills filled creeks and marshlands, whole neighborhoods reclaimed from the sea. The city began swallowing the sky, buildings stacked higher and higher, balconies jutting out like footholds, aerials bristling on rooftops. Houses were churned into flat buildings, sinks and rails and tiles preserved. Shacks sprang up beneath flyovers, no hint of shelter wasted. Construction workers swept the sandy grit from gravel mounds to make cement. The trickle of a brackish creek served for washing. A prostitute emptied her bank account to ward off a police beating. A customs official pocketed cash to wave electronics into the country. Cows munched placidly along roadsides, their dung collected to burn as fuel. Fires burned in slums and on beaches, in oil barrels, refineries, rubbish piles, and holy lamps. The smoke did not dissipate but lingered around the neck of the city, a filmy dupatta in mauves, yellows, grays. In such a city, no one bothered to look for the bicycle. It had surely been swallowed whole.

Two days later, the Holy Name Choir performed their songs to conclude the morning service at Our Lady, Star of the Sea. It was the first day of the fair celebrating the birth of Mary, and the hillside was transformed by crowds and festival stalls. Flora could not close Pomfret on such a busy day, but she left Inez to cope while she ran up to hear the choir. At the end, she watched people pour out of the basilica until Celia emerged with a pack of friends. Flora hailed her for a quick hug and warned her to take care in crowds. She had already said goodbye when she turned back to press a few rupees into her hand: "Oh, and, Celu, light a candle for poor Mr. Almeida."

Celia sifted out of the throng to head back uphill and find her friends. When she saw a small black cylinder in the dust, she picked it up and pried off the gray plastic top. Inside, she realized, was a roll of film. She had never handled film before; she could not tell if it had been used or not. But she liked the feel of the container. She liked imagining what she might keep inside it: earrings, coins, folded notes. So she resealed it—she would ask someone about film later—and tucked it into her shoulder bag. Her mother disapproved of its thin leather strap; she said a thief would make quick work of it. But Celia wasn't worried. The choir sang well, her mother was proud, her friends were waiting. The only sign of trouble was a small boy wailing over his toppled ice cream. He was quickly supplied with his mother's but seemed bewildered and skeptical, dismayed by how fast events were moving—ice creams come and gone, tears streaking his face, his people urging him to eat quick-quick, before the new one melted. Finally, more wretched than joyful, he took a taste. His family clapped and cheered, and he looked at their smiling faces until at last he smiled also.

    A few paces behind them, a street dog applied himself to what had fallen, swallowing the cone in large bites, licking at the vanilla mound in the dust, leaving only a sticky pool for the ants and flies. By nightfall, even that was gone.

MAY 1996

The first time Anthony met a girl in a lodge was nothing he planned, more of an accident. And even after he agreed to the arrangement, his mind was so full of an argument with his father that he was shocked to open the door and find an actual girl sitting on the bed. He blinked, trying to take her in, and she smirked when she told him to close the door.

Her forehead was broad and her skin pitted on one cheek. She wore a sari with a sleeveless blouse: no special outfit, nothing revealing or immodest. She seemed close to his age. "One shot only," she reminded Anthony, and he touched the small foil packet in his pocket.

He'd blundered into the lodge after leaving his parents' house for good—or possibly for good; possibly until his father issued a proper apology. His departure, also, was unplanned, the result of a sudden rupture after Anthony caught his father with a cigarette. Smoking had long been forbidden for the whole family, one of the many limitations imposed by his father's weak heart. His father frequently slumped into coughing fits over secondhand smoke, sending Anthony to tell their neighbors to put out their cigarettes. These were moments of high mortification, made worse by his father's fanning the air.

His father stamped out the cigarette without meeting Anthony's gaze. "This is nothing to do with you."

"Nothing to do with me?"

"You sound like a parrot," his father grumbled, before reminding Anthony that it was not a son's place to question his father.

"We do everything to take care of you, and this is how you take care of yourself? Sneaking behind our backs?"

"What backs am I behind? I'm in my own shop."

They argued until both were shouting and his father's face boiled with color and his mother came rushing to scold Anthony—did he want his father's heart to give out entirely?

"He is well enough to smoke, then he is well enough to shout," Anthony flung back. It sickened him to see his mother bending over the mound of his father, begging him to take a little water. There was one last round of shouting while Anthony jerked open desk drawers—his father sputtering, his mother warning this would be the end—until Anthony found the pack, silencing them both. Then he thrust it into his pocket and left the shop. He was finished with tiptoeing around his father's moods, finished with his mother's dire predictions, finished with paint. He filled a bag with clothes, emptied the cash from his mother's purse, and remembered at the last minute to bring his camera. He'd obtained it with his bicycle a couple of years before but seldom found occasion to use it.

For a time, he cycled aimlessly through neighborhoods he knew, trying to decide what to make of this unsettling new freedom. He sat at an outdoor café and ate a dosa, which his mother didn't favor and never served. He smoked two of his father's cigarettes, choking on the bitter truth that he was eighteen and had never tried one before. He spent an hour in an air-conditioned camera shop, pretending to look at lenses, before buying a roll of film. Eventually, he ate again at a fish-fry in Varuna. The prawn potato chops were better than his mother's.

The afternoon tapered toward dusk. Anthony locked the cycle outside a cinema and bundled his belongings into his lap to watch a film and forget his troubles. Two hours later, he exited the theater into darkness, a disorienting shift. Night had fallen, and all his bright adventuring gave way to unease. He blamed his father for making it impossible to stay safely at home. Originally, he had planned to ride along the Queen's Necklace and enjoy the city's nightlife. He'd imagined girls in ice-cream shops, film scouts who could point to a boy and change his life. But the horns and headlights jangled his nerves, and he worried he would be a target for thieves.

"Yes, a room," the lodge manager agreed when Anthony wheeled his bicycle into a place near the station. "Full night? For you and your friend?" He raised his eyebrows at the cycle, but Anthony only nodded.

"Girl or no?"

Anthony was not prepared for such a question. He'd been thinking only of the flight from his family, the safety of a room. And whenever he imagined girls, they were the kind he could meet on his own. The manager spoke briskly through his confusion.

"These girls are high-class, very clean."

Anthony felt a wave of embarrassment when he said yes. But it would have been just as embarrassing to refuse, as though he were still a child. He had never been with a girl fully before, a barrier that was beginning to bother him, in case there were things he ought to know. The girls he'd linked up with in the village were too careful, too intent on marriage, though one agreed to use her hand until her engagement put an end to that arrangement.

It was a little extra for a girl, but not as much as Anthony feared. When the manager gave him a small foil packet, he was bewildered enough to consult the label.

"I'll find a nice one for you."

Was she nice? A little solid. Plump arms, round shoulders.

"What is your name?"

"Candy."

Was she sweet? Anthony wished she had smiled or softened when he entered. She must have been relieved to see a clean-cut boy instead of the men she usually encountered. He'd seen those men, the kind who went looking. They lingered on the bridge over the railway tracks, where sex workers waited in pairs or trios. Anthony had stopped before, just to see. The women were neither as ashamed nor as vulgar as he expected. Some could have been mistaken for mothers or aunts, middle-aged and faded; some were young, with bright mouths and painted eyes. Sometimes one went straight to a man and named a price. Whenever Anthony saw that, he tried to imagine being the man. Would he say yes or no?

Would he have chosen Candy? She was not as bold as the girls at the station. She did not seem like the girls he had heard about in Kamathipura, either, a place for men with no scruples. She was in a respectable place. And Anthony was nothing like those men. He had not come looking for her. She was a chance dropped into his path, a bit of roadside fruit, an unexpected windfall. When she said, "Come on, then," he complied.

―――

Within forty minutes, she was gone. Anthony wanted to ask where she slept but did not like to appear unknowledgeable. Already, she'd scolded him for not producing the condom quickly enough. Anthony wondered if that meant he could go again, but she twisted her mouth when he tried to resume and batted his hand away. The gesture seemed coarse and immodest, a reminder of the wrong things. He wanted to think she was thankful for the respite he provided—a man who was decent, a man who appreciated. When he turned away, annoyed, she laughed and ran her foot along his leg. He could feel how rough the heel was.

"What's your name, then?"

"Anthony."

"Like the film?" She sang, "My name is Anthony Gonsalves . . ."

Was she making fun? He was tempted to explain that he'd been named for that film, but it did not seem the right moment to tell stories about his mother—an Amitabh Bachchan fan who begged her husband to take her to *Amar Akbar Anthony* a week before her due date. When he refused, she marched off on her own, and that very night she felt the first pains. It was as if Amitabh himself had named Anthony: that was what she always told him. Sometimes Anthony imagined running into him outside a fancy beach club. Anthony would reveal that he was a namesake, and Amitabh would be so charmed that he would take on the role of patron.

Candy began to hum "Humko Tumse Ho Gaya Hai Pyar," and Anthony touched her on the hip. She did not shift out of reach. "I'm feeling lazy," she told him, and let him do what he liked for a few minutes more. When she sat up, he realized that, in the full half-hour they'd spent together, she had only undone one hook of her sari blouse. He wished he had asked her to remove it altogether, but already she was reaching around to refasten it.

The bed was good enough but strange, in a strange room. Anthony was used to village life, everyone connected. Darkness in an unfamiliar place felt darker, and it was disquieting to hear noises—a door, a voice, a cry—without knowing their sources. He slept badly. In the middle of the night, he removed the camera from his bag and stashed it beneath his pillow.

The light was halfhearted when Anthony woke. Some indeterminate worry curdled in his stomach. In the corridor, there was no sign of Candy or any other girls, but the manager occupied the same position as the evening before, though in a different shirt. He wished Anthony good morning, and this commonplace exchange began to calm Anthony's nerves. He tried to focus on the encouraging thought that at last, a few months shy of his nineteenth birthday, he was a man of real experience. He walked to the train station and ate steamed idlis from a stall, watching early commuters stream past. For a moment he had the wild idea to dance through them, singing, "My name is Anthony Gonsalves."

But the song also brought an image of his mother, heavily pregnant and pushing her belly through the crowd as she made her way alone to the cinema. One day she might be alone again, widowed and forlorn, like the mother in the film before she was reunited with her sons.

Anthony felt the power of that image rearrange everything. He was the only son of his family—and what good was Pinky to anyone? His father might shout, his heart might fail; all the more reason for Anthony to remain at his mother's side. He would be a hero, like Amitabh.

"Another night?" the manager asked when he returned to the lodge.

Anthony said he must go.

The manager tipped his head. "Come back whenever you like. New girls all the time."

Anthony did not intend to return. But he kept an eye out for Candy the next time he was in the area. It was pleasant to imagine that she might catch sight of him and suggest another meeting.

Eventually, he decided to stop in. It was mid-afternoon, a slip of time nobody would miss.

That day, it was Candy again. But afterward the girls were different. Anthony preferred to think of them all as Candy, though he kept the name to himself, a private currency. Once, by accident, he said it aloud. The girl that day was too skinny, all tendons and cords. Her mouth curled, less a smile than a twist of wry cunning.

"Yes, Candy," she agreed. "I am *Candy*. Sweet, sweet."

"Stop talking," he had to tell her.

The next time, Anthony asked the manager if Candy was about.

The manager handed him a condom in a single wrapped square, their ritual. Anthony preferred not to use them, although he accepted them as a function of courtesy. "That one is gone," he said.

Where did such girls go? Anthony wondered. They could never marry—used goods.

An hour here, an hour there. Usually less. It was easy to believe that his visits to the lodge made no real mark on his life. He never spent the night again; that was the point. He reconciled with his parents, submitted to family life, succumbed to paint. Those afternoons, maybe eight or ten, felt like wisps of vapor drifting beyond the stone pillars of his obligations.

Once, only once, he took a photo. He had begun to use the camera for promotional materials, taking shots of freshly painted boats and buildings, and he happened to have it with him one afternoon while he waited out a downpour in the lodge. The girl was clowning, her face behind her hands, her blouse tossed aside. It did not occur to him until later that he would have to turn over the film to be developed. The realization brought such keen embarrassment—such resentment over the injustice of what the photo-shop people would think—that he removed the film at once (a brand-new roll), and threw it away.

Still, he could not quite recover from the wrong ideas people would have about him if such a picture existed. He had never seen a connection between his actual life and these interludes, as insubstantial as dreams, but the act of taking a photo proposed something more tangible, something he could not reconcile with the person he understood himself to be: smart without wasting his life in study, successful without being a grind, loyal without being a pushover, deserving without having to chase cheap pleasures.

He had no desire to go back, he realized when he was next in the neighborhood. Abruptly, almost mysteriously, the lodge lost its allure, and Anthony pedaled away with a surge of abhorrence for the whole business. In hindsight, all his blurry notions and vague preferences resolved to new clarity: he did not belong in such places. The manager must have seen that at once but sensed Anthony was susceptible, reeling from the break with his family. Once those lines were crossed, Anthony gave in to natural curiosity, like any boy reluctant to push too hard with girls of his acquaintance. Eventually, the lodge trapped him in its powerful orbit.

It was exhilarating to find he'd spun free. The feeling was like coasting downhill on his bicycle, effortless motion, while certain memories fell behind. He need never think of them again. He felt different, stronger, ready for a future with a girl of his choosing. He imagined soft looks, a happy smile. That was the photo he would take and keep, a photo of his wife.

JANUARY 1997

At the end of his third contract with Diamond Cruise Lines, Jerome returned home for two months of mandated shore leave to the news that if he agreed—*See, son, the photos and letters, see what a friendly girl she looks*—he would propose that week to a girl called Alma from a nearby Koliwada.

Celia, who had studied the photographs for a fortnight before Jerome arrived, wondered what he would make of them. There were two, one of the girl's face and one of her standing on the Promenade, the Arabian Sea behind her, her arms carefully at her sides, the photo snapped in the moment just after she had been instructed to smile but before the smile had taken full hold. Her expression appealed to Jerome—a shy, budding look. He liked the soft curves of her shoulders and hips; she was plump in a way that seemed modest. He spent his days cleaning up after passengers who lounged near pools or the jogging track; he'd had his fill of ladies who kept themselves bikini-thin.

He also liked the close-up. She had a clean, fresh face that made him realize he was exhausted by glossy mouths and sunset eyes—not only the rich ladies but the women on the staff, who were encouraged by the cruise line to cultivate a professional demeanor through the tasteful application of makeup. He was a deck steward, and the women he knew best were waitresses and room stewardesses, working twelve-, thirteen-, fourteen-hour days, foundation painted over their fatigue, the recommended shades of lipstick fading. There was something in this girl's face that made him feel awake. He read the letters. He listened to his mother's comments about a good temperament. He asked for his father's impressions of the family. Within hours of hearing her name, he agreed to meet. Ten days later, they were engaged.

"What do you think?" he asked Celia, who found she felt shy with her own brother. She liked Alma when the families met. But Jerome with a wife? It made a stranger of him.

"Just wait and see," Flora told Celia. "This will set the ball rolling. You'll be next." She took the view that good fortune brought more good fortune, God's face turned to shine upon her family.

In fact, the family had fielded two inquiries for Celia already.

The first came from a widower in Varuna, whom Dominic refused at once: too old, he and Flora agreed. Celia was never told, so that she would not feel self-conscious when she saw him in the lane.

The second was brokered by their neighbor Esperanza, who thought Celia might suit her cousin's son. He was a lorry driver, in and out of Mumbai. At the very least, the prospect of a wife might lure him to the village and give Esperanza a chance to recommend her teenaged son as his apprentice.

Once a photo of Celia was favorably received, Esperanza arranged a day for the families to meet.

In the weeks running up to this introduction, Celia and Evangeline joked about the kind of boy Esperanza would produce. But whenever Celia actually tried to imagine him, her mind tumbled to her classmate's older brother, the boy she used to kiss. She'd felt perfectly calm when he left for university the year before. He had no part in this, her real life, in which she might marry the boy she was about to meet.

But she could not yet picture this new boy. It was the event that interested her more, the rite of passage. She was eighteen, a girl who liked things to happen, and most of her village friends had gone through such initiations already. Meanwhile, Flora took to reciting Celia's good points, rehearsing ways to tip the conversation in advantageous directions, and Celia relished hearing what a strong child she had been; what a bright student, hard worker, excellent cook. She could sew beautifully; she could read in English. When Flora took her to order a new choli, Inez pushed for a lower cut, and Flora shocked Celia by saying, "Such a good figure, why not make the most of it?" They laughed so loudly they annoyed the tailor. Suddenly, it seemed easier to be the daughter her mother wanted.

The night before the meeting, Flora opened a bottle of jasmine shampoo from Jerome's cruise line, which she had set aside for a special occasion. Celia washed her hair; then Flora brushed it a hundred strokes on each side. Celia closed her eyes, trying to concentrate on the rhythmic tugs and think of nothing else. It was unsettling to realize she must meet the boy and his family the next day, as if the whole point had been these days of preparation with her mother.

It ought to have worked, Esperanza lamented later. But everyone so picky-choosy, what could she do? The girl was not bad, her cousin agreed, but so much schooling for what? Her son preferred a simpler type. By the time Esperanza delivered this news, Dominic had decided he would reject a proposal. The boy showed no warmth, he told Flora. And it was not a clean life for drivers in those roadside dhabas. When Flora seemed puzzled, he said, "The lodges will have girls."

To Celia, he only said too much separation could cause problems in marriage. "You don't mind, do you? You didn't like this boy?"

What Celia took from the meeting was a feeling of being suspended, as though she were not quite herself but some older girl playing a part one moment, and a child about to burst into giggles the next. The boy spoke almost exclusively of driving. "I drive a Tata semi-forward," he told them. "For three years I was second driver; now I am the one who can take an apprentice." Bottlenecks, checkpoints, hairpin turns. The penalties for overweight loads. Celia listened, feeling rattled. Lorries were everywhere, and what did she know about them? What did she know about anything? The boy had a mustache and wavy hair, in which nested his aviator glasses. His jaw jutted out enough to make him look petulant. She struggled to imagine that anything about him would become familiar.

No, she didn't mind, she told her parents. She was relieved nothing came of it. But she wondered how her father squared his ideas about couples living apart with his son's engagement. In six weeks, Jerome would need to fly to the next port.

"So no point waiting," Flora said joyously. A long engagement was never favorable. At once, the family was swept into a storm of planning for the wedding.

In all the fuss, it was possible to lose sight of Jerome himself. But Celia noticed he used new phrases, whistled new tunes, announced new opinions. He luxuriated in sleeping late. He preferred beer to shandy. The Jerome she knew slipped in and out of the frame of the Jerome he had become, and it was difficult to know what to attribute to his engagement and what to his time abroad. Perhaps marriage would simply be another country he had seen and she had not.

The banns were read, the priests approved, and a month later, Celia drew a bright cotton sari between her legs for the pani celebration, two nights before the wedding.

Friends came thronging to the beach as soon as the village brass band begin to play: nine older men and a couple of sons. Jerome bent his head for Flora's blessing, then Inez's; then all the women of the lane came, one by one, to dab coconut milk on his forehead and wish him health and prosperity. He tried to dash out of range when he saw Celia and Evangeline with buckets, but his friends held his arms while his sisters doused him and the whole party cheered.

Working wells were hard to come by, so the band led a parade to Varuna Road, where Dominic triumphantly raised a garden hose attached to a spigot near Our Lady of Navigators. Jerome grinned through his ritual cleansing, waiting until he was completely drenched to try to grab the hose himself. Children shrieked and scattered, and Celia could not stop laughing at the sight of him, streaming with water and tossing his head like a good-natured bullock. There he was, happy and dripping and hapless and sweet, the brother she had always known. She joined the water fight, darting in and out of the spray until she stumbled backward into someone on a bicycle.

A boy. He was stopped at least, the cycle unmoving, his feet on the ground. He caught her with one hand, her head at his shoulder, his fingers tight on her arm. For a moment he was too shocked to release her. He saw a laughing girl, drops of water like beads in her hair; she saw the line of his jaw, clean-shaven.

"Sorry—" she gasped. His hand opened; she twisted back into the party.

He had pulled aside when he heard the band, intending to stay only a moment while the parade passed, then lingering when he found himself surrounded by the party. It was nothing he hadn't seen a hundred times before. These celebrations followed the same pattern: the old ladies with their jokes about wedding nights, the men tossing back shots, the churning tunes of the Koli bands. But there was a happy feel to the evening, a sense that the blessings the villagers offered this marriage would hold. After a little time, he asked an old man the name of the family. The fellow was leaning against a wall but hoisted himself up to point out the fish-fry restaurant down the road. "That is theirs," he said. "And a café also. That is the brother; there are the sisters."

The boy, who had eaten at Pomfret before, watched a little longer before taking out his camera to snap a photo of the young people near the shrine. The flash startled everyone. Then he edged his cycle past the courtyard to ride home.

Jerome was back at sea and Alma settled with the D'Mellos when the cyclist's family contacted Dominic. By the time a meeting was arranged, Celia had forgotten their encounter. Still, she felt a jolt of confused recognition when she saw the boy's face, and because she could not place him, the sensation took on an unexpected charge, the thrill of something to come instead of something that had already happened. She forgot her mother's instructions to smile at his parents and smiled at the boy instead.

The father was a big man, lolling back like a soft yellow

cloud. He spoke while the mother listened with narrowed eyes. They were fisherfolk but had moved into the paint business at just the right moment. It was the kind of future most Koli families dreamed about, the kind that hardly ever happened. Flora liked their good fortune: luck made more luck. Dominic liked the stability of an established business and the sense that the families were of similar means, neither stooping to the other.

"You enjoy the work?" he asked the boy directly.

"It's good work," he said, sounding surprised. "My parents are running the shop. Fishermen already come to us for boats, so I sell to builders. That is house paint, not marine. I go all over Santa Clara, Mahim, Juhu—wherever they are putting up flats."

Dominic approved of the boy's carving out something for himself. He mentioned that Celia might also be interested in pursuing a line of her own—with a sewing machine, she would earn well—and the boy's mother nodded. She had a sharp face, Flora thought, the kind of woman who was working sums behind whatever smiles she conjured. But the father seemed good-tempered, no sign of anything amiss, and the boy was promising: handsome in a poky way, clearly interested in Celia, and a good head of hair, which Flora appreciated.

"No medical issues in our line," his mother announced, before asking about any history of trouble in the family way.

Nothing, Flora assured them. No problems for mothers or children. Celia had been a nice fat baby, brimming with health.

"No bad habits?" the mother pressed. "No cigarettes?"

Dominic looked mildly puzzled: smoking was common. But no, he'd never had a taste for it. Certainly, Celia did not.

"I have a question." The boy turned to Celia with an attitude of such expectancy that it seemed to swell between them.

Celia glanced at her father, who gave her a coaxing smile. She could feel her mother sit straight up beside her.

"Do you know how to ride a bicycle?"

This was so unexpected that Celia nearly laughed. "Yes!"

Flora put a hand on her knee; better not to sound so amused.

"Good." He kept his gaze on Celia but spoke more generally. "I cycle for work, but I also like to ride in the evenings."

"Very nice," said Flora.

"I come all the way here sometimes." The boy stared so intently that Celia felt the pull of it and lowered her gaze. She was neither afraid nor modest, just seized by the impulse to defer what would pass between them, to let these first moments last a little longer.

Later, she would not be certain if he seemed kind or unkind. Kind, she decided, by which she meant he took an interest. She and Evangeline had to consult the photograph his family had provided to examine his face—Evangeline because she had gone upstairs with Inez during the meeting, and Celia because she could not recall his features clearly. She found the snapshot disappointing. What she remembered was the feel of him looking at her as if he would never see enough, her sense that such intensity could be the start of love.

There would be time to discover it, she realized. Her parents were pleased: a Koli family, steady earnings, the right age. No brothers; the business would go straight to him. One sister—a friend for Celia.

"And you could like this boy," said Flora again and again, almost a question.

Anthony Correia, thought Celia, testing the name. She told her mother yes.

APRIL 1997

After their first meeting came a handful of others, carefully chaperoned. Before they spent any time alone together, Celia knew Anthony liked films with happy endings. He liked Havmor ice cream from the stand on Creek. He liked to keep his bicycle in sight, even when it was locked. He assigned fanciful paint names to colors that caught his eye: mango lassi, eastern dusk, serpent green. He pretended not to hear when Pinky needled him, but waited for his chance to strike back. He did not care much for the shop, but he liked exploring the surrounding neighborhoods, striking deals with contractors that his father would not seek out.

"He never goes with you?" Celia asked.

"He stays in the shop." Anthony's voice was shut tight, like a door with a latch. Then he seemed to crack it open. "For him, the shop is everything. I don't like to be in one place every day, so I thought of training for something different. But my mother said this is our business, coming to you." He shrugged, rueful—the kind of son, Celia saw, who did not like to disappoint his mother. She liked this hint of sweetness. "If I'm in the shop with my father, we clash. So I thought we can sell house paint if we go meet contractors."

Celia could see their future as if it were a scene in a film: this boy, her husband, off to make a new deal while she sat at her sewing machine. Would he kiss her goodbye? Yes, she decided, and felt a charge run through her.

He was tapping his fingers against his leg, so close that it should have been a simple matter to brush her hand against his. But to move those few inches would be to push through a great force field, as if desire mounted its own barriers.

After a few weeks, her parents decided that Celia might go on a private outing with Anthony. But only if she didn't mind; would she feel comfortable?

"That's fine," said Celia. "When?" and hoped they could not hear her impatience. She felt both that she was meant to be excited and meant not to be.

Flora squeezed her daughter's shoulder. Lately, there were moments of unexpected affection, her mother holding on to some piece of her the same way she'd clung to Jerome before he went to sea. "Good girl."

At a separate meeting of the parents, it was determined that the D'Mello family would forgo the traditional bride price, still sometimes offered to Koli families whose daughters would perform the tasks of a fishwife, since Celia would not be obliged to bring those skills to her husband's home.

Flora's eyes filled with tears. Her daughter would not wait up at night worrying about a squall, or rise in darkness to take her basket down to the docks. Flora thought of her own days in the market. It was like living inside a tunnel, so dense with noise and smells that the great caged fans could hardly stir the air. The hours were waterlogged, three customers at once, then a blank stretch when she'd have to lift her voice and call. The floor slick with blood, seawater, melting ice, and fluid released from the organs of fish. There were constant jokes and chatter and squabbling, and the tiled walls batted every sound into a great echoing din. Women with shopping bags eddied back and forth, and from the next chamber, through an archway carved with angels, came a chaos of squawks, peeps, crows, and quacks from the cages of the poultry sellers. Sometimes Flora had one of her babies in a basket beside her, before they could toddle and must be left back at the village with other women, far from the wet, the blood, the knives, the flies, the hunting cats, the dread of disease, and the danger every moment of slipping on a tile and falling.

Celia's children would stay with their mother, all those bright hours in the fresh part of the day. In the middle of the meeting with Anthony's parents, Flora slipped her hand into Dominic's and felt the place where he'd lost his fingertip in a fishing accident, back when Evangeline was so frail, and Celia broke her arm, and Mr. Pujari lurked in the lane like a thief. They'd found their way from that moment to this. All the trouble in between seemed like a sea she could not believe they had crossed.

Everyone agreed that Celia could make clothes if she liked, to sell from home.

"She can stop when she has clothes of her own to make," said Anthony's mother.

"Soon," said Flora, beaming. Jerome and Alma would have their first in a few months. By next year, that baby might have a cousin.

In return for the waived bride price, Celia would keep her wedding gold, her saris, her sewing machine, and a work table that the D'Mello family would provide, all as her own property. Very well, settled. The conversation turned to dates.

29

MAY 1997

When Anthony arrived, Celia wanted to slip out quickly but restrained herself. She said hello twice, like a fool. "Hello," he said, looking stiff in a bright shirt.

"Hi," she said again. They might have gone on exchanging greetings indefinitely if Flora hadn't stepped forward with her "Welcome," and "How is your mother?," and "What a good color! You won't be lost in a crowd." Celia was both grateful and mortified. Finally, her mother said, "Off with you," and they were in the lane—neighbors turning to see, Celia ducking beneath their smiles. She did not know where to put herself in regard to Anthony. She tried to walk beside him, but in the narrow spots, one must fall behind the other. Celia had a quicker stride, a way of moving with surety through a crowd, but she curbed her pace and let him lead. It felt like a game.

They made their way to the small plaza near the shrine of Our Lady of Navigators. They were not alone. The statue and the little space preserved for it functioned as a meeting place: schoolboys jostled each other, sisters held hands, a woman shifted her handbag on her shoulder and peered down the road. A rooster strutted along the statue's base, then hopped onto a crate in a great flapping huff.

"Where should we go?" Anthony asked. Then, with a touch of apology, "I didn't bring my bicycle. It has a soft tire."

"Let's walk up Seaview," Celia suggested.

Anthony's mouth twitched, a tiny show of reluctance. She might have seemed too bold, Celia considered, suggesting a place where couples went to be on their own. She used to go sometimes to meet the boy she used to kiss. But it was a different matter altogether to walk up the hill with the boy who would be her husband. Whatever they said or didn't say, however long they waited to touch a hand, would signify. She was both intensely herself—feeling his nearness, the evening breeze on her face, the work of the slope in the backs of her legs—and anticipating the person she would become. It was exhilarating to think how important this night could be. No wonder Anthony did not speak; no wonder the air between them was charged. Their future gathered around them, right at the point of unfurling.

Celia felt his pace quicken as they approached the old Hotel Castelo. It was still abandoned, still standing. The pasted municipal warnings had parched and faded, boys had made games of rocks and windows, and lengths of marble had been pried up from the stairs.

"Did you ever go inside?" Celia asked.

"No! No."

She stopped opposite the deserted lobby. "Should we?" The idea came to her fully formed, like a book she had already read. They could go peeking into rooms together, a terrain all their own.

He shook his head and carried on walking. Celia had to run to catch up, flushed and chastened. For a minute they walked in silence.

"I don't like that place," he said at last.

Celia did not know how to answer.

"They should tear it down, don't you think?"

She nodded. Perhaps this chance to agree was intended as a kindness. He was speaking more earnestly now.

"It's not safe. There could be squatters inside. And people are thieving."

They hesitated again when they passed the ruins and reached

Land's End. Celia would have climbed down onto the rocks, but she was through making suggestions. Anthony chose a place on the seawall between another couple and a group of schoolgirls. He frowned at the laughter from their direction before offering to help Celia up. She took his hand, a small flat moment. Neither quite looked at the other.

The sun had just set. The bay had a perfect luminous calm. From a little distance came another burst of laughter from the schoolgirls.

"They're loud."

"We used to spy on people sometimes," Celia said. "But for that we kept quiet."

He turned to look behind them, and Celia laughed. His smile was like a glimpse of dolphins, as easily missed as seen.

All that was silvery deepened—blue, and then bluer. City lights glinted in the water as he asked about her brother. They spoke of the cruise ship, his training, fishing. Had Anthony wanted to fish? she asked. He shrugged; not really. He was so young when his father began selling paint. How did he decide to give up his boat? Anthony hesitated before saying it was a business move. His father sensed it was the right time. Was that the way it happened in her family also? Celia did not like to get into the full history of her arm and the moneylender, so instead she told him about finding plastic trinkets from the container wreck. "Everyone was off the boats anyway, so he opened a café and called it Holy Rosary."

The blank daytime sky gave way to soft black depths, stars behind stars. The lines between land and water, water and sky, subsided. The schoolgirls retreated down the hill. Celia glanced at Anthony. He had the vague air of a person thinking about something else until his attention was caught. Then his whole body seemed pulled into focus, lean and intent.

The darkness was liberating. She could look at him longer; he could brush his shoulder against hers by accident. When he put his hand beside hers on the wall, she kept very still. *Here is my husband*, she told herself. When he kissed her, she thought, *Remember this.*

30

AUGUST 1997

Francis woke slowly, letting the light persuade him. He could see Bombai, Bombay, and ancient Athens all hanging on the wall before him, their frames dusty, the shapes and colors indistinct without his spectacles. Below them, he had tacked up a map of the modern city, officially renamed Mumbai, and a current street map of Santa Clara. He used to know every home, every landmark around his neighborhood, but so many had gone, and it was possible to be bewildered by road signs. Over the years, several street names had changed.

The household felt vast and still before Essie woke, an empty bowl filled a drop at a time with the noises he made. The tug of pajama strings, water in the basin. After he washed, he stood at the balcony. It was already warm. The coast was to his west, a half-dozen roads away, but neither its scents nor its breezes could penetrate the trees and buildings rising before him. There was something desolate in knowing that even the restless energy of the sea could not reach him. Everything seemed faded, every strength spent too soon. Mornings had seemed fresher when he was young.

He wandered to the balcony to look out over his compound. The house had been built before Francis was born, by his father's family. Francis had surrendered the interior to Essie—bargain paint colors, dust, and damp. He never knew where anything was kept. But, well past his retirement, he took pride in keeping up the grounds. He directed the planting of flowers and the pruning of trees: mango, guava, papaya, jackfruit, chikoo, coconut. He oversaw the boy who scaled the palms with his leather strap, planting his bare feet on the trunk as he climbed. The children had watched from the balcony while their harvest pelted down. Then his grandchildren.

So it distressed him to see the current state of the garden. They had lost trees in the back for a lift he did not authorize, a project conducted a year ago, behind his back, when he was trapped in the hospital for surgery. That was all behind him—the warmed-over meals Jude brought to the ward, the moans across the corridor, the needles and the catheter. Only the lift remained, affixed to the house like an ugly brace on a perfectly good leg, grinding its tinny song whenever it was in motion.

"You couldn't find a quiet one?" he asked Essie.

"The music came for free," she said.

The lift was only the first of her schemes. After her seventieth birthday party, she spent several weeks lamenting its disappointments: Simon cut his visit short—his busy season, he explained; and Marian came alone, citing exams for Essie's only grandchildren. "You could have written to their teachers," Essie pointed out. "You could have mentioned my age. At my time of life, every birthday is a lucky chance."

Even Daniel had not bothered to accompany his wife, after pushing into the family against everyone's wishes and finding a warm welcome nonetheless. "It's the middle of his semester," Marian protested, and Essie reminded her that she knew all about university life; she was married to an emeritus professor.

But within a few months, Essie found a new focus. She would be upgrading the home, she announced to her children, and began enlisting them in detailed discussions about her plans. "This is all for you," she pointed out, when one or another objected. How many years did she have left to enjoy such renovations? And the addition she envisioned would impact the various ways in which the property might be divided for inheritance. It was a point of bitter irony that she could not alter the original footprint of the house without permission from the Historical Commission, from which Francis had recently stepped down after years of service. "But, of course, your father has abandoned that ship," she told Marian.

Francis was astonished and a little appalled by the energy with which she launched her projects. She began to stockpile building materials in one of his flower beds for a shrine to Mary. "That has always been a dream of mine," she explained to cousins, neighbors, priests, even the Koli woman who sold them fish. She was forever meeting with housepainters, collecting estimates, considering colors. She did not replace the original iron gate, but added an ornament whose brass gleam was so gaudy that each day Francis regarded it with fresh wonder: Who could have wanted such a thing, and contracted a metalworker, and agreed to pay for it? That it was his wife of nearly fifty years offered little in the way of explanation.

She was awake; he could hear the tumble of water in the pipes. Francis decided it was time for a cup of tea. By mid-morning, he hoped to be at his table in the gymkhana, exploring a new beginning of his own. He was toying with the idea of another book. This would not be academic or even committee work. He intended a more intimate history, a record of his memories of Santa Clara. Let Essie exhaust her strength on endless wrangles with contractors and gardeners. He would remove himself from the chaos and spend peaceful hours writing a kind of history that would surely come more naturally, more easily than any other. He would write about his own time and place, save from obscurity what he himself had witnessed.

There had been missed chances. He had not saved clippings. He had not even kept a journal of his private impressions. Had he failed to recognize history as it swirled around him? His father had understood more, insisting that Francis see the women extracting salt on Juhu with their makeshift stoves. But they had barely captured Francis's attention. He had not even realized how swiftly, how irrevocably, change could sweep into his own life. Agnes, for example. For years, he'd thought she would return.

Here was the project to capture what he had observed firsthand, the history that had sifted directly through his fingertips.

Two hours later, he sat at his table, enjoying the sense of momentum. Friends stopped to greet him, ask a question or two, note with neighborly pride that the Professor was back at it. "How are you?" they asked, and he could wave to the fresh sheet of paper spooled in his typewriter, the first passages already ventured. "Fine, fine! Working."

He began well enough, a few pages about his parents and grandparents. He would check dates later, find the family Bible, consult parish records. He discovered he was not sure of all the given names; nicknames had subsumed them. He noted such questions by hand on a writing pad beside the typewriter.

But soon the notepad was scored with queries, a sobering record of what he could not recall or never knew. The difficulty was that so many memories were incomplete. He wanted to describe the neighborhood when he grew up in it, the houses barely a generation old, the gardens filled with fruit trees, the community so tightly woven that everyone seemed to be cousins. But what endured were fragments, impressions, family lore—nothing that formed a reliable account. The simplest facts eluded him. When, exactly, had his father begun construction? What was the cost of such an undertaking? What were the exact terms of the arrangement with the parish association, who did not own the homes themselves but governed use of the land through a centuries-long lease?

"Working hard!" His friend Roddy clapped him on the shoulder. "Come and have a drink later?"

"Yes, why not?"

It cheered him to be recognized as working. He had made a start; that was the point. When it was time to go, he put the cover on the typewriter, feeling not only pleased but reassured that in some essential way he was still himself. Age and retirement had not stopped him. Lapses in memory were not insurmountable. The notepad was not a roadblock but a map to help him forward. It was still *possible* to move forward.

The walk home took him past more flat buildings than bungalows, a change that he generally registered with regret. But through the lens of his new book, what he felt instead was exultation: here, at least, was a history he had preserved. His camera had been lost a few years before—he could not think where, unless it fell victim to Essie's dubious housecleaning—but Jude had replaced it with a newer model, and Francis carried on taking pictures of the neighborhood. He kept them in boxes under his bed, but he must review them, he realized, and settle on a method of arranging the full collection. By date or by street?

It was an interesting question, one that distracted him from the painful flash of the new ornament on his gate. The welcome from the dogs on the veranda was heartening also; the pups were healthy and spirited, nearly ready to go to new homes. Bella was aging, and this would be her last litter. A sad milestone, thought Francis. But he agreed for the sake of Bella's health. Better for her, the vet had cautioned; better for us all, Essie added, as though gates and not dogs made a home.

Three of the four pups were promised to neighbors, but Francis could not bear to separate Bella from all her offspring, and the pup from two years before was in need of young company. A few dogs were easier than one, he explained to Essie, who thought only in terms of costs and barking. He would keep the one who had been overlooked, the short-legged fellow who could not scramble up the veranda step but waited to be picked up, whining when the others left him behind.

"Maybe *he'll* use the lift," said Essie, who resented her husband's rejection of such a costly renovation. "And how will you train him out of all that whining?"

That would come, Francis knew. He stopped to pet Bella and the pups before making his way upstairs. They must all be used to human touch, but he held the one he would keep a little longer. "What's all this?" he answered the dog's tiny cries. "What have you got to worry about?" The little fellow quieted as he curled against Francis's chest. "See? You know where you belong."

"You're late," Essie greeted him. "She's come and gone."

"Who?" Francis glanced at the table, where a single place setting meant the rest of the family had eaten.

"Celia, Frank! I told you she was coming."

This was possible. He could not attend fully to the great tides of speech that swept past him each day. "I've been working," he said, and held up his notepad, evidence of a morning well spent and a way to steer the conversation to solid ground. He was not entirely certain who Celia was.

She asked after Francis, Essie reported. She waited so long that lunch was delayed.

"She brought prawns from her mother, my favorite."

"She'll come again," said Francis, a bland enough prediction. He was still having difficulty placing her.

"She's getting married," Essie said severely. "She may not come so much anymore."

Francis tipped his head—yes, yes, it happened, but he was no longer scrambling to recall Celia so much as he was thinking of Marian at the airport the day she left home.

While he ate, Essie repeated all she had learned about the upcoming wedding. The groom's family owned a paint company, she reported with satisfaction. Now she was sure to get a good price for outdoors and indoors both.

Indoors! thought Francis.

"I thought three thousand rupees at first," she said of the wedding gift. "But in the end I gave five thousand. Four thousand *might* have been better, but five is a nice round number. And, poor child, she's lucky to have use of the arm after you crashed into her."

He felt a surge of relief and affection. Of course he knew that child, stampeding like a wild elephant.

"Married already!"

"*Yes*, Frank, aren't you listening?"

"The dogs are attached to her," he observed.

"Oh, the *dogs*," said Essie, exasperated for no reason at all, before admitting that Celia brought them bones.

OCTOBER 1997

Anthony was not sure what to expect of his new wife. He liked the way she'd been thrown against him the night of her brother's pani, as though fate itself had flung her into his arms. He liked the sudden laughing whirl of her, the water in her hair, the brief weight of her body against his before she spun back to the party. His mother lined up other prospects: girls she would want in the shop, girls whose feigned interest in paint oppressed him. Anthony met three, but waited until his mother was reeling from an unexpected refusal—a family who worried that his father's bad heart might be passed down to grandchildren—before he advanced an idea of his own: a Varuna family, café owners.

He was careful to say nothing about his chance encounter with the girl. Instead, he delivered the information he'd learned from a villager as though it came from a recent client. His mother seemed suspicious, but she was placated by a visit to the café, where she saw it was a going concern. She began making inquiries of her own.

By then, another prospect had come and gone, and Anthony had a clearer sense of what he wanted in a girl. Nothing hard, nothing calculating, nothing false. Pretty, of course, although, when the meeting was finally arranged, he was not immediately convinced that Celia was pretty enough. Her face was very round, perhaps a little plain. He kept his eyes on her, waiting to be revisited by whatever had caught his attention on Varuna Road. He liked her eyes, he decided, and then she laughed—or tried not to—and her smile had something conspiratorial in it, a lively intelligence that seemed to include him when she glanced up, as though they were already in on a joke together. She was happy, he realized, and understood for the first time that he was not.

He would be. After years of restlessness, of giving in to small temptations as recompense for a pale, bound life, he would make a fresh start with a girl of his choosing. On his wedding day, he was reminded of the way he had felt as a boy when he recovered his glider: the joy of claiming what belonged to him, the anticipation of what would come next. He and Celia posed for the photographer, looking straight ahead as though they could see the same bright future.

That night, she was hesitant, shy in just the way she ought to have been. "We're alone," he assured her, "they won't come for some time," and she pressed her face against his shoulder, murmuring something he could not hear. He felt an exultation so powerful that it was as if he'd been transformed. This was nothing like the lodge; this was real life, beginning. "Smile," he told her. "Smile for me." And she tried.

32

OCTOBER 1997

His mother wasn't easy: sharp looks, soon followed by sharp words. His father took pills every day and observed finely tuned rituals around sleep and meals. Everyone must be quiet when he rested. Everyone must take care with his food. When Celia brought fried prawns back from her weekly visit to Varuna, his mother took the package coldly. "I can see well enough what you are used to. In this house, we look after our health." She handed the prawns to Pinky to "throw on the rubbish pile," a bit of theater that appalled Celia, unaccustomed to waste, until she went outside and saw Pinky eating with her friends. Pinky winked, which almost felt friendly, but the family's habits were so odd, their moods so unpredictable, the jolts and swerves in a single day so disorienting, that Celia could not be sure.

There was no ease, she struggled to explain to Flora and Inez the following week. The family had no jokes together, nothing they laughed about.

"She's always been a joker," Flora reminded Inez, as if commiserating about a long-term affliction.

"It's not only jokes. And his father isn't well, but no one says what."

Flora frowned a little. "They said nothing about unwell . . . Is there drink?"

"No, no, not like that. He takes medicine."

"It may be blood pressure. Or—"

Inez bumped Celia's shoulder. "What's all this? Mother this, father that! How is the man himself?"

Celia smiled, bashful when she said he was fine, and Inez thumped against her again.

"Fine only! I'm waiting for good news."

"Leave her!" Flora said but laughing, too.

"Maybe a *little* better than fine," Inez coaxed.

It was better; Celia did not know how to tell them. He even looked better to her. It was as if he'd revealed himself to her bit by bit, and suddenly she could see that he was handsome in just the way she liked. There were still regions of unknowing, like dark holes to skirt past. He pretended not to hear when his mother scolded or Pinky teased. When Celia asked about his father's pills, he only said, "That is an ongoing thing." Another time, he spoke of building strength.

He seemed to drift out of himself when he was with his family, become a person she could hardly reach. That was when she missed her own family the most, so much that she sometimes ducked aside to hide tears. But when she and Anthony were on their own, he returned to himself, smiling, suggesting small outings, humming songs that made her laugh. He showed her his camera and taught her to take a photo. He asked questions about Jerome and Lina, which helped her feel less homesick. Sometimes when she was talking, he took her hand, almost idly, and played with the bangles on her arm. She liked the feel of his thumb on her wrist; she liked the feeling that what had once been new and startling was slowly becoming familiar. When he asked about her scar, she told him about the crash with Mr. Almeida, the broken arm, the suitcase full of clothes from America.

A few evenings later, he took her for a ride on the shop scooter. A surprise, he said. Should she dress up? He tipped his head—no need—but she put on a fresh tunic with red-and-gold embroidery, one she had made herself.

She expected to go toward the Promenade, but he steered them away from the sea, past Linking Road. Traffic thickened on the Western Highway, but the night was soft and warm, and Celia enjoyed the patches of music from open car windows. When they passed luxury hotels on either side, where rich people danced at weddings and parties, she tightened her hold on Anthony's waist. This was a part of the city she had never seen.

They followed a line of taxis off the highway, and Anthony zigzagged until they reached a clogged narrow lane of cheap shops and small hotels. He twisted past them to the end of the road: a fenced-in car park. The entrance was on the far side.

"We're going there?"

He pointed up. "Look!"

A cluster of lights, no bigger than a pendant, garnet and zircon, flashing topaz. Every second, the plane came thundering closer, so low in the sky that she clutched Anthony's arm when it dropped out of sight behind a high barricade.

"That one was landing. But from here you can see them take off." He helped her stand on a compound wall so she could see the blue lights studding the runway.

"Is it allowed?"

"Nobody ever comes."

For an hour they watched, flooded in the noise and lights of the planes, guessing their destinations. Dubai, England, South Africa, America.

"You would like to go to America?" Anthony asked.

Celia tipped her head—maybe yes, maybe no. It was not the next thing she wanted. She was happy outside the car park with Anthony, watching families come and go.

"Where would you go?" she asked.

He didn't answer at first, his face tipped up to watch another takeoff. Then he said, "It's the plane I would like," and she thought of him going so high and leaned against his shoulder.

33

JUNE 1998

Celia did not realize that Anthony's mother was keeping track until she said, "You're two weeks past, isn't it?"

Oh oh oh. Two weeks, was that right? Celia looked at her mother-in-law and saw that her smile had frozen to a question of such keen intensity that Celia wavered, tempted in this house of secrets to keep one of her own. She and Anthony had been married six months before he finally admitted his father had a heart problem. The only explanation he offered was that his father didn't like to talk about it, as though his father alone had concealed his condition. For the next few weeks, it was difficult to think of his family in the same way, and she fought the urge to go running to her own.

Her mother-in-law was waiting. No, Celia could tell her; you're wrong, it was lighter than usual.

The impulse shocked her, and she shook it off nearly as soon as it formed. Then her thoughts leapt from his mother to what might be happening. Every vague, far-off hope she had for a baby took shape so clearly, so irrevocably, that she felt herself swept out of the bland, dusty morning and into a vivid new day. She must know at once, it must be true, she must run to her mother and Inez with good news. Jerome and Alma's son, Akash, was nearly five months old, full of smiles; soon he would have a cousin. She felt pierced by longing and impatience and a joy too powerful to contain. "Yes! I think yes!"

Her mother-in-law held Celia's face the way a mother would, and Celia saw the way a baby would make both a mother and a daughter of her, the way a baby would change them all.

34

AUGUST 1998

The queue trailed out the clinic door and dissolved in the courtyard. Families regularly bullied their way ahead, occasions Flora registered by shifting her hips. Poor boy, she said of a spindly child who hoisted himself forward with walking sticks. His shoulders poked up, and his legs were thin and twisted. When he hesitated at the steps, his mother urged him on, throwing hard, flat looks at anyone who watched.

"See what God has given me!" She raised her voice when a man they passed hissed in objection. "And you can't give him a place to stand out of the sun?" The man turned away.

It was true, the sun bore down on the courtyard. It was the sort of heat to sand down whatever was sharp. Cotton faded. Plants blanched. Dogs sank to the ground, puddles of dogs. Celia, who had found her mother collapsed on the floor two days before, felt the jagged edges of her fears softening. It was hot, she was sleepy. She was thankful that the nausea of the first few months had passed. Soon, her mother told her, she would feel the baby move.

"We should have waited for a good appointment," said Flora. They had achieved the three wide steps at the entrance; another step and they'd be shaded beneath the veranda roof. "We didn't need to come rushing. A little blood only. What's a little blood to a woman?"

Celia gave her one of the worried glances the rest of her family had begun to exchange, like a language they hoped Flora couldn't understand. The last few times they were together, Celia thought her mother looked tired. Now she saw how her mother's body sagged on its bones, as if some internal gravity were taking slow but inexorable effect. Her cheeks hung slack. Her legs were thick at the ankles. How could Celia not have seen? She felt ridiculous, neglectful, blind.

"Mum." She touched her mother's arm. "Go and sit on one of those benches, I'll keep our place."

Her mother clicked her tongue. "This heat is not good for you."

"It's not much longer."

"Your fevers were so high when you were little. The sun gets into your blood." She raised a hand to Celia's forehead, and Celia fought the urge to pull away. It was like a joke—her mother checking her temperature in such circumstances—but a joke that left a bitter taste. In all the wash of fear and tenderness overcoming Celia, there were still these tiny flecks of annoyance, these small betraying judgments and smoky resentments. Celia did not like to be reminded of them.

"I'm *fine*, Mum."

"You don't remember." Her mother sounded accusing. "These fevers came on quickly. And if there is a problem with the heart . . ." She had been uncharacteristically quiet when Celia confided in her about her father-in-law. It was Inez who asked a series of sharp questions until Flora murmured, "Yes, yes, they should have said, but poor man." That was a few months ago. How long had her mother felt ill?

The queue dragged itself forward, and they climbed the steps. At the top, her mother stopped, rocking slightly, though her feet were planted.

"Mum, please. Go and sit."

"Only for a minute." But her body was inclined wholly toward the bench and her voice sounded faint as she crossed the little distance to rest.

AUGUST 1998

There was money for treatment. But they were past that stage, the doctor said.

Dominic came prepared for the appointment. He withdrew most of what he had in the bank and brought it in a zipped vinyl bag from Jerome's cruise line. He held it flat against his stomach while he sat in the doctor's office, listening to the diagnosis.

It was exactly what the doctor had told Celia and Flora four days before in the clinic, what Celia in turn had told Dominic. The same words, buzzing in the air between them, not quite landing.

Her mother said very little when the doctor broke the news, but her eyes went wide and huge and wet. "But a little blood only, Doctor?" It sounded like a plea: he must go back to his books and laboratories, interpret her body a new way.

"Maybe you've been passing blood for some time," he suggested, and she didn't speak or nod, only trembled. "Difficulty urinating? And there must have been pain?" He was infinitely gentle with her, inviting her to consult him at the hospital with her husband. He gave Celia instructions for her mother's comfort; he stood when they departed. Celia helped support her mother along the corridor.

Outside, the light was falling in long gold bars across the courtyard. They'd spent a full day at the clinic with nothing but tea and a packet of dry biscuits. Flora could only manage small shuffling steps. "Oh!" she said suddenly, a soft throb of sound, the first words to pass between them since the doctor's news. "My handbag!" Celia settled her on a bench and went back for it. She found the doctor at his desk, putting her mother's scans in a folder. "Maybe if she'd come in earlier," he said. These were the only words Celia did not repeat to her father.

Now he sat with the vinyl bag in his lap as the doctor pulled out a scan and explained again. Flora had not wanted to come, but Dominic insisted. "We don't know everything yet. A mix-up, a new scan—they may not know what we can afford." They sat stiff and upright in an autorick, Celia on one side of Flora and Dominic on the other. They had not yet told Evangeline or written to Jerome. "What point?" her father said. "Let's wait until we have better news."

In the doctor's office, Dominic listened politely before leaping up. "All this, sir." He unzipped the bag and held it up so the doctor could see the money inside. "If this is not enough, I can get more. I have a son in cruise lines, earning well. I can go to a moneylender . . ."

Flora looked at him in wonder, registering this small, sweet shock.

". . . I have a little property. We can afford treatment."

"I understand," the doctor said. "But at this stage—stage four, we call it—there is no cure. The cancer is too far advanced."

"No, no, not a cure, then!" He was eager to negotiate. "You are a doctor, not I. So you must tell us. If it's too advanced, how can we argue? I'm saying a little time only—medicine for a few more years. By then, who knows what new medicines will come." His voice changed. "You can see, her grandchild is coming."

The doctor offered Celia his congratulations. "Your mother may yet meet the child. We have no way of knowing exactly when a body's strength will give out. But no treatment will have any effect, not even to delay. The cancer has metastasized—that is, spread—all through the body. You've seen only one scan; now see this one. The bladder. This one. The liver. This is the right lung. You see these spots?"

He waited until the impact of what he was showing them seemed to press Dominic slowly back into his chair, with the bag slumped open in his lap.

Then the doctor faced Flora directly.

"All this time, the body has been fighting," he said. "Just as you have fought against pain. Yes?"

She nodded.

"And now the body is tired."

He stopped again, waited. Her eyes filled with tears, but she nodded.

"Then leave the rest to God."

There was a silence. Dominic hung his head so low that Celia could not make out the workings of his face. His shoulders were shaking. But Flora did not move. She met the doctor's gaze so intently that Celia thought she was afraid to break it and snap some last thin hope.

"What we can do now is manage the pain, so everything is peaceful. You understand?"

"Okay." Her voice cracked and she pressed her fingers to her lips. With the other hand, she picked at the fabric of her sari; she'd dressed up for the appointment. "Okay, okay," she whispered. Celia half-tumbled from her chair to kneel beside her. She put her head in her mother's lap, while from his chair, her father tried to cough to cover the sound of his weeping.

"Okay, okay," Flora kept saying. Celia took her mother's hand and kissed it. Her mother did not resist, but her fingers were limp.

Celia closed her eyes and pressed her own hand to the curve of her belly. She was almost halfway through her pregnancy and had not yet felt the baby move; at night sometimes, she imagined a baby made of stone. Now she imagined her own body and her mother's turned to stone also, all three carved as they were in this moment, entwined.

"Okay," her mother said a last time, and her hand came softly to life, stroking Celia's hair. The doctor nodded and explained what would happen next.

AUGUST 1998

Just before they reached home, Flora said in a trembling voice that she would wait to give Evangeline the full truth. Alma had taken Akash to visit her parents. Maybe when she came back. "What hurry?"

Neither Celia nor Dominic dared object. Through the open sides of the autorick, the road looked the same as it had a few hours before, the sun wince-bright, people chattering, the whole city a loud, brazen, foolish illusion. If they pulled one wrong thread, it would all unravel, thought Celia, the city felled and silent, her mother collapsed to weeping. She would not tug at anything. "Okay," said Celia.

She poured her mother a cup of cool water while Flora told Evangeline that the doctor was treating her for stomach pains.

"But what's causing it?"

"Oh, he showed us scans."

Evangeline looked to her sister for corroboration and Celia shook her head, meaning *Don't press;* or *Later;* or *Not true.* She did not know everything she meant, just *No, no, no.*

Dominic did nothing to challenge this account. His strength had been spent in the doctor's office. There would be no treatment. He left the bag of money brooding in a corner like an unwanted child and turned on the television. Voices sprang into the room.

Evangeline was late for a study group, but her gaze kept crossing from her mother to her sister.

"Go, darling," her mother told her, sounding a little forced but nothing more.

"Celu?"

"I'll come tomorrow or the next day," Celia said. She made her voice firm, as though she were making a promise that mattered. What would matter? What could she promise her sister? What would her mother want to hear? You will live long enough to see Jerome again, or to hold this baby, or to kiss Lina at her wedding. You will see Akash learn to walk. You will see my next child, and Lina's children.

"Have a nice time," her mother called when Evangeline had gathered her notes and was stepping out to the lane. "Study hard."

The strain of pretense lifted; the strain of knowing pressed down. Dominic must go to the café, but he would close early. He put his hand on his wife's shoulder, so heavily that for a moment her small body supported his. Then his hand went to his forehead, rubbing hard over the eyes.

"Inez is upstairs? You want me to get her?"

No, no, Flora shook her head. Her mother must give up Pomfret, Celia realized. Inez must be told. Every new thought landed like a stone.

"You can switch that noise off," said Flora once they were alone. Celia tried to persuade her to rest, but her mother only wanted to sit beside her. Occasionally, she roused herself from a thick, huddled silence: Had Lina eaten? When was Alma due back with Akash? Where was the latest letter from Jerome?

"Should we answer him?" Celia offered. "I can write it for you." Jerome must be told. They must find words to tell him.

Flora pressed Celia's hand. "Not now."

Celia stayed beside her mother until she could delay no longer. Only then her mother seemed to wake from her stupor. "Don't walk in this heat. Take an auto. You need cash? Come soon. Come soon."

SEPTEMBER 1998

Without much discussion, the family divided the crisis. Alma and Celia stayed with Flora and Akash. Dominic kept himself busy at the Rosy. At home, he did not like to sit still long, conceiving of sudden errands. He would pick up the next round of pain medication, he would bring Flora mango lassis, hoping to tempt her to eat. Once he came back with a cashmere shawl, the wool so soft and fine that Celia's fingertips felt too rough to touch it. It was blue, her mother's favorite color, and so voluminous that she looked tiny inside its folds. She gazed up at him with wonder and joy, and Celia caught a glimpse of how it might have been in the beginning of their marriage, before love became a kind of vernacular, in the tender weeks when each new word they wrote together was fresh and surprising. Then Akash, his eyes as bright and fierce as a bird's, reached out to seize a fold of the shawl, and everyone laughed.

It fell to Celia to fill the prescriptions: for pain, constipation, shortness of breath. She put them into a box and wrote instructions for her father to follow, but sometimes he did not like to force her mother, and it fell to Celia to insist. It fell to her to look up at the walls, where her parents had hung half a dozen laminated photos, and realize they needed more, dozens more.

It fell to Celia to break the news to Alma, who burst into tears in the lane.

On the same day, she told Anthony, who looked stricken. He took her into his arms and kissed the top of her head. Celia wept against his shoulder, not only for her mother but because she saw that she could. He would bring his camera, he promised. He would take photos of them all.

She told Anthony's mother, who asked questions about the cancer and clicked her tongue at the answers. She did not refuse when Celia explained she would go home a few days to help, only patted her hand with a grave reminder that Celia must not sacrifice her own health, even for Mummy.

She told Inez, who did not flinch or cry or gasp, only closed her eyes once, no longer than it would take to say Flora's name, then opened them again and said she would look after Pomfret and cook for Flora, whatever dishes she liked.

For a full day, while Evangeline was at school, Celia argued with her mother about telling her.

"Mum, she needs to know."

Her mother shook as though with palsy, tiny movements.

Celia put a hand on her arm and was unprepared for her to shake it away.

"She knows enough." Flora clutched her shawl more tightly around her, wrapped away inside, untouchable. "I forbid you to tell her."

"Of course we have to tell her—"

"I am still your mother! And hers!"

It was terrible to learn they could still wound each other. Alma slipped out into the lane, leaving them. Where *was* everyone? Celia would have demanded if anyone had been around to hear. Where was Jerome, where was her father? Why did this fall to her? She crossed to where Akash slept in a cloth cradle suspended from the ceiling. She hoped he might be waking, but his sleep was so heavy that he did not stir even when she stroked his head.

"It will put her off her studies." Flora's voice turned pleading. "She'll be frightened."

"She's *already* frightened."

It was terrible to win the argument. Flora pressed her fingertips to her lips, though Celia could see how badly her mouth was trembling. She picked up Akash, disturbing him just enough so that he whimpered and she could bring him to her mother to hold and comfort. Later, she took her sister for a walk and told her on the Promenade. On the way home, Lina slipped her hand into Celia's, the way they had walked when they were small girls, worried about money, a scolding, a shoe, a storm.

When she wrote to Jerome, Celia did not ask permission. She shaped the words herself, taking care with her handwriting. He had come home on leave for Akash's birth last December and was on a twelve-month contract, due home again in January. She did not know how to cope with this time line, whether there might be a special dispensation for crew with dying parents, whether he could break his contract.

Finally, she wrote, "I am due in February. The doctor says Mum might be strong enough to meet the baby."

Should she have said "might not be strong enough"? Would Jerome understand? It felt impossible to convey her mother's weakness. She was like a tent with the poles giving way, propped up on some last spindly strength.

"She can hold Akash for a few minutes before she feels too tired."

She thought of her brother receiving this letter in some chilly port. How long would it take to reach him? What was too much to ask?

"Maybe you can come home for Christmas."

Just the idea of Jerome ducking his head into the room made Celia want to cry with longing.

"Please try."

Once she had written "Christmas" and called her brother home, the holiday became fixed in Celia's mind as their new horizon. Surely, the family could cast their faith that far. It seemed better to dole out hope in small intervals—more responsible, more circumspect, as though modest prayers might win God's favor.

Without need for discussion, the rest of the family followed her lead and gave themselves over to the idea of the holiday. They hung five illuminated stars, so many that Akash blinked up from his sling, dazed by the bewilderment of lights. They leaned on talk of decorations and gifts to cheer Flora when her spirits flagged. They bought an extravagant outfit for Akash—an embroidered silk sherwani and soft leather shoes—because they knew what pleasure it would bring his grandmother. They spoke with confidence about bringing Flora to Midnight Mass—like a queen on a litter, Dominic promised, and she did her best to laugh. Jerome wrote to say he could not come in time for Christmas without breaking his contract. But his superior officer gave him leave to go nine days before the end of his contract, when they came into port. He would be back December 30.

"See, Mum! In time for the new year!"

In the beginning of November, Celia felt a strange fluttering: the baby. She was sitting on the bed with Flora, showing her the photos Anthony had taken while Evangeline was at school, both pretending she had come only for this errand and not because it was increasingly difficult for Flora to manage on her own. Flora was more asleep than awake, but after the first kick Celia pulled her mother's hand onto her belly, and after a minute they both felt the second, a clear jab. Flora smiled.

"Strong..."

Celia was transported by joy. The baby was well; the baby was growing; the birth was close, so close. She surrendered to laughter the way she might have to weeping, her whole body flooded with the force of her relief, her astonishment at the strange sensation, her gladness that her mother had shared this moment. She took it as dispensation: they could look a little further into the future together.

"Is it a boy or a girl, Mum? What do you think?"

"Either is nice."

"But you could tell with Alma."

"Could I? She was carrying high, maybe."

The baby thumped again, but Celia was left with the sense that her mother could not really attend.

"You're in pain, Mum?"

"My back, a little. Not much." Again she smiled; again the smile seemed posted from someplace far, faded in the mail.

"Only fourteen more weeks!" Celia kept her voice cheerful, but her euphoria was ebbing away. Where *was* her mother? Why wasn't she brimming over with advice and warnings? Why hadn't she scolded Celia for carrying a sack of rice, or for the dark circles under her eyes, which Anthony's mother had noticed at once? Why did Flora seem only vaguely aware of her family just when they were trying to keep her close?

Celia visited most days, watching Flora keenly. She appeared to be holding her own. The pain was not overwhelming. The medication eased some of her symptoms. She ate a little, without appetite but without complaint. She drank glass after glass of water to oblige them. But, slowly, Celia became aware of a kind of fog between them. What would once have delighted her mother—the Christmas decorations, the anticipation of Jerome's arrival, little Akash—brought faint, distracted smiles. What would once have outraged her could hardly capture her attention. Was it the medication? What would it take to recall her?

"I'm scared." Celia did not mean to say it, but the moment she heard the words aloud, she knew they were true. Maybe they were the truest thing about her; maybe she had always been scared. She thought of the nights when her father went out into the darkness, nights when Jerome, too, might have been lost. Evangeline with typhoid, the moneylender in the lane, the first months of the café. Maybe she was scared that her brother would hold a piece of her father she never could. Maybe she argued with her mother because she was scared Flora would never approve of her. Maybe all along she had been scared that they would land right here, her mother softly disappearing despite all Celia's efforts to hold her.

Her mother patted her hand. "No, no," she murmured. "Everything is fine."

This was so far from the truth that Celia ought to have laughed, but she was crying instead. She kept one hand in her mother's and tried to wipe her face with the other.

"It's my first baby."

Flora turned in bed, a careful relocation of her hips. For the first time in days, it seemed, Celia felt her mother right beside her. "Nothing will happen to you, Celu. You don't have to worry."

She sounded so calm, so certain, that Celia was almost angry. Anything could go wrong, at any moment. Isn't that what they were all learning?

"I went to Mary," her mother said. "When you were just a baby and you had a terrible fever. You would die, people said, or the fever would go to your brain. But I prayed to Mary to watch over you, and that morning, before sunrise, your fever broke." She shifted back again, wincing. "It's better on the other side . . ." She spoke to Celia without facing her. "Mary heard me. I put you in her hands. That is why I don't have to worry about you. All your fits and falls, all your breaks and bruises. And then you're fine again. This will be just the same."

Celia was left with the aching sense that she had learned something she could not quite believe. But her mother had heard her, her mother had spoken to her almost in her old way. She steadied her voice.

"Should I turn on the TV, Mum? You could watch something."

"No, no . . . Maybe I'll sleep."

Over the next few weeks, she slept more, or lay not sleeping, gazing up at the illuminated stars. A small dry cough never went away.

Anthony came often with his camera, but eventually Flora began to wave him off. On the first Sunday of Advent, the family dressed for Mass, and although Flora would stay home with Inez, Celia brushed her hair and put her own gold earrings in her mother's ears.

"For a picture, Mum. We can show Jerome."

"Why not just of you with your father, looking so nice . . ."

But Celia begged, and in the end, Anthony took a snap of the girls on either side of their mother. They had to support her. "Very nice, son," she sighed as she leaned back again. "Thank you."

Sometimes she told Celia and Evangeline stories of when they were small or of her own girlhood. Then she began to confuse Akash with Jerome. Outwardly, she was only a little weaker, nothing more. A little fatigued. "Let her sleep," Celia told her father in one of their low-voiced conferences in the lane. "Let her save her strength."

"Mostly she is tired," she wrote to Jerome, a letter that might not reach him because he was coming so soon. They lit the second candle for Advent, Christmas only three weeks away.

Two days later, Flora could not get out of bed. Evangeline phoned Celia.

"You should come, I think."

Celia wanted to argue with the way her sister sounded, so quiet that she knew Evangeline was not trying hard enough with their mother.

"But what has she eaten? She'll feel weak if she hasn't had food. Or juice. Have you given her juice?"

"She won't take."

"Is Daddy home? Can you lift her?"

"She can't, Celu."

Celia could hear the tightness in her sister's voice. She wanted to puncture it, to make Evangeline cry, to make her admit that she was giving up too easily. Only two days before, her mother had been smiling on her pillows, happy to see the Advent candle. Celia had posted her letter to Jerome. *Mostly she is tired.*

"She doesn't need the toilet." Evangeline told her. "It's been a full day and night."

"Of course that's what she'll say if she doesn't want to get up."

A brief silence.

"You may want to stay." Evangeline spoke so formally that Celia felt the rebuff as though they were children again, Lina swinging her face away while Celia still itched to argue. "Bring clothes for a few nights."

Her mother-in-law did not like the plan, but Anthony offered to take her. They rode together. When the autorick driver hovered at an intersection, about to turn toward the inland route, Anthony directed him to the Promenade instead. Celia was holding the rail to brace herself against the turns. Her face was rigid, her muscles were tight, all her thoughts trained on what must be done to stop her mother from sliding down.

When she felt Anthony's hand on her knee, she started.

"We can walk here in the evenings with the baby."

She could see the sea in bright bronze patches beyond him, but everything near at hand swam. She had to look swiftly down to blink away tears. She wanted to say yes, or thank you, or even please, as if any small kindness opened a channel through which she could beg for her mother's life. But her throat flooded with sobs, and she could only nod. He held her hand for the rest of the drive. *Here is my husband.*

Here is my mother. Flora looked up when Celia and Anthony came to her bedside, her eyes brimming over with what she could not say. Celia had studied the language of her mother's gazes all her life: warnings, directives, beacons, threats, entreaties, gratitude, love. She saw at once this was an apology. Her mother was sorry, so sorry. Her eyes raked Celia's face, pleading with her headstrong girl. *Celu, Celu. Look at me.*

She could not be saved. Not for Dominic, hunched in a corner, or Lina, making tea. Not for Jerome or Akash or the baby she would never meet. Not for Celia, not even if Celia lifted her from the bed in her own arms.

"Mum..."

Flora looked and looked at Celia before she spoke with effort to Anthony.

"Hallo, son."

He called her mother. *Here is my husband.* He pressed her hand and promised to come back the next day with her favorite guava chutney. She tried to smile, still eager to please. A careful pretense.

When he slipped away, her eyes came back to Celia.

"Good girl," she said.

Over the next several hours, she took a sip of water, nothing more. Dominic bought fruit of every variety, fruit that was out of season, hothouse berries. For a few hours, Celia offered small bites to her.

"Just a little, Mum? Just to taste?"

But her mother had stopped saying no. The pain had outstripped the medicine. Even when she seemed to sleep, Celia could see it traced across her face. When it was at its worst, her mother's face was the tracing and the pain was everything beneath, showing through so baldly that Celia wondered if they must go to hospital after all.

"The medicines will be stronger," she whispered to her father.

"Let her be."

Dominic surrendered the bedside to his daughters. He could not bear to linger, hearing the progress of each ragged breath, wondering how to measure it against the last. He kept a restless vigil in the lane, pacing the way he had when his children were born, darting in to see her at brief intervals.

"I'm here," he told her then.

Sometimes she stirred. He was reminded of her remoteness when the babies came, the way her pain and her labor locked her away on an island he could only circle at a distance. He remained at a remove even after the births, mother and child a world unto themselves for the first weeks. Was that true again? His daughters took up their places on either side of his wife, and he hung back.

Occasionally, he contrived small errands that took him away altogether. There was the relief of action, of his own quick stride up the lane, and the sense—increasingly illusory—that these were still essential undertakings. He brought her favorite scented lotion for the girls to rub on her hands and feet. He bought cough syrup nobody attempted to administer. When he came back with a canister of film for Anthony's camera, Celia said nothing, and Lina told him to put it away.

For Celia, there were hours and hours and no time at all. Her mother had drifted past all the questions Celia still needed to ask her. Celia's body throbbed with the force of them. She tried to imagine that the answers might travel like an impulse along a nerve, through her mother's hand.

She tried only once, waiting until Flora was fully awake. "What names do you like, Mum?"

Her voice cracked over this betrayal: the first time she admitted aloud that her mother would never see the child.

"Celu..."

She could say nothing more, even Celia could see that. She was crying when she answered for her.

"It's okay, Mum. We can wait and see."

"Lina," she said a few minutes later. "Celu." Their names more like breath, something to live on.

Celia and Lina continued to speak to her quietly, all night long. "There is a full moon," Celia told her. "Remember full moons when we were small? You used to take us to the beach to wait for Daddy?"

It seemed incredible, wrong, that her mother would not see a full moon again when it hung right outside their door. Celia had a wild urge to call her father: they would carry the bed into the lane. It was past midnight; the moon was setting over the sea. But even her mother's field of vision was contracting, pulled inward to a dim, warm circle. Lina switched off the illuminated stars hanging above the bed. She and Celia moved closer and closer. Eventually, Evangeline lay down in bed beside her mother, her face against Flora's shoulder.

By morning, their mother's voice had been subsumed, flooded by a great dense silence. By afternoon, Dominic sat hunched at the foot of the bed. He had been down to the beach to see the tide come in, two meters higher than usual. The ebb would be just as powerful, a spring tide. His wife would not survive it.

Celia sat on the bed, stroking her mother's arm, face, hand. Occasionally, she put a sponge with water to Flora's cracked lips. She did not know if her mother could still hear her voice, but she tried to keep talking into the maw of that great silence. Small words: *love*, *hand*, *here*. She did not say *Please*, she did not say, *Don't go*. She said, *Mumma*, like a child. She said, *We know*. She said, *Don't worry*. She said, *Okay*.

JANUARY 1999

Almost a year and a half into his book, Francis had come to accept certain limitations. At first, he kept a notepad beside his typewriter to record the necessary questions for a conventional history, while on typewritten sheets he tried to proceed with a running narrative. But he had not expected so many halts and fractures when his memories gave way. For a few months, he persisted with this system, increasingly dismayed, before he gave up the notepad and began typing the questions themselves. This gave him a refreshing sense of energy and momentum. The lists of items to be fact-checked—in what year this, which person said that—soon budded into descriptions or small reminiscences, which gradually, after a lifetime of a historian's scruples, Francis learned not to interrogate. What type of viper came to his chikoo tree? he typed, and as long as he did not require an answer, he could move freely into his recollection of the snake that once swayed down from a branch over Marian's head. When had it happened? She was old enough for field hockey, because he used her stick to thrash the snake from the tree. It writhed through the air, twisting down and away under fallen leaves until he finished it off with a few slicing blows. Tricky among the roots, he remembered, pleased that the moment came back to him with such force. His family treated him to endless prompts and corrections, but he held on to more than they knew.

Nearly every day, he could be observed at his table in the gymkhana, typing at a great pace. He had learned that pauses were deadly; if words eluded him, he left spaces to fill later. He did not know how these strings of recollections might coalesce, but personal testaments were useful, he knew, even with occasional inaccuracies. Later, he could ask others to contribute: the Golden Boys, old neighbors, even Agnes. What would she remember? He imagined the letter he would compose to invite her to the project. It was pleasant to anticipate writing to her, an impulse he would not indulge—had never indulged, all these years—without a clear purpose.

He kept his papers in a large file labeled "Professor Almeida." Usually, it was visible on the shelf behind the gymkhana check-in desk, where it was possible that Agnes had seen it on one of her visits. Francis liked to imagine her encountering this side of him, a respected historian still at work. He sometimes worried what impression he had made the last time they met at the Hotel Castelo. He hoped that impression might still be altered.

At home, away from his typewriter, his work was to finish transferring his neighborhood photos from collapsing boxes to his suitcase. Essie made pointed remarks about the proper uses of luggage, but Francis's days in stations and airports were over. In another few months, he would be eighty, beyond the age to submit to the discomforts of travel. Essie had returned the week before from a long visit to the States, and it was no surprise to Francis that she took to her bed to recover. He'd made the journey twice, when his grandchildren were young, and that was enough for him. They were grown now, old enough to visit on their own, only faintly the little girls he had known. What he remembered best from those years was their astonishing lack of reserve, the way they settled against him when he read them stories, the way they ran laughing into his arms. The last time they visited, they loped through his house like young giraffes, inscrutable and alarmingly tall. Their smiles were quiet, their manners polite.

"What do you think *now*?" Essie called down to Francis when she heard him on the stairs. "This girl is leaving us."

Quick as a shadow, Francis felt the echo of the letter Marian had sent long ago. For a moment, it was an effort to remember that her departure was behind them, already absorbed.

"What's all this?" He stepped slowly, as if to stamp the years into place.

"I've just told you, Frank, she's leaving! A post in Delhi. I arranged a meeting with these people before my trip, but they said six, eight months. And suddenly—what?—they're expecting. Now they want her in three weeks!"

Francis tipped his head. One month, six months . . . Awkward, but not a crisis. He took his place at the table.

"These people snap their fingers and think everyone should come running to their aid. How can she go to the Gulf without seeing her mother? Of course she must go home first. That means in six days' time she'll be gone."

Francis grunted and began to eat.

"'But the baby won't come for some months,' I told them, 'and if you take this girl now, you leave an old woman in the lurch. Be sensible, let her follow in April.' And what do they say to that? 'Not to worry, aunty, we'll pay the fare for her *sister* to come to you.' The sister! That was an idea, but nothing I was set on. I've seen photos of this sister. She'll be carried off by a strong wind."

Essie had not touched her food. "It's good," Francis encouraged her.

"Good," she agreed bitterly. "Two years it took me to teach this one to cook, and now I must start again with my shoulder to the rock."

Did she mean a grinding stone? Francis decided it was not worth asking. Already, Essie was on to the next wave of complaints, lifting her voice to be heard in the kitchen, even though the transition from one servant to another was a regular domestic disturbance. Every few years, the girls found husbands or better posts; usually, Essie had a hand in both. She trained them well and taught them English, which qualified them for higher-paying jobs. One of the girls, twenty years or so back, married after leaving their household and used to bring her two sons to visit. Francis remembered the pair of them in matching shirts and shorts, their hair combed back, sharing one large chair and eating sweets while Essie and their mother chatted. When they were still young, the husband decided to leave their mother and took the older boy away in the night. For years she could not find them. Essie took charge of educating the younger son, using her parish connections to find him a place in a decent school. Eventually, he trained as an electrician and kept his mother in a flat in Andheri. Whenever Marian visited, the mother came to visit and exclaim over the girls; Simran was her name.

"What is the name of that boy, Simran's son?"

"What are you talking about, Frank?"

It was perfectly clear that he was talking about Simran's son, the one she was able to keep. That's what happens, he would remind his wife if she were disposed to listen. These people come and go; they are with us a few years, and we grow attached, and sometimes they come back. He thought of the little boys, their legs dangling down from the big chair, and of Simran's quick voice—she spoke like a river in flood season—and of various students who kept in touch, and even of the village girl who once crashed into him on the road. For the moment, he had forgotten her name, but they had known the child since she was small, still in her primary-school pinafore. She used to come often to see the dog, and it was a pity she did not come anymore.

Essie was eating at last, all the while calculating the hurdles ahead. Bad enough that the girl would go so quickly, but Essie must drop everything to help her. She needed a decent bag, something that locked. "I thought of your suitcase," she told Francis, who looked up sharply, "but that should stay in the family in case anyone needs it."

I need it, he thought of reminding her, I'm using it right now, but there was no point opening that conversation. Essie moved on.

He lingered at the table after their meal was finished, waiting until Essie was stationed on the telephone. Then he nodded to the girl when she came to clear the plates. "Very nice," he told her, in acknowledgment both of the meal and of the changes to come.

FEBRUARY 1999

Celia ought to have gone home for the birth of her first child, but Anthony's mother was having none of that. "And who will look after you there? Mummy is gone. Sister is young. Brother is back on his boat. And his wife has her own baby to see to."

She was not unkind. She spoke with the stern tenderness of a mother waiting for a child to admit the truth. Still, Celia felt the plain, hard slap of it: her mother was gone. The months ahead seemed blank and terrifying without her.

You'll know, her mother had promised. *It might start as an ache, a little nothing, then—* But she had stopped with a sharp cry and gripped Celia's hand, her face small and tight. *It's not so bad,* she'd gasped when she could speak again, and Celia hadn't known if her mother meant her own pain or the pain that would soon be Celia's.

"Anyway, you've just come from there," her mother-in-law said, meaning her father's home, her mother's deathbed.

Celia protested that her father would want her to come home. She would go to Inez, who was like an aunt in her family, ready to help.

"That is the woman with no children? What Daddy wants is same as me, a good fat baby."

Celia put a hand on her belly. "He's feeling so sad. He needs something happy ahead."

"What's all this—he feels, he needs? This is the time to think of yourself. You go to a sad house and soon you're sleeping badly, you're forgetting to eat, you're feeling tears come. But what does the baby need? When a baby is coming, that is what you must think about, not every other sad thing." She clicked her tongue, decided. "You can visit after the birth instead. Then this friend can help, your daddy will be happy. But, for now, you need a mother looking after you."

Celia had no energy to argue. She did not know if the heaviness she felt was from the baby or from the way her mother's death had settled, a constant ache. As the eighth month passed and it became harder to sleep, she lay awake at night with the sensation that her limbs had been painted over with plaster and she was sealed inside, unable to crack open to air or light.

And it was true, her mother-in-law pampered her. Special dishes, soft cushions, cashew nuts for strength. In the ninth month, she insisted on cups of warm milk and ghee, which upset Celia's stomach.

"Never mind that; ghee will make the birth go quickly." She made a whooshing motion with her hand, as if babies tumbled into the world down slides, and for the first time in weeks, Celia laughed. "But take buttermilk also. Why not? Make the little man feel happy."

She meant the doctor they had just seen, so young he might have left school five minutes before, so slight that he gave the impression of a balsa-wood toy. Anthony's mother was not the sort to overlook deficiencies of age and stature. She made no secret of her preference for the older doctor, whose bulk seemed commensurate with her ideas of proper medical authority. "You only," she told him, "when the time comes for my daughter-in-law. This other little man can see us in clinic." She bullied the older one until he gave her the number for his private office.

But it was the young doctor who delivered the child—his thin face that Celia remembered; his voice telling her quietly what to do next. The older doctor had seen her a few hours before, when Celia and her mother-in-law arrived in an autorick. Her water had broken, two days before her due date. No pains yet, only a little blood. *What's a little blood to a woman?* The nurse put her ear to Celia's belly, shifted her head, listened again. Then again.

"In the night he was kicking," Celia said fondly. "Always at night. In the morning he sleeps."

Such a sweet, funny baby, wanting her all to himself, rolling and playing when no one else was awake and she alone could feel him. She used to wake Anthony to feel the pokes and jabs, but in the last weeks the baby had grown so much that his movements were smaller, more cramped, and Celia kept them for herself. Soon enough, she would share him.

The nurse called the doctor; the doctor came rushing. Celia did not understand why. She spread her hand wide on her belly, felt the body of the child just beneath, but the doctor moved her hand aside. The gel was cold, Celia felt cold. Her mother-in-law was chattering to the doctor, her friend, her favorite. "See, I knew you would be the one . . ." She stopped, shocked, when he silenced her. On the screen, a ghost child, white limbs curled tight, a round white head, tucked, ready.

"You said he was in a good position," Celia reminded the doctor, but already her voice was faint. He moved the wand in tight circles. There was nothing. She heard nothing. His hand slowed, he lifted the wand, and Celia seized it. She laid it over the mound of her baby. Poor sleepy boy, up all night. In a minute he would shift, his knee or elbow poking up, his heart flickering into view.

"I'm sorry." The doctor addressed her mother-in-law. "There is no heartbeat."

"Go," Celia told them both. "Get out from here." Let the baby have his way, shy little fellow; let him have her to himself. When they were alone again, he would rouse. Turn the lights off, make it night again, let her drift into a thin doze. Together they would sleep until he nudged her awake with foot or fist; night after night, he had wakened her. Why not once more? "Go!" she begged.

Instead, the nurse returned. The doctor left; her mother-in-law followed. The room was full of comings and goings; Celia could not keep track of them all. The nurse took the wand from Celia's hand and wheeled the machine to the corner. Someone else wiped the gel from her belly, leaving her skin sticky. Celia struggled to sit up, but the nurse eased her back down and took her hand. "Just wait quietly. Doctor is coming."

Time went elastic. It stretched so far that when it sprang back again her son would still be living.

Then the younger doctor came in and spoke to her gently, and the moment snapped, and her child was dead.

She must still deliver the baby, he said.

"What?" She did not understand him. The nurse gave her a cup and tried to help her drink. Celia let water slide down the sides of her mouth and her chin.

"Are you having contractions?" he asked.

You'll know, her mother had told her. But she had known nothing. She had not known the moment when, inside her own body, her son had died. She wanted to call her mother back from the dead and rail against her.

"Otherwise, there's surgery, but it's better this way. There's not as much risk."

Risk of what? She nearly laughed. But his face was full of earnest sorrow, so she did her best to pay attention.

"I don't know," she said finally.

"I'll stay with you," he said.

Her mother-in-law came back, stone-faced, to say she would go fetch Anthony. By then, the contractions were strong enough that when they peaked Celia could close her eyes and try to live within each flare of pain, to stay inside its jagged heart and burn there slowly and never come out again.

40

FEBRUARY 1999

The baby was taken. Celia lay still. All around her were brisk movements, swift and efficient, mostly silent, with a few low words between the nurse and the doctor.

"Where?" Celia asked. Her voice was hoarse and cracked, and she had the strange sensation that she, too, had died, that the girl she had been just hours before had been tipped to one side and poured away. All that was left was a dry husk. The room tilted.

"Drink." The nurse put a straw in her mouth, and Celia tasted something too sweet. "Your husband is on his way."

But Celia was not asking about her husband; she had forgotten about her husband. "The baby—"

"In a little while, maybe. Doctor is still working. First you must drink."

Celia sipped from the straw and imagined the juice leaking from a hole in her body and pooling on the floor. Was she still bleeding?

"Just a small tear," the doctor said. He kept talking, words drifting up and raining down—*You did well, no permanent damage*—and still nobody brought the baby. Everything was empty, as light as air. Celia could feel occasional tugs in the numbness where the doctor was stitching, like strings, yanked and broken. There was nothing to hold her down. *Now, lie still and rest* . . . No. No. Where was her baby?

At last, he stopped talking and nodded to the nurse.

The moment the baby was laid on her chest, she felt a return to substance, the weight of herself. She could not escape so easily, even though her son had slipped away. She must still be herself; he must still be gone; all the moments ahead must be gotten through, one by wretched one. There was nothing to be done but unwrap him from the blanket in which he had been swaddled, put his skin to hers, and remember this at least—the sharp liquid pain of it, but also the softness of his cheeks, the dark hair in bunches, his curled fingers.

She was sitting up when Anthony came, their son tucked against her. Anthony came to the side of the bed and peered into the blanket. The baby's skin had a delicate blue tinge, faint, like a bruise. His lips were dark.

"Do you want . . . ?" Celia shifted the baby against her, not quite offering him; she was relieved when Anthony shook his head no.

"I called your father. He's waiting there." He waved a hand toward the door, the rooms beyond, where at some distant point Celia would have to go. She could not bear to think of it. "Lina also, and my mother. Pinky would have come, too, but I thought . . . that's enough."

Celia nodded. She was crying but would not move her hands from the baby. She tried to rub her cheek against her shoulder.

"Here." He held out a handkerchief, but she would not release the child. She looked up at Anthony—a naked look, more pained and helpless than any he had ever seen. He wished he had not seen it; he wished he had stayed with his mother to speak to the doctor, far from this bed. Quickly, he blotted her cheeks and stuffed the handkerchief back in his pocket.

What had happened? One minute he'd had a pretty, pleasant wife with a child on the way; the next, this ravaged woman clinging to a tiny bundle. He felt sick with pity, and what was the use? What could he do? The business with the handkerchief filled him with revulsion. He wanted to be done with this—not a father after all, but a man who, through a trick of fate—some snip in the fabric of things—had no son. He looked down at the wife who still was crying, the baby she still held, and he knew that both were past his help.

Still, he stayed. He could not have said why. Better to go home, begin the long business of forgetting; better not to see the child at all. But Celia looked at him—a terrible, raw look—and it bound him to this room, the only room in which they would be all three.

He sat with his hand on the cotton sheet, not touching her hip. Once, when she loosened the blanket, he looked at the baby's head.

"So much hair," he said, and felt at once he had said too much.

"See his fingers," Celia whispered. "Such tiny nails."

Anthony rose like a marionette, all sticks and rods, and patted his shirt as though this interlude had left him in need of reassemblage. The full head of hair, the astonishing fingernails—everything in the body of his son that went to the great trouble of being created but came to nothing—filled him with a terror he had never known before. He had a flash of a commuter train moving out of a station, men hanging from the open doorways, more men running alongside, some leaping, hands reaching out from the packed cars to swing them up—so many men, crammed, back to belly, in car after car after car, ticking slowly past, until one train was spent and the next approaching. Men tucked beneath the bars of windows; men propped between other men's shoulders and swaying asleep; men pushing and being pushed; men smiling, glaring, watching, blind; men flapping from the doorways like pennants in a ragged breeze; men dropping lightly to the rolling gray expanse of the next platform before the train stopped. Endless women and children and men in this roiling city, every one of them fashioned with impossible delicacy—hair and fingernails, irises, veins, the tiny chain of bones in the ear, the knuckles, the nerves, the subtle curve of a kidney, all the elegant chemistry of a single passing thought—

and then a body on the tracks, the ungodly mess and waste of it. Passengers backed up, grumbling, while the lines were cleared, and a small child calmly squatted in the dirt along the rails to empty his bowels. Mess and waste, mess and waste. Anthony himself could come to nothing, as quick as that, and what would it mean that he could ride a bicycle, marry a woman, snap a photo? He'd thought a baby would give him meaning; instead came a flash of the abyss. He could not bring himself to speak, his voice too coarse in this room of useless marvels.

He would take his mother home, he told Celia. But her father and sister were waiting to see her. And a priest.

"To baptize him?" She looked at Anthony. "What name should we give?"

What did it matter? "You choose."

She nodded, her attention on the baby. Anthony might have melted from the room, incorporeal, already gone.

She did not see him turn at the door. For a moment, he flung himself into a wild fit of hope: Why not a miracle? A breath, a pulse, a fistful of hours undone—what was that to the God who had formed the body of his son?

Then he looked again. The child was dead, the mother broken, and God nowhere to be found—just a priest in the corridor who was sorry, so sorry, for any misunderstanding. He could not baptize a child who had never lived, only offer comfort to the afflicted, a blessing for the departed.

What did any of this matter? Anthony thought again. His mother was tired; he, too, wanted to sleep. He barely glanced at the priest.

"You tell her."

Celia listened to the priest's explanation without speaking. Her father and sister came in for the blessing, her father looking as faded as old newspaper, Evangeline weeping. Celia let them pray, her head pressed against her son's. He smelled of damp skin.

She waited until the blessing was finished. Inez was bringing food for Celia; her father and Lina went to meet her. The nurse burst in to say that in a few minutes she would help Celia try to stand. There was not much time. Soon someone would take her son away. But first Celia would baptize him herself.

"Wake up, now," she whispered when at last they were alone. "No? You only want to sleep?" She was crying again, but only a little, so he would not be frightened. There were footsteps outside the door. "Sleep here with me, then," she said, and called him by name.

FEBRUARY 1999

Celia let them take the baby—"to clean," they said. But she insisted that she and her family would hold a vigil; they must bring him back. When the nurses refused, she began to argue. Her father did not know on which leg to stand. Evangeline looked young and frightened. But Inez did not back down. "Then where will you put him?" she demanded. "He's in this building; why not here?"

Finally, the young doctor was consulted. To keep Celia calm, he relented.

"But you must promise to sleep."

"He won't wake me," she said in a voice so brittle that her father turned away.

There was a bassinet, but Celia kept the baby beside her on a soft blanket Alma had sent. Together, the family and Inez began to say the prayers of the rosary. Several times, nurses interrupted: Celia must drink, she must stand, she must try to use the toilet. One nurse stayed a few minutes to pray with them. Celia clutched the beads as though her fingers were hungry, one small hard stone after the next. She must think of Mary, she told herself; she must think of her son cradled in Mary's arms, safe and cherished; but she could not. Would her child suffer because she could not? The prayers rattling through her felt blank and useless. *Pray for us sinners now, and at the hour of our death. Amen.* At what hour had he gone, what minute exactly? She remembered her mother, festooned in rosaries from the shipwrecked container, and wished they could all land back in that day. *As it was in the beginning, is now, and ever shall be, world without end.* She wanted her mother.

Evangeline and Inez stayed the night. When Dominic went home to sleep, Alma took his place. Always someone was awake with the baby.

In the morning, her mother-in-law came to see her. "Yes, stay with them a few weeks. Then we can put all this behind us." The skin near her eyes was swollen. Celia reached for her hand. It was his mother who took her to clinic visits; his mother who coddled, scolded, cooked, massaged; his mother who laughed with Celia over the store of little garments they had readied, as if she could not resist the joke of how tiny a boy could be.

"Did you see him? He's here." Her mother-in-law glanced at the small form beneath the blanket, but no, she did not like to look.

"You can have more," she said. "Nothing is damaged. I've spoken to the doctor."

"Is Anthony here?"

"He needs to rest."

"When they say I can go, I'm taking the baby to Varuna, where we took my mother. Anthony can meet me there if he likes."

She frowned. "No, no, the hospital takes care of all that."

"They said okay."

"But there's no need. They won't be able to . . ." She shook her head. "And who is paying for all this?"

"My father arranged it."

She clicked her tongue. "It's a mistake. You shouldn't go ahead."

"I named him." Celia held his name close, a last secret between her and her son, but here was Anthony's mother, so stiff and sad and angry. His name, such a little name: she could carry away that much comfort at least. "And I put some water, and made the Sign of the Cross, and said a prayer. So he can be buried. There is a name for him."

Anthony's mother did not look at Celia or the baby. She stood, smoothing her clothes. "It's foolish to drag everyone through this. You're better off forgetting. You're only making things worse."

Celia said nothing. It seemed ludicrous to speak in terms of *worse*.

A few hours later, she was not so sure. Anthony's mother was gone. Anthony himself never appeared. Her father led them from the hospital, looking as if he might split apart from pity.

"It's bright," said Celia when they went outside. She felt confused, as if she had been released into the wrong day. She held the baby close against her in the autorick, thinking how strange it was that he did not feel the breeze.

"Sleeping well!" The driver grinned when the baby didn't stir after a blast of horns. "All night he'll be ready to play," and Dominic passed his hand over his eyes.

She walked gingerly toward Seven Sorrows Undertakers. The building was narrow, not much wider than a car. Plain wooden coffins were stacked high on one side, all open-ended so they could be adjusted for height. On the wall, a laminated print of Our Lady of Sorrows pierced by seven daggers; on the ceiling, a fan; on a worktable with fresh sawdust beneath, a small wooden box. Her father had placed the order the night before.

He walked close beside her, as if afraid she might fall, as two men came to greet them. One was her father's longtime friend; he took Dominic's hand and didn't let go. When he turned to Celia, his voice was quiet but steady. "I'm so sorry this has happened, my child." Then he introduced the younger man, his nephew. Also quiet, also sorry.

Celia barely heard them. She saw nothing but the box into which her son must go, the sharp corners where a baby could scratch a foot or bump a head. When she faced the undertaker, she was crying.

"Celu—" Her father looked stricken, but his friend touched

his arm and led them into the shop. He arranged a cushion on a chair for Celia and sent his nephew for tea.

"We can go slowly. We don't need to rush."

Celia wanted to thank him but could only nod, the baby on her shoulder. While they waited for the tea, the undertaker asked simple questions about Jerome until she recovered her voice. She was reminded of the way this man used to read the newspaper aloud to her father, every word calm and clear. She was much younger than his daughters, but his son was only a year or two older than Jerome. That was the boy with nosebleeds.

The nephew brought tea on a brass tray, and Dominic accepted a cup before realizing that Celia could not with the baby in her arms. He fumbled to put his cup back down, intending to take the child for her, when the nephew spoke.

"Could I hold him?"

Celia hesitated, then handed him the baby. The young man held him nicely, a hand behind the head. Her father watched them, looking lost, before explaining he did not have all the required papers.

"The hospital wouldn't give a certificate," he said. "I don't know what—"

"Everything is settled," his friend assured him.

"But—"

"I've spoken with the woman who administers these things. For years, we have worked together. Not to worry—she understands the situation. Normally, there might have been some difficulty, but in this case . . ." He turned to Celia. "We can put your son with your mother. They can be together."

Celia felt tears flooding her eyes again but said yes before she reached out her arms for the baby. Her father was crying also, shaking his head no, and meaning, of course, yes.

"Come, Dom," his friend said. "We'll walk a little. Let Celia drink her tea."

Her father kissed the baby's head before they went. Celia held him a few minutes more while the nephew arranged one of her blankets inside the box, and then she laid him down swaddled in another, the blanket Alma had given him. She kept her hand on his chest. After a minute, she opened his blanket so she could see him fully. His fingernails looked painted, dark like his lips.

"I met your brother when he was home. Your son looks like him, I think," the man said.

Celia studied her son's face. She had never seen his eyes, she realized. His lashes were long, like the lashes she had wanted as a girl.

"His lips—"

"A little darker, yes. That is natural." He spoke evenly.

"Jerome also has a son," Celia told him. "A year old. Akash. We've been telling him that he must share his toys with his cousin, but he holds tight." She smiled a little. "He likes so many things to touch, so many bright colors . . ." Her son had a small knit hat, white. A rosary beside him, glass beads, silver cross. Nothing a baby would want. How had she failed to think of it?

"Wait," said the man and withdrew pots of paint from a lower shelf—black, red, white, gold—which undertakers used to paint temporary crosses. "I have more," he said, as though she'd asked, and ducked into the back of the shop. "When I'm not working, I like to paint . . ." A crate with more pots, a tin can of brushes. "We can give him colors if you like." He dipped a clean brush in a pot of paint. With a few quick strokes, a scarlet bird took flight on the inside of the wooden cover.

Celia stared, watching it come to life.

"Yes?" he said. "Go on?"

She pressed a hand to her mouth—*yes*—and he painted a tree for the red bird, filled with fruit. A kite with an orange tail, a bicycle with round blue wheels, a dolphin with a friendly smile.

"Paint me," Celia begged.

He used pink for her clothes. He painted a small boy in a white cap, holding her hand. When he finished, she was crying as though she might never stop. He stepped back and cleaned the brushes one by one while she wept, then stood quietly while she wrapped her son in his blanket again. She kissed his head and his cheeks and his small, still chest and blundered out to the road, where her father and the undertaker were waiting near the Lady of Navigators. Every step from that moment would be another step away from her baby, she thought, and she did not know how to keep walking.

The next day, the box was closed. The pictures were out of sight. Anthony did not come. It was not a proper burial, only the box on the ground beside her mother's cross. Inez came, her arm wrapped around Celia's waist, and other villagers. The undertaker stood beside her father.

Celia did not notice his nephew at the back, but she thought of him when she wrote to Jerome. She did not have to say much; others had written. But she wanted her brother to know that the baby looked like him.

MARCH 1999

Because Pia worked in a house a full day's ride from her own village; because she must learn to cook and Memsahib was a strict teacher; because smoke and onions hurt her eyes and when she sliced tomatoes the knife might slip to nick her wet fingers; because the children in the schoolyard next door made such a noise that the air seemed swollen with shouting; because Memsahib preferred Pia's older sister, who had been in the house five years before taking a better post in Delhi; because Pia was darker than her sister, no matter what lotions she applied, and one cream even brought out a rash; because her sister would surely marry first, so Pia must wait and wait while the best boys in her village were taken; because Memsahib's voice was sharp if Pia forgot to buy garlic or took too long with the chopping or chipped a cup in the soapy water; because Pia's fingertips smelled of garlic and her nails were stained with turmeric like the fingers of a sick woman; because Pia wore four gold bangles and her sister wore seven; because Memsahib said what a quick girl Pia's sister was, so quick with her English letters and such a nice way with cutlets; because Badasahib often called Pia by her sister's name and sometimes did not seem to see her at all; because three times he soiled the bed and her sister had given no warning of such things when she persuaded Pia to take her place in the household; because Memsahib's face could be as sorrowful as the face of Jesus in the front room and Pia must dust the glass of that sad picture every week; because Pia remembered walking with her mother to the shops when she was small, running ahead with her sister and quarreling over what sweets were best, what bangles, what boys; because, when Pia was thinking of such things, she threw mustard seeds into hot oil and splattered herself with tiny burns; because she was saving for chiffon salwar kameez the color of spun candy, but saving took so long; because, with all her saving and Memsahib's strict ways, she could hardly ever go see films, though sometimes Jude-sahib let Pia watch serials on his television; because Jude-sahib sometimes flew away, so high in the sky that she worried he might fall out of it; because he might not find a wife, which would be sad, or because he might find one who would be cruel to Pia; because Badasahib told her snakes used to hang from the trees of the garden; because every time the dogs barked she thought, Oh oh oh, the snake; because the mother dog hurt her leg and the swelling was so bad that Pia thought maybe she was bitten; because Jude-sahib spoke so sweetly to the dog that it made Pia miss her mother and father and even her sister—Pia had good reasons to cry. When she did, Memsahib scolded and Pia cried more. She learned to wipe her eyes with her wrists after a terrible day when she had been grinding chilis and touched a finger to her eyelid. At once, the skin puffed up, and she sat for an hour with a wet cloth to her face.

That evening, Memsahib took an envelope and turned it to the blank side. "See here," she told Pia. "For every day you don't cry, I will make a mark. Today, I'll put one as a present. When there are seven marks, I'll give you two hundred rupees. You understand? Seven days with no crying."

Pia stared at the envelope and its lone tick mark, her burned eye weeping of its own accord. "I am not crying now, Memsahib. This is the eye only."

"Seven days," said Memsahib.

In the next four weeks, Pia won the prize only once, and only because she had worked so hard to snatch back her crying that she developed an ache in the back of her throat. "Well done," Memsahib said as she counted out the bills, and Pia was so pleased that she shared her plan to buy skin cream.

"Try coconut oil. Then you can save your money." Memsahib's gaze returned to the drawing she'd unrolled on the table, its corners weighted down by cups and saucers. Pia looked also. Her first impression was of a shelter for the mother dog; perhaps she would live in the garden while her leg healed.

"It's a small house?"

"It's a shrine to Mary."

Pia leaned closer. She knew about Mary; Memsahib had taught her all about the baby in the manger. Pia liked the part of the story when the angels sang, but she felt sorry for poor Mary, tired from traveling and poked by straw when she lay down to sleep. And that was only the start of her troubles. Memsahib told her what happened later, with the nails and the Cross, but Pia tried only to think of happy stories. Her favorite was when Mary visited her cousin, both expecting. Pia liked to imagine that her own life would contain such joyful moments. *Hail*, her sister would greet her, anticipating the marvelous child she would carry.

Memsahib pointed to the center of the drawing. "This is where she will go. Tomorrow, a builder is coming to look over the plans. And when the shrine is finished, Father Evelyn will offer a special blessing. You will come and stand with us."

Pia regarded the drawing again with pride and seriousness. She wondered if Mary would be anything like the Ganesha her father kept in a small shrine in their own home. He did not mind having his daughters work in a Catholic household. "God is great," he told Pia, meaning many gods—Ganesha, and Shiva, and Jesus with his sad, sad eyes. "God is not arguing this way only, that way only." From the way he spoke, Pia liked to imagine Ganesha, remover of obstacles, plucking the thorns from Jesus's crown.

Memsahib's shrine should have been a simple project, but the builder was held up at other job sites. He could only spare one or two workers for a crew, and these were always changing. They misread the plans at first and prepared a site on the wrong side of the compound. At first Memsahib scolded whomever turned up, but soon she no longer required their presence: her complaints streamed behind her as she walked through the house. Badasahib made himself scarce, gripping the stair rail as he descended into the chaos of the garden. He was off to work, he always said, and on bad mornings Memsahib asked what kind of work anyone did at a gymkhana. Jude-sahib went to real work. That left only Pia at home on the terrible day when Memsahib inspected the work site and found a spidery crack in her prized piece of marble. This was marble Memsahib had found years before and brought home herself, which formed the basis of her argument. Why would she salvage damaged goods? The builder must be responsible, one of his workers had been careless, they must compensate her for this disfigurement. A shouting match ensued, the builder walked off, and the crew did not return.

During the first week of the stoppage, Memsahib came several times a day to lean on the rail of the kitchen balcony and stare at the materials they'd left behind. She spoke bitterly of thieves, her grievances hanging in the air like the angry scent of fresh-cut ghost peppers.

At the start of the second week, Memsahib began to cry. If only Jude would deal with these people. If only Marian were not halfway around the world. If only Simon came to visit.

"Jude-sahib is coming soon!" Pia comforted her. His business trip had been extended, first one week extra, then two days more, but it would not last forever. "When he comes, he can tell them." She led Memsahib into the house for tea and put out the biscuits without being asked.

"You're a good girl," Memsahib said in a way that made Pia feel proud, but also lonely for her mother.

She also felt the absence of Jude. He was the one to make small jokes or suggest a pizza. He had a quiet way of putting his head to one side and telling Pia who was who when Memsahib mentioned people in conversation. Sometimes, if Pia's work was finished and Memsahib was watching television, Pia slipped down to his rooms on the ground floor. She liked to peer over his shoulder at the bright-green field of his computer screen while pictures of cards flipped neatly into rows. "Oh, there!" she said, when she began to understand the game.

She waited for Jude's arrival nearly as keenly as Memsahib. Then the worst blow of all: he returned with news of a transfer.

"One year only," Pia heard him promise. "It's not so long, Mum." He had to raise his voice to be heard over her weeping.

Pia fled to the garden. Half an hour later, Jude came down, looking weary. "She's talking to Marian."

"Marian also went far," Pia said, to show she knew who everyone was. But what was the point? Whatever she knew about the Almeidas was wasted. Without Jude, no one would appreciate her effort, no one would make her feel she belonged.

Jude took a pack of cigarettes from his pocket and shook one free. They could hear Memsahib on the telephone, her voice high and injured.

"It will take time to get used to, that's all."

"Where will you go?"

"Only Bangalore. I'll be back once a month, sometimes more." He blew smoke into the darkness.

Once a month. How would Pia last? Memsahib's battle with the builder had left her raw and bristling with rages, but there was nothing to be done when she began to shout. Sometimes, in the middle of a tirade, Jude winked at Pia, turning everything upside down: instead of wanting to cry, she must stop herself from giggling. There were nights when Badasahib had trouble getting to the toilet, and it was Jude who helped Pia those sour mornings, taking Badasahib to clean himself while she tended to the sheets.

Pia began to weep.

"What's all this," said Jude, not really asking.

She could only weep more. It was a house in which Memsahib never stopped talking, yet certain things were never said.

"Come. Tell me."

She might not like to stay, Pia said at last. Memsahib would be sad all the time. She would write to her father and ask to go home.

Jude's face reminded Pia of her father's own gentle expression. When she cried as a small girl, he used to nudge her with his shoulder again and again, a smile flickering beneath his mustache, until she laughed.

"You're doing well here," Jude said mildly. "It's only—what?—nine months? And already you've learned so much."

Pia thought about this. "I am making sorpotel."

"You make many good dishes. You will soon be a very good cook. If you stay, in two or three years, you'll be able to choose whatever house you like."

Pia thought of following her sister to the Gulf. Or a fancy home with an electric grinder.

"You know the word 'promotion'? It means a better job. I can take this promotion because I know you're clever enough to look after them. In a year, when I come back, I will have an even bigger job here, and everything will be easier." He stubbed out his cigarette. "Maybe you also need a promotion."

By the end of the evening, she had decided to stay. Jude would pay her extra each month—he put one finger to his lips so she knew to keep it quiet, although already she felt swollen with wanting to tell her sister. She cried a tiny bit more, because changes sometimes made her cry.

"Come." He gave her the key to the locked cabinet where he kept his computer and taught her how to switch it on. She had to wait for his nieces to appear, baby and chota baby. The picture was taken long ago, when they were small, looking so sweet that Pia waved to them. Then she must use the small handful he called a mouse to click a tiny picture of a card. As quick as that, she was playing.

"Solitaire," he said. "It means a game you can play alone."

A week later, Jude packed two suitcases. He would stay in a furnished company flat, so most of his things remained. He even left his razor and toothbrush, the scissors he used to trim his mustache. "I'll keep a set in Bangalore," he told Memsahib. "That way, I'm not carrying back and forth."

Memsahib's lips seemed pinned together.

Once he left, it felt as if no household pursuit would ever be finished. The frame of the shrine was in place, but the marble slab sprawled in the dirt like a reproach. Memsahib had stockpiled paint for the exterior of the house—a good deal through a village friend, she told Pia—but the cans had been stacked in the back of the compound so long that Pia wondered if paint could spoil. For a week, they picked at the same dishes of food, because Memsahib said she did not know how to cook for so few.

Even the mother dog was out of sorts. Pia put special ointment on her injured paw, the way Jude had taught her, but the dog spent her days in a shaded corner of the veranda, clambering up when anyone approached, sinking back to the tile when the person was not Jude. Pia did not like dogs as a rule, but it was uncanny to see her own sorrow reflected in the dog's demeanor. Sometimes she called Bella to come inside while she cleaned Jude's rooms, so they might both feel less alone. Bella made a hopeless circuit, nails clicking, before settling down among Jude's shoes. When Pia put them away, Bella dragged them out again, using her teeth so delicately that they left no marks.

"He's coming soon," Pia told her, but the dog only rested her chin on the toe of a loafer, her eyes meeting Pia's in dull acknowledgment that here was the best either could offer.

43

MARCH 1999

For seven weeks, Celia stayed in Varuna. To rest, her father said. He'd inherited her mother's worried tone, her trick of hovering from the far side of the room. Where was the father she'd always known? Perhaps he was gone, too, Celia thought dully. Perhaps they would all take up pieces of the ones they'd lost and lose pieces of themselves.

What would be left of her? She felt ghostly, drifting through the days, hardly leaving a trace. She slept as many hours as she could. Sometimes, before she was fully awake, she lifted a hand to feel the baby kick. Then something recalled her—a noise, the rush of her own heartbeat, the new softness where her son had been—and she was flung out of her life once more. She wept with her eyes shut or rolled to her side and pressed her slack belly to the floor the way she might staunch a wound.

Her milk came in. She bled. Lina and Alma spoke to her carefully, as though the wrong words might punch another hole in her, spring some new leak. Her father took down a framed photo of Celia and her mother, both standing, the first swell of the baby beneath Celia's hand. A few days later, he put it back up.

"I don't know." He looked at her, helpless. "Mummy was so happy."

"Leave it," said Celia.

Only her nephew behaved naturally. Together, they stacked blocks high and higher, until nothing more could be risked. For a single teetering moment they waited, Akash's face absolutely serious. Then he toppled the tower and laughed at the clatter.

Among the things her mother had saved, Celia found a canister of film she did not have the heart to develop—happy photos seemed like relics from a lost age—and the Travel Diary from Mrs. Almeida. She added Alma to the page of her family's names, then Akash, Anthony, and her son. On a new page, she described his length and his weight, his head full of hair, his hands and feet. She listed everything the man from Seven Sorrows had painted. Then she closed the diary and replaced it in the cupboard.

Twice a week, Anthony came on his bicycle to see her. "You're looking better," he said in the sixth week. By then, she had healed enough to perch on the bicycle with him, and they went to the cinema. On the way home, she leaned against him. The night was hot and heavy, but there was a tattered breeze when he gained speed.

When she returned to her husband's home, Anthony was careful, a bit distant, and Celia felt shy with him. His mother expressed satisfaction that Celia had kept to a good weight. Pinky rolled her eyes at this, like a friend from school. His father made a gruff announcement that it was good to see her looking well, very well, nothing to worry about going forward, and then went silent, as though he'd said too much. Nobody mentioned the baby. All signs of preparation for him had disappeared. Celia wondered where the tiny clothes had gone.

On her second evening back, Pinky brought home a pile of fashion magazines from the salon where she worked. Some of the pages were torn or ragged, but Celia looked through them again and again. The pictures offered a numb reprieve from the crush of her own thoughts. The pages were airy—the girls in the pictures also airy, their shoulders bare, their skin like milk. Celia imagined they lived in the flats overlooking the Promenade, flats so high their balconies jerked up like chins. A girl in such a flat could look straight out to the water without seeing any of the bustle or squalor in the streets.

A few days later, Pinky woke Celia early from her afternoon rest. "You're coming with me."

Celia looked up to make sure her mother-in-law did not object.

"Where? Why?"

"You'll see."

At the entrance to the salon, Celia balked. "I can't help you. I don't know how."

"No, silly!" Pinky giggled.

Pinky's boss, called Mrs. T. for Tamara Salon—though in fact, Pinky said, she was Mrs. Take Your Tips and nothing more—had gone on holiday to a wedding in Delhi. "Taking Weak Tea with her, thank God," Pinky added, meaning the daughter who usually presided over her absences. Instead, they had left a senior girl in charge. "That is Kalpana," Pinky said, and Kalpana grinned in welcome.

Room by room: haircut, waxing, threading, polish. Celia had not been to a salon since the days before her wedding, when her mother brought her to this very place, so she might come to know her future sister-in-law. Now Pinky presided over her choices of polish color with domineering affection. The girls were joking and laughing as if Celia belonged.

"You're fitting in nicely—you also should work here," said one.

But Pinky's voice rose over all the others: no, no, no. "Celia is staying home, to give Anthony a shock with her pink nails and have such a pack of babies that she can never leave the house again."

Celia smiled, her hands outstretched, her feet bathing in a small plastic tub. She felt wistful, wondering if things could still happen that way. It seemed like the wrong thing to hope for, or too soon to hope. But she listened to the friendly chatter of the girls and thought, with a flicker of pleasure, *Anthony will be surprised*. She tossed her head to feel the lightness of her newly cut hair.

"Hold still!" Pinky scolded, finished the last nail, and blew on Celia's fingertips. "There. What do we think?"

"Good, good!" the girls chorused and began to discuss the right shade for her toes.

44

APRIL 1999

Usually it was on nights when Pinky stayed late at the salon, when the girls lingered after closing to wax each other's arms and legs, thread each other's lips and eyebrows, buff and polish their nails. Salon girls must look nice, explained Pinky. They scrubbed their heels with stones and painted their nails bright candy colors. Usually Anthony was asleep by the time Pinky returned. Usually Celia was still awake. Usually she could see Pinky's painted toes beneath the curtain, which the family strung across the room for the young couple's privacy.

And usually Anthony was gentle. At first Celia thought it a rough business. She braced herself for the moment he pushed inside her, the churning and rocking that followed. She learned it was easier if she did not tense her muscles against him; she learned he would mistake a small cry of pain for something wilder, the animal noises he made into her neck when the house was empty and he did not worry about being overheard. Sometimes he pushed his mouth against hers, as if to bury his cries inside her, too.

"It doesn't hurt long. You'll get used to it," her mother promised when Celia had been married two weeks. But she put Celia's head on her lap and stroked her hair as though Celia were ill. "Give it time, Celu. Then, who knows, you might like?" She smiled, a playful smile. Celia swatted her mother's hand away, and both began to giggle. But Celia had seen something more in her mother's smile than teasing, something secretive and satisfied, like a possession she'd never known her mother had. She did not ask; she was not prepared for more revelations. To Celia, newly married, in a new home, the world already felt as if it were tipping. Something as simple as a rooster's cry could startle her.

Slowly, she grew accustomed to her days and nights with Anthony. When he went to work, she helped his mother in the house before she began sewing. At first she took in mending for women in the lane, but soon she made a tunic for Pinky and a shirt for Anthony in a deep-blue fabric she chose herself. Her days took on a new shape. If Anthony came home for a midday meal, he looked for her first when he entered the room. *Here is my husband*, she thought gladly. Sometimes it felt as if even her body were being shaped into something different: where his eyes landed, where his fingers touched.

Had this happened to her mother? She never asked. When her mother was alive, Celia was content to be soothed without putting words to such questions.

"You're fine? Everything fine?" her mother wanted to know.

"Everything fine."

After the first few weeks, it was. When he kissed her, she learned it was not to keep her quiet, but to speak to her. When he moved his hands over her body, she felt more words between them. Every touch a new word, her own fingers speaking. Sometimes afterward, he stayed awake with her, whispering in the dark. He liked to hum "My Name Is Anthony Gonsalves," which always made her laugh.

"Soon a baby, then," her mother said, stroking her head, and Celia thought, *Yes, a baby*.

Usually, the baby lived. But two months after they lost their son, it seemed as if everything Celia had hoped was gone. The baby gone, her mother gone, Pinky gone for the night. The prickly affection she had come to feel from her mother-in-law, gone. The interest her father-in-law took in the child she was carrying, gone. And wherever Anthony had been all day, he'd most recently been in a bottle. He came in smelling of liquor, a stench so heavy that she looked up, startled, as if he had spoken. But he did not greet her, did not even say her name. "Anthony?" He pulled the curtain closed as if something were being torn down. "Where . . . Anthony, wait . . ."

He did not wait. In an instant, he was upon her, his mouth pushing apart her lips, his knee pushing apart her legs. She tried to roll free, but he held her down. He was her husband and she was his wife and already he had one hand on her thigh while the other fumbled with his pants. She struggled a little, but he ripped her hand away and pinned her arm above her head and pushed, and pushed. She could not speak with his mouth tight on hers; the words she tried to form were sounds a dog might make, sounds he swallowed, and what words were left to her? She was his wife. She twisted her face away, and his head slammed against her mouth. She tasted blood. He was her husband, he pushed, and pushed, and she thought she might shatter beneath him, her bones smashed to nothing. Her mind spun away from the crush of him. She felt him jerk and heave once more before he fell against her. She was his wife; she did not move away, she stayed dead-still beneath him. After a minute, he pushed her away and rolled to his side, his back to her, his pants hanging slack around his hips. He had never removed his shirt.

Celia pushed her tongue against her lip and felt her teeth to make sure none were loose. Then she lay still, so still that no one would know she was there, not anyone in the main room who might have heard whatever it had sounded like. She lay so still that perhaps the tears running into the hair near her ears would stop, perhaps the rushing of her blood would stop—perhaps the whole world would slow and stop, planes frozen overhead, birds turned to stone, waves holding their breath. Only Anthony would be breathing beside her, her husband, whom she could not stop.

APRIL 1999

Celia slept a few tattered hours and got up before dawn, creeping away from Anthony to walk to the sea. It was dark, the moon a little thing. Lights from the city looked greasy on the water.

She thought of setting off for Varuna and arriving by daybreak. But she had just returned from a long stay. Her father would ask questions, and what could she tell him? Already, he was haunted by her distress over the baby. Celia was too tired to create a good reason for such an abrupt visit. She could think of nowhere to go but back.

Inside the house, she sat against the wall on her side of the curtain. If she'd extended her legs, she might have touched Anthony, but she kept them curled beneath her and listened as, one by one, the family awakened. It seemed to take a long time. His sister and mother made a big splash of noise in the morning. It was like listening to birds, cheeky, greedy, never shutting up. Celia had liked that Anthony was the quiet one. She had counted herself lucky.

Anthony didn't stir, but the rest of the household began to empty: Pinky to the salon, his father to the shop. Celia listened but heard nothing from the main room; her mother-in-law must have gone out as well. She unfolded her aching legs and winced.

She ached on the inside as well, and her lip was cut, hot and tender. She slipped into the front room, wondering if it showed.

Her mother-in-law sat on the floor, nothing in front of her, no grinding stone, no vegetables to peel, no pretense of a magazine. She looked up the moment Celia came into view.

"Asleep, is he?"

Celia said nothing.

"Let him sleep it off. I can smell him from here." Her eyes moved to Celia's face. "You've hurt your mouth."

Celia nodded, as though she agreed to this assessment of events. She did not know why she resisted speaking; her lip was not as bad as that. But proper speech felt like a high wall she did not want to scale.

"Bleeding? Put some sugar."

Her mother-in-law waved Celia toward the kitchen area: stacks of stainless-steel pots and pans, a small refrigerator, a two-burner plug-in, shelves for dry goods and spices. "Go on."

Celia coated the torn skin with sugar.

"There's congee, if you want to eat." She indicated a pot of rice in its starchy broth. "It will settle his stomach as well."

Celia, who cared nothing for his stomach, made a small sharp sound.

"Don't be foolish, girl. All men have a drink from time to time. It's nothing to cry about."

But Celia was not crying. She was dry and drier, dust and sand. She thought of Inez greeting them with her broken wrist, of the cupboard they'd hoisted onto her balcony, of the way Celia could slip inside it as a child, as though playing a game of hide-and-seek.

Clive had died a few years later, which no one quite called a blessing, but which allowed Inez to recall their younger, happier days. Flora was gone; Jerome back at sea. Even her father and sister felt distant, since she could not see them in this state. She meted out hope in small, blunt portions: an hour or two in an empty room, a few minutes to herself before Anthony wakened. She did not even know what she would do with them.

But her mother-in-law sat as though weighted to the floor. "He's not a drinker—that's the trouble. He isn't used to it."

Her speech had taken on a slow and winding quality. Celia could not bear the idea of letting those coils of words settle on her; she closed her mouth over the swelling in her lip and went to work with a whisk broom while Anthony's mother told long stories of men who took drink every day and were much, much worse. "I hope you know how lucky you are. Think what your life could have been."

Celia swept the dust pile into the lane. She had a sudden urge to swab the floors, to clean every surface.

"He's feeling unhappy, that's the trouble."

Celia looked up blankly. Of course they were unhappy—both families, his and hers. The baby died.

His mother's voice sharpened. "And what does his wife do? Nothing on top of nothing! Always glum, always with your mouth shut tight."

Celia flinched. Where had his mother got to?

"You think I'm blind? All this sulking, thinking only of yourself. What about him, hanh? Such a good boy when he married you. So certain everything will turn out well. How many times have I warned him: Be a little cautious, son. Not everything is happy-rosy." For a moment his mother seemed off on a different track. Then she glared at Celia again. "When he said this is the one I want to marry, I said, Think a little. A fish-fry! No, no, he said, this girl makes me happy. And what does he get? Nothing but scowls and frowns." She let her jaw droop and dragged down her eyelids, a grimace meant to imitate Celia. "Is this how you look after a husband? At least smile at him! Talk sweetly! Let him feel he is doing well in life. Otherwise, he gets upset, then see what happens." She raised her hand toward Celia's face.

"Upset?"

But her mother-in-law carried on talking as though Celia hadn't spoken. What a better girl her son could have had; she should have prevented the match . . .

Celia's thoughts were so scattered it was hard to catch hold of any one of them.

"Always with your chin in the air! This is what comes of too much school—a simple girl is best."

No, no, Celia thought, but she was too dumbstruck to argue. How long had this been her life?

"From the first, I thought the mother looked sickly, and then see what happened! Who knows what she passed on? Then a few months later—" She stopped. "There'd be none of this nonsense if he had a child."

Celia dropped the broom. For an instant she felt her baby in her arms, silent and still, the dead center of everything. All noise fell away before it could touch him. Then her son was gone again.

His mother kept talking; she had reached money.

"Stop," rasped Celia. She meant to shout but her throat was dry, her mouth sore. She ducked into the bedroom, but what was the use? Anthony lay stinking of drink, and his mother's voice filled the house. Celia tore at the room with her eyes; she did not know what she was looking for. Then she snatched up Anthony's camera and began taking pictures of him, flung on the floor like something dropped from a great height. He shifted, still sleeping, and his mother came running as though to avert some act of violence.

"What are you doing!"

Celia turned and pointed the camera straight in his mother's face. She snapped a picture.

"Put that down!" But Celia kept on, stepping forward while her mother-in-law stumbled back. She clicked until the camera was out of film, and still she held the camera to her face and looked at the room through the lens, one view after another, as though it might show her something true. She felt a trickle of fresh blood inside her lip and closed her mouth over the cut. She did not care that it made her look sullen. She would not be seen in this house. She would not be understood.

When she was done, she held the camera against her side.

"What's wrong with you?" His mother's voice shook, the question not quite an attack any longer. "Give me that film."

"These pictures are mine."

His mother stared at Celia, who lifted the camera once more and looked through the viewfinder. Flat cheeks, graying hair, a pouch beneath the chin. The eyes widened a little.

"I'm going to market," she said shrilly.

She collected her things while Celia watched as if throwing her out of the house. As soon as Celia was alone, she went to the bedroom and nudged Anthony with her foot to stop his snoring. Then she sat in the front room, a wedge of cucumber on her split lip.

She was frying onions when her mother-in-law returned two hours later. Anthony's mother put down her bags while she scanned the room, her gaze quick and wary, finally settling on the doorway of the bedroom. "Sleeping still?" She clicked her tongue. "You should wake him, he should take some water."

"He can get himself up."

The onions browned.

"Not so much!" his mother cried when Celia added the chili paste. She sounded afflicted when she reminded Celia not to prepare such pungent foods; Anthony's father did not like them.

"Because of his heart," said Celia flatly.

"I know what you're thinking! That had nothing to do with it!"

Celia did not answer. Her mother-in-law had no idea what she was thinking, which was that she was through with pretense. She knew what she knew. She knew her baby had been beautiful. He had a good heart; that was what she believed.

Her mother-in-law spluttered like hot oil but Celia was no longer listening. She picked up a piece of fish with two fingers, put it flesh-down in the pan, and lifted the next as it began to sizzle.

46

APRIL 1999

The following morning, Anthony still winced in sunlight. But he needed to photograph a project for an estimate. He passed a hand over his eyes and looked around the bedroom. "Where's my camera?"

"Where did you leave it," Celia said, not asking. She was folding clothes, just washed, with a hot salt smell from the rocks where they'd been laid to dry.

"I don't remember."

"You don't remember anything?" Celia folded a shirt, which would have to be unfolded to hang in the wardrobe.

"No."

She could feel him watching her. She did not look up when he cleared his throat, though she recognized it as a bid for conversation.

"Maybe my mother has it?"

"Wait," said Celia and unearthed it from the cupboard, behind her tunics. She held it before him, then made a sudden move as though to drop it. He seized it with both hands, looking pained.

"Does it work?"

This time she said nothing, only turned to finish the clothes. He put the camera down and laid a hand on her wrist. "Stay."

It had begun this way a few times before, when the house had been quiet. *Stay.* Would he tell her where he went, why so many drinks? He had not asked about the cut on her lip—because he remembered or because he didn't?

"No." Her bangles made a brief fuss at her wrist when she pulled her hand free. She expected him to object, expected her own anger to ignite, imagined a fierce conflagration. Instead, he dropped his hand. His eyes strained up to meet hers; then he winced again, looking forlorn and useless in his undershirt. She could hardly believe this person had hurt her.

"Later, we could go to a film—"

"No."

"Goodbye," he said when he left. "Goodbye," she answered. But nothing more about the offer of a film. He did not bring it up again.

OCTOBER 1999

Celia had her own mobile phone, in a jazzy case she chose with her sister on Linking Road. But at the clinic, when she tried to turn in her forms, the receptionist insisted that she provide Anthony's mobile number as well.

"Full family," the woman said without looking up. She was busy with files and pushed Celia's form back across the table. "Daddy as well as Mummy."

"No—I don't want—" Celia balked at having to offer an explanation. She did not know if she could explain the current state of her marriage to anyone.

Her mouth had healed without Anthony's asking her what happened. Because he knew, Celia decided. How else to account for the new gentleness in the way he treated her? He took every chance to respond when she spoke to him. He thanked her when she brought his plate. He was mild, almost tentative, when, after a week had gone by, he put a hand on her hip. She rolled away and lay with her back to him, as tight as a fist, waiting to feel him pull her back. He did not. Three weeks later, when she did not push him aside, it was not because she had forgiven him but because she was tired of feeling locked away, as though she were shut inside Inez's cupboard, cut off from the life she had once imagined. It was quick. No whispering, no songs.

Slowly, they stacked days and nights on top of each other,

building a wordless understanding. The rains came, and they spent long afternoons in their room, not trying to talk over the hum of Celia's sewing machine. But the quiet hours brought a kind of tranquility, if not their former ease. It was as if the earth had shifted, and they had both toppled down, and they were each finding a precarious new balance. Anthony did not directly acknowledge a rift, but he was more attentive to Celia, she noticed—deferential in a way that seemed freighted with meaning. Occasionally, she was tempted to force some larger admission or penance. But she felt reluctant to speak of that April night. She could not find the words to say what had happened to her. She doubted any words from him would suffice.

She told the woman at the clinic she could not give her husband's number.

"Why not?"

"I'm not telling him yet."

The woman's eyes flicked up before she returned to her paperwork. "You should tell him."

"Later." Again Celia tried to submit the incomplete form, but the woman shook her head.

"Full family, we need. Otherwise what happens? You're feeling faint or ill, Doctor says she's not walking home, we need a number for Daddy."

"I want to save the news."

Without looking up, the woman shook her head no.

"Once before, I had trouble. I'm waiting to be sure."

At last, the woman pushed her papers aside. The weight of her full attention struck Celia as a measure of sympathy. "That is why we say full family, so Doctor can keep everyone informed. That is best for your health." She slid the form to Celia again and gave her a cup for a urine sample. "When you're finished, Nurse will call you."

It was a small waiting room, with chairs and benches lining three walls. Celia had never been to this clinic before. Her mother-in-law favored a different one. She passed half an hour looking up whenever new people entered, checking faces to see if they were known to her husband's family, and examining the posters that hung at uneven intervals on the pale-blue walls. Pictures of cats vied with public-service announcements. "Be Smart, Never Start." "Health Is Wealth." A kitten dangled from a branch: "Hang In There!"

Eventually, a nurse led Celia to an examination room to take her weight and pulse, check her blood pressure, and fill three small vials of blood. Then she handed her a cotton robe. "You can remove." She waved a hand at Celia's garments, then added, "Everything off, you understand?" in the tone of someone used to being misunderstood. "Doctor will come in a few minutes." She took the urine sample and closed the door behind her.

This room, too, was dotted with posters. Celia turned away from the image of a pregnant woman sleeping beneath a mosquito net—"Malaria Can Kill Your Unborn Baby"—toward the happier possibilities of a mother with an infant against her chest: "Give Bottles a Rest, Mother's Milk Is Best." She laid a hand to her belly and told herself it was a child, a healthy growing child, and not the restless patterns of her mind that made her feel ill.

"Take a Cat Nap," advised a poster with a gray kitten curled inside a tiny hammock, and Celia thought of Jerome, who used to take pity on the wounded urchin cats around the market, giving them food. Her mother complained that he would start a hospital of howl and yowl the moment her back was turned—and as quickly as that, Flora was among the posters and announcements, the health tips, the slogans, the kittens. Her voice came to Celia with such startling clarity that she might have been beside her in the examining room.

Of course, she was not. That was the shock of it, her mother gone but never wholly so. When Celia prayed, she believed her mother heard her; when she encountered a surfeit of kittens, she could not believe in a world in which her mother did not scoff.

The door opened with a snap. The doctor—a lady doctor—came into the room with an open file folder. She was humming, a mindless sort of tune, making Celia feel that she'd caught her in a private moment. She noticed the graying hair and wondered if this woman had children of her own. Then the humming stopped, the doctor looked up, and everything righted: the doctor became a doctor again, and it was Celia in her short blue robe who was exposed.

A brisk set of questions. *Previous pregnancies?* A small murmur of acknowledgment, a scratch on the page. *At how many weeks?* More questions, more and more. *This was how long ago? And have you seen a doctor since that time? In which clinic?*

When the doctor closed her pen and put aside the file, Celia thought the questions were finished and began to lie back on the table for the ultrasound.

"Not yet," the doctor said. "Sit a minute more. You had a boy or a girl?" She asked with warm interest, the way she might have asked about a child who'd lived.

Celia, who'd thought she was prepared, felt a tremor pass through her. "A boy."

"Did you hold him?"

She nodded yes.

"Good. That's good."

Was it? No one had said so before.

"He was still. He looked . . ." But there was no way to explain how beautifully formed her son had been, sweet and quiet, a good, sleeping baby. She'd traced his ribs, opened his fingers to put one of her own in the palm of his hand.

"A pretty baby, yes?" When Celia could not answer, the doctor nodded. "Of course he was. When babies like yours die, it's an accident, like a bus hitting someone in the road. You see? Someone absolutely healthy, going in the road at the wrong minute. Nothing was wrong with the baby. And that means your body knows how to make babies." She smiled at Celia. "Go on, lie back now. Let's see what's what."

The doctor began to hum again as she worked. Celia lay with her head to one side, listening. The wall swam in her vision, posters blurred to spots of color. When she shut her eyes, she felt tears. *A pretty baby.* She wished her brother had seen him.

"This will be cold."

Celia flinched when the gel touched her skin but did not move. All around her, the room was shifting, the world remaking itself. Molecules aligned in unexpected arrangements—air, sound, flesh, and breath in new configurations, her son restored to her as she hardly dared to remember him, whole and perfect, such a pretty baby. She did not look at the screen. And then the doctor stopped humming and said, "Turn and see."

A few minutes later, Celia was dressed again. The doctor disappeared, and Celia went to the desk to make her next appointment. Already, she held her body differently. Back here in one month, the doctor instructed. Vitamins. Fish oil. Try not to worry.

Hindi, Marathi, or English? the nurse asked, and handed her pamphlets: *Which Fish?*, *Small Changes, Big Difference*, and *Taking Care of Baby Means Taking Care of Me*.

She would not say anything to Anthony yet, Celia decided. She would do nothing to disturb the delicate balance in which her children, both her children, felt near: her son, not quite as lost, a new child taking shape.

On her way out, a woman passed her in the corridor and smiled; in the waiting room were more women, women with bellies full and flat, faces calm and strained. Celia wondered how many had secrets of their own humming inside them. She pushed out into the hot, bleached day and walked to the next building. She would buy vitamins before starting home.

FEBRUARY 2000

Celia was in her twenty-ninth week when a nurse from the clinic called Anthony. Would he please come in for a consultation as soon as possible? He could bring his wife or not; that was his decision. But the nurse advised him to come alone and meet the doctor before mentioning the appointment, so as not to unsettle his wife at this stage of the pregnancy.

"But what is wrong?"

"Better to come, sir."

He went the next day, bracing for news of some complication. Celia had spent the start of her second trimester so worried that even his mother, badly stung by the loss of her grandchild, softened. In her fifth month, the doctor gave her a chart that used pictures of different fruits and vegetables to track the size of the growing baby. Almost at once, Celia sounded more hopeful.

"Look, we're past all these. Even mango."

Mustard seed, peppercorn, cherry, fig. Their baby was bigger than an avocado, longer than a banana. The parade of fruit cheered them. Lemon, papaya, aubergine, tinda. Only two weeks before the clinic called, they had laughed together at cauliflower. "Gobi Baby," they began to call the little one. Anthony envisioned another son.

Instead, an office with chairs. A man at the desk.

"But my wife is seeing a lady doctor." Perhaps there had been a mistake; perhaps some other husband was supposed to have been summoned.

This was his clinic, the doctor explained. He made a point of meeting families in difficult situations. Anthony felt light-headed.

Routine blood work. Positive test results. He said something quickly, something Anthony did not understand. "HIV," he repeated. "That is human immunodeficiency virus. The virus attacks the body's immune system . . ."

Once Anthony understood it was a sex disease, he shook his head no. It was not possible his wife had contracted such a thing.

"I'm sorry, sir. We ran the test twice, in case the first sample was spoiled."

Anthony kept shaking his head, the way a man tries to clear the fog of too many drinks. "At the moment, she is only HIV positive. We don't call it AIDS until the viral load has reached a certain level."

Anthony stopped listening. He felt like a boy again, trapped in a schoolroom with a set of facts that he was meant to absorb but which could have nothing to do with him. The doctor kept talking: government treatment programs, antiretroviral therapy. "So you must be tested as soon as possible."

"What?" He stared up at this man he did not know, this doctor.

"The virus is spread through blood or sexual activity. In cases of married couples, it's usually carried by both partners—"

"This is deadly?"

"There is no cure for AIDS. But with treatment—"

"Who gave this test to my wife? She asked for this?" Anthony seized on this point as crucial. Why agree to testing unless she thought she was at risk? What had Celia done to him?

"This is standard testing for all women expecting, so in cases of HIV infection we can try to prevent transmission to the baby."

"The baby?"

"HIV can pass from mother to child during birth, or later through breast milk. But with proper treatment, the baby may not pick up the virus at all."

Anthony felt a lurching despair. He had not thought—it had not occurred to him—he had not put any of this together. Of course the baby would be sick. The baby came from the mother, and the mother was diseased. He could not keep hold of all the ways his thoughts were running—Celia laughing over the fruit chart, his mother dropping hints for names, the tiny curled fists of his first son. He thought of a time before Celia was pregnant when he caught her scrubbing brown stains from her clothing, other times when she set out with a plastic bag to dispose of whatever she and Pinky used each month, the night he tried to touch her after she turned over and his fingers came away with blood. She remained as she was, curled to one side, too embarrassed to face him, and he got up to clean his hands. For how long had her blood been poison?

Long enough to contaminate his child. The baby would not live; he must give it up as lost. He could not be the father he had meant to be only a few minutes before. And there was his own death to consider, the pain his mother would feel.

The doctor was asking questions: had he ever, did he ever.

What? Anthony blinked up at him, his mind snagged on the question of how. Was Celia to blame or was he? For a while after her lip was cut, she had turned cold and hard. Was she only sulking, or did she turn elsewhere for affection? He barely encountered the idea before it ballooned in him. Who? Who would she have chosen? Men flicked through his mind: the young barber, their customers, the delivery boy his father had hired. He recoiled from the idea. She would not. She would not. Everything he knew of Celia argued against it. She was honest, she was modest, she was not so beautiful that she would draw attention, she was sullen at times but not deceitful. At any rate, she was with members of his family for most of the day; when would she meet anyone? How would she hide such a secret? And why? He was a good husband. What more could she ask?

With these pinpricks of sense, his rage began to drain away, but a new terror swelled. *No, no, no,* he answered all the doctor's questions, *nothing with men! No drugs, no needles.* Yet his memories of the lodge blazed, lurid, acidic, even as he said, *No sex workers*. What business were his private movements to this doctor? What laws had Anthony broken? What had he done that other men had not? It was not as if he had been a regular. He went maybe a dozen times in all. He was nothing like the middle-aged men with standing arrangements, nothing like the migrants pouring into Mumbai with no other chance at a woman. The manager had given Anthony a condom nearly every time, but Anthony preferred what he considered a true experience, no fumbling with foil packets in the middle of everything, and all along he was told that the girls were clean. Had he been deceived?

Their faces whirled in his memory. Their knowing smiles twisted to something more cunning. He'd once refused a girl with a sore on her mouth. "That is nothing," the manager said easily. "A small burn—these girls with their cigarettes. But let her go—why not? We have another." The next girl looked better, and Anthony remembered congratulating himself.

He could never mention such girls. His family would pin the blame on him.

The doctor was talking, talking, talking, but Anthony was not listening. The old feeling came over him again, his hands shaking, terror palpating in his blood like its own disease, like the truth he knew even before he was ushered to an examination room and an orderly with double gloves took a vial of his blood. He had killed them, killed them all.

The clinic rushed his results. It took only a week before he knew what already felt certain. Still his hands began to shake when the nurse handed him the paper, bearing his name and marking him for this painful end.

An orderly brought water, which Anthony sipped through waves of nausea. Eventually, he was ushered into the office, feeling so ill that the room, the desk, even the doctor's voice seemed to slide away from him. This was a private clinic, the doctor explained, dedicated to the care of women and newborns, so Anthony must seek treatment elsewhere. He suggested a government hospital. His wife would require prenatal treatment, which Anthony must authorize at once. Medication could save the baby. "You must think ahead to what might happen."

Something had already happened, thought Anthony. His child was already orphaned. What was the point of all this?

The doctor picked up his phone and buzzed an outer desk to ask the date of Celia's next checkup. "In ten days' time?" he repeated, making a note on his pad. Very well; Anthony should accompany her for a family consultation about protocols for an HIV-positive pregnancy. He nodded as though the appointment were ending on a high note, gave Anthony three pamphlets, and sent him on his way.

Anthony said nothing. He burned the pamphlets and huddled into himself, waiting for some unimaginable reprieve. None came. All the roads he could follow led someplace worse. He could tell her and . . . He could wait for her to go to the clinic, and . . . He could pretend the virus had come to him some other way and . . . Every dead end left him looping back to the beginning: paralyzed, silent, unable to seek comfort or aid.

Days passed, an inexorable march toward exposure, and his suffering became more acute. Celia brought out the fruit chart and he felt a sharp cramp in his lower abdomen. Was it the disease or nerves? He lost his appetite, cried out in sleep.

In the end, he told Pinky because he needed her. He waited outside her salon, and they walked to a nearby park, where sad-eyed ponies waited to plod in circles for a birthday party.

He started with Celia. Pinky's eyes narrowed.

"That isn't right. You misunderstood."

"Shut your mouth," he told her, so sharply that she was shocked into silence. Pinky never credited him with any sense. For once, let her listen without making him feel small.

He was angry enough to let the rest come out in jabs and blows. She was crying openly by the time he told her what he meant to do: slip away before anyone knew.

"But where?"

He would seek treatment. He might start at a hospital, but he had also been looking at newspaper advertisements. Some he dismissed as quackery—these fellows with their tiny storefronts, offering miracle cures over a raw plank of wood. But others were respectable. He would take advice from experts, not this doctor from a women's clinic who might not understand how the virus worked in a man. Or he might try holistic treatment, Ayurvedic centers where he could take up residence until his body was cleansed. Once he was free of this thing, he could send for Celia.

Pinky tipped her head in mute agreement, still crying. Anthony, who had never imagined she would be so grieved, let his own eyes fill. "It won't be forever. I'll come back when I'm well."

Pinky tried to smile, and he held out his handkerchief. There was a tiny stillness, a hesitation as slight as breath before she took it. He pretended not to notice. But his voice went rough when he said he'd need money. How much could she give him?

He delayed until the appointment was two days off. In private moments with Pinky, he said he needed to finish making arrangements, but in fact he was not sure where to go. Beyond the first mile or so of his flight—south, toward the good private hospitals—his plans dropped off entirely. He could not train his thoughts to climb down that precipice.

For his last nights at home, Pinky was unusually subdued—soft when she spoke with him, quick to suggest his favorite meals, once even tearing up when the household made plans about the baby. Celia was happy and open, laughing over names. Gobi Baby, she still called their child, although they'd reached coconut. Anthony found himself at the center of all his family's hopes at the very moment he must cut himself off from them. He saw that, quietly, without drawing attention, Pinky kept his drinking glass and Celia's aside even after they had been rinsed. He was like that glass—clean but not clean, already set apart.

Two nights before the appointment, Pinky woke with him in the middle of the night and held a small light while he collected his things. He took some changes of clothes, one pair of closed shoes, and a pair of chappals. He took his wedding ring, camera, and a small print of his wedding picture. He took the paperwork with his test results and Celia's, folded so that the words didn't show, in the bottom of his bag. He put all this into his bicycle rack.

His father kept tight hold of the money from the shop, but Anthony had skimmed what he could from cash payments. He brought his own stash, along with money from Pinky and the savings Celia had put aside from her sewing. He took his mother's gold bangles, her ruby pendant, and her gold chain. He had not realized that Celia had locked away her wedding gold, so instead he took the necklace he had given her when he learned she was expecting again. He hesitated before brushing her hair aside to unfasten it while she slept. He wished he could leave it, a sign of his good intentions. But the baby would die, and what life could there be for Celia if she lost her husband also? Her best hope was that he could find a cure for them both.

Pinky did not hug him, only gripped his arm tightly through the sleeve of his jacket. Anthony felt it less as a goodbye than as a fierce call to return. Then she crossed her arms over her chest, holding herself in place while he wheeled his cycle up the lane. A sliver of moon, a dim wash of stars. In another hour, men would head to the docks.

Anthony did not start riding until he reached the paved road, and then it felt strange to move so swiftly. On the outskirts of the village, he swept past a dog who sprang up barking. Anthony swerved sharply but kept cycling until the dog fell behind him. Soon it was just another noise in the night, like something that had happened to someone else.

MARCH 2000

Three days before Jude flew back to visit—"for three nights; that is two days only," said Memsahib—Pia was waiting, waiting, waiting. Since her promotion, the highlight of her days came when the long, flat hours of the afternoon finally thinned to heat and sleep.

Badasahib lay down to rest, curled like a dry leaf, but Memsahib lingered over the dismantling of lunch. When, at last, she moved heavily into her bedroom, she issued fresh directives from bed relentless as coughing fits, until a long pause finally gave Pia hope. She moved to the curtained doorway and heard the woolly sound of the old woman's breathing.

Half an hour later, Pia had just uncovered a card with ten fat red hearts, a sign that ten handsome boys would smile at her, when the dogs began to bark. She knew the commotion would rouse Memsahib, and she guessed the watchman, Ashok, might be sneaking a nap also, so Pia left the tempting chains of cards and hurried to the front.

Two men were maneuvering a column-shaped bundle from a three-wheeler. The bony one looked Pia up and down, as though she were his next bit of freight. The gate was padlocked, so she ran upstairs for the keys, but by the time she returned, Ashok had appeared and unlocked it himself. He waved the men inside, paying no attention to Pia in an effort to pretend that he had been there all along.

Pia lingered, for surely this was Mary, come at last. The men deposited her near the steps and began pestering Ashok for a tip. There was nothing set aside for them, the dogs resumed their barking, and suddenly there was Memsahib, hair rumpled, feet bare. She peered down at the men from the landing before calling to ask what they wanted.

Pia lifted the sackcloth at the statue's base. Underneath was clear plastic sheeting, through which she saw that beneath Mary's carved foot was the head of a carved snake. At once Pia backed away. Memsahib had never hinted that Mary faced such dangers. Pia thought of Jesus with his sad, sad eyes and thorny crown, a god in anguish, and worried that his mother had endured attacks also. She tried to think of Shiva's serenity while the serpents twined around his arms, or of Mary's story safely told, all dangers overcome.

From the landing, Memsahib's voice cracked like a whip. Pia decided to wait in the kitchen. But she was uncertain how to take her leave from a holy figure in such a compromised condition. Mary seemed more puzzled than powerful, blinded by wrappings. Still, Pia slid off her chappals and bowed, as though at temple. Then she climbed up to the back balcony.

When she looked down, she saw mostly what she always saw: the tangle of vines along the wall, Ashok's tarp roof crisscrossed with palm fronds, the work site for the shrine. The only new feature was the statue, which seemed to have already absorbed the sad and dusty resignation of all that waited in the Almeida compound. Pia wanted to fly ahead to the moment when Mary would be unveiled, then to the relief of Jude's arrival, and on and on, rushing forward, until the day when she herself would be a bride unveiled.

Only when she went to fill the kettle, when she heard the sound of water rushing through pipes and knew Badasahib was awake, when she heard heavy footsteps on the stairs and knew Memsahib would be kneading a fresh lump of complaints, when she heard the shouting of the last schoolboys on the game court, the sign that afternoon would churn to evening and evening to night—tea and washing, dinner and washing, the swabbing, the bedding, the dogs—only then did she remember the card game she had abandoned and the ten of hearts, still waiting.

The next morning, Pia woke with the rasp of crow calls in her ears. On dry nights she slept on a pallet on the kitchen balcony, beneath a net of clotheslines that could be raised and lowered with a crank, and for a few minutes she gazed up through the ropes to the morning sky, tinged with yellow like milk gone sour. After a minute, she felt the day begin to hurtle down on her—tea and washing, breakfast and washing—and rolled to the side. Down in the compound, the statue was gone.

Pia sat up. Other work-site materials seemed untouched. Only Mary had disappeared.

What had happened? What to do?

The house was quiet, Memsahib and Badasahib in their bedrooms. The road would soon shake itself awake, but for now the rumble of distant motors might have been snoring. Pia, who slept in cotton salwar kameez, pushed her feet into rubber chappals and hurried to wake Ashok.

His shelter was in the rear of the garden, directly back from the gate but tucked out of sight behind the trunks of twin palms. This was in deference to the bylaws of the St. Hilary Road Association, which forbade temporary structures in favor of hiring day and night watchmen in revolving shifts. Memsahib recited these laws to Ashok whenever he annoyed her, or disobeyed, or asked to borrow money for another sick relative; it was on his head, she told him, if she was forced to pay a large fine or thrown into prison.

Now Pia worried that the disappearance of Mary would also be on Ashok's head. They were not friends exactly—a man much older than her father—but she found comfort in his company. Once, soon after her arrival, the household had emptied for a wedding and Ashok made a brush fire. He and Pia sat in its flickering light, where the smoke kept away the mosquitoes, and spoke of small things: the neighborhood festival, the school next door, the way Jude's company driver was always checking his mobile, like a child feeling a loose tooth. This garden had no snakes, he assured her. Not for many years.

When Pia saw his shelter was empty, she circled the compound. The gate was still locked. Then the dogs, who spent their nights on the veranda, lifted their heads at a soft noise behind her, and Pia turned to see Badasahib. He wore pants only, no shoes or chappals, no proper shirt with buttons. A thin vest, no longer white. He looked angry, as if he had just been stung but could not find the insect.

"You there! Where is my bicycle?"

The search for his bicycle was nothing new. Several times, Badasahib had checked the post where it used to be chained and reported with fresh alarm that he had been robbed. Lately, he complained that one of the children had gone for a ride without his leave. What children? Pia wondered in bewilderment, until she realized he meant the ones who had already grown, Jude-sahib, and Marian, who telephoned, and another brother, who did not. Once, Badasahib berated Ashok for working in league with bicycle thieves, shouting so bitterly that Memsahib left her television program to see what was wrong. Pia expected her to end the matter at once, but instead she stood on the last step and only said his name again and again: "Frank. Frank. Frank." Later, after Jude came and coaxed Badasahib back inside, Memsahib told Pia to bring Ashok two mince-and-potato cutlets, fat and nicely browned, even though he prepared his own meals.

Pia felt sure he would accuse her next. "That is gone a long time, not today only," she managed before she hid her face in her hands and began to cry.

But Badasahib did not shout. "What's this crying?" he said presently. "Who has been worrying you?"

Pia peeped between her fingers. The angry look had gone from his face.

"I must get to work," he said gruffly. "But go and have some tea. I will speak to her later. She shouts sometimes—that is nothing. Don't make yourself ill."

Pia lifted her face to look at him, and suddenly Badasahib seemed puzzled. "Marian? Where is Marian?"

Pia did not know how to answer—gone, or sometimes on the telephone—but Badasahib was looking this way and that, in the garden.

"Such a girl," he said. "Always tucked away with a book." He turned to Pia again and seemed to take her in properly. "Tea is ready?"

At last, a question she could answer. "I'm making now," she said, and hurried up the front stairs.

From the landing, she scanned the compound once more. Mary did not appear, Ashok did not appear. The morning light was thin and golden, something wet on the verge of drying, and it seemed to Pia as if things must change quickly or not at all, that the household could not wait to recover Mary. From where she stood, Badasahib seemed no longer menacing but small and useless, poking around the garden in his bare feet. She must wake Memsahib.

As she passed through the house, Jesus watched her from his place on the wall. Memsahib said he could hear thoughts and prayers as easily as voices, so Pia silently assured him that Holy Mummy would come back. Then she slipped into the bedroom.

The light was dim. Curtains hung to the floor, lank against the thick walls and furred with dust at the hems. Memsahib and Badasahib lived as brother and sister, eating and quarreling but nothing more, so Badasahib kept to his own room at night. But Pia could see the small gray hillock of Memsahib's head on the pillow. She slept facing the window, where a seam of light fell through the narrow parting of the curtains and over the hooded figure of Mary. She stood at the bedside, right over Memsahib, her arms softly open. Her hand, if she could lower it, would touch Memsahib's hair.

Pia stared. The green walls lost their twilight feel and began to glow like seawater. The school next door burst into shouting like a tree full of starlings disturbed from their perch.

It was only when Memsahib shifted that Pia withdrew to the kitchen. Despite her confusion, she did not feel vulnerable to an attack of crying. She did not wish to consult her sister. She did not trouble herself to understand this latest expression of the unfathomable workings of the Almeida household. She put the water to boil and began to lay the table.

Her thoughts flicked again to the portrait of Jesus. Holy Mummy is here, she reassured him. After a moment's consideration, she put out an extra cup.

Twenty minutes later, she heard the dogs barking. It was another minute before she heard Ashok's voice and the creak of the gate. Memsahib was still in her bedroom; she had not yet turned up at the table. Badasahib was washing.

"Who has come?" Pia asked in a quick high voice when she heard footsteps on the wooden stairs. She was not frightened exactly, but she did not like to greet a visitor on her own. She wanted Memsahib to overhear and come pushing through the curtain to help her.

Instead, a girl heavy with child appeared on the landing. Pia took in the wet lashes, the plain sandals, the hair loose beneath a shawl. The girl put one hand to her belly, so large and round that it seemed to Pia as if the baby might arrive at any moment. In the other she held a bag. She looked as if she might sink to the ground, but she did not set the bag down.

Pia understood. It was not quite the way of the stories: the colors all wrong, the shawl gray, the eyes dark, and from the veranda below, dogs baying instead of sheep and oxen and an ass.

"Is Mrs. Almeida home? Please?" Her voice shook a little. "Or Mr. Almeida?"

See! Pia thought to Jesus. She smiled widely at this girl, whose child would not need a bed of straw.

"Come! We are ready for you!" She led the girl past the front room, where visitors always waited, past the dining table, with the teacup Pia had known to prepare, straight back to Memsahib's bedroom to be reunited with the other Mary.

50

MARCH 2000

Believe what you will, Easter Almeida had not intended to sleep with Mary beside her.

But she felt an unexpected tranquility as she watched dust tumbling in the channel of light from the window, drifting toward the statue. Mary was lit from behind, her chalk-rose cheeks cool and shadowed, her hands uplifted.

Then Essie heard a mild cough and turned to find Frank in the doorway. He cleared his throat again, his version of a greeting, and waited. It was as though, after fifty-two years of marriage, he'd taken a sudden interest in what she had to say.

"What is it, Frank?" She tried to recapture her sense of the glowing presence beside her, but some mystical possibility had vanished, some communion she and Mary might have shared. Frank had blundered into a significant moment with his yellowed undershirt and mindless cough and ruined everything. When Essie looked at the statue again, she saw a weary parable, Mary's arms raised to no purpose.

He patted one pocket after the other, so Essie knew what was coming. He was always looking for his money, his watch, his photograph, his bicycle. Or even his children, grown and gone.

"I'm missing some cash. You haven't taken any?"

"Don't be ridiculous."

Essie both regretted her sharpness and resented that she

had been driven to it. She glanced at the statue, whose serenity composed a gentle reproach. *But you see what I put up with*—an appeal not to the statue, exactly, but to Mary herself.

It was clear Frank saw nothing. Her husband, once a man of dignity in a top university, was peering beneath the bed as though his money might have rained down from the mattress.

"I think it was ten thousand."

"Oh God, Frank."

He looked at her and, perhaps for the first time, registered the figure beside her. Essie did not think she could explain why she had brought Mary to her bedroom—an impulse so difficult to describe that the story of all her days might not suffice. But she felt an unexpected current of anticipation. Then his gaze slid past her. "You think it could have fallen somewhere?"

Essie sat upright and reached for her spectacles. The softness of the morning sharpened to hard edges and aggravating truths. "It's like living with the thieves in the temple," she said aloud to Mary.

"Damn thieves!" her husband said in a burst of fury. "They've taken my bicycle!"

"You lost that yourself." But there was no point explaining that his bicycle had disappeared years before, no point looking for money he might have lost and recovered a dozen times, or spent, or gambled, or never had in the first place. "You should check the bathroom," she said instead. He was forever worried that his belongings would disappear into the plumbing, and Essie must have a few moments of peace before facing the day. Already, she heard voices, someone at the door.

Frank glanced down the passage toward the bathroom, then turned to the statue. "What's that doing here?" Then he shambled away.

MARCH 2000

The servant, a wisp of a girl, smiled and jabbered about expecting her. Celia did not understand; how could anyone know she would wash up on the Almeidas' doorstep? But she was so startled by her reception, so staggered by the events of the past few hours, that she did not protest when the girl led her straight into Mrs. Almeida's bedroom.

"Here she is! She has come!" The girl's thin face was radiant with joy. She has mistaken me for someone, Celia realized wretchedly, one of the family. Her mind flicked to Nicole, the granddaughter whose clothes she once wore, but it was too late: Mrs. Almeida turned to face her. She was standing near the wardrobe in a cotton nightdress, her feet pushed into old, soft slippers, her hair still in spikes from its argument with her pillow.

Why had Celia come crashing into this room? Why had she come to the Almeidas at all? She swung her gaze aside to preserve a last hint of privacy for the old woman. But she found something intimate wherever she looked: used tissues, a tub of Vaseline, the rumpled bed, and close beside it a statue of Mary. She fixed her eyes on Mary's face. And because Mary reminded Celia of her mother, because she wanted her mother so badly, Celia began to weep.

She was barely aware of the girl scuttling away, or her own

bag dropping to the floor, or her movement to the bed. She sank to the mattress and could not stop crying, even when Mrs. Almeida sat beside her with an her arm around Celia's shoulders. "What is it, child, what's happened?" she said again and again, so gently that Celia knew, for a while at least, she did not have to answer.

MARCH 2000

The servant, Pia, came at once when Mrs. Almeida called for a glass of water. By then, Celia's tears had passed, and she did not know where to look or what to do. She felt physically depleted, as though she'd wept away her strength.

"I'm sorry . . ."

Mrs. Almeida gave her the glass and told her to drink. "Do we have buns?" she asked Pia, then directed her to make chapatis. When she had gone back to the kitchen, Mrs. Almeida sighed. "My son used to bring home nice buns, soft, with plums inside. He had a company car, you know, so on the way home from the city he could stop. But it is too far to walk, and Jude has gone . . ."

Anthony was gone, too, but that was the least of it. Celia did not know how to explain what had happened; she could not hold on to all the pieces herself. She thought of the day she had taken his camera and made small flat squares of whatever she saw.

". . . even the statue," Mrs. Almeida was explaining. It was meant for the garden, but she preferred not to keep it outdoors until the shrine was ready. "And I can't leave it in the front room. Sometimes Frank sleeps like the dead, sometimes he goes stumbling through the house like a lost soul. Once, we found him standing in the bath in his pajamas. I don't know if he was awake or sleeping."

When she had taken some water, Mrs. Almeida sent her to the table. "I'll just put on some clothes and come."

Celia moved to retrieve her bag, but Mrs. Almeida said, "Leave it. You're not rushing away, are you?"

There was fresh tea in a dented kettle, a cup and saucer at her place, a plate of fruit.

Outside, the light was strong. Above the din of shouting children, a school bell rang. It seemed incredible that it was still morning, only a handful of hours since she rose just before dawn, needing the toilet, and found her mother-in-law and Pinky waiting in the light of a single lamp. The bag Celia had brought into the household two years before was at the door, but Anthony did not appear to be back.

He had left early the day before, setting off on his bicycle before anyone was awake. Only Pinky had spoken with him. "He has business," she told them. "Maybe two, three nights."

Celia had been confused. Anthony never spent nights away. His father decamped to the shop, intensely irritated; his mother hounded Pinky all morning, so many questions that Celia's head ached. She lay down to rest and woke two hours later from a thick sleep to find both Pinky and her mother red-eyed.

"It's nothing," insisted Pinky, "onions"; and her mother gave a quick, tight nod. Celia was fed up with them both, so hellbent on secrets. "I am in this family," she reminded Anthony's mother, and though the older woman would not acknowledge her in words, she eventually tipped her head to acquiesce. Later, she asked Celia to do Anthony's washing and fold it away. They passed a quiet evening.

But the next morning brought a flood of words, such torrents that Celia could hardly hold on to their meaning. Anthony was gone. No trip, no business. He had left them all.

Celia looked at Pinky in disbelief. Pinky looked at the ground.

It was still dark out, her father-in-law still asleep. Go on, get dressed, her mother-in-law said, and for a few minutes Celia thought that the three of them would go after Anthony together.

Then came more: A blood test. A disease.

"Wait—" said Celia, but her mother-in-law would not stop.

They were careful in this family, always watching out for health. So who brought this sickness into their house? Who ruined their son?

"No, no—"

She was unclean, diseased, a danger to them all. They would not keep her.

"What are you—"

"Get out from here."

"But the baby!"

His mother shook her head, stone-faced, through whatever Celia said. No, no, no.

Celia turned to Pinky. Did Anthony know what they were doing?

Pinky flinched.

"Where did he go?"

Treatment—a hospital, maybe. She didn't know.

"Without me?"

Pinky said nothing, her face a pale thumbprint in the dim room. She had agreed to all of this, thought Celia.

"You took me to the salon," she said, and Pinky began to cry, and Anthony's mother pushed Celia's bag out the door.

Celia looked at her sewing machine on its table, her box of fabrics, the colored thread she'd just purchased, and remembered her sewing money. She went to the wardrobe; the purse was gone. A hand to her neck; the chain from Anthony, gone. The locked box with her wedding gold, gone. What had they packed, and what had they stolen? The thread was new; she must take the thread, she thought numbly. The other women kept far from her while she filled a shopping bag. She put a hand on the table to steady herself, then moved to the door.

"This is your *grandchild*."

Her mother-in-law wet a rag and began scrubbing the place where Celia had laid her hand on the table. Pinky sank into a corner like a frightened child. Celia followed her bag into the lane and began to walk.

The dark sky was draining to gray. On the shore, where hut people scratched a living from foam and rock, thin spires of smoke rose from cook fires. There had been no chance to use the toilet, and the baby, due in six weeks, bore down against her bladder. Celia picked her way behind a straggle of scrub and weeds and squatted with her hands in the dirt, her face turned away from the trickle between her feet, her mind hardened against the idea of anyone catching sight of her.

The bag chafed one hand, then the other. Her thoughts were thin and bitter, like coins on the tongue. The first southbound bus that stopped was full, but she climbed aboard the second. People sifted on and off, she slid one way and another; eventually, she sat beside a window. She looked between the bars and watched whatever she saw slip away.

She reached Santa Clara in full daylight, offices open, schools in session, the morning rush subsumed into the thick trunk of a Mumbai day. But she could not imagine returning to her father's house, thrown out by her husband's people, bringing nothing but death and disgrace. The only place she could think to go was the graveyard of the Church of the Loaves and Fishes. She could sit with her mother and son. The dying could not hurt the dead.

Her route took her straight down St. Hilary Road. She came to the Almeida gate without paying attention to where she was. Then a dog began to bark, setting off others, and she looked up and saw Bella, the one she had helped rescue, moving stiffly to the edge of the veranda. The younger dogs kept up their barking, such a din that the ancient watchman appeared. Bella sat, waiting calmly for Celia to come to her.

The watchman recognized her and opened the gate. Celia was not thinking of the Almeidas, not thinking past the dog, whose welcome seemed so radical that she sat on the veranda steps, her head buried in the dog's warm fur, her eyes shut tight, as if she could sift back through the years to that bright morning when everything seemed on the brink of ruin and, in this very place, her mother had come for her.

Upstairs, waiting at the table for Mrs. Almeida to appear, Celia began to feel afraid. It was a relief to sit quietly, the heat and blare of the day at a merciful remove. But the world outside was muffled, not gone. Mrs. Almeida expected Celia to confide in her, and what could she possibly say? Abandoned by her husband, discarded by his people, contaminated. She did not know how this disease was spread, or how she herself had contracted it. What if she had passed it along to Mrs. Almeida already?

For the first time, Celia felt the full force of what she had been told. She would die. How quickly? How painfully? Would the baby die also?

"May I use the toilet?" she began, too faintly to be heard. Then she was hurrying to the landing, a hand to her mouth. She leaned over the rail, certain she would vomit, and closed her eyes. When she opened them again, she tried to focus only on what was before her: the rooftop games court of the school next door. Boys were passing footballs. The nausea began to pass.

"Dropped something?"

Mr. Almeida was more rickety than ever, the ring of his hair damp-combed in front and springing up behind. He did not seem surprised to see her and did not remark upon the pregnancy.

"I myself have lost something. A little cash, actually." He sounded stern, as though someone else had been the culprit. "I walked in the garden earlier," he added, more to himself than Celia. "Should we have a look?"

"I'm waiting for Mrs. Almeida."

"Acha, acha. Any minute she'll come."

She could run away before Mrs. Almeida asked her anything, Celia realized. Could she abandon her bag? What was the difference between having nothing and almost nothing?

"Remind me, you are—?"

"Celia. You called me a wild elephant."

"Ah well." He smiled sheepishly. "I did crazy things when I was a boy."

Celia laughed. It came as a shock that she could. "You were already older."

"And you are what? A friend of that one—what is her name—" He forced a laugh, striking his head with the heel of his hand as though to dislodge the word he needed. "My daughter," he said at last.

"That is Marian," she said softly.

"Yes. Sometimes I think of the other one," he added, by way of apology.

Had he forgotten he had only one daughter? Celia did not know what to say.

"So you've come to see Marian." He spoke with an air of finality, relieved to have settled that much, and Celia saw she was pouring water into a pair of cupped hands. He could not hold on to what she told him.

"Yes, I'm waiting for Marian. She'll come soon."

This calmed him. His expression eased. He forgot to look for his money. They stood together while he gazed out at the boys with their footballs in the milky air.

"The balls used to come flying over. Bang—right into the house. They had to put up a higher net." Celia saw the moment when understanding caught hold, a piece of the morning she could not distinguish from any other, snagging him so sharply that the soft drift of years fell abruptly into place. His face flooded with dismay. "Marian won't come, child! She left years ago. And Jude . . ." His eyes went pink and wet; she touched his arm.

"My husband left also."

She regretted this impulse at once. But Mr. Almeida only tipped his head. "What about the arm? That is healed?"

"You remember that?"

"Your face is the same. And now you will have a baby." He shook his head. "All these troubles, they come and come. You know what I live with? Statues in the bedrooms! That woman has always been crazy." He smiled at her. "But children are the reward. Now, let me ask, have you seen my bicycle?"

"No." Her voice broke a little. "That was lost."

"Really? Is it?" He sounded both polite and incredulous.

Mrs. Almeida called from inside; she would only be a minute more. Celia blinked away tears. She did not know what she would say to Mrs. Almeida. But she thought of Mr. Almeida, still looking for his bicycle, and saw that the world would not drop away when she left this house, even if she wanted it to, even if she tried to stay with her mother and son. Some future would come, however little was left of it. She would be chased from the graveyard, the gates would be locked for the night, and she would either have to sit on the street with the beggars or find a place to go. Had she ever been anyone's reward? Maybe when she was small. Maybe now she could only be a torment. But, at least once more, she would go home to her father.

"I must get on." Mr. Almeida looked around vaguely. "A late start—I must get to the station. But don't worry." He made a gesture toward his house. "These people will look after you until Marian comes."

MARCH 2000

Essie tried to dress quickly, but what was quick anymore? She used to dash about from one thing to the next, but at her age, her body made its own claims. She could not read as long as she liked without headaches. Her back protested when she rose from her chair. When her joints acted up, she could not grip a knife. That meant Pia must chop the onions, which caused a flood. Her weeping set off Frank—*What has happened? Who has died?*—and it fell to Essie to calm everyone down. She tried to describe such difficulties to Marian and Jude, but they took the view that she got too worked up about onions. They did not understand how one thing led to another.

Essie could see how it would appear to her children, hauling a statue into her room. But, for all their knowing airs and united fronts, they had a way of looking at the wrong moment. At times, this inattention seemed deliberate, an offshoot of the same dexterity with which they swept past any mention of her lonely evenings, or offered hollow assurances about *coming soon* or *calling more*.

But the night the statue arrived, did anyone call? Essie sat for hours with the cordless phone in her lap, anticipating the moment when she could report the statue's safe delivery and the concession she had finally wrested from the builder. Instead, the girl swabbed the floor. Frank dozed in his chair. Essie coughed, a lingering symptom of a recent chest cold that her daughter knew about but evidently did not consider important. This was a mistake, Essie knew. At her age, the slightest infection could take hold.

Just after midnight, she switched off the television, feeling flat and restless. There was no answer when she tried dialing Marian. Somehow she'd landed in an ordinary night.

She got up with the usual exertions and stood on the balcony, gazing out as if from the rail of a ship. Essie had long considered herself its captain, but ten years before, about to have an operation, Frank had officially given her power of attorney. He'd made no objection: past seventy and diagnosed with cancer. Marian came charging in from America and ganged up with Jude to insist on all sorts of high-priced nonsense, second opinions, private rooms, a lift in the back of the house. In the end, the rush to his bedside was for naught. The cancer was cut away, Marian decamped, Jude threw himself back into his work, and they lost their three fruit trees for a lift Frank never remembered to use.

So, when Essie heard a commotion in the back, she went on her own to investigate. Frank was in another world even when he was awake, Pia was afraid of her own shadow, the watchman slept like the dead, and the dogs saved their barking for invited guests in broad daylight. It was left to Essie to steer the ship alone.

She crossed the length of the house, taking up a knife as she passed through the kitchen. Even before she reached the back balcony, she could hear the crackle of flames. Ashok squatted beside an open fire, which was strictly forbidden by the neighborhood association, with another figure opposite. Essie could not see his face, only his silhouetted form, larger and stronger than old Ashok's. They were roasting ears of corn, this stranger who had no business in her compound and this watchman who had no business setting fires. She thought of tossing the knife down just to hear them shout, but why waste her good knife on scoundrels?

And she preferred not to wake the girl. Ashok was always taking liberties; better not to put such ideas in Pia's head or the whole household would be picking corn from their teeth. So she stepped past Pia's sleeping form, put down her weapon, and made her way down the front steps. The younger dogs whined and pushed their noses through the veranda rail, but Bella only followed Essie with her eyes, an economy Essie appreciated. She underwent similar calculations when visitors arrived, deciding whether to remain in her chair or rise to greet them.

"Oho!" she called, surprising the men. Ashok reacted at once, struggling to his feet with his stock expression of dismay. The other fellow turned, and she saw the resemblance even before Ashok tumbled into explanations. Essie put up a hand; she understood. Here was a nephew or grand-nephew in need of work. Ashok meant to shelter him.

"Where? Not here. As it is, the neighbors are at my throat!" It had been a protracted struggle to secure a concession from the neighborhood association for a live-in watchman, and Ashok claimed to understand his precarious position. But she was forever having to remind him of his part of the bargain: no unsightly tarps to reinforce his roof, no cook fires, no additional people. Twice, Ashok had tried to bring his sons to stay, then a son-in-law. Once, she made an exception to harbor a grandson who showed promise, a child who stayed a few months. Later, Essie brought him back to serve as ward boy after Frank's surgery. Marian wanted someone with hospital experience, but Essie would not bring a total stranger into the house to sleep, and the boy was thirteen by then, strong enough to support Frank's weight, intelligent enough to change a dressing. He slept on a pallet beside Frank's bed and helped him to the toilet in the night. Essie set aside some of his wages for his education, and when Frank recovered, she placed the boy in a good school. She warned Jude not to pay his fees entirely, but Jude waved away her advice, and here was the next fellow, hoping for his share. If she was not careful, the whole family would come pouring in, the neighborhood board would have to take notice, and she would have to hire in shifts.

"How can he stay?" Ashok agreed. "No, he cannot stay."

"Then where will he go?"

Ashok tipped his head, acknowledgment that, yes, this was the question. "Very soon, he will have his own post."

"Soon, is it? What about tonight?"

"He can stay anywhere." Ashok waved his hand airily, taking in the compound, the street, the whole of the Mumbai night.

Essie refused to be diverted; she asked and asked until even Ashok could not twist free of the question.

"It's back from the road; no one can see." Essie detected a singed edge to his entreaty, a touch of sullenness. He glanced at his nephew before flicking his gaze to the back wall, where Essie saw a piece of sackcloth spread against a frame of branches.

"You've built a *new* shelter?"

"What shelter is this? In two minutes it can go."

"On my own property? Without saying a word to me?"

"Of course your property. See, no one can come. We are watching."

Essie looked from Ashok to the nephew, their faces taut with expectation in the light of their illegal fire. It was the middle of the night; she was exhausted. And where was her son? Ashok could raise a tent city behind her back, and what help would she have?

She cast her gaze about, ransacking the dark for some last solution, and found instead the statue of Mary, lying on bare earth with only clear plastic sheeting to protect her.

"What is the meaning of this?"

Ashok looked puzzled. She wanted to shake him.

"The statue fell?"

"Nothing fell. We put it down." He made a cradling motion, as though they had rocked Mary to sleep.

"In the dirt! Where is the cloth?" She turned back to the shelter where the nephew would sleep and saw it all. They had left Mary to molder on the ground while they harvested the cloth.

She wanted to shout at them like a fire they could not imagine, a great dangerous blaze, but the words would not come. Or maybe she had already said them a dozen times before. She felt old, like ash. Ashok was putting the statue upright, beckoning to his nephew to come and help. The sheeting covered Mary from head to base, with a piece of twine knotted loosely around the neck. Our Lady of the Asphyxiating Veil, thought Essie. Our Lady of the Cracked Slab. This was how the world was, warping her best endeavors.

The idea came so powerfully that it did not feel like an idea at all but the involuntary working of some large muscle. "Stand back," snapped Essie as she raised Mary from the ground and began to carry her to the steps. Ashok bleated offers of help, but the statue was as airy as a beach toy. "For heaven's sake, go see to that fire," she said.

The statue's length made the ascension awkward, but Essie pressed on, resting a minute on the landing before she angled the piece through the doorway and set it on the tiles. Then she cut the twine and tugged the plastic down to Mary's shoulders, unveiling her for the first time. The face was unmarked, perfect.

It took several more minutes to free the statue entirely. Carefully, Essie examined the lines of her drapery, the fingers, the base. Not a single scratch or chip.

Essie felt a surge of triumph. She balled the plastic into a great wad and dropped it over the rail of the landing for Ashok to dispose of in the morning. The fire was out; the men were nowhere to be seen. In the morning, she would deal with the nephew—by daylight, his shelter would be visible to anyone on the games court of the school next door.

For the moment, she must decide where to put the statue. Mary could not remain in the center of a dark room, where anyone might stumble into her. But Essie did not want Mary pushed into a corner or tucked behind a chair. She could not keep Mary beside the television, as though they were competing attractions. It did not seem right to stash Mary in the kitchen. As Essie rejected one idea after another, she became aware of a kind of foolishness taking hold. She wanted Mary out of earshot of Frank's snoring and the flushing toilet. She wanted her guarded but not hidden.

A car sped past, making the sound of a zipper's teeth being undone, and for a moment, the night hung open. Lately, the neighborhood had been turning a brash new cheek—trendy shops and clubs all along Creek Road—and Essie felt the loneliness of her position, young lives flying past her gate. Perhaps that was why she decided not to abandon Mary in an empty room. Such concerns had not attached themselves to a statue in the garden, but inside, Mary became Our Lady of the Vacant Couch, Our Lady of the Fruitless Vigil. On whom would she spend her blessing? No one will come, Essie wanted to tell her. Put your arms down, rest. No one is coming.

The words, forming only in her thoughts, nearly made her weep. Not a single person beneath her roof would understand the thoughts consuming her. Not her husband. Not Jude, either, even if he were home. Mary belonged to women. Essie imagined the force of her isolation rippling across the world, through dark hours and lit ones, over oceans and hilltops, through forests and cities, all the way to her daughter, who would feel the brush of this spiritual tailwind and think to call her mother.

The phone squatted. Frank snored. Fans churned. The girl slept.

Essie did not know how she had landed in this moment after a lifetime of drawing people to her. It was a kind of exile in the middle of her own home, something past enduring, something God should not permit. She retreated to her bedroom and rummaged through her wardrobe for her favorite nightdress, which Marian's daughters had given her years before. In another month, she would turn seventy-five, and only one of her children would be with her. Her grandchildren had not visited in three years. She was left with little more than this nightdress for comfort, old and dangerously soft. But Essie pulled it over her head. She washed her face, cleaned her teeth, snapped off the lights, and returned to the front room.

The darkness was as soft as muslin. Without light, the statue became a silhouette of itself, veiled and mournful, for here was another mother whose child had left her, here was perfect understanding. Essie felt a strange clarity take hold, available only to her. If she had been seized by madness, it was the madness of prophets and saints, the madness of Moses lifting his arms to the impassable sea. She felt in the throes of a great and merciful intimacy. She knew, as she had known in the garden, what she must do. Neither she nor Mary would be alone.

The morning brought its succession of difficulties. Essie regretted that half of Santa Clara had paraded into her room to find the statue close beside her; with two minutes to herself, she would have moved Mary near the wardrobe, a perfectly rational place. The fancies of the night before, even her great wash of loneliness, had thinned to vapor in the loud, bright day. Her longing for her children also changed in tone. She believed they should bear witness to the demands placed upon her: a squatter in the garden, a girl on the run. They might even see that, while they were ignoring her, others came flocking.

In the kitchen, Pia greeted Essie with a wide and baffling smile, but Essie did not have time to linger over the puzzle of Pia's moods. From the balcony, she saw that Ashok had cleared away the plastic sheeting but left the remains of the fire—stupid, she must tell him to shovel the ashes. The sackcloth was folded outside his shelter.

"Ashok is at the gate?"

And Frank in the garden; Pia mentioned no one else. The nephew must have gone off for the day—one worry, at least, that could wait.

"It's a pity about the buns," Essie told Celia when at last she joined her. She poured herself a cup of tea and took a first long sip, feeling she had earned it. "Now, my girl. What happened?"

MARCH 2000

Mrs. Almeida listened quietly to what Celia told her: Anthony had disappeared, his mother waited a day to throw Celia out, and Celia was meant to understand he would never come for her. She wavered over how much else to say. She was aware of where her hands rested on the kettle, of her breath in the air, of herself as contagion. But, however little she knew of AIDS, she did not think it spread through touch. It was a dark disease, belonging to drug users and sex workers.

She could not understand how she had contracted such a thing. Had something happened in the hospital, one of the instruments that went inside her after her son was born? Maybe God heard Celia's prayer and struck her down that very day, so she would not be parted from her son for long. Then she passed it to Anthony.

She did not mention the virus outright. But she decided she would not lie if Mrs. Almeida asked why the family had cast her out. She braced herself, knotting her hands as though to contain any infection in the nest of her fingers.

But Mrs. Almeida's questions went in other directions: how had she come, what money did she have, when was the child due.

"You have one bag only? The bag in my room?"

And a shopping bag with thread, Celia told her. She felt shattered by her own foolishness, snatching up thread when she no longer had a sewing machine.

"You packed your things yourself?"

"His mother and sister."

Mrs. Almeida blinked, startled as a bird. "We must see what's inside." She led Celia to the front room and called for Pia to bring the bag. "Here's Frank at last," she said as they heard footsteps on the stairs.

"He was in the garden," Celia said. "He was looking—"

"Oh, he spends his life looking. He has no idea what he has and what he's lost—his mind is going."

Celia flinched, but if Mr. Almeida heard his wife, he gave no sign of it. Instead, he peered at the table, empty plates and used teacups.

"We've had breakfast?"

"You see? He doesn't know if he's coming or going. In a *minute*, Frank. You remember Celia from a little girl. Here she is, back again."

"Acha, acha." He moved past them, taking in the bag Pia brought to his wife's chair. "Going somewhere," he remarked without quite asking.

Together, Celia and Mrs. Almeida sorted through its contents. Clothes, shoes, her few books. She kept letters, cards, and photos in a wooden box; these had been dumped into a plastic bag. Handbags. Toiletries. Shawls.

"This is it? Where is your gold?"

Celia shook her head.

"Check the pockets. Feel the bottom."

She found two bottles of nail polish that did not belong to her and nearly laughed at what passed as a gift from Pinky.

"Anything?"

"No." Celia looked at the sum of her belongings, disordered from the search.

"Chapatis!" Pia sang out.

"I left the sewing machine," said Celia. She did not mention her wedding sari, which her mother had chosen, or the bedding her parents provided, or the cushion covers Celia made. Would Pinky wear her gold? Where were the clothes she had prepared for the baby? Celia felt the slow burn of a new humiliation. She had gone from a wife and mother, a person of standing, a skilled seamstress, to a girl with nothing.

"Well," said Mrs. Almeida briskly, "these people have robbed you." Then she hoisted herself from her chair. Before anything else, she told Celia, they must eat.

MARCH 2000

Celia sat in an autorick. Places she passed, places she knew, looked strange and new. Time seemed to be running backward, like a film rewinding, taking her back to Anthony's house.

At Mrs. Almeida's direction, she had emptied her bag and left her belongings on Mrs. Almeida's bed. "Mary is watching over," Mrs. Almeida said, a little joke about the statue that stood in the bedroom, and because Celia appreciated the old lady's attempt to cheer her, she tried to smile also. They brought her bag with them, along with some bags of the Almeidas'. She would need all of them, Mrs. Almeida said, to carry away the rest of her things.

It was midday before they climbed into the autorick. The morning was devoted to a series of preparations, all devised by Mrs. Almeida. After she was satisfied that Celia had eaten, after she helped Celia compile a list of the property Anthony's family had retained, after she prompted Celia *not to forget this* and *what about that*, and read over the items, and told Celia to make a fair copy to take with them in case of dispute, after she directed Pia to find the large duffel bag and Pia came back to say it was on top of the wardrobe, where she couldn't reach, Mrs. Almeida paused.

"Ah," she said.

She went to survey the situation herself. "Even with a ladder, it's high for you," she told Pia. This was true. Pia was so slight, she reminded Celia of a little shaving of cucumber peel. When Celia offered to try, Mrs. Almeida did not even look at her.

"Wait, I'll just come . . ." she said. They heard her steps on the stairs, slow and heavy.

"See, she is looking for a high, high ladder," Pia said, her words so fast they sounded like a person tumbling downhill. "When Jude-sahib is here, never once does he send me up a ladder—"

"How can she carry a ladder?" said Celia.

In fact, she brought a rake. She poked it up and snagged the full nest of bags, dragging them down from the top of the wardrobe in an apocalyptic cloud of dust. Pia beat a further layer of dust from the chosen duffel while Mrs. Almeida ran a soft cloth over the statue of Mary.

"I used to dry off my granddaughters when they came out of the bath," she told Celia. "I used to pretend the towel was a little mouse trying to bite their toes, and they would laugh and laugh." She could not bend down easily, Celia could see; she only brushed off the top of the statue. Then she sent Celia to eat some yogurt. "You are not hungry, but what if Baby is?"

When it was time to go, Mrs. Almeida took up the rake and Celia carried the duffel, with several other bags stuffed inside. Celia's thoughts were moving slowly, as though she had to fashion the joints between each one, but it occurred to her that they were an old woman and a pregnant woman, easy to rebuff. Her mother-in-law might laugh at them, or shout at Mrs. Almeida, or hurl something.

At the bottom of the steps, the pups waited, snuffling and wagging at the veranda rail. Mrs. Almeida paid them no mind, but Bella pulled herself up, a painstaking process, and came to greet Celia. She had not yet lost everything, Celia realized. There was more to lose. Anthony's mother would expose Celia as sick, and what would Mrs. Almeida do then? Celia could not risk this haven, where the dogs knew her, and the people welcomed her, and she could look at Mrs. Almeida and see a woman who thought well of her mother.

"We can stay." She was suddenly in tears. "I don't need those things."

Mrs. Almeida had a small head, like the pit of a fruit, but she was a person of some heft, with staunch hips and creaking knees. She was no longer in the business of quick turns. When she turned to face Celia, it required a series of movements, the way Jerome described an ocean liner changing course.

She paused to look closely at Celia before speaking.

"Your mother died."

Celia was taken aback. "Yes."

Mrs. Almeida sighed. "I went to America for ten weeks. That is why I didn't know. When I came back, and a month or two passed, and she never came to see me, I asked Inez. I buy only from her, because that is who your mother gave me. This was quick, I think?"

Celia tipped her head.

"And the baby also." Mrs. Almeida's voice softened. "Mummy told me you were expecting. Such a happy smile, so proud! Do you know she used to come and see me? Every few weeks, she brought dishes for us—bangda cutlets, butter-garlic crab. Harnai bombil. That is something my grandmother made when I was a girl . . ."

There was a storytelling feel to the way Mrs. Almeida was talking. Celia had never imagined the old woman in the first years of her life, her small head weighted with braids, her smile breaking open around her front teeth.

"These people," she said in a different voice, "your husband's people. Stealing from you, sending you off with nothing. What would your mother say to them?"

Celia put a hand to her mouth.

"They think they can do what they like with you. They think Daddy may let this go quietly, if he doesn't want people talking. They think, *What can she do?* Because you are a woman alone, no mother to help you. Now let them see. You are not alone."

Celia made herself look directly at Mrs. Almeida. "They say I am sick. They say—this baby also will die."

Mrs. Almeida tipped her head. "Then you will go to a doctor and see. Thieves may well be liars." She peered at Celia a moment longer. "Come. Think what Mummy would do."

She marched to the gate, and Celia followed. Pia slipped downstairs and hovered behind them like a shadow to see them off. The watchman took the rake.

"Where is this nephew of yours?" Mrs. Almeida said. "And none of your stories—working here, working there. I have a job for him."

Pia's eyes went huge when Ashok produced a tall young man from the back of the compound.

"This is how he goes looking for a post? Hiding in the back?"

He would meet a theater manager later, the watchman explained. "That is for shows. Big crowds, night security. Very good post."

"Never mind that. Today he is security for me. What is your name?"

"Akhil."

In this way, they became a threesome. Mrs. Almeida put Celia in the autorick first and squeezed beside her, with Akhil on the outside. She spoke to him, but Celia heard only the sound of their voices, not the words. She turned her face to the road. It was pleasant to let her thoughts blur, the way stalls and bodies blurred. The air off the pavement was as warm as breath.

Mrs. Almeida took her hand. "When we get back, we'll eat lunch." She spoke as though the outcome of their errand were assured. "Then you should lie down and rest. No arguments—such a morning you've had! After that, if you're feeling ready, then you can go home." Her father's house, not her husband's, which could never be home again.

The baby moved in her belly. The road flowed backward. *Five Raid a Den of Thieves*, thought Celia, though they were only three. She imagined a second rickshaw behind them: Mr. Almeida and Bella the dog, grinning in the breeze.

MARCH 2000

Essie watched Celia closely. She was tired, frightened, shocked. But Essie was pleased that, when they reached the causeway, Celia leaned forward to direct the driver. The situation demanded a show of strength; this was one of Essie's objects in recruiting Akhil. There was a time for weeping, and times when weeping might be used to advantage. But for the next hour, better if Celia did not break down.

It was after midday when they pulled aside near the turning. With a brief lament over what a help Jude's car would have been, Essie instructed the autorick driver to wait. He agreed with such alacrity that she sighed over the expense. Celia was last to disembark—slowly, Essie saw, which she attributed both to general reluctance and to swollen ankles. Akhil took the duffel.

"You understand what is happening here?" Essie quizzed him.

He cocked his head in Celia's direction. "We are getting her things."

He had accepted Essie's commission without fuss, but without curiosity, either.

"How old are you?"

"Twenty."

An age when boys were interested only in themselves. "You're not married?"

"No."

She sighed again. An illegal tenant was bad enough; an unmarried boy right beneath Pia's nose was another problem altogether.

"This is one time only," she reminded him. "Not a job you can keep." For a moment, she indulged the image of herself as an avenging angel, traversing the city to rescue destitute girls with this fellow acting the sherpa. "Come. Let's go."

She took care to keep her voice firm. Essie had raised three children; she knew that softness at the wrong moment might unravel Celia's hold on herself.

Outside the house—a solid-looking place; there must be money—Celia hesitated. The door was open, but a curtain kept out the dust.

"Here?" said Essie and pushed the curtain aside. She stepped inside, making sure Celia kept close. Akhil remained in the lane. "Hallo? Who is here?"

A dim, square room, with barred windows on the back wall and curtains indicating additional rooms on either side. A girl near Celia's age emerged from one, clothes and hair rumpled; clearly she had been resting. When she saw Celia, she stopped, pricked suddenly awake.

"We've come for her belongings," Essie announced, aware of a magisterial quality to her tone. There should be no mistake: she was not asking permission. "Celia, where should we start?"

"In the back. We share with Pinky." She began faintly, but her voice landed with more strength on the girl's name, as though to emphasize a claim. Pinky blanched when Akhil stooped his head to enter behind them. It was a good idea to bring him, Essie congratulated herself.

She did not have to order Pinky out of the way. The girl skittered from the doorway as soon as they approached and kept far from where they busied themselves. Akhil sat near the door, waiting for the bags to be filled.

Essie let Celia do most of the packing, only prompting her occasionally: "Did you bring this quilt? . . . What about shoes? . . . Where is your gold?" When Celia shook her head, looking helpless, Essie marched back out to Pinky.

"Bring her gold now."

The girl did not move until Essie said, very well, she would begin with Pinky's shelves.

"Stay where you are!" she cried, her voice high and shaky. She ducked behind a curtained doorway—the parents' room, Essie guessed—and returned clutching a small lockbox.

"Akhil will take that," said Essie briskly; she had no intention of a tug-of-war. He brought the box to Celia, who said "thank you" weakly, possibly to them all. "You have the key?" Essie asked Celia. "Check inside."

"It's all there! Nobody wants to touch your things!"

She sounded on the verge of hysteria, but Essie would not tolerate such attacks, and Celia was looking faint.

"Bring water for this girl," she said sharply.

Pinky did not refuse. But she put the glass on the floor and stepped back, the way she might have offered water to a dog.

"This is how you treat her?" Essie handed the glass to Celia. "She's carrying your niece or nephew!"

"I wanted a niece." Essie looked up to see Pinky was crying and realized they must finish soon. The duffel bag was plump with bedding, two smaller bags were ready, and Celia looked lost among the last items on the floor, some cushions, a leather bag with cheap clasps, and her wedding sari sheathed in plastic.

"These can go in the shopping bag," Essie said. "You pack up the sewing machine. It has a case? Good. And nothing else is missing?"

"One chain is gone. That wasn't in the box; I was wearing it. But that went missing before today." When Essie asked, she answered steadily enough, "When Anthony went."

"So he has taken that."

"He is the one who *gave* it," cried Pinky. "That was his to give and take."

Essie did not deign to answer but spoke loudly enough to fill the room. "Very well. We will make a claim later. For furniture as well. What about the sewing table? Is that from your father?"

Celia was nodding her head yes, "But no, please, let it go"—there were other tables. She wanted only to be gone. Essie liked giving the sister something to think about, but she saw the sense in leaving. Akhil stood at the door, the duffel over his shoulder, three smaller bags in one hand. When he saw Celia pick up the case with the sewing machine, he stopped her gently and took it himself. Celia looked around—not scanning for anything left behind, Essie realized, but taking a last account of the place where she had lived. As though it were still her job to tidy up, she bent to pick up the glass she had used to put in the dish tub.

"Take it," shrilled Pinky. "Just go."

Celia froze, the glass still in her hand.

"He's *sick*," Pinky flung at her. "He's gone for treatment. What should he do? Stay home and die? What is better, a living husband or a dead one?"

"What's *better*?" Celia echoed.

"We are going," said Essie, but Pinky would not be stopped.

"He'll be cured! He'll be cured! Then, when he comes back . . ." She broke off, tearful. When she spoke again, she was almost pleading. ". . . he can come for you then."

"He can't come for me," Celia said, in a voice so clear that Essie was transported back to the day when Celia had first turned up at her house—a child emerging from a dead faint, bruised and frightened, her wrist hanging wrong, sitting up to tell Essie, *I want to go home.*

Celia looked straight at Pinky. "I am gone. The baby is gone. Not one of you can come anywhere near us."

A voice rang out from the doorway. "What the hell is this?"

"Akhil," said Essie. "Take Celia's things." For, oh ho ho, here was the mother.

Akhil gathered up the bags and sewing machine. His way was blocked by a middle-aged woman, but he used the duffel as a wedge to move past her and out the door.

"We'll leave the table for now," Essie added by way of a parting shot. She held out her hand to Celia. "Come, Celia . . ." She did not want to risk a commotion in the lane, with the neighbors rallying.

But Celia stood as though unable to move, her eyes fixed on her mother-in-law.

"Wicked, wicked girl. You walk into my house and take what you like?"

"She's taking what is hers," Essie said sharply.

"I sent her with more than she's worth."

"Should I come back with the police? In one hour, I can come with them: three, four, as many as you like. My husband taught the Commissioner. Who will they believe?"

For the first time, the mother dragged her eyes from Celia and looked directly at Essie. "Who the hell are you?"

"I am her guardian." She stopped short of *angel*. "Celia. You have nothing to say to these people."

This time, Celia did come, the glass still in her hand.

"Take it, then, take it all," said the mother, and Essie thought of a cobra spitting venom. "Just get out from here and never come back."

Celia followed Essie to the door. She did not turn back as her mother-in-law continued to harangue her.

"We would have burned it! Everything you touched!"

"You will burn," said Essie and stepped outside into shattering sunlight. A few women had gathered to see the fuss, but no one made a move to stop Akhil, who was walking up the lane. Celia stayed close to Essie, blinking. Her arm with the glass dropped, spilling the last of the water.

"Whore!" shouted her mother-in-law.

Celia let the glass fall from her fingers. It did not break but rolled on the ground, the wet spots quickly coated with dust. She was not crying. Her eyes looked blank. Then the scene before her seemed to register—the lane, the women, Akhil with her belongings, Essie waiting beside her. Her eyes filled with such fright that Essie leaned forward to support her.

"I don't know what happened," she said.

Essie felt the echo more than she remembered it, her mother

after her father died. *I don't know what happened. I don't know, I don't know.* Essie had been six, fatherless for only a few confused days, and already she could see that her mother would not have the strength to conduct Essie through the years ahead until some other man could take over her care.

I don't know what happened. Mary might have said the same to Joseph, two thousand years before. This had always been the lot of women. A woman swept aside—abandoned or widowed or even chosen by God—must above all feel afraid.

Not Essie, whose grief for her father was shot through with a first, bitter taste of revulsion. She watched her mother stumble through the days—increasingly incompetent, increasingly unstable, reduced to pleading with Essie's uncle for a corner of her childhood home in which to bring up Essie and her brother. Essie had resolved that she would never be so lost and helpless: when she was grown, she would run her own household, on her own terms. She declined one match before agreeing to the marriage her uncle arranged. Even now, with her husband's mind thinned to strings and knots, her children telling her what she could and couldn't do, Essie stood firm. No wind would uproot her. If she'd thought the old wooden sewing table was of any importance, she would have ordered Akhil to carry it out, on his head if necessary. If she had a notion to build a shrine, or bring a statue of Mary to her bedroom, or harbor a cast-off girl, she did not waver.

So it pained her to see that Celia was not only afraid of the villagers, or her husband's family, or her father's reaction: she was scared of what Essie herself would think.

A show of reassurance would be too flimsy, Essie decided. She must give the girl something else to think about. "You used to cook with your mother, I think? You know her recipes?"

"Yes." Celia spoke hoarsely, hardly more than a whisper.

"Then you can help me. I bought rawas from Inez at market. Six pieces, for lunch today"—she steered Celia up the lane, past the staring villagers—"and your mother had such a nice touch with fish-fry. Very delicate. Pia cannot get it right. Heavy, greasy . . . I don't know why. The spice paste is fine, I think. Maybe she puts too much flour."

"Or the oil isn't hot enough." Celia's voice was steadier. She could see Akhil ahead of them, putting the bags into the autorick. "Thank you," she said to Essie, with such feeling that Essie felt the weight of it.

Essie kept hold of Celia's arm. This was not the end, she understood. The father might not take her back. God only knew what treatment the husband had gone for, or what a doctor would say after checking Celia. But it was best not to think too far ahead.

Only when they were seated tight beside one another, the sewing machine perched on Akhil's knees, did Essie permit herself to venture a few hours into whatever future was in store for this mother and child. "All this back and forth, your ankles are swelling," she told Celia. "Straight after lunch, you must put up your feet."

MARCH 2000

After lunch, Mrs. Almeida took Celia down to the veranda, where the high wooden doors to the ground floor reminded Celia of a church. The dogs twined around their legs while Mrs. Almeida fitted the key into the lock. This was where Jude stayed, Mrs. Almeida explained, but he was in Bangalore. No one would disturb Celia.

Bars of dusty light slanted in through the windows and landed in tilted patches on the floor and furniture. Again Celia thought of a church: the tile, the dim light, the chalky cool during the hottest part of the day. The ceilings were high, with threads of cobwebs running toward the walls like cracks in the paint. When Mrs. Almeida switched the fan on, they shivered without breaking. "Sleep," she told Celia, and waited for her to lie down on the guest bed before returning upstairs.

The floors and ceilings were thick. Outdoor noises dulled to a thin drone against the walls of the house. The bed was so large that when she stretched her legs she could not touch the edges. She curled herself tight around the baby and pulled a cover over her shoulders. The quiet took on a stony quality, like petrified wood. Then she heard scratching.

It took effort to heave herself up and unlatch the front door. The pups had flopped in a corner, but Bella stood at the threshold, gazing up at her. Celia unclipped the lead from her collar and let her inside, closing the door on the green-gold haze of the afternoon. Bella made a slow circuit of the rooms, her nails clicking on the tiles, before she returned to the bedroom. Celia lay down again, and the dog waited while she adjusted a cushion to support her belly. Still Bella stared, until Celia thought to put a pillow on the floor for her. Bella considered the pillow. Then she gathered herself and sprang. "Good girl," said Celia, almost laughing. They settled together on the bed, Bella curled into the crook of Celia's legs, Celia listening to the sound of the dog's breathing. She slept.

———

When she woke, her throat was dry and the light gone. It might have been any hour of the night. Without Bella, Celia would not have known where she was. She lay still a minute before she realized that someone had switched on the lamps in the front room.

"Hallo!" Pia was sitting at a desk, her face illuminated by the glow of a computer screen. "You slept and slept. Memsahib said, if she does not get up soon, how can she sleep in the night? She says you will stay if you like."

"What time is it?"

"See!" She beckoned to Celia and showed her the hour, 8:07 p.m., at the top of the screen. She was in the middle of a game of solitaire. "This gives exact time. So I know when Memsahib's show will be finished."

"Could I use the toilet?"

Even after Celia splashed water on her face, she did not feel fully herself. It was as if the quiet had closed over her, encasing her in a hard shell. The house did not seem the same, either, the rooms larger and lonelier. How many people would it take to fill such a house? She went to sit close to Pia, who played the game in fits and starts, flicking cards madly, then stopping to frown and think.

"There." Celia pointed when Pia overlooked a black nine.

"Oh oh oh!" Pia leapt to action. She smiled at Celia, rueful.

"That is because I am always bad at nines, even in school. I like fives. So nice—five, ten, fifteen, twenty."

They played to the end of the hand, which they lost. The next game they won. By then, it was 8:24 p.m., and Bella gave a small whine.

"She needs to go out." Pia sighed and switched off the computer, pulling a dust cover over the keyboard. "And Memsahib's program will finish."

Outside, the night air was a little warmer. "Go up," Pia urged Celia. She took Bella's lead and disappeared around the side of the house. "Where is your nephew?" Celia heard her ask Ashok.

But Celia hesitated. Upstairs would mean another large room, this time with the Almeidas. She was not afraid of them. She knew Mrs. Almeida would continue to help her; she knew Mr. Almeida as a kind of friend. It was not the people that daunted her; it was the empty space around them, the lonely rooms, the silences. Even if she and Mrs. Almeida talked all night—she believed Mrs. Almeida could—their voices would be like a thin column of smoke disappearing into the sky. She wanted to run home to her father's house, so crowded that they must step over one another.

An hour later, she was ready to walk back to Varuna with a single bag. The rest of her things would stay in the guest room.

"You and your father can pick them up tomorrow," said Mrs. Almeida. "Or, if there is any difficulty, you can come back here tonight," she added tactfully.

"What difficulty?" Mr. Almeida wondered.

"Oh, Frank!"

"She is going to her father's house?"

"*Yes*, but—"

"Then? Why should there be any difficulty?"

"Frank, you're upsetting her!"

Had he? While Celia walked, she tried to prepare herself for a version of her father who might turn her away. She did not feel so different from the person she had been on her last visit, a few weeks before, laughing with him over her nephew's pursuit of sweets.

"But will you share with your cousin?" her father had teased. "When Baby comes, you must share."

Akash had recovered quickly. "My sweets! That baby will be too small."

Was she still the person who dropped a shower of chocolates into Akash's lap? Once all was known, who would her father see when he looked at her? The shame of her rejection would be his shame also. This disease, whatever its terrors, would come into his house. Akash must be protected, and Alma, hoping for a second child, and Evangeline. Her mother had taken such pains to guard their health; what would she say to Celia, putting them all at risk?

Celia might have turned back without the echo of Mr. Almeida's voice—*She is going to her father's house*. The sound of the words—the ease with which he'd assumed her welcome—kept her moving forward. The moments when Mr. Almeida recognized her seemed more important than the moments when he didn't. She wanted to put her faith in what he knew.

She reached Varuna Road just after nine-thirty, a lively time. Friends and neighbors came to greet her, exclaiming over her belly, making predictions.

"You're looking more like Mummy every day!"

"See her hair, thicker than ever! That means a boy, Celu."

"How long will you stay? For the birth?" Inez grasped her hand. "Any little pain, day or night, you send for me."

At her own door, Celia hesitated. There was a new rangoli pattern, a green-and-pink pinwheel. Celia knew Alma meant nothing particular by it; she had taken to rangoli as a way to relax when her work was finished. She liked to sit and chat while sand shifted through her fingers; she liked to please Celia's father, who was reminded of his grandmother. Rangoli was a way of passing the time, a way for Alma, who reminded Celia of a plump bird with plain feathers, to sing a loud, bright song.

Still, Celia hung back. *Diseased*, her mother-in-law had called her. Some villagers believed rangoli designs prevented evil forces from crossing a threshold. What evils would she bring her family?

"That is mine!" Akash announced in his funny, sharp voice. She heard laughter; heard that her father was home. Then the curtain swung open.

"Celu!" Evangeline smiled with such happiness that Celia could hardly bear it.

"Celu?" Her father crowded behind Evangeline, smiling also but puzzled when he saw Celia's face. "What is it, girlie?"

"I can't go back. They won't have me." She did not expect to be so blunt. But she could not bring herself to step over Alma's pinwheel until her father knew. "They say Anthony is gone and I am sick." She kept her voice steady until she had to say, "The baby also." Evangeline looked as if she'd been struck. "I have a place to go if you don't—" But her father brushed past Evangeline to come into the lane. He held Celia so tightly that when she began to cry, no one could see her face.

Then, without letting go, half-carrying her over the doorstep, he brought her inside.

MARCH 2000

The house was quiet once Celia left. A news anchor rattled through the events of the day while Frank sat with his face inclined toward the television, the way a flower faces the sun without appearing to notice it. Essie sank into her chair. Her back and knees ached; she was too old to go running all over town. Still, she did not want to go to bed, in case Celia was turned away.

The newscaster kept on and on with a voice like a wool sweater in June.

"Frank? Are you watching that?"

"What?" He looked around. "Where's that child gone?"

"To her father's house. You *know* this."

"Acha, acha."

"He must have taken her back or she'd have come by now."

"And tell me once more, what is the connection?"

"There's no connection; she's a village girl." Essie did not have the energy for all this round-about. "The only connection is, you hit her with your bicycle."

He seemed to regard this as old news and turned back toward the television. Essie checked the cordless phone to be sure it was working.

"Sometimes she reminds me of Marian. Or that other girl."

Our little one, the baby." He tapped his head with his knuckles to remember her name, which Essie had not said in years.

"Theresa?"

He smiled when she supplied the answer, as though they were young again, winning a round of charades at a party. The babies had come too early. Jude's twin was born first, a little girl who lived only a few hours.

"I go sometimes to see her," Frank went on.

"You go to the cemetery?"

He tipped his head—where else? The baby was in a permanent family grave, one of the last before the church moved to a system of temporary plots and niches, or bone wells for the poor. "This village girl. She must be around the age the baby would have been."

He got up and crossed to the front railing. He had probably lost the thread of the conversation already, thought Essie. There was no point reviving it.

"No," she called to him finally. "Celia is younger. The baby would be Jude's age exactly. Forty."

"Forty!" He laughed in disbelief. "Such a little thing. I held her, you know."

Tiny limbs, ragged breaths. They had sent for a priest at once, and Frank's sister-in-law stood as godparent to both. Impossible woman, Essie did not want her, but she was home and the baptisms could not wait. At first it seemed that neither twin would survive, but Essie named Jude for the patron saint of lost causes, who must have interceded.

Frank wandered back into the room. "I think of her as a young girl," he said. "Then this one turns up expecting!"

Essie did not know what to say. They had not spoken about their child in decades. What did it mean that, when Essie thought of the baby they lost, she saw the ankle, as small as a knuckle bone; she saw the eyelids? She had felt the small body against her chest, the tiny fluttering heartbeat. She lay in bed and held them both, one on each side, for as long as she could. One by one, Frank lifted them from her arms to be christened. Then the boy began to cry, a small, crumpled noise, and she had to shift to feed him. Somebody else took the girl; was it Frank? She was not with Essie when she slipped away.

Afterward, someone brought her back to the bed and held her close enough for Essie to say goodbye. She blessed the baby, touched her cheek, kissed her hand. But no, no, take her. She tried to train her eyes on the little boy's face. Her son was still alive; if she must lose them both, she could not miss his last hours. Even though she was not crying—she was not, she was praying with an intensity she had never felt before—tears streamed from her eyes so that she could hardly see. His slight weight on her arm, the scant pounds of him wrapped in a blanket, seemed to be the only thing holding her on earth. Otherwise, she might have floated off with her daughter.

"Her face was not so round as Jude's," she said. "More like Simon's. She was smaller."

It was strange but unexpectedly companionable to talk about her. When had they decided not to mention her? Perhaps at first they were being careful for the older children. Marian was ten, Simon only eight. Essie tried to point them firmly ahead. She tried to fill their heads with Jude. *Who would like to feed the baby? Who would like to sing to the baby? Go and wash your hands properly so you can hold the baby.* She tried to fill her own. He was smaller than the doctor liked; she needed to keep track of his feedings. He looked only to one side, a condition of the muscles, and she called to him from the other side to encourage him to turn his head. "It's like a stiff neck," the doctor said. "This can happen with twins, when the babies are crowded." She tried not to imagine her son's body forming around his sister's. She tried to feel thankful for the child God gave her to keep. When she wept, she made certain to be alone, waiting until Simon and Marian were in school and Jude was asleep. Even then, she left the room so her grief would not harm the baby.

When she gave her confession, she went deliberately to the new young priest, the one who did not know her. "I want more than God has given me," she told him. Sometimes he said what she knew already, that God was not finished giving, that God's blessings were all around her, that God would give her strength.

One day, he only said, "Yes." She walked out of the church feeling lighter, and then she began to run, terrified that such lightness might mean Jude would also be taken.

What did Frank feel? What did he do? She wondered how often he visited the grave. But they'd ventured into unknown territory; best not to go too far at once. Anyway, he was pacing once more. His legs were the fittest part of him, Essie thought, carrying him around and around his house in search of something to do. But what could she entrust to him?

"Why don't you check on the dogs, Frank?"

"Is that statue staying?" As though Mary were a visiting relation, off in the morning to get a train.

"Yes, of course. We're building a shrine."

"In the bedroom?"

"In the *garden*, Frank!"

"Ah," he said, and headed down the stairs.

"The dogs," Essie called after him, in case he reached the bottom without knowing why he had gone.

She must have dozed. When she woke, the night had shifted, as though she'd missed a round of musical chairs. Frank was gone, the television talking to no one. The door was wide open—their daytime habit, but it was full night.

Essie pushed herself up from her chair. Frank was fast asleep, a sheet pulled so high on his shoulders that she could see his heels. Pia was nowhere to be found.

Essie called from the kitchen balcony. No answer. It was after ten-thirty, not an hour when Pia should be out of hearing. It would serve her right if Essie bolted the door. Instead, she started heavily down the steps. How many girls would she need to rescue in one day? she wondered grimly.

She spotted Pia before she reached the bottom. The girl was in the road with Akhil, walking back from God only knew where, perfectly clear in the light from a streetlamp.

"Pia!"

You see? she wanted to tell her children. She could not close her eyes for two minutes without some fresh nonsense. Then she realized Ashok was with them, *Memsahib, come.* Pia was crying openly. Akhil carried something in his arms. The dogs on the veranda were barking, barking madly, but when Essie looked she saw only the pups.

 She found she could still run, right through the pain in her knees.

MARCH 2000

Memsahib never seemed to like the dogs. She sighed over the food, the expense, the noise, even the "breaks" Pia must take to go and walk them, although these were not exactly breaks, Pia felt, only a chance to leave the house, and anyway it was not Memsahib dragged through the neighborhood at such a pace that once Pia lost her chappal and had to yank the pups back to the heavyset man who had picked it up. He laughed at Pia and had bad teeth, so there was no happy-ever-after Cinderella story, only the tug-tug-tug of the pups and her foot dirty from the road. After that, she told Jude-sahib that the pups pulled too badly. She took them for a quick loop each morning, but otherwise she let them off their leads to chase each other around the compound. Then Memsahib sighed over the flower beds and the messes they made, although it was Pia who had to remind Ashok to clean up their dirty business and sometimes even to point out the piles, because he grumbled that he was too old to go hunting. Otherwise, the pups stayed on the veranda, tied to the rail with a bowl of water that Pia must keep filled. They barked so loudly when visitors came that they set off Memsahib also, and again and again Pia must hear the story of how Jude convinced his mother to keep first one, then the next, before accepting a transfer south. "They will outlast me," she said, which might be true, thought Pia, since the pups were only five and three, although Memsahib's exact age was beyond her calculations. After Pia's second spring in the household, she realized that Memsahib's birthday fell on different days each year because Memsahib did not bother about the numbers. She was born on Easter Sunday, she was named for Easter Sunday, so Easter Sunday was her birthday.

Memsahib also sighed over the nice mother dog, Bella, but Pia enjoyed looking after her. She must be coaxed up steps but still enjoyed a walk, and this was one of the duties Jude assigned to Pia, giving her an hour to wander through the neighborhood without Memsahib scolding. Sometimes they went to Varuna, for Bella to sniff the cats and fish. Sometimes Pia met her friend, who worked in a house on St. Vitus, to walk along Creek Road. The friend liked a bank guard who wore a uniform; Pia preferred a clerk in the hardware store. When she stopped, Bella did not tug but waited so sweetly that it seemed she approved. Jude taught Pia that dogs sensed the goodness in people.

So it was terrible that it was Bella, with all her quiet ways, who was hit in the road—such a loud, bad thing to happen. And terrible to see Memsahib take one look at the dog in Akhil's arms and go pale and drawn, like a lovesick girl.

"She's alive?"

Yes, she was whining, staring up at them, trying to follow their voices with her eyes. The underside of both thighs were huge open wounds, scraped raw, as though she'd been dragged.

"What happened? How did she get out?"

Akhil said nothing. Ashok tipped his head sadly, an acknowledgment of fate, bad luck, the unpredictability of life. Pia began to cry again, knowing it had been Badasahib. Ashok would not say so in front of Memsahib, but he saw Badasahib open the gate to take Bella for a walk, the way he used to. Ashok was not at the gate when Badasahib came back; he did not see that he had returned without the dog, or he would have gone looking at once. He could not watch the gate every moment of the day; he was one man only, he defended himself to Pia when they discovered Bella was missing. "Even with two of you, there is no one at the gate," she cried, then burst into tears; she had not known misery could make her cruel. Ashok did not answer, which made her feel worse. He insisted on coming when they went to search.

They found her two streets away, the lead still clipped to her collar. Something must have distracted Badasahib, and he dropped it. Or maybe Bella pulled free, Ashok suggested, though Pia knew Bella never pulled. "Bring her in, quickly. Pia, run and get towels."

What could they do? It was too late at night for a vet. Ashok stayed outside to calm the pups. Akhil carried Bella into the bathroom and held her head so she would not snap while Memsahib tried to clean her wounds. But the dog only whined, twitching so weakly when the towel touched her that Pia thought she must be near death. Memsahib found a tube of antibacterial cream, and they cut a clean sheet to use as bandage. Akhil held her while Memsahib and Pia wrapped her hind side as gently as they could.

"Can she stand?"

She could not. They saw no further injury, but her back legs collapsed beneath her, and she cried so sharply that Pia cried also. In the end, they spread a towel on the floor and laid her on her side, the side that seemed a little better. She shifted feebly, but no position could be comfortable. Akhil kept his hand on her head. She gazed at Pia when Pia brought a bowl of fresh water but did not lift her nose to drink.

"Keep her far from the pups—they'll go for the bandages. And see if you can get her to take some water. We'll see what the vet says in the morning." Memsahib sounded tired but more like herself, making plans. "It's better if she stays down, in case she needs to go out. You'll have to sleep here and carry her," she told Akhil. "Only tonight," she added sternly. "Pia, you come up with me."

A few minutes later, when Pia was nearly asleep, she heard Memsahib come quietly to the kitchen, saw the cold white light of the refrigerator. A minute later came Memsahib's footsteps, heavy on the front stairs. Pia was asleep before Memsahib came up again.

60

MARCH 2000

It occurred to Essie that the dog might take meat. She rejected the chicken—too pungent for a dog—but she took down a plate of sorpotel that was not so highly spiced. The pups were asleep, curled around each other in a corner; they rose to greet her as she stepped past them but for once did not bark or beg, as if they recognized the gravity of the moment.

Inside, Akhil still sat on the floor with Bella. He dipped his fingers into the bowl of water and put them to her mouth. She licked them, a weary courtesy.

"She takes a little," he said.

Essie gave him the plate of meat. "You have eaten?"

Yes, before they found her. He offered Bella a small piece of pork and she licked it lightly before letting her nose sink down again. Essie thought of the night her mother died. There had been breakdowns, public episodes, spells of ranting, several years when they were careful not to let her leave the house unattended. It was a relief when her body began to relinquish its frantic hold. Her mother, so jagged and shrill, so impossible to contain, finally quieted, as if a large hand—the hand of God—had smoothed over her edges at the end. She was peaceful, composed, dying softly. It was a relief to Essie to perform the duties that any daughter would, to send for the priest and recite prayers at her bedside. For once, nothing was out of order.

Essie looked at Bella, who was gazing at her from the floor, and wished she could call someone to pray over the dog. It felt empty, a little wrong, just to leave her.

"If anything happens in the night . . ." She stopped. She had thought it was better to keep Pia upstairs; the child did not have the disposition to cope with emergencies and she must be chaperoned with men about. But if Bella suddenly worsened, what could this fellow do? The upstairs door must be locked. Essie could not have him creeping through the house to wake her. "You think she will live?" she asked suddenly. It was not her custom to seek answers from others when her own judgment was perfectly sound, but the day had worn her down. She found herself wishing she could consult Marian or Jude. A long time ago, it would have been Frank, she thought with a pang. Tonight, there was only the watchman's nephew.

"How old is this dog?"

They did not know exactly. She was a stray, lured home from church. If it had not been Christmas Day, Essie would never have agreed to keep her. "Ten or eleven, we think."

"That is many years."

No, then, thought Essie. *He thinks this is the end.* But she was not a person to say goodbye to a dog. "Good night," she told Akhil instead.

Her legs felt waterlogged even after she lay down. The statue of Mary was still in the corner near the window. It did not quite face the bed, but Essie let her eyes fall on Mary's face before she slept. A sidelong view for a sidelong prayer, one she did not form in words. She was not a person to pray for a dog. Her mind simply filled with a vision of Bella jumping up to greet Jude, something that had happened so many times before that, despite what Essie knew, she could not break the habit of believing it might happen again.

MARCH 2000

There, thought Essie triumphantly when she came down in the morning and Bella looked up at her. She could not rise, she moved only her eyes, but she had lived through the night. She took a little water, Akhil reported. "Not enough. She is weak." He did not say "dying," though the dog's gaze struck Essie as sad but knowing, too dignified to ask to be saved.

But there was no stopping Frank, who was so distressed when Essie broke the news at breakfast that he insisted on accompanying her to the vet. Neither could carry the dog, so Akhil came as well, Bella held softly against his chest. Frank kept a hand on the dog's head, so the two men moved in tandem, as awkward as a parade float. This was just like men, thought Essie, slowing everything down for no good reason. "Hurry!" she called, before predicting beneath her breath, "Or that dog will die in the road." She was the one to walk to the corner and hail an auto.

She hoped the vet would conduct a quick wound check and let them go, but they waited over an hour to learn that the dog must stay. There would be antibiotics, a hydration pack, scans to rule out further injury.

"And what will all this cost?" Essie wanted to know.

"We don't know yet if Bella will need surgery," the vet began. She was a short woman with hair so wild that Essie, already taken aback by the parrot in the waiting room, recalled the days when her mother called her uncombed hair a bird's nest. "And there is danger of infection."

"Whatever she needs!" Frank said, as though packs of money roamed the streets like pariah dogs, waiting to be lured home. As though Akhil were not sitting beside them, bound to think they could afford any number of watchmen.

"Frank—"

"Let's go one step at a time," the vet said, and Essie tried to persuade Frank to come home with them. When he refused, the vet patted his shoulder.

"*Welcome* to stay, Mr. Almeida. Your wife mustn't worry; we can make you very comfortable in our lounge. These pets—they're like our children, no?"

No, thought Essie, aggravated nearly past restraint. Could any mother think so? She once sat in a hospital, waiting for news of her child, and so had Frank, if he could remember it. But Frank would not listen to reason, so Essie enlisted Akhil to stay with him. Then she took the vet aside and explained that she alone held the purse strings. "No procedures without my approval. Unless you are offering them for free," she added.

The vet pressed her lips together, all talk of dogs as children finished, and directed Essie to the billing counter to submit her deposit.

"These scans cost more than my own," Essie told the girl behind the desk.

"The machine is the same," said the girl.

"You must bring him home in time for lunch," Essie reminded Akhil. Then she raised her voice, to be sure Frank heard. "I am not packing up food to bring back here."

He tossed his hand to brush her away, a gesture she would not normally permit. But she saw he could not speak.

Your father is heartbroken, she thought as she left, a preview of the calls she planned to Jude and Marian.

At first Essie was not sure about Celia's father. He came with Celia before lunch, and hung back in the yard even after Essie urged him inside. She found herself remembering the first time she met Celia's mother—Flora's dismay over the strange house, the broken wrist. Still, she had managed to keep the child calm, to accept the money she needed to accept, to do all that was required. Would the father be capable? He looked a simple man, in his loose trousers and sandals, handing her a bag of fresh fish with hardly a word. Essie had to point out that at her age she could not be expected to carry packed bags and sewing machines; he really must come inside. Then he jumped as though she'd set off fireworks beneath his feet. Essie felt an unexpected twinge of loss, thinking Flora would have shared her amusement.

He looked ready to dash down the road the moment they gathered Celia's belongings. But Essie told them to sit. It was one thing and then the next this morning, but she could not let Celia go without certain assurances, not only because she was fond of the girl, but because she must act on behalf of Flora. They had been friends in a way that others might not credit or recognize but which meant something to Essie: a welcoming smile in the market, the certainty of fair treatment, the gift of a meal when she did not expect it. Her sons and husband had no idea how pleasant it was to be surprised by a dinner she did not have to supervise. Her daughter had lived with fixed prices so long that she had forgotten what a difference a fishmonger could make. Every time Essie thought of prawns, she thought of Flora.

Of course, it ought to have been Flora looking after Celia, but Flora was gone. Essie ought to be occupied with her children and grandchildren, but they had cast themselves off. Essie and Celia were left behind. There were days when Essie found it difficult to trust God's hand in such a mishmash, but hadn't Jesus entrusted his own mother to John? She would not turn her back on this child.

Half an hour later, she was satisfied. Dominic would take Celia that very evening to the clinic. If Celia did not like to continue there, they would find another near Varuna.

Essie faced him directly. "You know there may be something wrong. These people spoke of illness. I don't know what."

He tipped his head.

"But she will stay with you?"

He said yes so openly that Essie pressed to be sure he understood.

"Even if she is sick?"

His face settled into a resolve she had not yet seen. "Celia is home. And the baby also."

Then it was only tea and biscuits before they went.

"You gave me these when I first came!" The strain of the past days lifted, like a piece of tracing paper, and there was Celia, as bright and happy as a child. Essie nearly laughed aloud to see her.

"These are my favorite, from abroad. We used to have them only when Marian visited, but now you can find them in special shops. Jude brings them from Bangalore."

Essie's knees ached, and her back. Still, she walked them down when it was time to go. "Where's Bella?" Celia asked when the pups leapt up to hail them. "Still sleeping?"

Essie looked at Celia, holding a parcel of biscuits for her sisters and nephew. For the moment at least, the child was managing not to think about the clinic or her husband or the troubles ahead. "Sleeping," Essie agreed. "Come soon and see her." She turned to the father, speaking firmly to be sure he took her meaning. "I want to know how she does."

Essie watched them go, his hand on Celia's back as he ushered her across the road. In another month, Essie would turn seventy-five. Would she always wonder what her life might have been if her father had lived?

They turned the corner, out of sight. Essie turned also. It was time to begin lunch, and still no sign of Frank. Should she get in an auto and fetch him? But her knees, her back . . . No, let him be. Soon the poor dog would die, and that would be the end of it.

MARCH 2000

Francis came to the table, but it was a wrench to leave the poor dog in such a bewildering place with only strangers to look after her. The whole business left him tearful and queasy.

"Eat, Frank," Essie kept saying.

He took a bit of rice. It felt as if something had lodged in his throat, which even hot tea could not dissolve.

"A little more. You must eat with these medicines." Every morning, he took pills to thin his blood, strengthen his kidneys, boost his memory. When they upset his stomach, the doctor advised this and that; Francis did not keep track. But Essie was watching, always watching.

She waited until he took a small helping of chicken before she began fussing about a person named Akhil, for whom she would have to make arrangements. Was he a houseguest? She did not exactly address her remarks to him, but they rose around her in a cloud.

"Let him sleep in Jude's room," Francis said, by way of dispensing with the matter, but Essie frowned and said they had already put him there once; now they must be careful. She must find a good solution. Until then, she had so much to do, she slept so badly in the night, possibly she could send this Akhil back to check on the dog.

The dog! It all came flooding back, as sharp as a cramp. Francis must get back to her. He knew the street—he could see the building—but he could not remember the name to tell an auto driver.

"But what is the name of that place?"

"Don't upset yourself, Frank, eat."

The dog's name slipped out of reach. *Good girl*, he thought, which was what he always told her. To Essie he said fiercely, "We must bring her home."

"I *know*, Frank. But it could be some time before she's ready."

"What time did they say?"

She did not answer properly but called Pia to clear the meal and said maybe she'd better go herself; otherwise, what kind of bills was she racking up.

Bills again, thought Francis. Her conversation generally found its way into certain tracks. He watched her go, her legs looking thick and painful. When he remembered the couple they had once been—her slender ankles, the breadth of his shoulders—Francis could hardly believe the directions their bodies had taken.

It was easier to hold on to his thoughts once she left, easier to keep to a single purpose. He must get back to the dog. He would ask the watchman—then, suddenly, with no warning, his bowels seemed to buckle. He clutched his abdomen and cut through Essie's bedroom to get to the toilet, but could not make it. He bent double in a corner, praying no one would come.

The accidents came without warning, a side effect of a new medication. "We'll try a few months to see what his system can tolerate," the doctor said. "For now, just put a cloth beneath him." Essie kept an old towel over a vinyl chair and frowned if Francis went near the sofa cushions.

He did not know what to clean first. The girl was in the kitchen; Essie could be anywhere. Gingerly, he removed his soiled clothes, took fresh ones from his wardrobe, and locked himself in the bath to clean himself. At first he tried to rinse the slacks as well, but in the end he stuffed them into a plastic bag with his underclothes and hurried to mop the floor with a towel.

The mess was not as bad as he feared, but Essie kept a statue of Mary in her bedroom—an icon of her capacity to bewilder him still—and it was unsettling to crouch before the statue in such a state of mortification.

He could not risk the chance of discovery, so he slipped off to discard the soiled clothes and towels in the rubbish bin behind St. Anne's. Then he walked home, trembling with effort. That was the medication also: fatigue.

The girl was in the kitchen when he returned. Francis went straight to his room and collapsed on his bed. He would rest a few minutes, then go find the dog.

When he woke, he was cold, the sun setting, his mind fogged, the day lost.

Essie was in her chair in the front room, watching a news report. "I've been running all over town, and you slept right through," she told him. "In a little while we'll eat—Jude is coming for the weekend. Any minute he should be in."

"Good, good." Francis brought his hands together in a single clap of approval and went to the balcony, in part to look out for Jude but also to see the neighborhood come to life for the evening, people laughing and talking in the streets, children chasing down the last daylight, visitors ringing bells, commuters making their way home. Across the road, in the place a small cottage used to occupy, was a five-story flat building with balconies. On one nearly level with his own, Francis saw a gray-haired woman in a wheelchair sitting quietly among her potted plants. He knew her, of course, had known her for years. The cottage had once been hers. She was recently widowed, but her children had taken flats in the building above and below her. It was pleasant to think that, although the shapes of their homes had changed, they were still neighbors.

He ought to find the photos he had taken of her cottage, he decided. He could show them to her, and they could speak of the days when they were young. He might write up an account for the neighborhood history, though his typewriter was no longer stationed at the gymkhana. Jude had brought it home and set it up on a small table on the front balcony for the mornings when Francis felt able to work. His papers—pages he had typed and research he had collected—were safely ensconced with his photographs in a suitcase. Everything he needed to work was near at hand, though most days the typewriter remained shrouded beneath its dust cover. Francis had not given up the project, but the medications took a toll, and the disturbances of home, and the limits of his own strength.

On the back of a stray sheet of paper he wrote "cottage across." That was enough—a quick note, so he would not lose ground. The day had gotten away from him, but he would try again tomorrow. In the morning, his neighbor's name might come.

He drifted through the front room—past Essie, frowning at the television; past his chair with its towel—and circled again to the balcony. His neighbor in the wheelchair had gone in. The night was slowly settling, the way a large animal—a bullock or camel—lowers itself to the ground in stages. He was not at all cold, now that he was up and moving. Perhaps he and Jude would go for a walk, the way they used to in the evenings. They could take the dog. Good girl. She liked a bit of exercise at night.

APRIL 2000

She was home, Celia kept telling herself. But she felt so dazed that nothing could anchor her—not her place beside Lina, where they used to sleep as girls; not the plans anyone made for her; not the items she prepared for the baby, which she unpacked into a small box, folding and refolding the clothes, wondering what she had forgotten.

The days tossed her up and batted her along, one to the next. A doctor, another doctor. Yes, she was HIV positive. No, that was not yet AIDS. Yes, the baby was doing well. No, no sign of any problem. Yes, perhaps they could prevent the virus from passing to the baby.

"But how can you cure the child and not the mother?" Her father sounded angry. He sat beside Celia in the doctor's office, his hand on the arm of her chair as though they were both on small boats and hers needed steadying.

More explanations. A pamphlet.

"And what should we do to prevent?" he asked carefully. "She will be staying with us. What cautions . . ."

Another pamphlet, which Celia held tightly. Yes, she could feed Akash with her fingers, but no, she could not breast-feed the baby. Yes, she and Lina could drink from the same bottle. Yes, she could hug people, kiss people. Yes, she could prepare food. But if she cut her finger . . . if she needed injections . . . if she engaged in sexual activity . . .

Celia looked away from them both, to a corner of the room.

No, it was not dangerous to sneeze, cough, vomit. Yes, she could use the same toilet.

"Then how did she—"

"Anthony," Celia said. Here was something she knew, a clear shaft of light through all her bewilderment. She did not know how or why, only that he had fled out of shame.

The doctor waited for her to say more. When she did not, he addressed himself to her father. "Usually in such cases . . ."

Celia spread her hand on her belly and waited to feel a kick, a roll, a swell of movement. Was the baby asleep? She was haunted by the fear that these might be their last days together, their clock ticking down.

"Celu? What do you think?"

She blinked. Her father waited, the doctor waited. "Can you say it once more?" she had to ask.

A meeting she should attend. Her father peered at the flyer before passing it to her. EKATRA was printed at the top, a transliteration of the word "together" in Marathi. Together what? Celia heard the doctor's voice—*community, information, support, services*—without connecting the words to their meanings. She saw that the meeting was in a parish building of St. Anne's.

"This is not our church." Her voice barely scratched the air. She cleared her throat and tried again. "We are at the Church of the Loaves and Fishes."

"It's only a meeting room," the doctor said. "Anyone can go."

Celia nodded as though she understood. She kept missing things, the bridges from one idea to the next or from a fact to its conclusion. She would go to a meeting in a different church; why? She had this virus; what was it doing to her? She had a question about every twinge, every ache, every night she lay awake, exhausted. What was illness and what was pregnancy and what was her husband running off? She wished to be a schoolgirl again, for teachers and drills and the chance to put her hand in the air and ask questions outright.

"Will I die?"

Her voice was too loud. The doctor stopped whatever he was saying. She had to ask again.

"The virus will kill me?"

He tipped his head, prevaricating. "Not directly. Being HIV positive only means you have the virus. The trouble comes when too much of the virus builds up in the system. That is the last stage of infection—what we call AIDS. We can still treat a patient with AIDS, but we cannot cure it. Eventually, the body cannot fight off opportunistic infections, and the patient succumbs."

Succumbs, thought Celia. She wondered if her father knew the word, but he was stuck on another.

"But Celia does not yet have this AIDS? She is virus-only?"

"That's right. We say 'positive.' And we can treat her with medications to delay the virus from taking hold."

"What medications? How long can they work?"

"In some people, the virus is dormant a very long time. With treatment, she may be strong for many years."

"How many years?" her father wanted to know. "What is the longest?"

Celia did not have to hear the doctor's answer, because the baby moved beneath her fingers. She cupped her hand over the knob of a little froggish heel or fist and hummed beneath her breath in case the baby could hear her. Their voices washed past—the doctor proposing and her father countering—making arrangements, as though Celia were embarking on a new marriage and her father was determined to secure the best possible terms.

APRIL 2000

Celia had no interest in support groups. She wished only to stay with her family. In the early mornings, while the others slept, she stared at the same patch of wall she had faced as a child and pretended she was a girl again, her mother alive, her own life fresh and new. It was only when she must push out of the house and walk up the lane that she was forced to return to herself, nearly twenty-two, with a husband whose desertion she had not revealed outside the family and a disease that would make her an outcast if anyone knew. She let people think she had come home for the birth and tried not to speculate about how long such pretenses could last.

But her father regarded the community meeting in the same light as a medical appointment. He kept the flyer in a folder of materials from the clinic, which he consulted again and again.

"Today is the day!" he announced the morning of the meeting, the way he might announce a birthday or surgery, some momentous occasion.

But nothing will change, thought Celia. I have this thing. I will have it always. She hinted that she was feeling tired. Maybe she should wait until after the birth?

"It may be more difficult with a little one . . . Better to make a start, no?" He would hate a delay, Celia knew. The doctor had stressed the importance of early intervention, and whatever he advised, even in passing, was sacred to her father. Foods, vitamins, grassroots meetings. Prescriptions filled at once. If compliance could save his daughter and grandchild, they would live.

"It's for support, this says. Nothing tiring. Should I come with you?"

Celia put on a fresh outfit, as though going to church, and folded the flyer in her handbag so no one would see.

"I can come with you," her father offered again, his face a little lost. Celia did not have the energy to worry about him.

"Next time," she said. "Tonight, I'll see what it's like."

The meeting room was in a parish building just past the church. A paper sign on the wall said only EKATRA, nothing to indicate HIV or AIDS, with an arrow that directed her up an exterior flight of stairs to an outdoor passage. Shoes were piled outside an open door at the back. Celia had walked slowly, a delay she regretted when she heard a single clear voice from inside the room. Clearly, the meeting was under way, and she could no longer slip inside unnoticed.

Instead, she lingered among the shoes. Men's, women's, children's, even a small red pair that reminded her of the day she had lost a shoe as a child, when this jumble might have seemed the answer to everything. Would she have taken a pair? She did not think so, but she could not be certain. What she remembered best was fear, a fear that seemed strangely disjointed so many years later, because what exactly had she been afraid of? Not a scolding, not really. Not poverty, though she knew how badly that frightened her mother. She was afraid to let her parents down, afraid to see the care and worry she cost them, afraid the shoe might expose her as more trouble than she was worth.

How much had changed? She had lost her mother, she had lost her son. In any way that signified, she had lost her husband. She might lose her new baby. Eventually, the virus would overtake her and she would lose her life. Yet those fears weren't the ones holding her back. They seemed almost beside the point on a warm evening in April, her back aching from the steps she'd just climbed, her thoughts fully occupied with whatever the next few hours would hold. She was outside the door because she was afraid to be seen, and she had come to the door because she was afraid to disappoint her father.

This was what finally drove her into the room: with so much else to face, she would not be conquered by a meeting. A woman in a cotton sari came hurrying along the balcony and kicked off her slippers, nodding briefly at Celia before entering. Celia followed.

The room was full. She tried not to look at anyone in particular, but her gaze raked over the rows of people in chairs, with more standing behind and others cross-legged on the floor. Children played in a corner, the little ones looked after by older siblings. Celia began moving to the back, but at once a woman got up from her chair and motioned to Celia to sit.

The speaker was in her early forties, Celia guessed, with a broad face and strong voice. She held up an example of a doctor's certificate and explained that people with immune deficiency could receive concessions on bus and train fares. "Sometimes you may be turned away," she warned. "But even if you feel embarrassed, you must fight against such discrimination. Remember, you are fighting also for others. Many positives need these fares to go and seek treatment. And people with other illnesses—cancer, heart conditions, kidney problems—all are eligible. Why not us?"

She sat down, and the next speaker got up, a man who spoke about screening centers. Next came adherence to ART protocols—a patient, not a doctor. "For four years, I am positive, and still feeling strong. HIV is not the end of life." Speaker after speaker addressed the group, a brisk round-about of information about drop-in centers and hotlines, an update on the youth outreach program, a report on the link between HIV and TB. The woman who had given Celia her seat announced job openings at the support center. "We train you to work in your communities as teachers and counselors."

Half an hour after Celia arrived, the first speaker stood again to share her personal story. Her name was Saroja. She went home for the birth of her second child, and after a routine checkup, the doctor asked that she summon her husband. Saroja explained he was working in another city and could not make the journey, but her father was with her and asked to know the problem. For over a week, the doctor refused to discuss her condition with anyone except her husband. After several days of this impasse, Saroja's father finally said: I am the caretaker for my daughter, I am here with her; just please tell me what is the problem with her blood. Finally, the doctor sent Saroja out of the room and told her father that she was infected with HIV; her husband would need to be tested.

"So my father told me. The doctor would not tell me himself."

The doctor said she must begin treatment, but Saroja could only think of her older son. "He was six years old, waiting at home for me, and I thought, What will happen to him if I have this?"

When it was time for the delivery, her husband came. He went to a private clinic, where the doctor told him, "There is nothing you can do. You and your family will all die of this thing. Try to enjoy the time you have left."

Saroja and her children stayed at her father's house, but her husband returned home to his job. Within days he took an overdose of his father's blood-pressure pills to commit suicide. He lived, but his family came to know of their status. "Before, we were like one family, but from there, a separation began." They did not believe the new baby, another son, was HIV negative. To them, if the mother had it, the child must also be infected.

Saroja looked right at Celia. "This is not true. A baby can have a different status than the mother. But so many people had wrong ideas."

Her husband never regained his strength. The shock of the doctor's advice left him too depressed to work, and his family refused to go near him. He did not take medications properly, because he felt so hopeless. Finally, he came to stay with Saroja and her family, but Saroja herself was struggling. The new baby was negative, but Saroja could not breast-feed—again she looked at Celia—"because the virus can pass that way." Formula upset the baby's stomach. Saroja was also troubled by the secrets she had to keep. Her father worried about the stigma and made her promise not to reveal her status. "And I said okay, because we had seen this problem already in my husband's family."

In the end, nothing changed except Saroja herself. "I had the baby to look after. Our older son was positive; we didn't know what to do for him. I had to come out with my status so I could learn what to do next."

By then, her husband needed treatment for an open sore on his leg. But when he went to the hospital, the orderly sent him outside. "He saw his status and refused to treat him." So Saroja and her father took him to a clinic for HIV patients just north of the city.

One of its founders, Sister Agnes, greeted them.

"She is not a young person," said Saroja. "But she bent down and rolled up his pants herself. She touched his leg without feeling afraid. She was running this clinic, she must know what is safe and what is dangerous, yet she herself wrapped the bandage. That gave us confidence."

The next day, Saroja came back with her son and Sister Agnes saw that his teeth were not good. "We were giving him sweets whenever he liked, because we thought, He won't live long, what harm can that do. Sister Agnes said, 'No, you must stop.' She told him, 'See, you must take care of your teeth, because you will need them when you are older.' This was the first time since we learned our status that I thought our boy could grow up. We could live a life." Sister Agnes gave the boy a Spider-Man toothbrush.

"That day, my life took a new direction," Saroja said. Her husband needed treatment; her elder son needed ongoing care; but nobody was working. After a few weeks, Sister Agnes suggested that Saroja could take a job at the clinic. Her family would be eligible for free treatment, she would be earning, and she could help others who needed support. Saroja began training as a counselor. Within two years, she became a team leader. "We help families get over the first shock, but we also help them plan for the years ahead. My husband lived three years, not three months. He might have lived longer if he had not suffered so badly after everything the first doctor told him. We thought a doctor's words are like God's words, but sometimes we are the ones who must teach the doctors." Her sons were five and eleven, both strong, though the older boy had changed schools when his status became known.

"His adult teeth have come in," she finished. "He has a good smile again."

Two other speakers shared their stories, a man and a woman. The man spoke about things Celia had thought she would never hear directly: sharing needles in a park at night, waking to a policeman's baton. He turned to drugs to escape his life; then, once he was positive, he realized he wanted to live. The second woman spoke in a monotone, rattling through her story as quickly as she could. She had learned her status when she was pregnant, but did not tell her husband. He used to drink alcohol, and she did not like to set him off. When he came to know, he decided not to get tested: he was confident he had stopped all his bad habits, so how would such a disease come to him? He said they must keep her status a secret, so she gave birth at home. That baby died before a year. The following year, when she was pregnant again, her husband finally agreed to be tested. Even when he found out he was positive, he refused treatment for all of them, so their families would never know. But this time she listened to the clinic. She argued with her husband until he gave in. They began giving her medicines before the child was born.

For a long time, she agreed with her husband that, above all else, they must keep this secret. And he was right: they were shunned when people learned they were positive. He began to drink again. Her worst predictions came true.

But after that, she was surprised. Her husband began falling ill with fevers again and again; that stopped his drinking. They were still married, raising their child together, though they lived as brother and sister. Slowly, his family learned more, and his mother and sister came to see them. If something should happen to her, they agreed to take the child, who was negative. When she looked backward, the things that used to scare her had all happened, but none meant the end of her. What she regretted was not doing more for her first baby.

She put her head down and moved back to her seat. The meeting finished with an announcement about timings for the following week. Some people went at once—the woman who had just spoken, a few men, some mothers with infants—but others stayed to talk.

Celia made her way outdoors to find her chappals and watched the children go running to the compound for a game. She could not tell which were positive and which were negative; she both wondered and felt wrong for wondering. She pitied and envied, admired and mourned. Every feeling she had seemed to collide into another, her thoughts so chaotic that, although she intended to leave at once, she could not move.

A hand on her arm startled her—Saroja. "Let me help you with your shoes. No, no, don't bend down. You're in the last month, yes?"

Celia almost held up her fingers, like a child too timid to give her age. "Three weeks."

"This is your first time coming to EKATRA?"

Celia nodded.

"Very nice, welcome! But you're feeling tired, I think. Is anyone with you?"

Celia shook her head. "I'm not tired." Then, "Maybe a little tired."

Saroja had a big smile. "I was the same after my first meetings. Don't worry. You grow accustomed."

Accustomed to what?, Celia thought. The meetings, the virus, the treatment, the fear? "Do you come every week?"

"Most. Not every time."

"And you always speak?"

"I make announcements, but not my full story. I haven't given that in many months. See, every person in this room has a story. We ask people to share when they are ready, not before. It can take a very long time. Pooja has been coming for two years, and tonight she spoke for the first time. But she was feeling nervous, so I said, Let me go first. Someone with confidence needs to make a start."

"I don't know how people do it," said Celia, meaning not only the stories, but all of it: the train passes and the drug regimens and the people she must tell. Inez, she thought, and remembered Inez's hand over her own, guiding the knife when she taught Celia to clean fish.

"With HIV, the stigma is very bad. For some people, that is the hardest part of learning their status. I tell my patients the stigma is like a high wall, cutting us off from the people around us. We must begin to pull down this wall, so we can live our lives. If Pooja can tell her story here, in a place where people will listen, she breaks down another piece of the wall. She is not so cut off; she is not so lonely."

Celia looked out to the passage, where people were smiling and talking and taking their leave the way they might after any regular occasion, a Mass or a concert. "She went away without talking to anyone."

"It all comes back, no? The little one she lost . . . But next week, Pooja will feel lighter, because her story is no longer a secret. Maybe she will chat with a few people. Maybe you, if *this* one"—she laughed at Celia's belly—"doesn't cause trouble. You can come back and see. But tonight, it's enough, nah? Come, we'll see if anyone is walking your way. I live near Mahim—are you that side?"

Celia hesitated to reveal anything concrete. Then she thought of Inez again, the next person she would tell. Soon, she thought. Before the baby. "I'm in Varuna."

"Oh, but that is where Ivo stays. You know him? Ivo Dharmai? He is right on the village road. Wait one minute—" She plunged back into the room, straight through Celia's protests. Celia knew the surname, but she could not remember anyone called Ivo. She hoped Saroja wouldn't find him.

When Saroja reappeared with a tall man behind her, Celia knew him at once: the man from Seven Sorrows, the undertaker's nephew, who had painted pictures for her son.

She was dumbfounded, but he just nodded hello. "I saw you inside; I didn't like to disturb you."

"You know each other, then," Saroja said briskly. "I thought you must—good. Ivo, you'll see she reaches safely? But come again, come often." She pressed Celia's hand and left them. Celia did not know what to say. It was unnerving to know only impossible things about each other.

"Ready?"

They made their way downstairs. Ivo smiled but did not stop when people greeted him. On the street, he kept behind her until they had to skirt an open pit; then he briefly took her arm.

"What do you hear from your brother?"

Celia was grateful to him for finding some safe ground.

"He'll come in three months, before his next contract."

"That little one is just like him." He took another step before adding, "Round."

Celia laughed. "But his mother is also round, so we don't know who Akash will look like in the end."

"And your brother likes his work?"

Could Ivo possibly like his? Celia wondered. Was he actually an undertaker, or just helping from time to time? But they kept to Jerome, his life with the cruise line, the places he had seen.

"You would like to travel also?"

She told him yes, though she did not feel the way she had as a girl. She would like to see new places, but with her own people. She would not like to leave so much behind, the way Jerome must. "And you?"

He tipped his head yes. "Maybe without so much water in between."

She laughed again, though his expression remained thoughtful. She couldn't quite tell if he intended to be funny.

"There's so much to see here," he said. "I would like to drive through India."

"You have a car?"

"No," he said mildly. "I mean someday."

They came to Varuna from the park. She could see Seven Sorrows ahead, a stack of fresh-cut caskets poking into the road.

"Where would you go first?"

"Anywhere. My cousin—the one who went to school with your brother—he is living in Thane now. Even that train ride is interesting."

"He hasn't stayed here?"

"He didn't like this work, so I came in his place, and he trained as a phlebotomist." When Celia shook her head, he said, "He takes blood. In hospital."

"Oh!" she said.

"What?"

"I was just thinking, he used to get nosebleeds. So there was sometimes—"

"Blood, yes. We have the same disorder. Our mothers are sisters, it comes through the family." He looked into Seven Sorrows, where a teenaged boy waved from the back. "You're okay, then? Good night."

He made no mention of the next meeting or running into her again; he simply took his leave. A minute later, Celia realized she hadn't told him her name and felt a little foolish, though they were clearly past the usual introductions. Was everyone at the meeting positive? Maybe Ivo came to support a family member. Maybe he was negative, with his plans to drive through the country *someday*. Maybe he was wondering how the virus came to Celia, how she had gone so wrong. She wanted to run back and tell him she didn't know, to take back everything he assumed about her and begin again with her name.

At home, her father waited eagerly, hope spilling everywhere. What did they do, what did she think, would she go again? Celia did her best to sound keen.

"Good, good!" he said. But his voice sounded hollow, and she realized they were both performing an enthusiasm they did not feel. She thought of Saroja, who smiled so easily, her face breaking open like a Christmas package, and of Ivo, who had not really smiled at all.

"I'll go back soon," she said, and hugged him.

MAY 2000

Two months after his departure, Anthony called Pinky to report good news. He had finally found the right treatment.

"Then you still have it?" she asked.

It was always this way with Pinky. He checked in occasionally from public call offices, carefully planning times when she would be at the salon, looking forward to this sole contact with his family. And then came these moments of deflation, the kind of blunt outlook that made treatment at home impossible, he reminded himself. A person in his position could not expose himself to such relentless negativity.

Still, he had begun his journey with an idea that he would not need to go far, a private medical clinic. His original test results were tucked into his bag, but Anthony decided not to reveal his status to the intake desk. Even during his examination, he found it difficult to say he was positive. Perhaps they would find something new, some explanation that was not HIV. He let a gloved technician fill a vial of blood before saying, as offhandedly as he could manage, that he had come to take advice for treatment.

"So you've tested already?" The technician sounded matter-of-fact in a way that irritated Anthony. "The result was positive?"

Anthony nodded, a tick of relief in not saying the word himself.

"Have you had a baseline taken? We'll need a full set of counts." The needle was still in his arm. Anthony watched, feeling ill, as the technician removed the elastic around Anthony's arm and applied a double bandage. Then the technician checked boxes on a form and handed it to Anthony. "Out and to the left. You pay at the counter for blood tests, then go back to Reception and ask for the counseling office."

The blood tests were more expensive than he expected. When he counted out the money, he tried to shield the operation by keeping his hands in his bag. He did not want anyone to guess how much he was carrying.

"These tests are all necessary?"

"I'm the receipts clerk," the man reminded him.

It was the voice Anthony recognized: a boy from his school days, two or three years ahead. Anthony could not remember his name, but he used to walk with a slight waddle. Anthony kept his face low while the clerk marked the receipt.

"Name."

Anthony panicked. He could not risk his real name and he could not think of another. "Anthony Gonsalves."

Stupid! The film, the song—did he think he would avoid notice by naming himself after Amitabh Bachchan? Of course the clerk peered up at him; Anthony might as well have burst forth from a giant Easter egg.

"Singer, is it?" He smirked and handed him the receipt. "Keep this. In three days' time, bring it back for your results."

Anthony mumbled okay, turned to go, and walked as swiftly as he could without breaking into a run. He did not stop at Reception; he made no inquiries about the counseling office. He already knew he would never come back.

The chance encounter alarmed him. He would have to leave the city, he realized; he could not risk being recognized in a clinic catering to AIDS patients. He would leave his surname behind as well, so that no trace of this business could be attached to him once he was clean. He flicked through a few possibilities—cricketers, film stars—before deciding to stay with Gonsalves. The clerk was so distracted by the joke of it that he'd hardly registered the actual Anthony, and at least the idea of the name had come from his mother.

He had always imagined that when he first ventured from Mumbai it would be by plane, the full sweep of the city unfurled below him like a map. But when the moment came, he was not sure what papers were required, or how high the costs might soar, or how to bring along his bicycle.

So Anthony Gonsalves rode to CST, bought a ticket on the Deccan Queen, and boarded the 14:30 train to Pune. He arrived in the glazed light of late afternoon, rubbish on the tracks, and pigeons stalking the platform. For two nights, he stayed in a hostel near the station; by day, he wandered the city, considering various medical centers. At Sassoon Hospital, a plaque commemorated a successful appendectomy for Mahatma Gandhi in 1924. Tacked below was a laminated photo of a painting depicting the surgery, which was conducted during a thunderstorm by the light of a hurricane lamp.

This history of good outcomes seemed promising, but Anthony could not see the sense in paying—twice—for tests that could not heal him. He sought a more constructive approach at an Ayurvedic center a little distance from the city center, which he discovered while cycling along the Mutha River. Here was an ancient form of healing, outside the negativity of clinicians. Far better to boost his system and bring his mind and body into balance. He found a room and signed up for intensive therapy. There were purification rites, special diets, and early-morning routines of meditation and yoga, all in pursuit of true health.

"Meaning what exactly?" Anthony asked six weeks in, with the sour feeling that came from wondering whether he'd had his money's worth. Did he actually feel stronger? Some of the remedies upset his stomach; he was forced to lower his doses and slowly build tolerance. He chafed at the dietary restrictions and rigid bedtimes. Spikes of fear and anger disturbed his nervous system. He lay awake when he was meant to be sleeping, felt his mind fill when he was meant to drain it.

"True health is total health. Mind, body, and spirit."

"But is HIV still in the blood?"

"That may be. But with a strong mind and body, you can withstand."

This was not altogether satisfying. It was one of the other patients who told Anthony that a healing center in Hyderabad claimed to have eradicated the virus in at least one patient. "It's where the drugs themselves are manufactured. They have access to the newest treatments."

Anthony saw the sense in such a confluence. A week later, he and Jankesh, the other patient, booked their tickets and waited together for the train. Jankesh slept deeply on the platform, his bag tucked beneath his head, but Anthony could only doze, worried about his bicycle. Several times, he got up to check that no one had tampered with it, and he paid off a baggage handler to be sure it was loaded properly.

"You worry too much!" Jankesh doffed an imaginary top hat. He was far too jokey for Anthony's liking. Whenever he decided Anthony needed a laugh, he broke into a song-and-dance routine—"Your name is Anthony Gonsalves!"

Anthony already felt nettled by their association. There was the difference in station: Jankesh had been a night security guard in the container yards. He had no money, no standing, nothing valuable to lose, so how could he understand Anthony's concerns? And he was being treated for herpes as well as HIV, a double affliction that Anthony regarded as a sign of unclean living. Anthony himself was a man of decent habits; the few occasions when he might have been exposed were aberrations. But these distinctions—made clear to Anthony by a sore on Jankesh's lip—were not always recognized by others. Over the nine-hour rail journey, Anthony became more and more sensitive to attention from other passengers, looks that included him as well as Jankesh. He did not want to be dragged down by a temporary alliance.

Once they reached the center, it was easier to maintain distance. Not all patients could afford the full treatment: a trio of cutting-edge drugs, available through this center alone, combined with a secret herbal supplement. Jankesh was among those who chose a less expensive route. But his results, while beneficial, would not be as spectacular as those of the tri-stream patients. In one case, the viral load was undetectable; several others were following the same promising trajectory.

Anthony did not hesitate to enter the optimal treatment program. Here was the cure he knew must be possible for people with money and purpose. It grated that Pinky did not seem to understand.

"A full cure," he said. "This is the only place in the country getting such strong results."

"But what about the past two months?" she wanted to know.

That was a program to build up his strength, he explained. Now he could withstand the intensity of these medications. He was aware of a slight distortion, presenting the move to Pinky as though it had been his plan all along. But perhaps he was simply discerning a greater truth in his actions, which had led him from one treatment to another at just the right time.

"This is why I couldn't stay. There's nothing like this clinic at home."

"Okay."

Anthony was at a loss to explain; nothing seemed to penetrate. "You can tell Mum I'm in good health. And Celia."

He had not brought up his wife directly during their previous calls, waiting for the moment when he could share good news. Pinky sounded impatient when she told him Celia was gone.

"What do you mean, gone?"

"She stays with her father."

"For the birth, you mean." He felt his chest tighten. Usually, he tried to push aside thoughts of the baby, but it was difficult to forget so much so quickly. He kept track without meaning to: another week at most. Watermelon on the fruit chart.

"Not only the birth," said Pinky.

"What are you saying?" he asked, and he had to close his eyes against the rush of his pulse while she answered. He had imagined Celia and his mother brought closer in their grief for him. Instead, a whole new raft of troubles awaited him at home. Why hadn't Pinky stopped it? Why couldn't the world keep steady long enough to give him a chance? He would manage everything when he returned, but it was ridiculous, maddening, to have to contend with additional strain.

"That is an argument, nothing more," he told her. "Once the baby comes, once Mum realizes I found a cure—"

"Mum says we're finished with her. Even if the baby lives." For a moment Pinky sounded tearful, then her voice stiffened. "When people ask, she says Celia was sneaking drink, she poisoned the baby, in the end we had to throw her out."

A silence before he asked what their parents said about him.

"They say she ruined you."

"Tell them nothing about this cure. Let them feel they've lost their only son."

"They don't—" she began, and he rang off before he had to hear any more.

Nothing had changed, Anthony told himself as he stepped outside into searing light. The turmoil at home was temporary; none of it could touch him. He was the same man with the same cure as he had been an hour before. Yet dread swept through him, corrosive, obliterating. Anthony leaned against the lurid yellow wall of the call office with one hand on his bicycle. The day swelled with heat, like a wound waiting to be lanced by the monsoon. He was at the edge of an outdoor market, and a tumult of voices and colors and movement slowly tipped into his awareness. He closed his eyes and breathed deeply, the way he had been taught to fill his lungs at the healing center.

Eventually, the feeling passed through him, and he was left spent and ravaged, like the beach after a storm. He considered going back inside to call Celia, but it was too easy to imagine scenarios in which her father would pick up the phone. And what would Anthony say, even if he reached her? She did not want to hear that he hadn't been able to bring her with him. She would have been like Mary on the donkey, forced to have her child in God knew what circumstances, and he would have been consumed with their care. Better that she stay put, better that the baby pass in and out of life quietly. Anthony's cure would be effected in six months, maybe twelve, and what was that, in the long run? With his own recovery as proof, he would appeal to Celia's father to put up money for her treatment, and in two years they would be as they were, with time for more children.

That is where he tried to fix his thoughts as he wheeled his cycle past vendors on either side. He moved slowly, the heat so bad that he bought a bag of sweet limes and ate one where he stood. It was not until he saw a steel cart with a man serving winter-melon juice that he got on his cycle and rode.

FEBRUARY 2002

For months after Anthony had gone, Celia imagined his return. He would appear on her father's doorstep in various states of penance and dishevelment, needing this or offering that, apologizing or demanding, with love or without. The story changed as she told it to herself, bending this way or that, carving its own bed like a river through rock.

But over time, the river dried, first to a trickle, then to cracked earth. Anthony was gone. He was not coming back. Celia spoke of him only in passing and avoided any mention of his family. Dominic followed her lead, so, although Celia was aware that he periodically contacted Anthony's father, she was never sure why. Was he insisting on some recompense for her? Did he think Anthony might return? Did he imagine they could reconcile? The conversations were brief, as far as she knew—not hidden, exactly, but conducted when she would not have to overhear. Even when she caught a few tight words of a phone call, she did not ask what had transpired. If her father had news, he would tell her. Month after month, he said nothing.

So, when a phone call came two years after Anthony's departure, she was wholly unprepared. A woman asked to speak with Celia, and within minutes came the revelation that Anthony was staying just over Vasai Creek. Celia had always imagined his return as a journey over some vast distance, a pilgrimage back to her. It was disorienting to think that he was in easy reach—about sixty kilometers north of Varuna on the western commuter line.

Only a slow train would halt at the Naigaon station, so the ride took a little over an hour and a half. She traveled in a Ladies Only car, able to sit after Andheri. A woman beside her was knitting, and Celia wished she had brought something to occupy her hands. She had only a small paper, folded and refolded to cottony softness, with the directions the woman had given her. From the station she could take a bus or an autorick.

Celia had agreed to come. But suddenly the prospect of seeing Anthony in a quarter of an hour was too much. She walked the bus route, trying to stamp away each fresh wave of apprehension. It was late morning, the sun fierce. She did her best not to think about what would happen next, and when she failed, she imagined her thoughts melting in the pool of heat shimmering on the top of her head. Twice, she let herself be overtaken by buses.

Even the walk turned out to be short, no more than an hour. She passed the junction where the bus would have dropped her and turned down a quiet road: salt pans on one side, their shallow water reflecting the sky, and a line of green mangroves in the distance. She could see three figures, dark against glittering white, raking salt into small dunes.

The clinic was a complex on a large site at the end of the road. Inside the gate, where she gave her name and waited, were three white buildings, two stories high, with shaded courtyards and gardens between. A yoga class was under way in the biggest courtyard. Signs taller than Celia were mounted on either side, listing the Twelve Steps in Marathi and English.

A nun approached, dressed in white, and greeted her warmly. Celia recognized her voice from the phone, although she was older than Celia had guessed. Her face was soft and wrinkled, and she wore round glasses with thick black frames. "Welcome, welcome."

She led Celia to one of the buildings in the back, pointing out flowers alongside the stone path. "When I have a little time,

I spend it in the garden. Some of our patients do also. It's good to feel we are working together to help things grow."

"Anthony . . ." His name felt rusty in her mouth. "How long has he been a patient?"

"Four months."

Longer than Celia had expected. Was he one of the patients who worked in the garden? She wanted to know everything and nothing; she wanted to stay clear of him, and to see him at last, and to hear what he had to say, once and for all.

"Here is my little patch." Sister Agnes smiled with pride. "All pink. That is for my sister. She used to drive my mother mad when we were small, wanting pink this and pink that. She used to say she would be married in pink."

"My sister likes pink also," said Celia.

Sister's office was dim after the bright midday garden. A cluttered desk, a kettle on a hot plate, two bookshelves, not the same height. On the wall above a metal file cabinet was a print of Christ and the lost sheep. Sister offered tea, but Celia asked for water.

"Now, for Anthony," Sister said, matter-of-factly. "It's a long time since you've met, so you may feel shocked when you see him. He's lost weight. He's quite weak. He has neuropathy in his hands and feet, which means he cannot move them." She paused before adding, "He doesn't have long."

Celia felt a lurching sensation, as if the past two years had fallen away and she must pull back from the edge of a cliff. "He doesn't have long," she repeated, trying to let the words penetrate so she would know what to feel. "That's why you called."

Sister Agnes shook her head no, with a calm that seemed like kindness.

"Many patients go quietly, without saying goodbye. I called because he asked."

FEBRUARY 2002

Celia saw the room in patches: an open window, a pitcher of water, a chair, and Anthony. He had sunk into the bed as though to relieve his body from the sharpness of his own bones. He tried to lift his head.

"Here is Celia," Sister Agnes said, the way she might announce a regular visitor.

Sister poured water and held a glass to Anthony's lips. He swallowed visibly. Someone had shaved him, perhaps two days before, Celia saw. Then the glass came away, and her gaze brushed across his; she caught the huge, liquid force of his stare and looked away again.

The idea that she must be with him felt large and suffocating, as though she hadn't expected the morning's journey to lead here. It seemed more sensible to follow Sister Agnes out of the room and back into the garden—she had the impression of Anthony as a cut flower, the heavy bulb of his head drooping on its narrow stem—and then the door shut and they were alone.

She felt his stare, a heaviness she wanted to shrug out from under, and reached for the glass of water. "You want—"

"No, no"—the merest brush of sound. Was his voice what she remembered? She could not tell. Another moment passed. She kept her hands in her lap. Before setting out that morning, she had removed her wedding ring and locked it away with her gold. She'd continued to wear it out of habit, or a sense of history, or simply to discourage questions, and gradually the ring had less and less to do with Anthony. It became something that belonged to her, a feature of her hand, a gleam that caught her eye when she was washing or writing or lifting a child. The prospect of wearing it in front of him brought a sudden sharp anger; she would not do it. Then, just before leaving, she unlocked the cabinet and put the ring back on. She was not a child with a grudge; she was a grown woman who had lived a certain life. There was no point pretending otherwise.

But at Anthony's bedside, the ring felt conspicuous, a message she did not mean to send. She glanced at his hands on the papery sheets. His ring was gone. Would he think she meant something hopeful by wearing hers?

Then she looked at him again—his arms, his collarbone—and saw that such hopes were beyond this room. Whatever Anthony wanted, whatever prompted this summons, was not about a future he would see.

"You're looking nice." He seemed to have to gather his voice from within his chest, to push out the words with such effort that they had a peculiar force.

She tipped her head, part thanks, part resistance to this line of conversation. "Sister says you came some time ago?"

He paused to reckon. "Before Christmas."

She wondered if his mother had spent the holiday with him, or maybe Pinky, but she did not like to ask.

"I came here from Belgaum. That is a nice city. Quiet, easy." He tried painfully to sit up a little more. Celia knew she ought to help but couldn't bring herself to touch him; instead, she looked out the window to offer the pretense of privacy. "I lived outside the center in a village called Ghataprabha. I took a job in a travel office."

"A travel office?" She did not try to hide her surprise.

"Just a small place, local tours. There is a bird sanctuary." He tried to laugh, all breath and strain. "Actually, I rode there myself sometimes to see. It's best to go early. At sunrise you can see huge flocks of cranes—a special crane, the koonj. You've heard of it?"

She stared at him, incredulous.

"They dance," he told her. "They are mentioned in poetry, compared to beautiful women." Then, as though despairing of ever conveying his meaning, "They have a graceful look."

Had he noticed so much as a crow when they used to walk in the evenings? How could this be the man who ran away in the night?

But he was. She saw him at once, half a dozen Anthonys or more: the boy who had been so earnest the first time they met, the husband whose bed she had shared, the father who had lost his son, the man who had struck her, the man who had fled, a stranger she could hardly bear to meet. It was the last who made her angry. She had expected to confront the man who abandoned her; here was a man with whom happiness might have been possible, speaking gently to her about birds. She looked at him and remembered his expression the first time she invited him to feel the baby kick—shy, nearly formal, as though he knew it was his privilege but worried he might be found wanting.

"Our daughter is almost two," she told him.

"Our daughter?" A rasping breath. "And she is—?"

She had made a mistake. She did not want the baby in this room, she did not want Anthony to lay claim even to thoughts of her. But his face! The shock had given way to yet more Anthonys, some stricken, some flaring with hope.

"How *is* she?"

"Negative."

She meant to throw the word at him, but her private relief came flooding back. Anthony's body seemed to sink even farther into the mattress. He looked both calmer and weaker, inclined more irrevocably toward rest. Would this be the way it happened? she wondered. Not the passing of time so much as the human demands of every hour, each encounter taking a little more? Would he die faster because she had come? He turned his head on the pillow to face the window, breathing slowly, as though to take the view into his lungs.

"Can you see the garden?"

He looked at her with tears in his eyes.

She put another pillow at his back. He could not sit up unassisted, so she had to support him. She followed the line of his gaze to Sister Agnes's pinks, a tree-patched sky.

"Better?"

"Thank you."

"Water?"

He closed his eyes against the suggestion. When he opened them again, the effort of looking at her seemed to require unusual strength. "What is her name?"

She hesitated. "Isabella."

His eyes drifted shut, and she saw a slight smile. "Gobi baby. You remember?"

She felt a knife flick of anger. "Don't."

His eyes widened but he did not argue. His shock faded, and in its place arose a deep and sorrowful resignation. Here was his apology, she realized: all she was likely to get. And perhaps she had also reached the limits of what she would say to anyone too feeble to answer. It was not only Anthony who had run out of time. They were caught in the same ruthless geology, as if a giant force had compressed every living strand of feeling and made fossils of their marriage and parting. They were reduced to brief looks, bare handfuls of words.

He carried on watching her as though afraid she would slip his gaze and go. "Pinky told me you had the baby. I didn't think she would live." He swallowed painfully. "Later she said nothing."

"Your family was happy to let her go."

A ghost of a smile. "They are happy to let me go also."

"They haven't come?"

"Pinky, once. She had to sneak away. They think it's unsafe."

"And your mother?"

"Maybe this week. Pinky said she'll talk to her." A pause. "And she is well? Isabella?"

"She's well." Celia thought of her daughter—her bright eyes and firm pronouncements—and laughed. "She's *very* well. My father spoils her."

"Isabella. A pretty name."

She had meant to keep the baby to herself. But it was a relief to think of something outside this stifling place. "We call her Isha."

"Isha . . . And she has playmates? Jerome's boy—"

"Akash. And Sidu. He's ten months; she treats him like her doll."

Was she bright? he wanted to know. Was she strong, was she happy? "Not quiet," he guessed. For the next few minutes—carefully, but not entirely falsely—they talked about their daughter.

A knock on the door, and a ward boy came to check Anthony's pulse. "How are the hands?"

"A little burning, not bad."

And the feet?

Worse, Anthony admitted.

He would come back in a few minutes, when the visit was finished, the ward boy said. Massage might help.

Anthony nodded.

Celia had been in such rooms before. She had seen men and women as young as she was or even younger, their bodies assailed in ways she could not forget. She tried not to look too far ahead, but here was Anthony, dying one piece at time, and it was terrifying to imagine this might be her end, too. She'd learned to surmount these swells of fear by repeating what she told her clients at the clinic, where she had joined Saroja's team of community counselors: *We don't know what will happen. We don't know when a cure will come.* When that didn't work, she thought of Isha.

What did Anthony think of? He faced the window, and they sat quietly. Celia wondered at what point she should go.

"A tailorbird! There—"

She saw a flutter of leaves, the bird disappearing into a bush.

"They're small, shy." Every word its own breath. "They

stitch leaves together to make their nests." He paused to rest. "You're still sewing?"

She tipped her head yes.

"For a tailor? Or home?"

"Listen"—she fumbled past the intimacy of using his name—"I have to catch a train." Just the thought of the station came as a relief. In two hours, she could be home: Inez on the stoop pretending not to be waiting, Alma beginning the evening meal, Isha running to greet her, her arms closing tight around Celia's knees. Her father would ask half a dozen times how she was. Ivo would come; he liked to walk the shoreline when he finished at Seven Sorrows, and often he asked Celia to join him. They could climb Seaview Hill to see the lights; they could stop for ice cream. All these things were still possible for Celia.

"I should go soon." She meant to speak gently but in her confusion—would he ask her to come again? should she say yes?—her voice struck the room like iron on rock, nothing to soften her departure.

"I meant to come back for you."

His vehemence startled her. Celia tried to make a small parrying motion with her hand. "You don't need—"

"I went ahead to find treatment. Later I was going to . . ." He took another ragged breath.

"Leave it," she said, trying not to sound unkind.

"After I ran out of money, I had to sell whatever I could. Gold. My camera. My wedding ring." He closed his eyes and opened them again. "By then, my counts were low, so I started ART. That is free treatment."

Celia nodded. How much they had learned, each on their own. Would it have been easier together? She could no longer imagine it.

". . . But I kept the bicycle. That is the one thing I never sold, even when I had nothing. I kept it to come back . . ." Again he had to pause for breath, so long that he let go of whatever he meant to say next. "I have it here. Sister Agnes keeps it in the shed. That is for you."

Later, she sat facing backward, with the train rocking, and

watched the salt pans fall away. The motion of the train made her feel that time was speeding up. Power-line poles ticked past; the scalloped dips of cable between them blurred like minutes in which nothing much happens. A pack of slum children clowned on the embankment; a bevy of waves and shouting, and they were gone. The muddy creek looked like something she would have jumped across as a child. Building by building, field by field, she was borne away from Anthony.

At the last minute, when she was standing to go, the room had looked so empty that she gave him the photos she was carrying in her bag. The first was of Isha in the cloth cradle where she had slept as a baby, her head popping up, all wild curls and mischief and laughter. *You are too big!* Celia tickled her. *So big, so big!* Anthony could not move his fingers well enough to take it, but Celia held it up for him and he seemed to breathe in the sight of his daughter's face. She left it propped against his cup with another, more recent: Isha, dressed for a wedding in a froth of blue lace with the little triangle of a smile she produced when posing, like something a child would draw.

"Tall . . ." he said, in a kind of wonder.

"She had new shoes." Gold, with straps and tiny heels. Celia could look at this picture and see their trip to Linking Road, Isha holding tight to her hand, looking thrilled when a shop boy threw boxes down from the storage space above the ceiling and another boy caught them, as neat as a circus trick. They had just traded back her baby earrings for her first small gold hoops, and every few minutes Isha reached up to check them. It was dizzying to think of all Anthony had missed.

"You'll come again? For the cycle?"

She tipped her head yes, an assurance that they did not have to say goodbye, and he let his eyes close. He was asleep before she left the room.

"Come again," Sister Agnes invited her warmly. "I'll phone you if anything happens."

They walked back along the garden path. "The bicycle is just there." Sister pointed to a low shed beyond the courtyard. "You don't want to take it now, do you?"

"Not today," said Celia. She was aware of small birds hopping from one branch to another—perhaps the same kind Anthony had tried to show her. She could not recall its name, which troubled her a little. "I'll come back," she told Sister, thinking maybe there was still time to ask him. Maybe she would.

FEBRUARY 2002

The light had changed when Anthony woke. His mouth was dry, his throat raw; his hands were not strong enough to manage the cup. Useless, really, his hands. His fingers could barely pluck the edge of the sheets. His feet were like the tin-can stilts they used to make as schoolboys.

When he was first bedridden, he had tried to fill the long drifts of time by imagining he was on his bicycle, pedaling hard, just about to crest a hill and go ticking down the other side. But time was turning inside out. Hours passed like minutes in wisps of sleep, and spells of pain stretched minutes into days. He no longer wanted to fill time so much as to give it a shape and hold it. Sometimes he lay in bed and recited the lyrics of film songs his mother used to like. "My name is Anthony Gonsalves," he heard in Jankesh's big rolling voice, which had somehow overtaken Amitabh Bachchan's rendition.

Jankesh must be dead. The sound of his voice running through Anthony's head, the image of his song-and-dance nonsense—how much else remained of him? And those fragments would disappear with Anthony. He wished there had been time and strength to tell Celia more, even mention Jankesh's name to her, so that all he remembered was not entirely lost.

They had spent five months together in Hyderabad, though Anthony ran through his cash after three. He sold his mother's bangles, then her pendant and chain; a fourth month. For the fifth, he tried to negotiate with the head clinician: What good could come of stopping abruptly? Once cured, he would be a walking advertisement. From this he wrung a further week before they cut him off.

He left messages at the salon for Pinky to wire the necessary amount and sold the rest of his belongings. The only items he held on to were the bicycle, the camera, and Celia's necklace. He liked to imagine their reunion, when he could give it to her once more.

He waited a week before any word came from Pinky, who sent a quarter of what Anthony hoped. Still, he made the most of it, putting down the full amount as a deposit to finish the treatment and pledging that his family would pay double in the end. He felt cheated when the clinic treated the payment as cash for one week more.

When he was forced to decide between the next dose of medication and a roof over his head, he decided he must borrow. Jankesh was earning, working late nights in a restaurant to save for more treatment, but his weight was low and he wore long sleeves to cover lesions on his arms. What point throwing good money after bad? thought Anthony. He himself was a better investment, the one with a real chance at recovery. But Jankesh would not be moved. He stood, silent and mutinous, smelling of garlic, shaking his head no when he'd tired of saying it.

Anthony stopped paying his hostel bill, coming and going at odd hours to avoid any unpleasantness. At the healing center, he pleaded his case to various clinicians, whose refusal to administer a blood test began to offend him. He only gave up when a dispensary attendant pointed to his wedding ring and estimated its worth at another four days, maybe five.

That night, Anthony visited Jankesh for the last time, meeting him behind the restaurant to eat leftover food from the kitchen. This was an arrangement Anthony had contrived when his money ran too low for meat, but Jankesh's illness made him timid. He had retired his imaginary top hat; he no longer sang his teasing song or smiled when Anthony appeared.

"I can't do this again," he warned.

"No, no, not again." This was the full extent of Anthony's goodbye, despite a pang of loss. It was easier on the road with another person, a companion for the lonely hours, someone to watch his belongings when he needed to run into a shop. But even if Jankesh could be induced to leave, the scales had tipped. He was too far gone. He could only hold Anthony back.

Anthony stole away before daylight, mounting his bicycle in the dark. He was several miles away, sunrise curdling in the eastern sky, before he stopped to rest. A mosquito shrilled past his ear, and when he slapped his neck to kill it, his hand came away smeared with blood. Clean, he told himself. What difference, really, would another month make? Anthony had sacrificed so much; surely, he was clean.

Yet some little doubt lingered, some trepidation about returning before his family would be inclined to believe in a cure. And he acknowledged that his homecoming would be complicated. It seemed possible that the longer he stayed away the more he would be missed, and after all his ordeals, it was pleasant to cherish daydreams about the fatted calf. So he rode to the Lingampalli station, but instead of rushing back to Mumbai, he boarded a train west, which he viewed as the beginning of his route home. At first he thought of Goa, but high season loomed, so instead he bought a ticket to Belgaum. The source of the idea brought a twinge of sorrow: Jankesh used to speak of their visiting together after another patient told them stories of its lush forests and rivers. Anthony felt no particular attraction to natural wonders, but Jankesh's voice came back to him—*We've got to go, man*—as a kind of commission, a way in which he would not quite leave their friendship behind, if in fact they had been friends. Besides, one place was as good as another.

Anthony had to part with Celia's necklace for the fare, but his confidence surged the moment the train pulled away from the station. He had money in his pocket. He had slipped out from under his debts. He was free of Jankesh, whose deterioration was painful to witness. He took a seat near the window and felt his troubles falling away. By the time he disembarked in a new city, they had dissipated like mist. He would buy Celia a new necklace when he returned.

A few weeks later, he called Pinky to report that he was in the final phase of recovery. It was a version of the truth, he decided. He no longer required treatment, but the stresses of the past year had left him worn and anxious, and at last, he felt his spirits returning.

"That's good," said Pinky, as limply as if he'd won a schoolboy prize. Her ignorance was staggering, offensive. He wished he could give her a glimpse of Jankesh, the way he'd looked when Anthony last saw him, so she could know what her brother had escaped.

Instead, he announced that he would soon return, thinking this news at least would spark a reaction. In fact, he had not committed to any time line. He'd found a job through a travel agency, snapping photos of tourists at nearby waterfalls, and holiday travelers would be at their peak. He might enjoy this last season before resuming the burdens of life at home. "I may be in time for Christmas," he added. "You can tell Celia."

"Celia?" she said, incredulous, before her voice took on a prim formality. "We have nothing to do with Celia. Or the baby."

"That is my *wife*," he said. Then, "The baby?"

"She had a girl."

A girl. A girl. It was painful to know such things. He had lost a son and daughter both, then.

"I'm getting married in January," Pinky told him. "Maybe after is a better time to come."

Three days later, he experienced severe chest pains. He went to a city hospital, thinking here was his father's heart after all. A nurse came to take his history, and Anthony mentioned that he had received treatment in Hyderabad. He had been given various medications.

"But you don't know the names of the medications?"

"It's a new regimen, only available at one clinic."

"And this was treatment for?"

"I used to have HIV."

"You're HIV positive?"

"Not at all. I've had the treatment."

The nurse asked more questions and brought in a doctor to examine his chest. "The pain comes and goes, but it gets very bad," Anthony said. "Right in the area of the heart," and it was true—pain so intense that he had doubled over when it first struck. He began to explain his father's condition, but was asked to lift his shirt.

When the exam was finished, an orderly escorted Anthony to the doctor's office. Even before the fellow spoke—"I understand you've tested positive for HIV, Mr. Gonsalves"—Anthony felt everything starting again, a wheel that would crush him.

"No, no." He held up his hand. "There's been a mix-up. All that was a year ago. But I've been fully treated, I'm no longer positive. I've come about a heart problem—"

"Not your heart," the doctor interrupted. "Shingles. A viral infection. It can be quite painful. People who are HIV positive are at higher risk—"

"I'm *negative*." Anthony struggled to stay calm. "For months, I took intensive treatment designed exactly for this."

"Unfortunately, treatment cannot eliminate the virus."

"These are new drugs, cutting-edge. Most doctors aren't aware, but the results are totally proven."

"Mr. Gonsalves, your blood work indicates—"

"There must be traces from before. I'm telling you, I'm negative!"

"I'm sorry, sir. I don't know who has treated you or with what. There are sham cures, quacks. Or maybe you were given treatment to keep your viral load low. But nothing can eradicate HIV from your system. What we must do instead . . ."

Anthony could not hear. Pain flared in his chest; panic howled through him in great gusts. He might have been hollow, with only the single band of pain tethering him to his body. After a while, he asked the doctor, "There is nothing the matter with my heart?," and his voice sounded rusty, as though the burning in his chest had scorched his throat.

He accepted a prescription slip the doctor gave him for the

in-house pharmacy—tablets for pain, tablets to sleep—but he stuffed the second note, a referral, into his pocket without a glance. He stood in one queue to pay for medications, another to pick them up. It was a problem with the test, he told himself, a careless lab worker, switched results, these fat-cat doctors bleeding him dry. But cold currents of doubt ran beneath every assertion. He went back to his room and passed a sleepless night. When the pains came again, he thought they might crush him.

He put in a call to Pinky to ask for more money. "There is a problem with my heart."

"I'm sorry." She did not ask what.

"This is nothing to do with the earlier issues," he said as firmly as he could. Saying it aloud was like trying on his favorite clothes and finding them ill-fitting.

Pinky did not argue. "I can send a little," she said, sounding tired. "Not as much as you want. I don't have it."

"Ask Mum for more," he said, and she said nothing.

Main duniya mein akela hoon. I am alone in this world. He roamed the parks and gardens, hoping the cool green spaces might soothe him. But his mind raced, the pain raged, fear clutched at him with wild hands. When he found a Catholic church named for St. Anthony, he accepted the sign of his name and went inside. It was tiny by Mumbai standards, with nothing for him beyond a statue of St. Anthony holding the Christ Child. His prayers felt flat and lifeless, already denied.

Outside, Anthony sat on the lip of the porch where he'd left his shoes. A statue of St. Gabriel presided over the sunbaked courtyard, his trumpet nearly as long as his wings, the bell tipped to the sky. Anthony dropped his gaze from the statue itself to the shadow of the trumpet falling across the courtyard. It seemed to point in the direction of the train station.

His next steps came to him with grim precision. He left the courtyard, returned to his room, and arranged his belongings—his bag neatly packed, his bicycle ready, his identity papers. He wore his wedding ring, but the rest of the gold was gone. The money from Pinky had not yet arrived, though he checked at the MoneyGram office one last time. He did not feel troubled by this. Instead, he found a pawn shop and sold his camera. He did not haggle long; he would not need much. For his last night in Belgaum, he decided on an early meal and a film.

He chose a romance whose posters looked lush and tender; he did not expect the heartbreak ending. Another sign, he decided. He walked to the railway tracks with his sleeping tablets. He took a handful of pills, washed them down with alcohol, and lay across the tracks to wait for sleep to come.

The next day, he woke sprawled in the dirt on the side of the tracks. Maybe someone had dragged him to safety. Maybe he'd staggered up and collapsed again. He had no memory of the black hours between the bottle and the midday sun. When he could stand, he shielded his eyes and bought water from a street vendor. He located the key to his room, still in his trouser pocket. Nothing had been discovered yet; his bag and bicycle were still waiting for him, as though he'd dreamed the whole episode. He discarded the clothes he was wearing, filthy from dirt and drink and vomit, and bathed, splashing dipper after dipper of water over his body. He shaved to scrape the residue of the night from his skin. For the rest of that day and much of the next, he slept. Then, with no plans or objectives, only an impulse to be in the open air, he wheeled his cycle outside.

He thought he might be too weak to ride, but he stopped at a bakery for bread and ate it warm. When he found he could keep it down, he ate more. His chest pain came in waves, but the lulls left room for other sensations. It was late afternoon; the sun dipped in and out of the trees. He rode north. A sliver of creek twisted along the side of the road like a bit of string, leading him on. The road ended at a fenced compound with a small ticket booth: a bird sanctuary.

He parked his cycle near the last two motor scooters in the lot and went to the window, curiously unbothered by the entry fee. But the woman waved him in for free. There was less than an hour till closing, she told him. "If you like, come another time and pay."

He followed broad paved paths lined with signs about birds: the osprey, the marsh sandpiper, the wire-tailed swallow. The lesser whistling duck had a faint orange breast and a lifespan of twelve to fifteen years. He had lived twice that long already, thought Anthony, and he would not have twelve to fifteen years left. It felt reckless but strangely palliative to let this idea take hold and find that he could still breathe, still feel the remains of his headache, still take in the greens, browns, and golds of the land around him.

The paths led to a boardwalk over the wetlands. He wished he could have told Celia something of that first visit—the sanctuary almost empty, the mild evening sky with a small kindling of color low to the west, and the boardwalk itself, wide and well made, just high enough to let him feel he was floating over the grasses and water.

At the end of the boardwalk, the lake was quiet. At first he couldn't see any birds, a scarcity for which the abundance of signs had not prepared him. Then he spotted two ducks swimming in and out of the rushes. Did birds keep track of the seasons? They might have been in their fifth year or their fifteenth, the end of their lifespan, but there was no way to know. They moved serenely, as much a part of the landscape as the trees that would outlast them or the lake itself. He also would die, thought Anthony. He let his mind rest there, and beyond his despair he felt a pearly calm he had never known before. It was certain, but not certain when. Until then, he was alive.

A sudden chaos overhead, and more ducks came streaming in, churning the surface of the lake as they landed. In the light from the western sky, Anthony could easily see the orange breasts. He felt strangely elated: *there*, just as the signs promised. He wished so keenly for his camera that for a moment that loss outstripped the rest. Instead he watched, trying to carve a memory too clear to be lost.

When he reached the entrance, the booth was locked and the attendant stood by her motor scooter, looking annoyed. "Next time you pay," she reminded him. Two days later, the money from Pinky arrived, and Anthony traveled north to the health institute named on the referral. He ticked the box for "positive," the first time he had shared his status openly, although he gave his name as Anthony Gonsalves. This seemed simplest, the name on his most recent prescriptions and the name, he felt, to which the rest of his life belonged. He did not become Anthony Correia again until the neuropathy in his feet became too pronounced for him to walk. When he told Sister Agnes, he thought maybe his mother or father would come.

He composed lists to carve footpaths through the foggy hours: places he had cycled, birds he had seen. Sometimes the lists spooled into fantasies. He imagined carrying his son, who had barely stirred the surface of the world, to see a waterfall in Belgaum. Or he would conjure his father beside him on the boardwalk, talking companionably, or Celia, or Jankesh. He imagined conversations that had never happened—perhaps could never have happened—but which felt so real and vivid that they expressed a kind of truth, if only because he could conceive of them. He liked to linger in those imagined spaces, which seemed to give a different meaning to his life, or the end of it.

Main duniya mein akela hoon, he heard in Jankesh's voice. But he was not entirely alone. Anthony looked at the photos of Isha, her wild curls like his own when he was a boy. Two snapshots. He could see her the way he used to see birds, a glimpse at a distance, a flash of life and color. She seemed a happy little thing. He began to imagine the ways he could still make her laugh. He could puff out his cheeks. He could teach her the silly wheezy donkey call of the whistling duck. Perhaps that was a story he could share with Celia, a memory that would not die with him. Perhaps she would come again, and he could tell her a little more.

MARCH 2005

Mrs. Almeida said she would buy the fish herself.

For already the day had got ahead of Pia. Here it was, nearly ten, and she had only just finished washing up after breakfast. Her hands were wet past the wrists, her eyes wild and wide while she surveyed everything she must do next: the spices to grind, the rice to rinse, the tomatoes to chop, the onions, the garlic, the ginger, the chilies. Inside the pressure cooker, lentils were soaking; inside the refrigerator, chicken thighs nested on a chilled white plate. In three, maybe four hours, they must serve lunch to nine people—twelve if the Delhi cousins arrived.

"Ooh . . . ooh . . . ooh, Memsahib, see the time!" Pia's gasp of a laugh was mostly nerves, Essie knew, with a slight touch of performance for anyone who might overhear from the dining table. All morning long, the family had been barging in to make a pet of Pia, with no idea how much their attention distracted her.

And there was work to be done, more than Essie could manage alone. The house was full, top to bottom, every bedroom in use, every meal a production. Jude was on a week's leave from Bangalore, with friends dropping by at all hours. Marian had flown in with her family, traveling on Good Friday over Essie's objections. A pity for them to miss the Stations of the Cross; nor did it seem right to sit comfortably on a plane through the hours of Christ's agony. Besides, they cut it very fine; the party was the next day! Essie worried that the girls would be jet-lagged—girls, she called them, though they were in their late twenties, both the size of circus animals, loping through her house and stooping to hug their grandparents.

They came with news: Nicole was engaged. "We wanted to tell you in person." Essie felt the shock as a rush of air, puffing her up then leaving her limp. "Who?" she asked, a small, foolish sound. She learned his name was Paul, though nobody volunteered that the family was Catholic until Essie asked outright. Her granddaughter had known this person for over a year, but Marian had met him only a few months before. He studied samples of earth from the sea floor. "And this is a job with salary?"

Essie inspected the photos; the boy was barely as tall as Nicole. His face was slightly round, though not bloated in that worrying American way that meant he would soon go fat. A nice enough smile. Why so many hats? Was his hair thinning? "He must wear his hair cut short," she ventured. But she held back most of her questions. The girls had chatted for only an hour before Marian sent them down to Jude's spare room—not the arrangement Essie favored, in which her granddaughters would share the large bed in her room with her.

"There's room enough for three—"

"They're not used to that, Mum."

Not used to their grandmother, thought Essie. The next morning, she rose early, determined to savor a few minutes with them before the day took hold. But the girls turned up late at the breakfast table, yawning through their cups of tea, and minute after minute drained away in loose conversation.

Essie felt her list of things to do coiled like a spring inside her. All very well for Jude and Marian to pipe up suddenly about chairs and decorations, a meeting with the caterer, an airport pickup ("But who, son? Let them take a taxi!"), a trip to the salon ("I'll run over with the girls; do you want a haircut, Mum?"), a plan to tidy the yard. They had not set anything in motion; only Essie knew the state of her arrangements. The girl who cut her hair was coming to the house at three, she informed Marian. A seamstress was coming also, with the sari blouse she had altered.

"That is Celia. You know the one, I've mentioned her. The girl your father ran down in the road."

"What girl? I haven't run down anyone."

"With your *bicycle*, Frank, don't you remember?"

She returned to the kitchen, where Pia had only just begun her chopping. Pia's eyes were full of tears, Essie saw at once. Was it the onions? The girl no longer wept at every turn, but she was apt to go watery over trifles, and Essie knew she must speak carefully or risk total collapse.

It was a shock, a constant astonishment, to find that, in her eightieth year, she must defer so incessantly to the feelings of others. All morning long, she had felt prevailed upon to make everyone else comfortable. Frank just rambled at the breakfast table without a single thought for all she must manage, his stories so pockmarked with gaps and errors that no one could make sense of them. She waited until he left the table before confiding in her children.

"You see how it is. He's gone totally bonkers." He didn't hear, of course. He only walked slowly through the front room with the same expression he wore at the balcony, not paying any attention at all. But Jude hushed her. Marian encouraged him with a false bright voice, the same she used when she kept Essie from waking the girls for early Mass: "Such a long flight, Mum. Better let them sleep so they'll be ready for tomorrow."

"If you had come a few days earlier . . ." began Essie, and Jude put a restraining hand on her shoulder.

And here was Pia, twenty-four years old, nearly six years in the Almeida household, all her prospects advanced after Essie's careful training in cookery and English, the chance of an offer to work for a young family in the Gulf the following year entirely due to Essie's efforts, and still Essie was compelled to guard Pia's feelings. Why not the reverse? she wondered. It came of giving too much. She constantly put other people first. If she could start life again, would she do it all differently? Her mind drifted to Frank before she returned to the matters at hand: the dal, the chicken, the paste for the fish.

"Oh oh oh!" At least Pia had conscience enough to look mortified. "Memsahib, there's no fish!"

Essie thought of the five loaves and two fishes and sighed. She must also buy fresh bread. "You keep on here. I'll go to the bazaar."

Usually, Pia regarded an outing as a treat, but she didn't pull a face. "You think we'll finish?" she giggled as though Essie were a co-conspirator, not an elderly woman who must try to spare her back. But there was nothing for it. Essie changed out of her housedress and checked her pocketbook for her coin purse.

"I'll come with you, Grandma."

Essie looked up, smiling but doubtful. It was one of the difficulties that arose when her family visited: after months, sometimes years of longing, they came, but it was not always easy to find the right fit when they tried to join their days together. Everyone on different clocks, used to different foods, with different ideas about what to do next. She would like to sit quietly with Nicole, to ask all about this boy who wore hats, to give both her granddaughters the readings she had chosen for the prayer service at the start of the party. She must make time later to hear them practice.

But such a morning! Essie could not afford to be slowed down. "I'm only going for fish, darling. Nothing fun."

"Fish will be fun!" Another of those bright, enamel American notions Essie could not argue against. Down they went, the stairs creaking while Nicole flew up and back again to retrieve her sunglasses. Ashok made a flourish of opening the gate, and they were released into the Santa Clara morning, stepping carefully around pits and chasms. St. Hilary Road was torn up again for some mysterious trouble with pipes. The roadwork went on and on, like a man who had forgotten his way out of a story.

Already, Essie's progress was slower than she liked; she could not greet neighbors quickly, she must stop and introduce her grandchild. Nicole smiled at each of Essie's friends, then at one of the laborers, who was carrying a basket of rubble from the ditch in the road. The woman grinned back.

"Do you think she's my age?"

"Come, my girl," said Essie. "We'll miss the best fish."

The market road was packed tight with vendors: fruit and vegetable carts banked on both sides, baskets of produce balanced on crates, ropes of flowers strung on bamboo racks. It was unusually crowded for late morning, all the Catholic ladies out to do their Easter shopping. When Nicole paused to photograph mounds of garlic and ginger, Essie took her by the hand and led her through the crowd.

The road broadened to a plaza at the entrance to the indoor market. Strings of pennants crisscrossed overhead, their shadows fluttering on the pavement like ideas of birds. A statue of Jesus, Fisher of Men, wore a crown of roses and marigolds. Essie made the Sign of the Cross.

Inside was hot and close. The floor and tiled walls were slick, as though the building itself were sweating, and the whole chamber smelled of low tide, with a gamy iron streak from the meat stalls in the next hall. Birdcalls ricocheted beneath the corrugated roof. Cats bided their time. The Koli women sold from a raised platform cluttered with tarps and plastic tubs. They sat on whatever they had: a low stool, an overturned bucket, a crate. Whole fish were fanned out on tarps or newspaper, baitfish and shellfish piled in plastic tubs and baskets, a few choice offerings arranged on trays. Milk sharks, pomfret, anchovies, rawas, surmai. Delicate fillets, and slabs as thick as steaks with pinkish stains on the flesh. Heads, tails, and fins cast to the side in thin pools of blood. A cat sniffed the air below the platform before stretching up to seize a fish head in its teeth.

"My favorite one used to sit just there," Essie told Nicole. "She died some years ago—that was a sad thing—but we are still connected to the family. Now I go to her friend, only sometimes she leaves early. I hope we're not too late—no, there she is! She's seen us!"

Three stalls down, a woman called out to them, and Essie smiled broadly. The sight of Inez brought something more than relief; it was as if the world had slipped back into proper alignment. Here was one who knew Essie, who would ask about her back and family before freely offering news of her own. Here were good fish, plump and fresh, from a fishmonger who knew what Essie liked and was sure to give a fair price. And here was Inez herself, laughing even before they said hello, delighting so fully in meeting Essie's granddaughter that, for the first time all morning, Essie could delight in her also.

"Here is my daughter's girl! All the way from America. She's come for my party."

Inez rolled her head, well satisfied. "Good, good," she said in English, grinning at Nicole, and then she spoke to Essie in Marathi: "The face is yours—the nose, the mouth—only this girl goes halfway to the roof."

"She says you look like me," Essie told Nicole. It was a pretty thought, not one she was accustomed to hearing. She looked at her granddaughter, this tall, fair girl, so American in her movements, who might yet carry a bit of Essie in her features, and it came to her that she was no longer accustomed to being seen—her husband's gaze sliding past her, her children barely in residence, Pia unable to see past the shape of an old woman. But Essie had once been as young as these girls, a child with plaits, an uncertain bride, a mother with babies. In those years, she had not realized how young she was, or that youth was always beautiful. Even bony little Pia, with her thin arms and worried eyes. It was the life ahead of her that made the difference, casting her in an almost sacred light that Pia herself, fussing over trinkets and lotions, could not recognize.

Essie had passed out of that light, invisible as any old woman. When she looked in the glass, she did not see the face she expected. When she glanced at her hands, she could not believe they belonged to her. The arms gone slack, the soft folds beneath the chin, the swelling ankles: these things had happened to her but were not her. The Essie she had once been, Easter Pereira, was both her true self and a kind of secret, shining out at odd moments. How pleasing, how gratifying, that Inez had caught a glint of it. How strange that this moment—in the din and reek of the Santa Clara fish bazaar, where the women at work all the long mornings did not even have a public toilet—should be when Essie began to feel the party spirit.

They went out as they had come in, the bag in Essie's hand swinging with the damp weight of a task accomplished. Nicole carried a bag of prawns. "For the party," Inez told them, and put her hand up to refuse any money. This gesture, the first of its kind between Essie and Inez, launched a disorienting interval during which their typical haggling turned upside down: Essie insisted she must pay, and Inez waved her off. But neither could sustain such pretense. The mock argument collapsed, Essie primly tucked the bills into her purse, and Inez's smile broke over her face like a wave as she gestured to Nicole. "So much like you, she'll like what you like." A chorus of thanks and assurances. Essie would come back in three days, the next market day for Inez. She would save Inez a fat slice of cake. She would bring Nicole to see Inez again—and the other one, Tara, also.

"We'll see who she looks like! Maybe she is not liking prawns." Inez laughed and laughed. She had not met many Americans, and it was hard to get over the joke of it, a family flung across the globe, this beanpole girl fetching up at her stall with one of the customers she knew best, their crisscross of foreignness and resemblance. She was still laughing when she wished Essie a happy birthday in Marathi, which she could see the girl did not understand. "You also be happy," she added in English, startling the beanpole, who had been looking all around as though at a kind of marvel.

They emerged into the plaza, the blaze of light, the quick dark shadows. Nicole put on her sunglasses, and Essie peered down the lane through her regular specs. For a moment, sundazzled, she did not see forms so much as spots of color, flickering like leaves. There was a sensation of the lane itself moving, alive like the limb of a tree, all the separate leaves connected in a single vast life that encompassed even her. She glimpsed this, and then it was gone, the lane a lane, the people people, her eyes clear. Jesus, Fisher of Men, stood with his arms outstretched. The day was wide as the sea. "Come, darling," she said to Nicole, and plunged.

70

MARCH 2005

Celia did not usually go to the clinic on Saturdays, but she dropped into the office for a few hours to update the charts of the households she visited. Each was mapped with its occupants, different-colored bindis indicating men, women, or children; negative or positive; those in treatment, those attending meetings. She and Ivo worked together, counseling a community north of Santa Clara, where a spike of AIDS-related deaths had sparked rumors that the virus could be transmitted by touch. In fact, several residences belonged to policemen, who were inclined to discount their contact with sex workers if they did not pay for it. It took months of going door to door for Ivo and Celia to make headway. They rode the train together but separated once they arrived, Ivo seeking out the men and Celia working with the women.

Eventually, they helped establish a grassroots resource group for support and education. At the first meeting, three widows shared their stories, and Ivo, to encourage the men, told his own. He spoke about growing up with a bleeding disorder, the apprehension whenever he fell or bumped his head, the feeling all through childhood that he would not live long. Twice, he required transfusions, before blood-bank donations were properly screened.

He looked briefly at Celia when he said, "Sometimes people

feel differently about me when they think this is how I contracted the virus. They think, *Oh, this guy didn't live an unclean life. This guy doesn't deserve HIV.* Even we—together in this room—might think in such ways. But nobody deserves HIV. It is a virus, not a sign of who we are."

The first time Ivo shared his history with Celia, they were in the counseling office. She was both appalled and relieved that his exposure might have come through a transfusion—a terrible mistake, but not one of his making. "Then *that* is how," she said, as if he had solved some mystery, and he looked at her with shattering calm. "Does it matter how?" She had no good answer.

That was one way he might have contracted the virus, but not the only way, Ivo explained to the group. He had felt rebellious as a teen, tired of being cautious, determined to chase experiences he might never have if he died young. For about a year, he had engaged in high-risk behavior. But slowly he realized he had survived all the falls as a child. He had survived the transfusions. He had an eighteenth birthday, then a nineteenth. He began to think about the life ahead of him, not the way it would end.

On the train, Celia chose not to ride in the Ladies Only car, but stayed with Ivo in a mixed car. It was nine in the evening, January, uncrowded. They stood near the open door, which framed picture after picture of the passing night.

"You have never been married," she said.

"No."

"Maybe that is one of the life experiences you thought you'd never have. When you were a boy, I mean."

He rolled his head—maybe yes, maybe no.

"All this . . ." She touched the notebook with their records: which families split, which households suffered deaths, which children might be orphaned. "It doesn't give a very happy idea of marriage. A person doing this work might think only of the negatives."

"That could happen. Like working in a funeral home, thinking only of death."

Celia was unprepared for the swerve to Seven Sorrows, but Ivo had a way of tipping things off kilter. She was working out what to say next when he added, "There is a great deal of love in a funeral home, you know. That is another side to it."

The mention of love startled her. "After hearing such sad stories, a person might be nervous. About marriage, I mean."

"I suppose so," he said easily.

"What do you think of marriage? Have you ever been . . . curious?"

"My parents are married. And my brother, my cousins. So, no, not curious."

In another ten minutes, they would reach Santa Clara and she would have said nothing at all.

"You have been married," he reminded her. "Maybe you also have reasons to be nervous."

She looked at him. He was not smiling, but she could see a kind of playfulness in his eyes.

"No," she said. "I'm not nervous."

"I see." They walked all the way back from the station, letting buses go by, speaking of other things. They were on Varuna Road before he said maybe she should marry him.

Evangeline and her husband lived in the next lane—near enough, said Dominic, to wake him whenever she sneezed. The Rosy seemed a little plain beside the fancy new cafés popping up in Santa Clara, but some preferred an old-fashioned place, and students liked what was close and affordable. There was money enough to settle on both his daughters and their husbands, money enough for Lina's computer courses. She would finish three months before their first child was due.

Jerome was on his last contract before coming off the lines for good. He would take over the running of Pomfret—meaning, the family knew, that he would obey Inez in all things. Alma and the children stayed in the family home, her boys growing up as brothers to Isha. In July, when Celia and Ivo married, they would live in one of the tiny flats behind Seven Sorrows.

In the evenings, if she was not too tired, Celia set up her sewing machine on a folding table outside her door and watched Isha play in the lane. She made clothes for many of the women and children, usually simple tops or cotton play clothes, although she had just finished an Easter dress for Isha and was altering a sari blouse for Mrs. Almeida. Mrs. Almeida had hoped to wear a favorite sari to her party but was dismayed when she realized the blouse no longer fit. Celia offered to take a look.

"I can get another made in plain silk, but the color may not be as rich," Mrs Almeida said. "Or the tailor says he can cut out a panel and add a plain back, but then so much of the pattern is lost."

It was only a matter of a centimeter or two, Celia saw at once, and Mrs. Almeida sent her home with it to see what she could do.

Celia often brought Isha to visit the Almeidas. Mrs. Almeida kept a small bag of picture books, which Isha pretended to read aloud. But on the day before the party, Celia only had time to drop the blouse and go. She wanted to check the stalls on Creek Road for a length of ribbon—a sash for Isha's dress—and she had promised Alma to bring sweets for the Easter baskets.

The Almeida household would be busy, she was well aware. Celia wondered if Nicole and Tara, whom she had never met, would remember any of the clothes they had passed along to her family. Her mother had saved the dresses and raincoats, she could tell them. Her own daughter would wear them in a few years.

But the visitors were out.

"They said they needed haircuts," Mrs. Almeida said, looking harried. "And Jude is running back and forth to the airport like a taxi—I don't know who he's picking up now."

Mr. Almeida was in his chair near the television set. He turned from the screen with the air of one who could settle the matter. "He's taken his car. Not a taxi."

"I *know*, Frank. Any minute the caterer will arrive with the tables—actually, I should have called you to sample the menu. The prawns were very bland, not so nice as your mother's. I told him, don't even bother with this dish. I know a girl who will bring me better."

She described various other misgivings while she ducked

into her bedroom to try on the blouse, which Celia hooked with no difficulty.

"There, you see!" Mrs. Almeida crowed. "Just think what that tailor would have done, cutting it to pieces!"

She had not even removed the blouse when Celia said she must go, but she promised to return with prawns the day after the party.

"Stay a little longer," Mrs. Almeida pressed. "Any minute, these people will come. Tell her, Frank!"

"Tell her what?"

"I'll come soon," Celia promised again.

She hurried down to the garden but paused for a last goodbye. Bella was lying with her back against the shrine, which had been finished at last. Mary had taken up residence six weeks before, atop the marble slab (crack facing down) in the niche with a high arch. Mrs. Almeida had confided in Celia that her only regret was not including a fountain—running water would sound very pretty—but that could be her next project.

The dog lifted her head, but before she struggled to rise, Celia bent beside her. "Good girl," she said. Bella put her front paw on Celia's leg, pinning her in place, and Celia smiled; the dog was not so helpless as she seemed. "You wouldn't mind a fountain, would you?"

She heard Mrs. Almeida calling out for Pia as the church bells began to strike the hour. "You hear that?" she said to Bella, who gazed up at Celia and pawed her again, as if she were a dog of such meager understanding, as if she had no idea it was past time to go.

MARCH 2005

The party for Easter Almeida's eightieth birthday was held on Easter Sunday itself. The claim to a March birthday, when her last was in April, disturbed one of her cousins. It was the fellow who lived in a ledger book, Francis remembered, doing accounts for the Bureau of Standards, his attachment to figures so ingrained that even after retirement he could not resist applying standards to Essie also.

"I understand you *celebrate* on Easter. That I accept. I'm only asking, when is your actual birthday?"

"Today, of course!"

His eyes narrowed. "But chances of that are very low. Frank, you must know?"

"I have no idea," Francis announced with vigor. He was enjoying himself.

"Then you may not be eighty!" the cousin told Essie.

Essie laughed and turned to friends at another table. She held a chicken lollipop—a drumstick coated with cheese and deep-fried—in her hand like a scepter. Nothing could upset her, Francis saw. The party was at its peak, with more than a hundred guests beneath strings of lights in the garden. The caterer had turned up on time. The statue of Mary was flanked by Easter lilies. At the last minute, Essie amended the afternoon prayer service to include an extra reading. The family had kept back their grand surprise until the night before, when Jude came home from the airport with Simon. Francis was as shocked as Essie. "Son," he repeated, wiping away tears and laughing. "Son."

"It's *Simon*, Frank!" said Essie, so jubilantly that he did not reproach her. Of course he knew his son, who kept his arm around Francis's shoulders when they looked together at his map of Athens.

Essie was unable to stay far from Simon—getting up from her seat whenever he crossed into another room, following him when he went to bed. Did he need another blanket, should she lower the fan, would he like a glass of water? "Oh, son! The service tomorrow! I must find a reading for you!" Her absorption in this task gave Simon a narrow window in which to fall asleep.

In the end, all her children and grandchildren took part in the service, her full family gathered around the shrine in tribute, Mary's arms spread to bestow her blessings. Simon had left the church years before, a painful point Essie did not raise, but she felt she found an elegant solution in giving him the lyrics of "On This Day, O Beautiful Mother" to read as a poem.

The evening's mishaps were minor. Firecrackers were planned after the cake, but the firecracker wallah accidentally set off a few early, and a dud sent a shower of sparks into the garden at just the moment when the family had gathered for a portrait. A tiny hole was singed in the sleeve of Tara's silk kameez, but the pattern was lively enough to hide small flaws.

And, inevitably, there was an argument over the sari that had once belonged to Essie's grandmother, rose Banarasi silk embroidered with gold. A century later, six cousins shared the heirloom. Essie, her cousin Mary, and the Jos, a quartet of sisters named for a brother who had died in infancy, all took the sari in turns. It ought to have been simple arithmetic, Francis thought, but his wife's family never failed to muddle the equation. Every year brought a fresh crop of inequities, alliances, negotiations, rifts. The sari was too valuable to be trusted to the post, but subject to fully booked railcars or airports seized by fog. A small stain shook the family for years.

Five of the six cousins were present at the party, and a squabble broke out over the timing of that day's turnover. Francis did not try to follow the dispute, but he saw that, after the prayer service, two of the cousins disappeared to change clothes and re-emerge. It was Joelle, the youngest of the sisters, the oddest and his favorite, who wore the sari during the party. She had always lived in the care of one sister or another—like a child, the family said, simple. She sat beside him, as thin as a broom in the lustrous folds of the sari, her hair in the single braid she had worn as long as Francis had known her. He tugged it gently, a joke so old—Jo-elle, Jo-bell—that it had become something sweeter, a bit of affection. Her smile had the quality of a wave breaking over rocks.

"You're looking nice," he said.

"Oh yes," she agreed. "It's my turn."

Jude stood to raise the first toast. Then Marian followed, a bit nervous. Francis smiled fondly. Beautiful girl, intelligent girl, but she had never liked being the center of attention. Essie's cousin Joanna offered a dignified account of Essie's family and girlhood. Father Evelyn thanked her for her work in the church. Francis's friend Bertie gave a gallant account of the couple's first meeting: her dazzling smile, the way young Francis had followed her with his eyes long after their dance had ended. "And after all these years and a beautiful life together, still he is looking!"

Francis ducked his head, submitting without complaint to such fictions. He drank to whatever anyone said, overcome with emotion by the sight of his children, grandchildren, friends, and neighbors all together in the garden. He looked from one side to another, trying to gather them all into his sight. For a moment, he was struck by the notion that Agnes had come, a bright glint of yellow at the edge of the crowd, like light sifting through layers of leaves. He peered into the shadows. His parents and his brother, Peter, might be beneath the trees, too. The little daughter he had held for only a few hours might be waiting in the house, still in reach. On most days her name drifted away from him. He could not fathom how old she would be. But he could feel her small weight in his arms, both grief and solace.

"What is it, Dad?"

Marian had gray hair, but her face was not so very changed.

"Nothing, my girl." He smiled at her. For the first time since the speeches began, he looked at his wife and saw that she was perfectly happy. *To Essie,* he said with all the rest, though what he meant was not exactly her but something larger, a circle he might draw with her at the center, the way people said *home* when they meant a life they once knew.

Women clustered in the doorway with a great raft of a cake, its candles casting a warm yellow light on their faces. The singing struck up, and slowly the cake was borne out into the garden, as though floating on a current of hands and voices. Pia followed, her hand curled against her smile, too thrilled to let the cake out of her sight, too jittery to help carry it. "Oooh!" she cried, when it landed safely in front of Essie, and her laugh broke free of her fingers. Essie puffed her cheeks like a child. People began to clap and cheer long before the candles were out.

The sing-along began once the cake was served. Jude pulled a keyboard onto the veranda; guitarists perched on chairs, singers crowded the railing. Francis sat with a plate of cake on his knees, taking an occasional taste and listening to his sons sing together, the way they had as boys.

Joelle applied herself to her cake with seriousness, ignoring the dark frowns of those who feared for the sari. "This is very good," she told Francis. But there was hardly time for him to take a bite. The party might have been for him also, people flocking to him in droves. Men and women who had once been his students pulled their chairs into a circle around him.

"Come, Professor! Let's have a song from you! You sang in my lecture once—do you remember?"

Francis laughed as he put up his hands: no, no, not tonight. But he *could* remember.

Yes, he told anyone who asked, still at work. A history of the neighborhood, with photographs. He had not expected such interest, such eager questions; tomorrow he must go through his papers properly. For the moment, it was pleasant to hear so many bright voices. He let their news sift past him: Babies, jobs. One fellow was an airline pilot.

"Where would you like to go, Professor? Say the word, I'm ready."

Francis thought of his suitcase filled with pages and photos. "I'm happy here," he said, and the pilot clapped him on the back.

After a time, Joelle took his plate to finish his cake. When neighbors from the flat building opposite passed near his chair, he lifted his hand to hail them.

"Where's Mummy?" he asked, meaning theirs. "You haven't brought her?"

"Not this time, Uncle. Her back is bad tonight."

But when, at the appointed hour, the firecracker wallah took up his position, Francis caught a glimpse of the woman on her balcony. Her name wouldn't come, but he knew her, he had always known her. A sturdy girl stood behind the wheelchair, holding its handles, and the older woman leaned forward to look down into the party. Francis raised his hand in a wave, which she did not see, because the fireworks began. How sudden they were, how splendid—blooming in wild abundance and lingering for just a moment after opening. Like lives he had or might have had: his life with Essie, or a different life with Agnes. Like the life of Joelle, clapping like a girl beside him, or the life of his neighbor on the balcony, her face aglow from the colors. Like the lives of his students, or the village girl who had once knocked him down in the road. Like the dog who lived when she ought to have died, still dozing by his chair each evening. Like his children's lives and the lives of his grandchildren, so far-flung that it seemed a miracle to find them all in his garden. Like the life of the child he had lost, the life he imagined she might have had.

A last string of pops, a last shower of sparks that seemed to fall like confetti and melt into the darkness. A round of applause as the church bells chimed. It was the hour when the neighborhood noise ordinance went into effect, when bands must unplug and public functions cease. Francis looked over his shoulder to the balcony opposite and saw that the woman in the wheelchair had gone.

But he remained in the garden. He enjoyed being at the center of so many laughing people, feeling he was known by them even if he did not recall their names or faces. They were connected to him; that was the point. They came to him, clasped his hand, told him jokes or stories. Linus arranged a snapshot with Francis and his former students, fourteen in all, smiling around his chair. Bertie pulled a chair beside his, and they spoke of their days at university. They toasted their old friend Roddy, another Golden Boy, who had died a few years earlier. How many are left? they wondered. They ticked off names before letting the conversation flow toward gentler questions.

Father Evelyn began an exodus with his goodbye. "Many happy years!" he wished Essie, his voice rolling over the assemblage, and people rose to go as though he had released them from the pulpit.

"We'll see you, we'll see you soon," Francis said again and again.

A smaller party began to coalesce on the veranda, mostly Jude's friends, glasses at their feet, cigarettes tapped into ashtrays, guitars tuned and strummed. Francis listened from his chair in the garden, looking up through dark palm leaves to the dark night sky. When he could not last any longer, Marian helped him to his feet. "Good night," he said to all who remained, and a chorus of voices answered him warmly. "Good night," he said to his wife, who occupied a cane chair like a throne. She peered up as though she could hardly see him through the fog of an almost perfect moment. This did not worry Francis, who saw her through his own kind of haze—not love, exactly, but all their shared years, as though the days had become particulate, suspended in the air between them like the city's film of smoke.

The household slept late the next morning. Even Pia did not get up until after eight, and only to help Bella, whose legs had never fully recovered. Pia waited until the dog relieved herself before helping her to a shady patch near the shrine. The granddaughters rose only to settle down again by degrees, reading old Penguin editions of books they had read on their last visit. Jude and Simon emerged after eleven. Essie remained indisposed, a victim of chicken lollipops. Marian went back and forth from her bedside until her brothers appeared, bare-legged and rubbing their eyes like boys.

She was headed out to meet a schoolfriend, she told them. Mum had taken antacids already.

"But you're coming back?" Francis frowned.

"Yes, Dad! In time for lunch."

Francis stood at the balcony, watching her go. The garden had the look of an abandoned wedding hall, but he gazed past the compound to the neighborhood beyond, the last few clay tile rooftops among the flat buildings, the treetops in the dusty light. He felt the day roll before him, unimpeded. He would put on his good trousers and walk to the gymkhana. Later, he could show the children his archive, a glimpse of the place they once knew.

He heard the gate, a ruckus from the dogs, a voice he recognized. He met her in the garden: that child who had banged into him in the road, grown and holding a small girl's hand.

"How was the party? Isha, say hallo nicely to uncle."

"Wild elephant," he said, as the girl hopped beside her mother.

"Yes!" said the mother, sounding pleased. "And we brought you a present—right, Isha?"

The child held up a bag of prawns, and Francis tipped his chin toward the kitchen when he said, "Ah, that is for Essie."

"*This* is for you." The elephant gave him a packet of photos. "I found a roll of film in a box at home; I don't know from where. But I thought they'd be nice for your collection."

Pictures of the basilica, the Hotel Castelo, Holy Name School. "I've been looking for these!"

"Should I take them up? You're going out?"

"No, no. Checking on things here." He gestured vaguely around the compound. He did not like to disappoint her. The gymkhana could wait.

The little girl tugged her hand free. "Mumma! Mumma!"

"Yes, okay. For a few minutes you can play, then come and wish aunty."

Francis peered at the child. "How old are you? Old enough to play on you own?"

"I am six," she said with total conviction.

"She'll soon be *five*," her mother said, laughing. "But ever since she's been fitted for glasses, she's feeling much older. Isha, stay in the garden. And mind the flowers."

Francis made a slow circle of the property—past the veranda, where the little girl was petting the dogs; past the coconut palms, back toward the shrine.

There, against the wall, was his bicycle.

He felt a sudden ease, the release of a tension he had not fully registered. He had lost track of it some time ago—a neighbor borrowed it, perhaps, or it had gone for a tune-up—but suddenly here it was, back again. He eased a leg over. The seat was a little low, but the frame was in good condition. He rode along the back of the house, wobbling slightly.

He looked up to realize a small girl was watching, a child with wild hair and glasses. She came running to meet him while he climbed off.

"Teach me to ride!"

Not Marian. His other girl, delivered up to him? No, he was being foolish; one of Marian's daughters.

"Soon." He put a hand on her head. "When you are a little older. Your feet must reach the pedals."

It was midday, the sun high. The dog he loved best was not tied up with the others; she moved slowly, but she had the run of the compound. She was—although nobody knew it—in her sixteenth year. For most of the morning, she rested, creeping nearer and nearer to the shrine to follow the narrowing bands of shade. All were gone now; she was in blazing sunlight. The red clay ground was as hard as stone.

It would be several months before anyone in the household noticed that Bella's hearing seemed to be improving. How? they wondered. But only idly. The dog had lived so long past anyone's expectations that they had grown accustomed to such miracles. And they were consumed with other matters. Pia took a position in the Gulf. Essie undertook the training of a new girl, an endeavor so absorbing that she attributed her spells of fatigue—the first stage of what would be her final illness—to the demands of the household and her confusion over Jude. Only days after he came home to stay, he announced his engagement to a woman who had recently divorced. It was not the woman's fault, exactly; Essie could accept that she had been mistreated. But to permit her son to make such a connection—would this consign him to the fringes of the church? Father Evelyn was lax about such matters, aggravating Essie, and she had no other supporters. The rest of the family thought only of Jude's happiness. She was left to come to terms on her own, pouring out her misgivings to the statue of Mary. There were nights when she wished the statue still stood in her room, days when she was too tired to descend to the garden.

It was Bella who attended the shrine daily, Bella who registered a recovery in her hearing long before anyone else did. She could not walk freely after her injury, so when noises began to drain from the world, her life had diminished to a small parched circle. Her sense of smell had diminished also, though she waited patiently for scents to knit themselves out of faint whorls of air. She came to rely on touch. But each day since the statue took its place in the shrine brought an incremental broadening. Scents deepened, and sounds. She heard the child; she heard Francis. She heard the quick mineral trace of the cycle's path in the back of the compound, a sound too thin to recognize. What she understood was an idea of motion, a current through the still noon air.

She had even regained a little strength, though her hind legs could not bear weight for long. She struggled to the lip of the shrine and rested briefly, her chin on the slab. Then she heaved herself up. The marble was as cool as rain, smooth beneath her flanks. Noises filled her ears, as rich as good soil. Scents bloomed like flowers. The world widened, rolling out from the place where she lay. She banked her head against the pedestal—*Good girl,* she heard as Francis passed—and closed her eyes to sleep.

ACKNOWLEDGMENTS

This book began with the warmth and generosity of my family's community in Mumbai. I thought in particular of my uncle Keith Suares, whose kindness was not only a feature of our visits but of the neighborhood at large, and whose affection always extended to dogs. I am especially indebted to Naresh Fernandes, who has provided help of every kind, and to Lorna Fernandes, a patient, gracious guide.

In 2008, I received an invitation from Negar Akhavi, on behalf of the Bill & Melinda Gates Foundation, to write an essay for an anthology about HIV in India. I am grateful to her, Prashant Panjiar, Chiki Sarkar, and all those involved in the publication of *AIDS Sutra*. My heartfelt thanks to those who shared their stories with me in Karnataka: people I knew as Ashwini, Saroja, Jayanthi, and Basavaraj. I think of them often, with great admiration.

The book was expanded in innumerable ways by my reading of *Beautiful Thing* by Sonia Faleiro, *City Adrift* by Naresh Fernandes, *Bombay, Meri Jaan*, edited by Jerry Pinto and Naresh Fernandes, *Riots and After in Mumbai* by Meena Menon, and both "The Last of the Ustaads" and *A Free Man* by Aman Sethi. I also relied on the indispensable "Report of the Justice B. N. Srikrishna Commission on the Mumbai Riots of 1992–1993"

ACKNOWLEDGMENTS

and eventually the "Bombay Riots Timeline" published in 2018 by Citizens for Justice and Peace.

Carol Janeway encouraged me to begin this novel, despite its obvious challenges, at a time when I was home with one baby and expecting another. "That only means you will write it *slowly*," she said. I am deeply grateful for the support she and Sonny Mehta offered, which was far more sustaining than they knew.

My festival crew have been an unending source of good cheer: Louis Edwards, W. David Foster, Kerry Grombacher, Danny Melnick, Greg Miller, Nancy Ochsenschlager, Dixie Rubin, Jill Sternheimer, Jerry Ursin, and Carol Young. Darlene Chan and Quint Davis are lifelong heroes. Charlie Bourgeois, Marie St. Louis, and George and Joyce Wein are never far from my thoughts. I'm especially grateful to Laura Bell, Tracy Reid, Chrissy Santangelo, Clarence "Reginald" Toussaint, and Nicole Williamson, charter members of Murphy's Theatricals; to Carrie Hood, an intrepid travel companion; and to Deborah Ross, a friend for the ages, who provided a foundational experience with bicycles. My thanks also to Branford Marsalis, who persists in believing I can finish things years before I begin them.

I'm grateful to friends and colleagues who have offered encouragement and guidance, including Elisa Albert, Elizabeth Boquet, Samantha Cole, Dan Dyksen, Bob Epstein, Jennifer Fritz, Dennis Keenan, Lauren LeBlanc, Alyssa Lodewick, Pete Nelson, Karen Osborn, William Patrick, Robyn Roope, Guy Sanders, Jan Sanders, Alan Santos, Hollis Seamon, Karen Shepard, Caitlin von Schmidt, and Baron Wormser. My warmest thanks to Gordon Haber, Elizabeth Hilts, and Eugenia Kim, who outdid themselves entirely, and to Sonya Huber and Rachel Basch, whose thoughtful feedback helped usher the novel through its earliest stages.

Binnie Kirshenbaum has been a generous advisor since my days in her classroom; her advocacy and enthusiasm have made a world of difference. Sarah Manguso's support has been an unexpected gift. Dave King and Franklin Tartaglione have dazzled me with their kindness, and I'm especially fortunate that

Dave has been my fellow traveler in reading and writing. Marice Rose has endured far too many conversations about an imaginary world while helping me endlessly in this one. Thank you to them all.

Thanks to Robin Desser, for her warm interest when our paths crossed. And, of course, my ongoing gratitude to Lexy Bloom for her editorial acumen, keen intelligence, and patience beyond all measure.

One person has read every version of this book: years of thanks to Genevieve Gagne-Hawes for her insights and companionship through many, many pages. My deepest thanks to Amy Berkower, whose faith in this novel seems miraculous and whose wisdom has saved me more than once.

Thanks to Eric, Gloria, Sophia, Keira, Hal and Fran Patrick; to Max and Finn Petersen; and to Kim Stevens; I'm lucky to be in their families. Helen von Schmidt remains my favorite person with whom to discuss books and prose; she is also a rockstar aunt.

I am hugely indebted to Jim Shepard, whose guidance has been impeccable, whose encouragement has been life-changing, and whose own work is a constant example of what is possible. And there is no beginning or end to my gratitude to Caryl Phillips, without whose generosity and counsel my writing—and life—would have taken very different forms.

Some of my strongest supporters will never read this book: Robert Cox, Gretchen Finn, Kelley Smith, and Robert L. Jones. But their influence endures in its pages and in everything I attempt.

I am forever grateful to my father; my mother, Marguerite Jones; and my sister and brother, Radhika and Chris Jones, the first people with whom I delighted in books and the first to believe I could write any.

Most of all, I am thankful beyond words for Drew, Phoebe, and Thalia Patrick. They have given more to this novel, and to me, than they will ever know.

A NOTE ABOUT THE AUTHOR

Nalini Jones is the author of a story collection, *What You Call Winter*. Her writing has appeared in *One Story*, *Ploughshares*, *Guernica*, *Elle India*, and *Scroll*, among other publications, and she has contributed to anthologies about politics, music, and families, including those affected by HIV in *AIDS Sutra*. She has been awarded a National Endowment for the Arts Literature Fellowship, an O. Henry Prize, and a Pushcart Prize. She lives in Connecticut and teaches at Fairfield University.

A NOTE ON THE TYPE

This book was set in Janson, a typeface long thought to have been made by the Dutchman Anton Janson, who was a practicing typefounder in Leipzig during the years 1668–1687. However, it has been conclusively demonstrated that these types are actually the work of Nicholas Kis (1650–1702), a Hungarian, who most probably learned his trade from the master Dutch typefounder Dirk Voskens. The type is an excellent example of the influential and sturdy Dutch types that prevailed in England up to the time William Caslon (1692–1766) developed his own incomparable designs from them.

Typeset by Scribe,
Philadelphia, Pennsylvania

Designed by Casey Hampton